"… I enjoyed your book! With the sheer amount of description of life in the different places in those times … Just loved it and absolutely flew through it … Absolutely fascinating."

Marg Eddy, Greenvale, Victoria, Australia

"… absolutely enjoyed every page. The detail is so graphic throughout the book, one's imagination can have a holiday … Jane becomes a very real person, your heart goes out to her so often … A wonderful read!"

Barry and Cheryl Smith, Tamworth, NSW, Australia

"… a wonderful read. What a story. And so much research … I purchased two more copies for friends."

Ron Lowe, Cheltenham, Victoria, Australia

"… A wonderful story of one woman's strength and determination to bring her family to what she hoped would be a better life in Australia … Extremely well written, would thoroughly recommend."

Diane Opie, Bendigo, Victoria, Australia

"… a great story and very easy to read. I enjoyed it from the beginning to the end."

Peter Beard, Geelong, Victoria, Australia

"… I enjoyed the book. It was a history and geography lesson as well as being an enthralling novel … Looking forward to the next."

Les Morrison, Wyong, NSW, Australia

"Just finished Max Beck's wonderfully rich and evocative book, *A Different Earth* … A great saga! Highly recommended."

Bill Barlow, Writers Group Convener,
Genealogical Society of Victoria, Melbourne, Victoria, Australia

A DIFFERENT EARTH

Cornish pioneer miners to Australia

The story of Jane Dunstan and her family:
Cornwall to Burra and overland to gold

MAX C. S. BECK

CORNWALL EDITIONS

This edition first published 2016
by Cornwall Editions Ltd
52 Gladsmuir Road,
London N19 3JU,
UK

ISBN 978-1-904880-34-9
A *Different Earth* © Max C. S. Beck 2014
A Cataloguing in Publication record is available
from the British Library.

First published in 2014 by Max C. S. Beck

Designed and typeset by Helen Christie

Printed and bound by Lightning Source UK

Front cover image:
The New Rush
S.T. Gill from *The Australian Sketch Book*
Courtesy of the State Library of South Australia

In Memory of

JANE DUNSTAN (later RODDA)

Born Wendron, Cornwall 1814

Arrived at Adelaide, South Australia, on board the barque
Trafalgar on 17th January 1849

Died at Vaughan, Victoria on 12th March 1886

Dedicated to all the strong women of this world

About the Author

After graduating from Monash University with the degrees of Bachelor of Laws and Bachelor of Jurisprudence, Max practised as a barrister and solicitor for twenty-two years and was then appointed a Magistrate and Coroner for the State of Victoria where he served on the bench for fifteen years. As a lawyer, much of his time was devoted to work as defence counsel in country Magistrate and County Courts dealing with all sorts of people and issues. Experience gained in the law developing skills to determine relevance, research authorities and weigh and fairly assess evidence has served him well as an investigative writer of historical fiction.

Although *A Different Earth* is his first novel, writing skills have always formed an important part of Max's life in the law and as a Magistrate and Coroner. Raised in a country hotel where his father was licensee, he worked as a labourer on the Snowy Mountains scheme, was a truck driver in the Mallee and still has his truck licence. He has travelled overseas to twenty different countries and is comfortable in the company of people from all walks of life.

His research for the book included two trips to Cornwall, UK, and a week's voyage on board a tall sailing ship heading south and west out of Hobart into the roaring forties. *A Different Earth* is based on the true experiences of his great, great grandparents Richard and Jane Dunstan. Max has enjoyed the process of research and writing *A Different Earth* and is looking forward to his next writing project.

You can contact him at mcsbeck@bigpond.com.

ACKNOWLEDGEMENTS

I record my thanks for the willingly given help and assistance I have received from personnel at the State Library of South Australia including the Mortlock Library, the Burra and District Community Library, the State Library of Victoria, the libraries of Deakin University, the office of State Records South Australia, The Royal Geographical Society of South Australia Inc. and the Cornwall Records office at Truro in the UK.

I am greatly indebted to my wife Prue who has tolerated the years of my self-imposed isolation while I have researched and written this book and whose supporting word processing and computer skills have been invaluable along with her proofreading, critical appraisals and encouragement.

Author's Note

Based on a true story, *A Different Earth* is a grand narrative rich in the details of history derived from extensive research.

To tell this story properly and with sufficient intimacy the blanks left between important recorded dot points of history have been filled with imaginative reconstruction and gaps in the lives of the main characters, who were real people, have been dramatised and fictionalised to help the narrative come alive.

Throughout the book the measurements of distance, weights etc, current at the time, have been retained. A conversion scale is included at the back of the book for those who would like to work out the metric equivalent.

INTRODUCTION

Max Beck's new book *A Different Earth* is certainly different. Hitherto, the story of Cornwall's nineteenth-century 'great emigration' has been an essentially male narrative, a tale of miners, engineers, quarrymen. Their female counterparts – wives, mothers, daughters – have generally been introduced as bit-parts when necessary to flesh out the domestic detail. In the history of 'Cousin Jack', 'Cousin Jenny' has been given a decidedly minor role. True, in 1949 Phyllis Somerville produced her *Not Only in Stone*, a novel based on fact, with its female protagonist Polly Thomas the wife of a Cornish miner on South Australia's northern Yorke Peninsula. But that was a long time ago, and historians and novelists alike have singularly failed to respond to what perhaps we should call Somerville's feminist agenda.

Until now, that is. For hiding behind Max Beck's subtitle *Cornish Pioneer Miners to Australia*, is a remarkable reading of the emigrant-settler experience through feminine eyes – those of Jane Dunstan (later Rodda), born in Wendron, Cornwall, in 1814. It is no accident that Max Beck has dedicated his book 'to all the strong women of this world', for the Jane Dunstan who emerges in this story – and again, it is a tale based on fact – is one of stoicism, courage, and ultimately the triumph of the human (or at least feminine) spirit over adversity. Demonstrating an assured mastery of the historical context – he has clearly read widely and carefully – Max Beck traces Jane's progress from Cornwall to Burra in South Australia and later to the goldfields of Victoria.

Max Beck's experience as a Coroner has given him important insights into the nature of life and death, and he uses these to great effect, not least in dealing with the tragic loss of Jane's husband and two of her daughters. And, perhaps unusually for a man, he has the ability and sensitivity to imagine the everyday life of ordinary women in nineteenth-century Australia, and to understand and sympathise with their predicament. In narrating the story of the Burra floods, for instance, when many Cornish families are washed from their dug-out homes along the Burra Creek, he observes, as we might expect, the 'frightened' and 'weeping' women, who are guarding their children and what is left of their belongings. But in a touching and well-observed aside, Max Beck also tells us that many of these unfortunate women are also 'holding their pregnant bellies', giving us a fleeting yet vivid and surely authentic picture of female anxiety.

Telling insights such as this pepper the book. Fortunately, Max Beck avoids extensive use of invented first-person dialogue, always a difficult device in historical narratives based on fact. Wisely, he restricts himself to story-telling, of which he is an accomplished practitioner. Sensibly too, he avoids Cornish dialect, always a trap for the unwary. The result is a compelling and extremely well-written addition to the literature on the Cornish in Australia, and an especially important contribution to our understanding of the experience of women on the colonial frontier.

Professor Philip Payton,
Flinders University, Adelaide, Australia

CONTENTS

LIST OF ILLUSTRATIONS

Part One

Cornwall

1847–1848

Chapter 1

TOLCARNE

1847

Jane knew what hunger pains were. Living in Cornwall in 1847 with six children aged two to eleven years and a Cornish miner husband, there had been many times when she had foregone her fair portion at meal times for the benefit of her children and their father. But the pain she felt this night as she lay in bed with Richard was an experience known to her that had no connection with hunger. She considered all her symptoms for some time before waking him. Well experienced in dealing with the approaching trauma, she did not want to cause any false alarm. As the spasms grew stronger and closer together Jane found herself screwing up the rag blanket in her hands. She elbowed Richard in the ribs and he woke in a flash.

"What is it lass?"

"The baby I think."

Richard scratched flint and steel to light tinder and then the oil lamp made from an earthenware dish with two flaxen wicks dangling over the side – a task that took several minutes. In an endeavour to not wake the children he carefully put a small log of wood on the fire smouldering in the hearth. The heavy smell of sardine oil burning in the lamp soon wafted around the small cottage. Comprising one room only, it was more of a hut than a house. The children slept on the boards of a mezzanine floor built beneath the rafters of the thatched roof and extending halfway over the ground floor. Access to this loft was gained via a ladder and here they would all huddle together like a litter of kittens to keep warm on cold nights. At least Jane had the parental bed on the ground floor. But it was a wretched affair made from ropes and cloth crossing from side to side and covered with a thin old sagging hessian mattress stuffed with straw. The ground floor was exactly that – trodden down earth.

There was one tiny window that had glass but did not open. A large fireplace and hearth was the centrepiece of the cottage. This was the family's chief survival device and social hub, providing food, comfort and warmth to stem the chill winter winds that blew through the cracks of the cottage door, window frame, walls and down the chimney.

They agreed not to send for the midwife yet as there were still several hours before first light. Jane had done this six times before and she viewed the coming ordeal with grit and resignation.

At 33 years of age and the mother already of Richard Junior 11, Ben 10, Henry 9, Wearn 7, Mary 5, and Anne 2, Jane may have been an ordinary Cornish miner's wife but, as a person, she was far from ordinary. While being a little below average in height she was not diminutive in character or personality. Mentally tough, she would not hesitate to cut the head off a hen to feed her family but wouldn't tolerate gratuitous cruelty to any animal. More than once she had yelled at a man whipping a horse in the street to "Stay ya hand!" With a stocky build and wide hips some would argue as to whether her figure was attractive. But she had a quality that caused men to give her a serious look. Her impish button nose, large dark brown eyes you could drown in and small straight mouth with full lips commanded attention. Long raven hair which she brushed methodically each day and neatly tied back gave an assertive aspect to her face. She smiled readily, was physically and intellectually strong, intelligent but uneducated.

Richard was always alarmed at these times. The entire business of birth frightened him. He did not understand it (although you would think that by now he should). He worried about Jane. She was his entire motivation, his complete reason for being. Nothing was more important to him. He held her hand and felt helpless. He wanted to go for the midwife now. Jane said no as it was the middle of the night and the midwife would be asleep. Richard lit another oil lamp, returned to her side and kissed her. He noticed perspiration on her forehead and what he thought was a hint of fear in her eyes.

"I'll be back in a short while love," he said, and fled in the dark to fetch the midwife.

Less than five years had passed since their friend and neighbour John Coombe had lost his wife as she gave birth to their first child. It was now a continuing struggle for John to raise his boy as a single parent on a miner's income. He would not have managed at all without the assistance of the boy's feeble old grandmother.

Jane, like most women, feared childbirth. Death was a hazard they all faced in the process as well as other consequences such as uterine prolapse, and tearing or ulcerations for which the only available treatment was extremely basic. Toxaemia, haemorrhage and puerperal fever (known as "child bed fever") were notorious killers. The latter was the main cause of maternal death after childbirth. It was a very serious form of septicaemia arising from an infection of the uterus caused by bacteria. It led to toxic shock syndrome in hours, not days, and killed swiftly.

The main cause was the lack of appropriate medical hygiene standards of the time which often resulted in doctors and midwives transferring infections from one patient to the next. But nobody had any understanding of the germ and bacteria theory of infection as a cause of sickness and there was no such thing as an antiseptic or antibacterial available, no antibiotics, no modern drugs, no effective painkillers, no place that could be called a hospital in the modern sense and the skills of doctors and midwives were limited. The cottage environment was not conducive to personal hygiene. There was no plumbing and, at best, home-made soap was available some of the time for washing. Cheap factory made soap was not available to the poorer classes until about 1880. It would be a week or two after the birth before Jane would be out of danger.

Dawn was breaking as Richard returned with the midwife. Jane had confidence in her as she had attended her on previous occasions and was a person who had received some medical instruction from the local doctor. She was skilled, conscientious, clean and knowledgeable, and took a pride in her calling. She instructed Richard to boil up a big pot of camomile tea which was for her own sustenance more than anything else, although it also gave him something to do. At around midday, a mixed cry of glee and relief came from the midwife.

"Success at last! We've got a girl. We've done it!"

Richard had been hoping for a boy. Although, in a poor family any child was yet another mouth to feed, it was also a potential wage earner. From his point of view boys were better than girls because they were paid more money and in Victorian England most men thought women were clearly inferior to males.

Richard Dunstan, aged 23, and Jane Roberts, aged 20, were married at Wendron Parish Church Cornwall on the eighth day of June, 1835. Illiterate and unable to sign their names, they placed marks on the parish register. They had both been born into large and poor families living in small mining hamlets in the parish of Wendron. In 1835 work was plentiful in local copper mines and as a skilled and industrious miner Richard easily found employment. The family settled in a little hamlet called "Tolcarne" which had come into existence solely to serve the mines. The surrounding area had many rich lodes of copper and tin ores with more and deeper mines than any other part of Cornwall. The nearest towns Camborne and Redruth, then the centres of copper mining in Cornwall, were respectively some four and five miles away.

For a rental of a few shillings annually Richard had been able to lease a couple of acres of hungry land on which the cottage sat. It measured some twenty four feet by thirteen feet with the thatched roof purposely made higher than the walls so there was room left for the sleeping loft for the children. The cob walls (made from a mixture of clay, gravel and straw) were built by Richard himself with the help of his friends or "cobbers". Being built entirely by eye with no plans, there was not a right angle or true horizontal in the place. The walls cost nothing, and only the cheapest of farm tools were needed for the job. The roof rafters and mezzanine floorboards were made from rough sawn timber scavenged from old mine workings. A good overhang of thatch and whitewashed exterior walls, re-applied annually, helped to preserve the cob. The threshold at the single door was marked with a grey slate flagstone.

There were only fifteen cottages in the hamlet which rested in a shallow valley where a stream curled around the base of a rising hill. A shaky little footbridge on the downstream side allowed careful pedestrians to cross over. Upstream from the bridge, the cottages were sprinkled along the lower bank and from a distance on a clear winter's day they presented a picture of almost perfect serenity with their whitewashed walls, thatched roofs and smoke rising slowly from the chimneys. Winding muddy pathways formed a web of shortcuts, knitting them together along the edge of the stream, made dirty by mining activities which had caused the removal of most of the trees except for the odd pine dotted here and there. Next to the cottages were small cultivated plots sprinkled sparsely among the slag and stone left by earlier spent mining operations. Here the women and children worked at tilling the family's crops. The occasional cow, goat, sometimes a pig, could be seen; and little clutches of ducks and hens dabbled and pecked about.

Each cottage had a tarred water barrel standing against its outside wall to catch rainwater trickling off the thatch. This was their best quality water which Jane used mainly for drinking, cooking and making tea. A respectable distance from the cottages, on the other side of the vegetable garden, there were toilets comprising a single deep pit with a seat over. Sharing of these with neighbours often led to disputes over rights of priority of use, who was responsible for the current stench, and whose turn it was to carry out the next service. Toilet rolls did not exist. Old newspapers were not used. They were too expensive to buy and no one could read anyway. Wooden scrapes, old rags and handfuls of any suitable vegetable material from grass, straw or leaves and a dish of cold water were employed. There was no follow-up use of soap on hands because it was generally too expensive and unavailable and no one knew why you should bother to use it.

Most cottages, including the Dunstan's, kept a pig in a lean-to sty around the back. The oozings and drizzlings from this drained down into a nearby depression designated "the muck heap", upon which was flung pig manure, dirty dishwater and any household refuse the pig refused to eat. There, everything happily composted into a nasty, stinking, black and green reception centre for all manner of germs, bacteria and obnoxious bubbling gases. Open drains or ditches along the fronts of the cottages were the next recipients of this decaying conglomeration when the muck heaps overflowed, as they did when they and the drains were finally flushed out by a good rain. Everything then finished up in the stream.

Rats were a constant problem – they had runs from muck heap to muck heap and pigsty to pigsty – they dug into and sometimes tunnelled the full length of the cob walls of the cottages and damaged and nested in the thatch and made noises at night. They stole food, carried diseases and sometimes bit babies and children.

A total of seventy-eight people resided in the fifteen cottages of the hamlet with a poor family in every one. Money was in short supply and families would save for months to buy a pig. Each dwelling had little more than the one small room with an open fire and poorly functioning chimney resulting in much of the smoke weaving its way through the blackened rafters and out through the thatched roof. This, together with the fumes from fish oil lamps and candles made from rushes dipped in grease, eventually coloured everything with a pervading hue of dinginess and left a prevailing pungent smoky smell.

What from a distance may have appeared to be a picture of perfect serenity, upon closer examination was a life a little less than that. But the twenty or more children, dressed in rags and eternally dirty, who happily played among the cottages were ignorant of anything better. To them this was happiness. They ran and stomped, played marbles, made mud pies and houses with sticks and stones in the dirt, lay on their tummies in the grass, splashed in puddles and laughed and cried and fought; and then hopped and skipped and jumped some more. They made the best of mischief before all too soon they would be drawn into the hamlet life of doing their fair share of work. They grew up, for the most part, with a large proportion of pluck and tougher than some.

Jane had now contributed a new addition to this happiness in the form of a baby she named Elizabeth. It had been three weeks since the birth and Jane was now beyond the danger period for contracting childbed fever. But Elizabeth had other perils to face. Throughout England at the time, deaths of babies before one year old were persistently at fifteen percent. While in the poorest working-class families twenty-five percent or more of babies died before their first birthday. The risk was highest in the first few weeks of life when they were most susceptible to diseases of the chest or bowel.

Gastro intestinal disorders, with diarrhoea and dysentery being the most common complaints, were the main causes of infant mortality. Such common infections were bred and fostered in the unsanitary and dirty conditions and spread by flies which accompanied the piles of rubbish and animal manure in every village and hamlet. A common infant diet called "pap" contributed to the problem. It was a mixture of bread and water sweetened with a little sugar or treacle and coloured with a dash of milk. Elizabeth and other babies were spoon fed with this mixture which was often kept warm all day near the hearth gathering bacteria.

Whooping cough, a highly infectious disease caused by a bacterial infection of the respiratory tract was a common recurring ailment in young children at Tolcarne and often fatal. Toddlers suffered bouts of violent coughing leaving them so breathless that their inhalations made a noticeable and distressing "whoop" sound. It was incurable and had to run its course.

Diphtheria, when it came, caused inflammation of the mucous membranes to the point where breathing became virtually impossible, resulting in the death of many children. Then there were the common or garden types of influenza and coughs and colds, all of which had the potential to develop quickly into serious complications in the environment of Tolcarne. Jane, and every mother lived in constant dread of her baby contracting any of these "fevers" and an array of more serious maladies that visited villages and hamlets from time to time, including measles, cholera, typhus and typhoid, smallpox, and scarlet fever. In the mining parishes of Cornwall there were times when all the children in a family were wiped out, leaving a healthy couple childless.

The major underlying cause of these diseases and the subsequent mortality were the conditions of poverty in which people lived. A bewildering array of folk "cures" were applied to these ailments ranging from soaking a thick piece of toast in vinegar and binding it to your neck in a rag, eating cakes made from barley and the child's urine, taking linseed or castor oil, gargling with molasses vinegar and butter, or eating live snails. People were desperate for cures and were willing to try anything. Doctors were too expensive but the local chemists in the nearby villages of Redruth or Camborne would, for every available illness and for a manageable fee, readily prepare a powder that had no efficacious effect whatsoever. There were then no legal qualifications required to operate as a chemist or druggist.

Elizabeth, like the majority of babies, was breastfed – the cheapest and best way of rearing her. Through Jane, this perhaps gave her some immunity to the array of threatening fevers of the time that she would otherwise not have had. In any event, there was not much alternative apart from the "pap" mix diet of water, sugar, bread and milk. There were no modern techniques of bottles, teats, sterilisation and powdered formulas available to assist baby rearing. While she managed to avoid any major complaint she was still plagued by re-occurring bouts of diarrhoea and it seemed to Jane's great concern that she was not thriving in the same manner that her other children had done at that same stage. Because she was unwell she was an unhappy child and cried and grizzled a lot. In desperation Jane consulted the chemist in Cambourne who prescribed "Godfrey's Cordial" – an opiate based formula which was commonly used to quiet fretful and crying children. Quietness and sleep were thought essential to the rearing of healthy babies. Unfortunately, the substance merely masked the effects of gastrointestinal complaints. It did not solve the problem and its long-term effects were more adverse than beneficial. Child mortality remained high in the parish of Wendron. More than half of all the deaths each year were in children under five years of age.

Chapter 2

COTTAGE AND MINE

Life in the cottage for two adults and seven children was certainly living at close quarters with everyone cheek by jowl. That it functioned as well as it did was due to Jane's home management skills as well as the dictates of necessity. At night baby Elizabeth slept in her mother's arms at first and later was transferred to a small wooden box cot beside her parents' bed. Ann, aged 2, had been sleeping in the same bed as her parents but, with the arrival of Elizabeth, had joined the other children in the loft where old wooden boxes were also kept for storing clothes and things. To deal with the chill winter nights Jane made rag rugs by stitching together whatever material she could find to form simple patchwork quilts. On very cold nights old coats and even sacks would be added to keep in the warmth.

Apart from being used as the matrimonial bedroom, the ground floor space was the sitting room, kitchen, nursery and wash house combined. Jane had fanatically scrubbed and cleaned the surface of the long rough table in the centre so much that the grain was worn, ribbed and whitened. For seating there were two home-made wooden forms made out of the first cut of a log, flat on one side and round on the other, two basic stools with legs of natural unfinished round timbers jammed into holes, and two rickety old chairs reserved for parental use only. On the end wall, opposite the bed, some old boxes had been placed for storage and a couple of planks run between them to form a shelf. Here, Jane placed her tinplate canisters that contained flour, tea and sugar. Underneath she kept a wide copper preserving pan and a large wooden tub used for curing sides or flitches of bacon from the family pig. A small woven willow basket hanging on the wall contained half a dozen brown hens' eggs. A wooden salt box with leather hinges for the lid sat near the hearth to keep the salt dry. Apples, cored and dried and bunches of herbs dangled from strings tied to the rafters. Flitches of cured and smoked bacon hung on the wall beside the hearth.

The fire burned simply in the centre of the hearth on a flat stone foundation. A large blackened iron crockpot hung from a hook at the end of a chain suspended from a crossbar in the chimney. Much of Jane's culinary magic took place in this pot. Sometimes the pot would be replaced with a cast-iron frying pan with a semi-circular handle allowing it to be suspended by the same chain. A three-legged cast-iron baking pot or cauldron with a lid (that in Australia was later called a "camp oven") was placed on the ground near the fire and often used for baking. Finally, there were the ever-steaming large cast-iron black kettles that burbled away all day on the side of the hearth.

One piece of equipment that was vital to the proper functioning of the premises was the large earthenware family pot kept under the matrimonial bed on the ground floor and used by all who felt the call of nature during the cold winter nights. It was the task allotted to young Wearn, aged 7, to empty it each morning into the muck heap. In Tolcarne everything took place in these tiny box houses – sleeping, cooking, eating, washing, procreation, childbirth, urination, defecation and death.

It was Jane's mission in life to convert this micro-space into a home. Within her limited means and capabilities she strove from before dawn until after dark each day to create the best workable and happy environment she could for the family. Always the last to bed at night and the first awake each morning, she would be up at or even before the first crow of the cock. Oil lamps lit, fire stoked, kettles filled and boiled, and breakfast prepared. Though there was no watch or clock in the cottage she knew it was time to wake Richard, and the boys Henry, Ben and Richard Junior, when the first whistle blew at the mine signalling a change of shift in an hour. Although the three boys were only aged 9, 10 and 11 respectively they were already full time workers at the mine. From an early age they had been given home-made toy picks and shovels so they could pretend to be miners like their dad. The father and son relationship was of fundamental importance to Cornish mining skill. It was expected and accepted that as soon as a boy was old enough, usually less than 10, he would go to work with his father to get experience and gain the skills of a miner. Henry, being the youngest, worked on the surface but Richard Junior and Ben had already joined their father working underground where they could earn higher wages. While the work was hard they enjoyed heading off each day with their dad as young men of the world.

Breakfast was usually barley bread with dripping or barley gruel made with rough-milled barley flour mixed with water or milk, if there was any available. If it was a good week, an oatcake might be had – with treacle if there were any left. There was never any real tea as it was too expensive but an acceptable herbal brew made from the dried leaves of mugwort was usually around.

As Richard and the boys left, Jane handed them a small calico bag containing their lunch. Today it was a baked solid mass of flour and water without any leavening called a "hogan". With luck it might actually have bits of pork or bacon mixed in with it. In better days, before the potato blight, the workers would have taken with them one of Jane's famous Cornish pasties but it had been some time since they had been so fortunate. With a peck on the cheek for Jane, a quick remonstrance to the other children, who by this time were grizzling awake, to be good for their mother, Richard grabbed his pipe and tobacco, picked up a lantern and headed out the door with the boys to the mine. The lantern was nothing more than a candle in an old treacle tin with holes punched in but it was of considerable comfort to them when leaving for work in the early black hours of midwinter with no assistance from any outdoor or street lighting.

From the hamlet it was a thirty-minute walk downstream along the bank, then up a rising lane dotted with hawthorns and brambles to the mine engine house on the side of the hill. They could see an array of lanterns exiting the other cottages, moving slowly at first and then jigging up and down in single file along the well-trodden winding path to the mine. Similar lines of other twinkling lights were coming down the hills from the other hamlets to converge and meet at junctions where they would briefly stop to form a collection of glowing yellow specks. As they progressed towards the mine the tiny lights met more lights that winked in recognition and joined the procession. There was just a faint hint of dawn by the time the lights and men, women and children of all ages reached the mine. Young Henry farewelled his father and brothers and joined the women and other mine surface workers.

Before entering the mine Richard and the boys changed from their day clothes into thick flannel shirts, and coats and trousers made from canvas, donned hardened felt hats and pulled on heavy boots over sockless feet. Candles were stuck on their hard hats with lumps of sticky clay. Then began the descent down 1,000-foot or more of ladders, lasting perhaps half an hour. The mine was always wet and in several places during the descent water spurted out of the rock face at right angles to squirt Richard and the boys in their faces. The constant dripping of water off the walls and rungs of the ladder soaked them thoroughly by the time they got to their working level. The deeper they went the hotter it got. One mine at the 1,104-foot mark recorded the temperature of the water springing out of the rock face at 100 degrees Fahrenheit. Another mine at the 1,764-foot mark had recorded an air temperature of 96 to 108 degrees Fahrenheit. They worked naked to the waist with the sweat streaming off their faces and bodies in the oppressive heat and humidity. The only light came from the candles on their hats and others stuck randomly on rock ledges, giving off a yellow glow.

The boys had started their underground careers as operators of manual air machines or fans at unventilated tunnel ends. Since then they had progressed to barrow boys wheeling laden barrows of ore or spoil, using a sling from the barrow handles and then around their neck to support the substantial weight. To avoid raw knuckles when wheeling through narrow tunnels they bound the backs of their hands with leather strips. In future, their training would extend to developing skills with picks, sledges, mallets, crowbars and the various other paraphernalia used in mining.

Richard did not own a watch and had to calculate the passage of time working underground by the number of candles he used. At times they would be working 600 feet or more from the nearest shaft from which air could circulate and candles would not burn in the thin, rotten air near the workface. To get any light at all to work in, Richard had to place the candles twelve or eighteen feet behind him where the air was better. Sometimes candles would not light at all until he belted his shirt about to stir the air up. If all the candles went out he had to use flint and steel to light tinder as there were no matches. In black-on-black zero visibility this procedure could take at least three or four minutes.

Some years ago Richard had experienced being lost in the bowels of the mine without light. Towards the end of his shift a sudden massive fall of ground in front of him killed his partner, buried Richard in rock and dirt, and knocking his hat off in the process, tore his clothes and extinguished all his candles. In the ensuing panic of extracting himself he also lost his spare candles. He searched for an age in the dark, trying to locate them without success. He had no choice but to try and find his way back to the surface alone, and in total blackness. He slowly walked, feeling the sides of the drive as he went, then crawled up rises and along old levels and cross cuts until, exhausted and almost overcome with confusion, he felt, intuitively and from the change in the resonance from the sound he made as he progressed, that he was approaching a vertical shaft. Picking up a stone he threw it in front of himself and heard it tumble and fall till it splashed into water more than 100 feet below. Searchers found him next day drained of all energy lying in the soft mud at the edge of the shaft.

Chapter 3

WORKING

Twenty-eight percent of Cornish miners died before they were thirty due to disease and accidents. Every mining district had men missing one or two fingers or one or both eyes. Miners under twenty-five years were twice as likely to lose their life as those in any other occupation. It was a good old age if a miner lived to be fifty, but on average most did not live beyond forty, and if he were still able to work underground at the age of thirty-five he was exceptionally robust and lucky. Richard, now approaching the age of thirty-seven, was nearing the end of his working life. Nearly twenty percent of miners in the Gwennap area (some five miles from Tolcarne) died in violent mine accidents in 1847. In the following year the mean age at death in the mining area of Redruth was recorded as twenty-eight years and four months.

While wholesale earth collapses from "bad" ground was a common problem, there were plenty of other hazards, including machinery failure, gunpowder blasts, drowning, suffocation, disease and falling stones from which miner's felt hats gave little protection.

Chest diseases killed twice as many miners as people in other occupations in Cornwall. The cause was fine dust, foul air and poor ventilation. Black gunpowder used for blasting produced volumes of acrid smoke full of unburnt carbon particulate that took hours to abate and each blast created clouds of fine powdery dust. The candles Richard and his boys used were made from crude yellow tallow that burned with an offensive smell, made a soot laden flame from their thick hemp wicks and contributed to the bad air. After each blast, Richard, in visibility down to six inches, would stumble up to the ore face with a rag over his mouth, take off his shirt, and belt the air to disperse the smoke and dust so he could see again to work. Many accidents were caused through reduced visibility underground due to the ever present dust and poor lighting.

After years of breathing this mixture Richard's lungs were so lodged full of particulate that the least exertion caused shortness of breath. He developed a chronic cough in an attempt to eliminate constant excessive mucous secretions and in this condition became more susceptible to colds and flu which could lead to bronchitis, pneumonia, pleurisy and ultimately death. Every morning on awakening he coughed, hacked, brought up dreadful black stuff and cursed black blasting powder.

After working in these conditions for eight or more hours Richard and his boys Richard Junior and Ben, tired and exhausted, had to deal with an arduous and painful climb, which could last more than an hour and exceed 1,000 feet to the surface (often carrying heavy tools) on scores of different ladders, many of them lying at odd angles and some poorly fixed and quite shaky. Candles provided the only light and dripping water causing slippery rungs

The remains of a Cornish mine engine house, situated not far
from Tolcarne.

[Photograph by Libby Luke.]

on loose ladders meant there was a constant danger of injury or death due to a fall. Many miners died this way.

In the depths of winter they went below before the sun rose and surfaced after it had set so they hardly saw daylight and had pale and yellow complexions.

During their climb out they would leave behind temperatures in the high 80s (Fahrenheit) to arrive at the surface in weather conditions sometimes below freezing. The Dunstans were lucky to be working at a mine where warm water was available from the engine house to wash in before they put on their surface clothes. On their morning walk to the mine from the cottage they were at times so drenched by Cornish rain that their wet and cold clothes had not dried by the time they had surfaced yet still had to be worn home – often walking into the teeth of a howling wind.

Having done his own hard day's work at the surface, young Henry was pleased to join his father and brothers. The walk home always seemed further than the walk to the mine in the morning. Little groups of lanterns formed clusters as women and children surface workers joined their mining husbands and fathers to navigate home through the rough mining terrain. While Richard, feeling the exhaustion of the day, plodded in sober silence, the boys chatted and yarned all the way home, but there was certainly no hopping, skipping or leapfrogging.

Nine-year-old Henry had spent the day "picking" ore at the surface which involved basic sorting of ore by removing rubbish rock from the heaps. This was the first job boys were given when they started work. It was boring and monotonous, hot and dusty in summer and wet and muddy in winter when the boy's hands had to be protected with rag bandages or old worn stockings from the continuous handling of cold, wet and dirty ore. At times Henry worked in wind and rain until he could not move properly because of the cold, and was then allowed to stand in front of the boiler furnace where the steam soon rose in clouds from his clothes. Then it was back to work again in a waste landscape.

The surface mine area was dotted with hillocks of ore, spoil and cinders, interspersed with toxic puddles of water and sludge, occupying every available space between all manner of stone huts, wooden sheds, horse whims, thatched air shaft vents, washing floors and the steam engine pumping house. A constant blanket of noise came from the roar and hiss of the boiler, creaking and groaning mining pumps and winches, the clatter and thump of pounding hammers breaking ore, the scrape of shovels and the rattle of ore trucks pushed along rails by hand. In the absence of a stiff breeze a cloud of dust, steam and smoke hung like a shroud over the lot. A string of mules saddled with panniers heavily laden with ore clippity clopped their way through the women and children spread over the workings engaged in picking, sorting, washing, crushing and all the requisite tasks involved in the exploitation of precious ore.

Richard worked on a contract basis with the mine owners as a "Tributer". In simple terms this meant that the more good ore he won, the greater was his income. On the other hand if he struck a patch of dirt that returned little ore, then so too was his income less. A very good patch of ground might yield £70 a month but really poor ground might yield as low as £1 pound a month. The boys never saw their earnings as their wages were paid direct to Richard. Young Henry, as a surface worker earned four pence a day. Richard Junior, 11 years, and Ben, 10 years, working underground as barrow boys, were paid less than £2 pounds a month each. When Richard brought home his and the boy's pay he made a point of handing the lot over to Jane at the front door of the cottage in full view of the rest of the street so that all could see that fair play had taken place. Jane would then dole back to Richard and the boys their allowance.

While the consolidated revenue from these funds, all derived from mother earth, went to supporting the family of nine it was still essential for Jane to make a contribution by working her own patch of dirt at the cottage vegetable garden. The two-acre plot on which the Dunstans' cottage was built was rocky, fairly steep and not very productive. Here they grew mainly potatoes, which were an important staple of their diet, turnips and barley. About half was left uncultivated to graze the family cow shared with their neighbours. A few apple and plum trees had been planted and a herb garden that Jane was very proud of grew parsley, thyme, sage and rosemary for cooking and lavender to scent her best clothes.

The plot required much work from the whole family to make it productive. Jane donned a hessian pinafore and worked every available moment she could. The younger children Wearn 7, Mary 5, and Anne 2, would join her and "help" as best as they could. It was normal for a mother to call for her children to help almost as soon as they could walk. Infant Elizabeth, now referred to as "little Lizzie", tucked into a crude box cradle with dried herbs tied to the corners "to keep the fairies away", joined the others and asserted her presence by raising chubby fists above the edge of the box, grasping and ungrasping handfuls of air. When they were 8 or 9 years old they would all be joining the balmaidens or women surface workers on the ore dressing tasks at the mine. In spring and early summer and other times when the plantings demanded it Richard, Richard Junior, Ben and Henry after doing a day's work in the earth of the mine, would come home to work again in the dirt of the family plot, sometimes late into the moonlight or dark.

Jane's day was always full with no time left to work at the mine. Top priority was seeing to the children, making sure they learned the skills they would need in the future for their own homes and generally nurturing them along. Then she cleaned, dusted, tended to the fire, washed, did the cooking, topped up the oil lamps, planned purchase of provisions, fetched water, and in what time she had left worked in the one-acre garden. To Jane, cleaning was a moral duty that had been instilled in her by her mother and through her attendance at church where she learned that grime and filth were certainly bad if not close to a sin and that through the efforts of cleanliness you could certainly travel some distance towards the goal of "nearer my God to thee". While the pursuit of cleanliness advanced the Protestant ethic that work was good for your soul it was also good for practical reasons. It was known that a clean cottage was a healthy cottage although it was not really understood why. In pre insecticide and vacuum cleaner days fleas were everywhere and bedbugs and lice, or "crawlers" as Jane called them, were common. They all harboured disease and thrived in dust, grime and filth. It is quite true to say that each day Jane "religiously" swept out every corner of the cottage with a birch broom and shook out and aired the bedclothes and straw mattresses. She paid particular attention to scrubbing the stone doorstep which she could not bear to show any dirt to passing neighbouring cottagers.

Given the environment she lived in, Jane had to accept a certain amount of dust and discomfort as normal. Secretly, she longed for a proper house like the Rev. Pascoe's she had visited on a trip to Redruth with her Methodist church group. If she had a house like that and not one made of dirt like the mud cottage she lived in then she could really keep it clean.

Being energetic, and above all else determined, she insisted on supplying the family regularly with clean clothes. It took all of Monday each week to do the wash for a family of nine and required considerable strength and stamina. Jane carried water from the stream in two wooden buckets suspended from a yoke to fill a barrel shaped wash tub outside the cottage where clothes were soaked, pounded, rubbed, scrubbed and rinsed. Hot water was available from the big black iron kettles that sizzled constantly on the hearth. She made her own alkaline detergent liquid, called lye, from wood ash and employed various agents to remove stubborn stains ranging from lemon and onion juice, vinegar, milk or even urine which latter substance, containing ammonia, was freely available and very effective in bleaching linen and cotton. Naturally, afterwards, a final freshwater wash was administered. Clothes were draped on nearby bushes to dry, whiten and sterilise in the sun or hung on a line strung between cottages. Little ironing was applied to work-week clothes but Sunday best dresses and shirts were pressed with flat irons heated on the hearth.

Clothes for herself and family were obtained by Jane from the parish charity or the second-hand clothes dealer in Cambourne or Redruth. She could seldom afford to buy anything new. They all wore "hand me downs" which were patched and darned until they were plainly irreparable. She would make a blouse out of two old shirts which were beyond patching. There would still be good material left, mostly in the sides and tails, so long as she avoided the most worn spots. She was the sort of person who, regardless of life's challenges and misfortunes would find ten good reasons for being grateful for what she had and would make the most of her lot. Her well equipped sewing basket was her most treasured and important possession. With it, in addition to making new clothes out of rags, she replaced ripped sleeves, re-seated pants, patched knees in trousers and darned socks. Around the fire at night she taught the younger children her sewing basket skills, and there was always knitting to be done.

Chapter 4

LIVING

Jane always worried about Richard and her three boys working at the mine, praying each day that they would come home safely. At night she would listen for every step until she recognised their familiar tread. On the worst wintery nights she would take her own lantern and walk to the hill on the track to the mine and wait for them. Her great happiness came from the knowledge that she was the indispensable centre of family life. She was in charge of the family budget. She took responsibility for making ends meet, and did everything possible with the means at her disposal to achieve this goal, but there was never enough money. The children were always hungry. Every day tummies rumbled and thoughts turned to food.

Moments after the mine workers returned home Jane dished out the main family meal of the day. It was usually based on a few home grown vegetables. When available, potatoes, boiled or roasted were the mainstay with parsnips or turnips, served with mugwort tea and perhaps barley bread with treacle for dessert. At times, local salted Cornish sardines, home cured bacon, or maybe a few eggs – always in small quantities, were served with a great dish of potatoes. In season there might be plums or apples from the trees in their garden. Food was served first to Richard then running down the children by age and ending with Jane who always gave Richard and the three older boys the best food because the whole family depended on their physical efforts as the main breadwinners. The rules were, "no talking at the table with your mouth full" and "nothing was to be left on the plate". Richard's job was to enforce the rules and he kept a handy strap available for that purpose. But the rules themselves were mostly made by Jane. They both strove to teach the children behaviour, manners and speech that were thought proper and to instil a sense of right and wrong in them.

Fresh meat was a luxury with only a few pennyworths of the poorer cuts of mutton bought in the market at Cambourne on Saturday to be cooked up in a meat pudding as a special Sunday treat. The meat was chopped and mixed with potatoes and onions, dropped into a dough lined mixing bowl then capped with a dough lid. Bowl and all, were then wrapped in a pudding cloth and lowered into the large iron boiling pot hanging from the chain in the hearth. This meat "pudden" was a favourite of Richard and the boys. Tripe was cheap and often bought by Jane – heated up in the iron pot with onions, potatoes and thickening it was a good sustaining meal for the family. Toasted barley bread was a favourite side dish with salted dripping, homemade jam or treacle if available.

Jane made a basic dessert pudding from a mix of flour, baking powder, dripping, sugar, a pinch of salt, water and whatever she could find to add to taste or substance be it stale bread, herbs, dried apples or fresh fruit if available. This was whisked together, plopped in a grease lined mixing bowl wrapped in a pudding cloth, dunked in the boiling pot for an hour or two and served hot with a drizzle of treacle. Puddings were an economical and sensible food for poor people.

The family pig was important. A nice fat one in the sty meant a good winter. Everyone helped to collect grass and greens to feed it. When piggy was fat enough he was butchered after sunset. A grisly sight as the silhouette of the pig, hoisted by the rear trotters, squealing and defecating, was blooded and dispatched in the flickering candlelight. Richard always did this on the waxing of the moon, otherwise it was thought that the meat would go bad. Jane took the next couple of weeks to cure the pig by rubbing salt into its flesh every day in a large curing trough holding the pig and a brine mix, after which it was hung in the chimney over a smoky wood fire for several more days. Before being eaten, the meat was soaked for up to thirty-six hours and then boiled.

As most fresh foods would not last more than a couple of days and needed to be protected from rodents, flies and insects, a good deal of Jane's kitchen time was spent in pickling, curing, smoking, salting, making jam and generally trying to preserve food. She had nothing that could be described as a kitchen appliance. The items she used as much as any in her preparations were her mortar and pestle. Something always needed to be pulverised. She had a couple of whisks, a colander, a cook's basic chopper and cutting knives. The most cherished and expensive item in the entire kitchen was her large copper preserving pan. This she used when she could get fruit to preserve or make jam which she put into earthenware jars sealed with corks and melted wax.

The Dunstan's cow, shared with neighbours, was fed and

milked by Jane on alternate days. Fresh milk was poured into a bowl and covered with muslin to keep out flies. Cream rose to the top overnight and was skimmed off next day. Some of this Jane churned with a whisk to make butter which was heavily salted and stored in an earthenware crock to preserve it. The rest was made into clotted cream by being slowly and gently heated for most of the day – making sure it did not boil. When cooled, a very thick, yellow, crusted, wonderfully caramel tasting cream was skimmed off. The procedure also helped to preserve the cream.

As all funds coming in were fully spent in the maintenance of a family of nine they could never save any money. If Richard struck a bad patch of dirt reducing his earnings, or the potato crop was insufficient, or the home cured pig had already been eaten then a more hungry time arrived. Feral birds might then be added to the menu. Sparrows, blackbirds and thrushes were caught at night by throwing nets over the hedges where they roosted and then ringing their necks in the light of a lantern. The eldest boys Richard Junior, Ben and Henry enjoyed very much going with their father on these hunting expeditions. As many as two dozen sparrows could be used to make a birdie pie. Sometimes a single bird would be roasted on a fork in front of the fire. The old nursery rhyme of four and twenty blackbirds baked in a pie is based on a foundation of truth.

There were no shops in Tolcarne apart from the "pot shop" that sold beer and cheap cider to the miners, although peddlers and tinkers called in from time to time. On Saturdays Jane and the children walked the tracks, paths and roads four miles to Cambourne or five miles to Redruth to buy provisions at the markets. Jane would not think twice to walk these distances to purchase a reel of cotton or any other small item if she needed it. The markets were the best place to buy cheap food and goods. Poor people were their main customers. Jane enjoyed the extravagant spiel of the stallholders, the cheap hot soup, the buskers, the bargains and the smells. It was a great source of free entertainment for her and the children.

Long rows of stalls stretched out with fowl, flesh and fish at one end and cakes, sweets and breads at the other. In between were boots, drapery, boxes, jams, baskets, sealing wax, beds, old books, chairs, hardware, crockery, cutlery, clothes, sauces and farmers' wives with great baskets of butter, cheese, poultry, fruit, eggs and cream. You could buy anything from chamber pots, thimbles and needles to snuff boxes, song sheets and potions – all offered for sale with an entertaining banter of more value than the goods. Knife grinders rang bells, peddled their stone wheels and created sparks. Fiddle, tin whistle and concertina players busked for a few pennies thrown into their hats. Horse, cattle and pig vendors haggled over the price. People walked, talked and laughed. Jane and the children loved it but could not afford to spend much. If she had to buy anything extra such as clothes or a pair of shoes for one of the children, then she and the children would simply eat less.

One person they did not like at the market, but still had to do business with, was the itinerant tooth puller. Mining families did not practise any dental hygiene. There was not a toothbrush in the entire hamlet. Stained, decayed teeth and bad breath were standard with toothache a recurring problem. The family had no access to qualified dentists and had to either employ a tooth puller or treat themselves through such methods as applying a small bag of hot salt to the ache. Anyone with a pair of tongs and a bottle of brandy could set up as a tooth puller. While no anaesthetics or sterilised instruments were used the fee charged was reasonable.

By today's standards Jane, Richard and the children were smelly, dirty and lousy. Their clothes were verminous and their hair full of lice. Richard used tobacco juice from his pipe to kill them. There was nothing like shampoo and proper soap was expensive as it carried a government tax which, in effect, operated as a tax on hygiene and cleanliness. Deodorant hadn't been invented. There was no piped water at all in the hamlet. No one had a proper bath to wash in and there was no other readily accessible means available for thorough and frequent washing. Cold water was available from the stream but that required numerous arduous trips carrying heavy wooden buckets dangling at the end of a yoke a considerable distance.

Poor people bathed infrequently at best and usually only the hands, neck and arms were washed piecemeal using a basin and a pitcher for a stand-up wash or a small low tub in which they sat for a sponge bath. Only babies, like little Lizzie, and small children had regular full baths. But, once a week Jane would lock the cottage doors, strip, step into a foot bath and wash from waist to toe thoroughly. On Saturday afternoon Richard would have his weekly shave.

The younger children, Wearn 7, Mary 5 and Anne 2 were a rowdy grubby lot as they were impossible to keep clean in the austere hamlet environment. But their childhood was orderly and although much of it was spent on household chores, there was always some time left for play. Skipping and rhyming games for girls, marbles and ball games for boys. Street games followed rules and conventions made up and passed on over the years.

Jane was a tough disciplinarian and imposed codes of family behaviour and well understood rules of conduct so that the family of nine could live, eat, sleep and successfully function in the one room cottage. Their very circumstances dictated that they would learn much about tolerance, cooperation and understanding of others. The children learned to be kind to each other and obedient and respectful to their elders. In default parental punishment, as deemed appropriate, was doled out for breaches.

Jane and the other women in the hamlet had no effective knowledge of birth control or practices and wives like them were usually locked into a continuous round of pregnancy and childbirth. She was now thirty-three and already had seven children after twelve years of marriage. She explained to the children that God put babies under gooseberry bushes and that was where they came from or that they were brought by the midwife. Sometimes, when they were older she told them that babies came from her body, but they were left with the impression that the exit point was her naval.

In a sense the greatest and most constant deprivation suffered by Richard and Jane was privacy. It was unattainable in a small cottage with seven children. In such circumstances it was impossible to have what we today would call a satisfactory sex life. They were not free to behave as they wished without being overheard if not observed. Overcoming adversity through necessity, they dealt with the situation with applied furtive cunning and skill to develop the art of copulating quietly in bed at night, while during the day they did not outwardly show much affection towards each other. Unless they went for a long walk together, lack of privacy in the cottage meant also that the couple could not discuss, argue issues or have a fight without involving the children.

There were disagreements. Richard claimed his place as chief breadwinner, head of the household and protector of the family. Jane and the children were expected to be obedient and submissive to his rules. The Victorian male thought he was rational, stronger and more courageous than women who were unreasoning, feeble and timid by comparison. The only problem with this attitude was that determined and strong minded women like Jane hotly disputed their assigned position. As far as she was concerned the home was her sphere of influence – a place where she knew she could impose moral authority over important issues such as religion, unselfishness, love and the demon drink. But try as she did Jane failed to get Richard either into a church or a chapel or to stay out of an inn or pot shop. His view was that a man's faith, or lack of it, was a matter for his own conscience. He respected his wife's religious zeal but did not embrace it himself. He preferred, in typical stout hearted Cornishman style, to join his mining friends in drinking, swearing and high-spirited fellowship.

Mainly due to lack of funds Richard was not a heavy drinker, but occasional bouts of prosperity when he struck a good patch of dirt in the mine allowed him to submerge his troubles in alcohol for a short while which sometimes led to family embarrassment from his conduct. While never a violent man at home he was not known to turn the other cheek if challenged in the local pot shop. Apart from his reputation as a first class miner he was also respected as a formidable man in a fight – particularly when he was younger. He had enormously large hands planted on short, powerful arms with broad shoulders and a strong back tapering to narrow hips on short solid legs supporting his frame measuring less than five and a half feet at full stretch. His hair had been black but was now salt and pepper grey, with more salt and less pepper showing as each year passed. His well shaped nose now displayed black spots from years of in-ground mining dirt and his full light brown eyes, no longer brilliant, were now bloodshot with bags developing underneath. A pallid complexion and drawn cheeks confirmed that at the age of thirty-six he was well past his prime.

The local pot house in the hamlet was the social centre for the men who gathered there after work to savour their half pints, a sip at a time to make them last. Just a few pennies would buy a cheap ale or cider. Richard argued that alcohol restored the spirits after work. It was not just a source of pleasure but a rejuvenator as well. Miners seldom got drunk as there was never enough money for that. There was always a lot of talk, good-natured ribbing, hearty singing (rather than good) and lots of mateship to go around. Sometimes men brought along their fiddles or tin whistles to provide entertainment. Only a few men from the hamlet did not attend and they were thought to be over furnished with religion, scarce on pennies, or both. It was a homely place with rustic wooden benches and tables around a big warm fireplace. There were half a dozen brass bound wooden barrels piled in the corner, battered pewter mugs on the tables, a low ceiling, flickering candlelight, a smoky atmosphere and a large, buxom and cheerful host named Hetty who cackled and joked her way through life. All who attended there got very happy on very little. Customers were served by a pot boy who brought drinks to their seats. In addition to any refreshment and entertainment provided it was also a good place to learn about local news and obtain information from your mates on any subject. Men like Richard who could not read would have newspapers and broadsheets read to them and it was here in the pot shop that he learned about the possibilities of emigrating to Australia.

It was not acceptable for women or children to go to taverns or pot shops. Women who did so were looked down upon. The centre of Jane's social life was the Methodist religion which had very strict ideas of right and wrong. It was a sin to smoke and drink and she prayed each day that Richard would abstain and be saved from these evil habits. As there was no proper church in Tolcarne, every Sunday evening she attended a service held in one of the hamlet's cottages dubbed "The Meeting House". It was an ordinary cottage converted each week for the purpose by clearing out the few basic items of furniture and installing some hard scrubbed white benches to sit on. Up front there was a little table covered with a white linen cloth upon which was placed a lamp and a Bible. The fireplace glowed and flickered. A faint smell of smoke and burning wax from lit candles pervaded the place. People packed in. It was warm and cosy. It was friendly and cheerful. Everyone gained from the fellowship. Hymns were sung without musical accompaniment and sometimes with if a member of the congregation had brought his fiddle, squeezebox or pennywhistle.

Prayers were offered. God was thanked. More hymns sung. Hymns sung again. The designated preacher then preached the gospel of love and forgiveness of sins and the brotherhood of man. The Lord was praised with eloquence and fervour. And more hymns were sung. Afterwards everyone always felt much better. As religion goes it was plain and wholesome; a poor people's religion that gave comfort and support to those who were struggling. It brought Jane happiness to know that she was counted among the saved and that she was part of God's plan for the universe. She loved going to the Meeting House and while Richard never went he was nonetheless a man of principles who still believed in God. His creed was to do the right thing, help your family and friends, be straight and honest, pay your way and have the courage to stand up to your beliefs.

During the week, the women from the Meeting House congregation would gather at evening social groups such as sewing circles or Bible readings if they had the time and energy left after a long day's work. Recipes were exchanged with gossip and those who could took turns to read to those who could not from the Bible, broadsheets and newspapers. Jane particularly loved hearing the newspapers being read. Group evening classes gave a basic grounding in literacy to the children in reading and writing and instilled them with the values of industry, punctuality, orderliness, cleanliness and godliness. This was their only formal education apart from those times when they and Jane went to Cambourne church on Sunday morning and the children attended Bible teaching classes at Sunday school.

Chapter 5

FAMINE AND RIOT

Potatoes were the most important source of food for the poor families in Tolcarne. When the previously unknown fungus *phytophthora infestans* hit the potato crops Cornwall was one of the worst affected areas. There was widespread hunger and deprivation with mining families suffering acutely. The blight wiped out the entire crop leaving nothing but a black, rotting, putrid inedible mess. Potatoes were a source of vitamin C and as they were a major food staple their absence from families' diets during the potato famine (1845–1848) caused symptoms of scurvy including aching joints, lethargy, bruise like patches on the arms, bleeding gums, wobbly teeth, nosebleeds, skin sores, a foul-smelling breath and a general feeling of unwellness and depression. Everyone in Jane's family felt poorly. The cure was fresh green vegetables or lemons, limes or oranges. Unfortunately these were beyond the budget of the Dunstans and other people in the hamlet.

The harvest of 1846 proved a disaster and sent grain prices skyrocketing to almost double the price. The winter of 1846 – 1847 was harsh and cold with great distress among the poor. On a night in early February 1847 something quietly happened outside the cottage. It snowed. Constantly, silently and efficiently it fell until by morning three inches or more had been laid. Icicles hung and glittered from the edge of the thatch and snowdrifts formed on the outside walls. Snow blew through cracks around the ill fitting door and window casement leaving a cover of the finest white powder on the floor in which the family left their foot prints on awakening. Condensation formed ice patterns on the inside of the single window pane and there was a solid crust of ice on the surface of the family chamber pot. Snow was rare in the hamlet and normally melted quickly due to the proximity and tempering effects of the sea.

This snow stayed for days. All food became very expensive and everyone in Tolcarne was greatly undernourished if not half starved. Often, the best Jane could do for breakfast for the family was to make up some gruel from three parts water and one part milk thickened with barley flour. That was it. Supper was often stewed turnips (in the absence of potatoes) with barley cake or just barley on the side. After buying food there was little money left to purchase fuel for the fire. The cold in winter created a desperation to stay warm. Little feet turned to stone. Shoes left wet all night could be frozen in the morning. Trying to stay warm and getting enough to eat were the family's two main problems.

Richard was angry, and at times nearly driven mad, because he could not earn enough to properly feed his wife and children. He was not alone. Dead fires, empty stomachs, wasting children and an ailing wife were powerful incentives to riot. In June 1847 the price of grain peaked. A crowd of angry miners, many accompanied by their wives, began to assemble outside Redruth where a number of millers had their mills. It included Richard and Jane and most of the people living at Tolcarne. Their grievance was against the millers and merchants and the high prices charged locally for flour which the low-paid miners could not afford. The event was heralded by the Redruth town crier who ran around frantically ringing his bell to warn that a large mob of miners, about 5,000, was marching on the town. With shops lining mud and cobbled streets it was a rough and rowdy place at the best of times. Somewhere within earshot there was always a domestic argument going on with traumatised children screaming in the background. Dogs barked often and fought regularly. A complex array of odours from the dwellings mixed with the smell of horse urine and manure in the streets. Horses, oxen and the occasional donkey, pulling a variety conveyances clip clopped through the lot.

Responding to the crier, innkeepers and shop proprietors hurriedly shut doors and shuttered their windows. The Riot Act was read by a local JP standing at the front of Andrews Hotel. The mob ignored him and marched off to a flour store where the women helped themselves to the accompaniment of rousing rebellious songs from the men. Jane did not hesitate to join in and grab some food for the family. Desperate times produce desperate people. Eventually a group of constables forced the women out of the store and Jane then realised that she had become separated from Richard. Being of less than average height she was unable to see where the crowd was sweeping her. Men and women were pushing her from all directions and several times she received an elbow in the ribs and then a kick in the shins which took away her breath. Sometimes the crowd would stop and sweating men would shout and curse out their grievances before surging off again. Several people fainted and were trampled underfoot. Eventually the crowd stopped outside another large grain house yelling "Sell us corn at a fair and proper price!", and then to her relief Richard's arm appeared from the crowd and held her tight around the waist. In anticipation of trouble a squad of soldiers had been brought in from Penzance and when they turned up the crowd dispersed.

No one was seriously hurt although a group of constables had been pelted with a barrage of stones and two men were injured. But flour mills and stores had been broken into and goods stolen; people who had tried to stop the rioters had been dealt with very roughly. Reflecting about it later Jane was quite upset at being caught up in it. Of those offenders who were arrested and later convicted and sentenced, two were given seven years transportation while five other men and five women were imprisoned with hard labour.

Despite all Jane's frugality, prudence and good management, Richard and the children remained undernourished and Jane even more so as she gave some of her food to Richard or divided it among the seven children. As the main breadwinner Richard's needs were given absolute priority and to that end Jane could always eat less. The problem was, she began to realise, that what amounted to her slow starvation would eventually reduce her ability to perform the formidable task before her.

There had been talk among the women at the Meeting House that in the Australian Colonies more money could be earned, cheaper food could be bought and that life was much better. When Jane learned that it was possible for a family to obtain a government assisted or free passage to get there she began to take an acute interest in the scheme which at the time was also actively promoted and supported by her Methodist church as part of its ideology of self-help and improvement.

An increasing number of people began to see emigration as a

logical way to escape hard times and embrace new opportunities. To Jane that seemed like the answer as she could see little hope of improvement for the family at home. Richard too had heard about the idea of emigrating as it was a constantly recurring subject for debate in the pot shop. But he was not as keen as Jane. He confidently believed that he and the family would all live and be sheltered forever in the cottage he had built for them. He did not look for change.

A number of Cornish people from the environs of the hamlet, including some from the villages of Cambourne, Redruth and Helston had already emigrated to South Australia. Their praises of the colony contained in letters sent home soon reached Tolcarne via word of mouth. Government agents promoted the benefits of emigration through public meetings, the local press and the publication of placards, posters and handbills. Such documents quickly found their way to the Meeting House and the pot shop where they were read out aloud by those who could read for the benefit of those who could not. On one of her regular visits to the Meeting House Jane had the following document read to her:

Emigration to South Australia

"Mr. I Latimer (Agent for South Australia), having been requested to explain the principles of colonization adopted by the South Australian Commissioners with regard to this colony begs to announce that he will deliver a FREE LECTURE on Monday evening next, July 26, 1847 in the Market House Redruth. As the lecture is particularly intended for the instruction and benefit of the WORKING CLASSES it is hoped that all those who feel interested in the subject will give their attendance punctually. The lecture will commence at seven o'clock precisely and at the conclusion the lecturer will be happy to answer any questions relative to the colony."

FREE

EMIGRATION TO PORT ADELAIDE,

SOUTH AUSTRALIA

Married Agricultural Laborers, Shepherds, Blacksmiths, Wheelwrights, Sawyers, Tailors, Shoe-makers, Brick-makers, Builders, and *all persons engaged in useful occupations may obtain a*

FREE PASSAGE

to SOUTH AUSTRALIA, where they are within the regulations of the Colonial Commissioners.

A meeting will be held by Mr. LATIMER, for the purpose of seeing the applicants and de-ciding on their eligibility

On *TUESDAY, October 15, at BODMIN, at Ten o'clock.*

In the meanwhile all particulars may be known on application to

Mr. I. LATIMER, Truro.

AGENT TO H. M's. COMMISSIONERS.

All letters must be *post-paid* or they will not be answered.

E. HEARD, PRINTER, BOOKBINDER, BOSCAWEN-STREET, TRURO.

One of Mr. Latimer's Posters.

[Courtesy of The Courtney Library, The Royal Institution of Cornwall, Truro.]

When Jane heard about Latimer's forthcoming lecture at Redruth she insisted that Richard attend with her and dragged him along notwithstanding his whining, complaining and general disgruntlement. There she learned firsthand about the exciting, but formidable, prospect of moving her family to South Australia. Numerous persons among the mass of people packed into the hall had travelled a great distance to hear the agent. The crowd listened intently to the reading of testimonial letters sent home by previous Cornish settlers extolling the virtues of the colonies. All reports spoke in glowing terms about the climate, the Aborigines, availability of work, potential mineral wealth for miners, the freedom, wages, conditions on board ship, availability of land, agricultural prospects, and the cost of living and so on. The combined effect of all this marketing propaganda on Jane was to convince her that emigration was a heaven sent opportunity that would undoubtedly provide a safe route to successful self-improvement and greater health and happiness for her and family.

Richard was less enthused and there followed many discussions between them, some quite heated.

"To go to Australia you might as well go to the moon," he said.

If they decided to go it would be a decision of absolute finality for it was most unlikely that the family would ever put together enough money in the colonies for a return journey to Cornwall. Then there was the country itself, its convict background, wild natives, rough bush, dangerous animals, different climate. Would they be able to deal with all that? And what about the dangers of the 3 to 4 months voyage at sea? Nearly all contact would be lost with friends and extended family members left behind. Would they be able to make a new life with new friends or be sentenced to a lifetime of loneliness? Once there, would they be able to earn enough money to support a family of nine? And, where would they live? Then, there was the question of cost. Although the voyage was promoted as a "free" or assisted passage it in fact entailed considerable expense including the cost of equipping the family with a compulsory onboard kit of clothing and the expense of travel between Tolcarne and the port of departure at Plymouth. It all seemed too difficult. Richard thought the family would do best if they stayed in Cornwall. A long sea voyage wasn't safe. When they got there a job wasn't guaranteed. To go to a strange land wasn't good. To leave the house he had built wasn't right. He wasn't happy.

Chapter 6

GUNPOWDER AND KNOCKERS

There was a certain magic in spending a winter's evening around a great open wood fire. The warmth from the fire, the smell of burning wood and the flickering flames lighting the cottage were a great source of nourishment to the family, providing a focus for holding them tightly together with feelings of well-being and sharing. Usually the fire glow was the only light. To people who could not read, the absence of good light did not matter. Talking, storytelling, reciting learned verse and even singing were the activities enjoyed during the long winter's evenings. The Cornish were great raconteurs and Richard had an extensive repertoire of old tales; many that got better with the telling. This was his favourite time of day. With the whole family seated around the hearth soaking up the warmth he would take the smallest on his knee, gather the others in closer and begin. He had stories about things that went bump in the night such as ghoulies and ghosties, and stories about the Little People which included the good-natured but mischievous Piskies who were always playing pranks and tricks on humans, when they were not sitting on their mushroom Pisky stools. One of their favourite pranks was to lead a lonely traveller at night away from his set path. But you could avoid being Pisky-led if you wore an item of clothing inside out – socks were the easiest. Then there were the Little People known as Spriggans who lived near the ancient stone circles, rock cairns and barrows and were quite different from the Piskies, being a humourless, nasty, malevolent branch of the family and always up to no good. They were to be avoided if at all possible.

The most important group of Little People were the Knockers who lived underground in the mines. They were central to Cornish mining lore. Their existence was taken as fact and novice miners were taught to both respect and believe in the Knockers. The stories that Richard told his children about the Knockers were always delivered seriously. He described them as small shrivelled beings about the size of a one-year-old child, with an ugly wrinkled old man's face on a large head and ungainly limbs. They were often heard close by the miners in the solid rock, tap tapping in the underground drives and tunnels during the intervals of the miners work.

The knockers knew the difference between good and bad dirt and the wise miner dug in the direction of their sound to get good returns. Down below, explained Richard, there were places where the ore was so rich it sparkled like diamonds. All you had to do was have the luck to find it. While the Knockers could be a great help to the miners they could also get up to mischief if it suited them. Sometimes their knocking sounds led not to rich ground but were a warning of danger. It paid not to offend them and they did not like disrespectful shouting or whistling in their presence.

Whistling in the mine was thought to bring bad luck and none was allowed.

The spirit of the earth was embodied in the Knockers. Their legendary tales served a practical purpose. Ground falls in mines were often preceded by cracking, groaning or knocking noises. Such sounds put miners on notice that it may not be safe to work in the area. The Knockers were warning them. If you respected the earth it would give you a good living, but it was not a safe environment and you always had to remain alert. A true believer, Richard wondered if the Australian earth accommodated knockers and if so, were they different to the Cornish ones?

By early October 1847 Richard Junior, now in his twelfth year, was working daily beside his father in the mine and had almost mastered the skills of picking, shovelling, drilling, blasting, sorting and carrying that went with the business of mining. On this day his job was to carry away "dead" ground as his father picked it and to dump it close by in an unused drive. They stripped to the waist because of the heat and worked in semi darkness as their candles struggled to burn properly in the bad air. Underfoot was wet and muddy with the walls of the mine damp and leaking water. Young Richard was happy working with his dad and was keen to learn.

They had now reached the stage where blasting was required, the pick being useless on the hard rock that their dig had uncovered. Using a hammer and a steel boring bar they hand drilled a deep hole in a carefully chosen spot on the rock face. While Richard Junior turned the steel drill his father beat it with a six-pound hammer. He took pride in the fact that he could beat the drill from any angle with either hand. By the time they were finished the end of the drill was beaten bright and shone in the candlelight, as did the sweat running down Richard's body. The hole was then charged with black powder from a powder flask, a hollow reed full of powder inserted for a fuse and the hole then filled with clay which was tamped down around it. As Richard was in the process of doing this by ramming the clay in the hole with his boring bar, he thought he heard a knocking sound and turned his head slightly to the left. When he did a spark created by the steel hitting the rock ignited the black powder charge. There was a short hiss followed by a flash and then an explosion as the rocks flew at his face and the steel whizzed past his ear to lodge in the roof of the tunnel.

Apart from being showered in rocks and getting a heavy dose of smoking black fumes, which caused them to cough and spit thick black mucous for hours, both miners remarkably survived without serious injury. Richard was deaf for a day and a half, his eyebrows and hair singed, had cuts to his face and vision that was blurred for a week. But aside from that and a more serious cut to his hand, he was fine, except perhaps for a certain tightness in the chest and a sharp rattling cough that seemed to linger on. Richard Junior was thrown back against the tunnel wall by the blast, covered in rocks and dirt, some of which he swallowed and breathed in, had the devil frightened out of him but was otherwise good.

Jane thanked God that Richard had survived his accident and thanked The Divine Father that he had also seen fit to spare her eldest son. To her the outcome was an uplifting and wondrous experience as she revelled in the glorious road to salvation. Richard reckoned that the Knockers had saved him as he turned his head to listen to a knocking sound. He just wanted to go to the pot shop to wash down the black powder and dust and everything would be fine. This time Jane was happy to give him some extra pennies to spend on himself as the explosion had revealed a remarkably rich vein of solid blue-green copper ore and it was apparent that, for the immediate future, they would have more money than they had seen for years.

The dreadful 1846 harvest that lead to the untenable price of grain peaking in June 1847 put pressure on credit and the currency due to the necessity to import grain at inflated prices. By September the price had dropped sixty percent and grain dealers who had invested money in the trade were ruined. The banking system was also under strain from rampant speculation in new railway developments and the effect of its own financial controls. The result was a financial crash in October 1847, the suspension of the Bank Act, a sudden increase in the number of unemployed and a wide and chronic depression that hit the whole of England.

Richard knew his income was never guaranteed. Illness, accident or a downturn in profitability at the mine might deprive him of his livelihood overnight. If another job could not be found and the family was unable to survive on any income Jane and the children might bring in, then the next step would be the workhouse. The fundamental principle upon which those places were run was to make life in them so terribly unattractive that any kind of miserable and miserly work elsewhere was preferable.

There were no such provisions as minimum wages or maximum hours to protect workers. If it came to going to the workhouse the rule was that a family had to be admitted as a whole. A man or a woman could not sacrifice themselves for the sake of the family which had to be admitted as a unit. On entering the house families were automatically broken up with wives separated from husbands and mothers separated from children. Standard in-mates clothes were issued, work was menial without wages and food was plain, monotonous and sparse. Diets specified by the Poor Law Board were about half of what a prisoner would get in gaol at the time. Inmates of one workhouse were so starving that they resorted to chewing meat remnants on putrid old bones they had been given to crush as fertiliser. Richard resolved that so long as he had breath left in his body he would not lead his family to the workhouse.

Jane had three main reasons that gave her the desire to leave for South Australia. Firstly, the failure of the potato crop had resulted in significant deprivation and hardship to her family from 1845 to 1847. There was, it seemed, just not enough food in Cornwall to properly live on. Secondly, she felt that there must be a better environment to bring up the children than in the dirty squalid conditions of what was more of a mining camp than a proper hamlet. And lastly, she worried about Richard, his health and the onerous conditions of his occupation underground in Cornwall. She had heard that in South Australia the mines were not nearly as deep, the air was cleaner, they were not as hot to work in, the ore bodies were better and the consequent financial returns to the miners much greater. It was a different earth. She had heard that the colony of South Australia was about three times as large as the whole of Great Britain and Ireland. Surely there had to be plenty of opportunities there. She persisted and eventually reached agreement with Richard that they would give emigration their best shot. To those who had large families and were hungry, the bottom line was well expressed by a Cornish migrant in South Australia who wrote to his friends – "There is no cry in our streets for bread."

Chapter 7

PAPERWORK AND RED TAPE

In 1848 a number of small pamphlet booklets were published and sold at four pence or less with information and advice contained therein on how to emigrate. They included details on how to obtain an application form and how to complete it, how to pack and prepare for the voyage, procedures at the port of embarkation, the sea voyage itself and how to deal with government bureaucracy and red tape. On a visit to Cambourne market Jane bought a booklet called *The Emigrants Friend* or *Authentic Guide to South Australia*. She liked the title the bookseller gave it and knew that her neighbour and friend Kathy Martin, who was a good reader, would be thrilled at the chance to read it to her. Indeed because there was so much interest in the hamlet in the entire question of emigration in general and the decision of the Dunstans in particular, Kathy Martin conducted readings of the pamphlet booklet to packed sessions in the Meeting House where she read out aloud: "… this is the place where the humblest house is fitted up with cedar – where the fields are fenced with mahogany and myrtle trees are burned for fuel, where the swans are black and the eagles are white – where the kangaroo, an animal between the squirrel and the deer, has fine claws on its fore paws, and three talons on its hind legs like a bird and yet hops on its tail – where the mole lays eggs, suckles its young and has a ducks bill – where there is a bird with a broom in its mouth instead of a tongue – where there is no quadruped with a hoof – where the animals mostly jump instead of run …"

You could hear a pin drop as Kathy read on surrounded by wide eyes and dropped jaws. The booklet described the coastland in South Australia as "… about one-third well-watered barren land – a large proportion rocky and mountainous – and the rest a fertile country – beautiful in aspect – highly productive, and healthy in the extreme. Here are no fevers – no periodical dysentery – no consumptions – no asthmas – no coughs – and no agues. Good health is in every countenance."

To the women assembled in the Church Meeting House of Tolcarne this sounded close to a description of heaven on earth and although the pamphlet did point out some less attractive aspects of colonial life in South Australia they did not register past the impenetrable enthusiasm of the ladies. The pamphlet went on to say that the discovery of copper mines offered a source of almost boundless wealth and that the mine at Burra Burra was admitted to be the richest in the world. It said that about half a mile from the mine there was a town with two inns and many stores and warehouses stocking at moderate prices clothing, hardware, tools, domestic articles, cottons "and indeed everything from a needle to an anchor". There were butchers, bakers, two breweries, several beer shops, a church and a Wesleyan Chapel.

Inexperienced miners were earning £12 to £15 per month and experienced miners as much as £30 or £40 a month. It only cost about £30 to erect a cottage suitable for a labourer. In England at the time many workers were earning £20 or less per annum. Richard usually earned only a few pounds a month. The details obtained about precisely what money miners might earn in South Australia reinforced Jane's determination to press on and even Richard began to show some enthusiasm for the proposal.

But the problem was that even if the family succeeded in being granted a "free" or assisted passage there was still a huge expense to be met. With the assistance of her friend Kathy Martin, Jane made a list of the costs from the information detailed in the booklet:

Passage Deposits:	Pounds
Richard and Jane at £2 each	4.0.0
Seven children at £1 each	7.0.0
Fee for more than two children under seven	7.0.0

Estimated cost of compulsory shipboard clothing and equipment:	
Richard and Jane	7.0.0
Four oldest children	8.0.0
Three youngest children	5.0.0
Cost of travel to Plymouth	2.0.0
Gen. sustenance – Tolcarne to Plymouth	1.0.0
Miscellaneous	3.0.0
TOTAL	**£44.0.0**

The total was equivalent to more than two years income for many workers at the time. But Jane was not deterred. The whole family would simply have to work harder to save more until they had reached the required sum. In any event Richard had now struck an excellent patch at the mine and was earning more than he had for years.

Jane obtained an application form from Isaac Latimer, the agent of the Colonial Land and Emigration Commission (CLEC) when she called to see him on one of his visits to Redruth. She sought the assistance of Kathy to fill it out. Like Jane she was bright and intelligent but also an accomplished writer as well as reader. It was a detailed and complicated form which required filling in particulars of name, trade or calling, whether parish relief had been received, address, marital status, name and address of employer and minister of religion. She also had to give details of names, ages, birth dates and smallpox vaccination status of each family member and if they could read indicating whether they could do so "very well", "well", "a little" or "not at all". Both Richard and Jane had to state on the form if they could write or not. It then had to be signed by Richard as the principal applicant (in his case with his mark) after he declared, among other things, that he would during the voyage conform to regulations established for the good governance of those on board and not leave the ship until it reached its destination.

The form was then witnessed by two "respectable house-holders" (publicans or dealers in beer and spirits were disqualified) who had to testify that the applicants were honest, sober, industrious, of general good character and not likely to become a burden on the colony. Next, a physician or surgeon had to certify that he had examined Richard, Jane and the children and that none of them were seriously mutilated or deformed in person, nor in his opinion afflicted with any disease calculated to shorten life or to impair physical or mental energy and that they were entirely free of every disease normally considered infectious or contagious. The signatures of the householders and the physician or surgeon then had to be certified as authentic by a Magistrate, Clergyman or Roman Catholic priest. Finally, the emigration agent had to sign a declaration that he had, among other things, carefully enquired into the validity of the statements on the form and that he was perfectly satisfied as to their correctness, that he had conducted all other enquiries in accordance with his instructions and that he believed the above parties to be in all respects desirable emigrants.

Dealing with this paperwork was a formidable task for Jane that she could not have managed without the help of her friend Kathy and the other ladies at the Church Meeting House. When they first heard that the Dunstans had made a decision to go to South Australia the women of the hamlet had zeroed in on Jane with endless questions, most of which she could not answer, but she did enjoy being the centre of attention for once. Everyone was supportive and readily offered their counsel, advice and encouragement.

To Jane it seemed like an age since she had delivered the family's application to emigration agent Latimer to send off to the London head office of CLEC. In fact only a little more than a month passed before an official government looking letter came to the cottage. She straightaway stomped off with it to her friend Kathy, two doors down, to get her to read it for her – cursing her own illiteracy with each stride. The letter included a long list of rules and regulations and, among other things, said that a decision on the family application would not be made until the CLEC received a surgeon's certificate of proof of smallpox vaccinations for all family members, a marriage certificate for Jane and Richard, and baptism certificates for each of the children. The letter said that until final approval was granted the family members should not leave employment, vacate their residence, sell any goods or chattels or in fact make any departure arrangements.

This was not what Jane was hoping for. She was angry at the prospect of having to deal with more paperwork, depressed over her personal incompetence, and embarrassed to have to call on friends again to help her out. Many times she thought that the business of emigration was all too hard and that she was too uneducated and ignorant to deal with all the paperwork and conditions that had to be met. Richard was no help. He was just as ignorant as her and after spending all day working in the mine was so tired that he often could hardly talk let alone engage in any serious discussion that involved an intellectual application. He relied on Jane entirely in such matters and was happy to leave everything to her.

Jane's friend Kathy was a saviour. She was sharp of mind, most particular on detail and read and reread the paperwork out loud to Jane until she was sure she thoroughly understood it all and could explain it back to her. Between the two of them they collected and mailed the information needed to answer the outstanding requests of CLEC.

Eventually another letter arrived from CLEC saying that having regard to the health, occupations, ages and characters of the Dunstan family members they had been accepted as suitable candidates for emigration. Jane nearly hugged all the breath out of Kathy when she told her what it said, thanked her at least a dozen times, then thanked God and then thanked Kathy some more. "Oh Kathy it would never have happened without you!" she said, "I can't wait to tell Richard and the children."

The bad news was that the letter demanded that the passage contribution deposit fees, totalling £18, should be sent direct to the CLEC office by postal order and that no departure date would be sent to the family until it was received. Jane had managed to save a bit less than £14. To save another £4 might take another couple of months or more depending on Richard's returns from his pitch in the mine. Then, after this payment, there were the further expenses of clothing kits and travel to Plymouth that could total between £25 to £30. Jane was almost at the stage of giving the whole project up when to her amazement and disbelief the women's group at the Meeting House passed a motion that the parish group would subsidise the Dunstan family's emigration to South Australia to the sum of £4. This was not an unusual thing for a church parish group to do but the catalyst for this generosity had been Kathy who knew Jane's circumstances and pressed the women's group to support the Dunstans. Jane was now just a few shillings short of the £18 she needed which she would make up in the next couple of weeks. The deposits would be paid. As for the rest, she would work out the details later.

In Cornwall things were not improving. The free-trade depression which was rife throughout Britain in 1848 was particularly bad in the far South West where Cornish copper mines were now competing with mines in Cuba, Peru and Chile as well as South Australia. The stoppage of many mines in Cornwall caused much unemployment and suffering. The harvest was again poor and potatoes continued to rot fast in the fields. There was too much poverty for all men to be honest. In the absence of social security the only way some jobless men could keep their family out of the workhouse was through crime. At Bodmin Assizes in March there were seventy-one prisoners for trial which *The Law Times* described as "an average (number) of the last two or three years, but a much larger number than formerly, crime having much increased in this county of late years." There were several cases of miners who were convicted and imprisoned for stealing ore from the mines.

There was also trouble in neighbouring Europe that the

Dunstans were aware of but did not understand. In Berlin, Budapest, Paris, Palermo, Prague, Milan, Naples, Krakow, Venice and Vienna mobs of middle-class liberals and working-class radicals crowded together to oppose and abolish the established order and then try to institute new systems of government. Revolutionaries dislodged conservative governments that had held power since Napoleon's fall in 1815. There was social chaos and political unhappiness.

In London a mass rally of thousands of workers on 10th April to demonstrate support for a People's Charter fizzled out after the government stacked the capital with police, troops and armed detachments. As a sign of the times a new book was published in the same month on *The Law Relating to Riots and Unlawful Assemblies* and before 1848 had finished Karl Marx and Friedrich Engels had published *The Communist Manifesto*. While there were a number of ingredients to the cake that cooked up these disturbances the issue of poverty was a significant part of the recipe. Lord Ashley told the British Parliament that more than 30,000 "naked, filthy, roaming, lawless and deserted children" lived on the streets of London.

Cholera broke out again in London. Public executions were still common. Convicts were still being transported to Australia. For a second offence of poaching you were sent there for at least seven years. In Redruth wooden stocks were still being used to punish offenders for drunkenness and other misdemeanours and poor people were still hungry. To Jane the prospect of leaving all this behind and relocating her family to the colony of South Australia was looking good.

Eventually, the order arrived advising that steerage accommodation had been set aside for the Dunstan family on board the ship *Trafalgar* and that they must all go to the port of Plymouth for purposes of embarkation on Monday the 16th day of October

1848. Further, that they must be in Plymouth at least three days before that in order to report to the emigrant's depot. Failure to attend as directed would mean that their deposit was forfeited and that they would be disqualified from further eligibility for assisted passage.

Chapter 8

Voyage Preparations

When the women of the hamlet heard that Jane and her family had been accepted as suitable candidates for emigration they came forward to give their moral support and endless advice and suggestions on what Jane should do to prepare and pack for the voyage. She listened carefully and made a mental note of things that made practical commonsense. The serious business of packing for a voyage of three months or more for a family of nine now had to be addressed. What to take and how to pack it were the two questions that occupied every spare minute of her mind. Adults were limited to twenty cubic feet of freight, not to exceed half a ton weight, which had to be divided into two or three boxes for easy handling and packing on the ship. Freight boxes had to be built and separate ones for the children. The box or chest containing clothes would be inspected by emigration officials at the port of departure and any emigrants with a worn or inadequate kit of clothes would not be allowed on the ship. While new clothing was not necessary it had to be sound, serviceable, and able to deal with the rough wear and tear of a long sea voyage. Required items for men included two jackets, two waistcoats, two trousers, two hats, six shirts, one pair of boots, one pair of shoes, four handkerchiefs, six pairs of socks, one pair of braces, three towels, a razor, shaving box and glass. Women had to pack six shifts, two bonnets, one shawl, a cloak and cape, three dresses, two petticoats, one pair of stays, four handkerchiefs, four nightcaps, four sleeping jackets, six pairs of socks, two pairs of shoes and six towels.

Jane was concerned about the problem of clothing for the family. She could not afford to buy all new things so she had to spend long hours with her sewing kit by candle light each night to select the family's best clothes and rebuild them where required so they would pass muster for the voyage. She decided to put the good clothes that had to be inspected in one or two boxes and in the other boxes, subject to the availability of space, she would stuff any old clothes with the intention of the family wearing them first when the ship was underway until they were dirty and then throwing them overboard. She had worked out that the ration of water per day per person for drinking, cooking and personal hygiene meant that washing clothes in freshwater was not going to happen. She thanked God that little Lizzie was now finally done with nappies for she had no idea how she might have dealt with that problem.

After weighing up the suggestions she received from the hamlet women and listening to the advice read to her from *The Emigrants Friend* booklet Jane finalised a list of extra provisions she would need for the voyage. She would take raspberry vinegar and ginger beer powder to mix with the water as it went "off" in the ship's barrels during the trip. She would pack some fresh eggs in salt (after first greasing them with butter) taking care to place them resting on their ends so as not to touch each other. She would take a bag of dried apples, a bag of potatoes and onions, a bag of flour and a bag of oatmeal. Also, jam, treacle, suet, cheese, salted butter, oatcakes and some lemons. If there was any money left over at the end of expenses she would then buy some tea and lump sugar. She would also take some candles, a ball of string, nails, hooks and screws to hang things on in the ship and a gimlet to fix them. Finally, she would take a well salted side of bacon and ham and some seeds of flowers and vegetables to plant in South Australia. To Jane this was a formidable list. Next, she turned her mind to a family medicine kit. It would contain bicarbonate of soda for upset stomachs, castor oil as a laxative and general cure all, linseed oil for coughs and colds, some cloves and garlic, vinegar, paraffin, the opium-based "Godfrey's Cordial" and some clean bandages. Finally, she would not leave without her most treasured and important possession – the well-equipped sewing basket.

In the past she thought she had been busy. Now there was much more to do about everything. But in her Methodist way she did one thing at a time until she arrived at the details she had to work out later; then worked out those details and moved on again to deal with the next problem. She had a mission. Methodical, unstoppable Jane. Each day brought her closer to her goal.

The first part of the journey from Tolcarne to Plymouth required considerable planning. It was a distance of some sixty-five miles. Although by this time there were 5,000 miles of railways in Britain with 200,000 labourers working hard at extending the system, in most of Cornwall it was still the age of the gig, the wagonette, the pony cart, the coach and all other types of horse-drawn vehicles. It was not until 1859 that the first train ran from Truro to Plymouth. The quickest and fastest method of travel was by coach but at the cost of sixpence a mile for inside accommodation the fare for one adult to Plymouth was more than £1.10.0. This was clearly beyond the reach of the Dunstans.

Poor people who did not have the money to travel by fast coach boarded a horse drawn wagon. This was Jane's plan. There were carriers based in each town operating on the main routes and servicing connecting towns. They regularly carried freight and people averaging three to four miles an hour. With Kathy's assistance Jane worked out that it would take three full days or a bit more to get to Plymouth when allowance was made for regular stops needed by the carriers to pick up and deliver goods. Another problem was that each carrier usually only travelled a short distance to the next town where you had to make new arrangements again with another carrier to get further, and so on. Then there was the question of three nights' accommodation during the journey for a family of nine. She thought that if it came to it she might make arrangements with the wagoner for the family to sleep on board the wagon. She then had to work out a plan of how to feed a family of nine during three and a half days on the road. The challenges kept coming – but she would feed them and would cook up and take with her, oatcakes, pasties and hogans with fresh apples and raspberry vinegar flavoured bottled water and cold bottled mugwort tea and whatever else she could think of and manage. It would be done.

Money was the question. Would there ever be enough. Jane had made sure that she had settled the few family debts they had. She sold her big copper preserving pan, which she really wanted to take with her, and their half share in the family cow. The few remaining items of cottage furniture were also sold and arrangements made with the landlord mine owners for a new tenant for the cottage. The family pig had been dispatched and cured. Half of it was sold to raise money and the other half would accompany them on the voyage. Fortunately, the blast that resulted in Richard finding a good pitch really did turn out to be a purple patch for the family. He and young Richard Junior worked extra long and arduous hours to extract the maximum return from the mine. In the end there was enough money and even some left for a small purse to take with them on the voyage.

On a chill autumn morning in early October two short, sturdy, muddied and steaming draught horses arrived outside the cottage pulling a long heavy four-wheel open box wagon. Neither Jane nor the children had slept much and all had been wide awake since before the first crow of the cock. They were dressed, breakfasted, packed, ready and waiting as the wagon pulled up. Family goods and chattels were quickly loaded to join the other freight onboard comprising sacks of flour and chaff and barrels of cider. As they were loading all the women of the hamlet came out of their cottages to wish Jane and the family well and present her with a patchwork quilt made out of all kinds of bits and pieces of cloth sewn together over many months at secret quilting bees held in the hamlet. Kathy came forward and gave Jane a comb because she knew she was always breaking them on her long black hair. They hugged and cried, Jane thanked everyone and everyone God blessed everyone else. Men and boys shook hands and Richard was quite moved when presented with a pocket knife from some of his old workmates who had clubbed funds together to buy it. They climbed on the wagon and with the sharp sound of a whip crack, the clop, clop of hooves and jingle jangle of harness the team moved off. The people of Tolcarne stood and kept waving until the wagon disappeared over the first hill.

They were unsprung, slow, unwieldy vehicles commonly painted blue with the undercarriage red or pink, a pivoting front axle and mostly pulled by two horses, usually in line. There were no seats and passengers simply sat on the floor or among or on the freight in uncomfortable cramped conditions for hours of jolting, lumbering and creaking along rutted unmade roads. With any luck the lurching and bucking had a soporific effect after a while causing the occupants to doze off. After the initial excitement, which lasted about an hour, nearly all in the Dunstan family were fed up with being rattled around and had their eyes shut. Not sleeping. Not talking. Just thinking, hoping – fearing. Jane held close to her a rolled up blanket from which the face of little Lizzie popped out. It seemed that she enjoyed the sway and jolting of the wagon and the clank and rattle of harness for she slept most of the time. Perhaps, what she really enjoyed was being held close by her mother for the longest continuous time since shortly after she was born.

The family settled in with their co-travellers of wood lice and silverfish left over from previous cargoes. There would be overnight stops at Truro, St. Austell and Liskeard and many stops along the way to pick up and put down freight. Every now and then herds of sheep or cattle blocked the road or extra slow speed was required to allow other wagons or coaches to pass. Because it was a noisy trip there was not a lot of talking. Every piece of leather trace and harness creaked, iron bars clanked, wooden parts of the wagon groaned, horses constantly clicked their teeth on bits and clopped their hooves while the big wheels crunched and thumped away. It was a long, tedious, jarring journey which reduced them all to a pathetic condition by the end of each day. Fortunately, the weather was pleasant except for the day they journeyed to Liskeard when it was cold rainy and windy. By the time they arrived they were all stiff necked, blue faced and frozen to the bone. That night the wagon was parked in a large barn which afforded the family some protection from the elements as they slept in the vehicle by prior arrangements with the wagon master.

As they finally crossed the Tamar River and entered Plymouth the tide was in and water lapped among the uneven stones on the foreshore. The wagon rattled on past sheds, warehouses and cottages all jumbled together in a disorderly manner. The smell of sea water was spiced with a hint of rope and tar from numerous luggers and barques making the most of high water to load and unload cargoes. Dockside wharves were scattered with an untidy collection of usual marine paraphernalia including rigging laid out being repaired, large coils of rope, rolls of sail cloth, nets, brass bound barrels, hand carts and wagons, sacks of flour and corn stacked high, squealing pigs in crates and piles of chests and boxes. Sailors yelled from ship to shore and shore to ship. Horses stood eating from a nose bag or defecating while they waited for their wagons to be dealt with and seagulls swooped or stood patiently in the hope of finding a morsel falling from the freight to peck at.

Jane and Richard had never been so removed from home before. They were now in England. Most people in Cornwall had never travelled that far. It was a long way from their comfort zone in the close-knit community of Tolcarne.

Chapter 9

PLYMOUTH

With little sleep and a lot of discomfort for three days the family were exhausted and lacking good humour by the time they reached Plymouth. The wagon master knew where the emigration depot was and unloaded them at the front entrance with their luggage. Jane was greatly relieved to be finally quit of the wagon as, covered in bits of straw and chaff, the family climbed down for the last time. The depot was a large three-storey building capable of accommodating up to 500 emigrants with two large rooms on each level. Although iron bars on the windows gave the place a prison like appearance the inmates at least had a good view of the beautiful harbour and surrounding hills.

They were met by the Depot Master and the Matron who welcomed and spoke to both Richard and Jane. The family then went through the usual formalities confirming their identities and making sure their documentation was in order. This procedure was conducted with military precision which was an indication of what was to happen next. Jane and her three girls, Mary, Ann and babe in arms little Lizzie, were ushered into a large room some forty feet by thirty-seven feet which was fully equipped with appropriate wash troughs and baths, an unlimited supply of fresh hot and cold water as well as all other personal necessities for ablutions such as soap and towels, and, to Jane's embarrassment, told to strip and wash. Clean clothes were set aside from their clothing boxes and the clothes they had been wearing were seized, washed, dried and inspected. If there was any suspicion that anything resembling an insect remained therein further decontamination was carried out in a hot baking oven. Richard and the boys were sent to the male ablution rooms for a similar cleansing procedure.

After the agonising wagon trip the wash room with abundant steaming hot water and endless soap seemed like the closest Jane had yet been to heaven on earth. She washed away not only the dirt from her skin but the aches from her body and the stress from her mind. This was the cleanest she had been in all her life. She thanked God for reaching Plymouth safely with her family and praised the Lord for their good fortune. Thanking God was something that she often did. But she made the most of the opportunity to do a proper cleaning job on the girls, thinking it might be their last for quite a while.

Inspection of their clothing kits took place next and Jane held her breath during the process as the inspecting officers counted everything even the number of socks. They closely examined clothes that Jane had darned, patched or otherwise rebuilt and caused her to blush when they praised her seamstress skills. Everything passed but she was told to make sure that before departure she bought two pounds of marine soap (which was supposed to work with salt water) from one of the local shops and that this would be noted as an outstanding requisition and checked again later. So long as permission was obtained first, the emigrants were free to go into Plymouth to shop and wander about.

Although tired and bewildered by their surroundings, hunger was the thing that was uppermost in their mind at this point as they had not had a proper cooked meal for three days. While pleased when food was mentioned, they were a degree nervous and timid when pushed into a large mess hall, equipped with a multitude of lined up benches seating eight to twelve persons each, and full of people in a state of activity and apparent confusion making much noise. The Dunstan family of nine fitted comfortably on one bench. When told by a group on the next table they had to have a Mess Captain Jane was unanimously appointed, issued with a ticket and instructed that when the bell rang she should report to the kitchen and exchange it for food which she should then dole out to the family. The food was basic but in abundance with plenty of roast mutton and potatoes, bread, tea, sugar, butter and salt with appropriate broth for little Lizzie. It was, in fact, considerably better than the food they had eaten at home in recent times. The meal not only satisfied their hunger but improved their disposition considerably.

The ship's surgeon arrived after dinner and each family member had to report to him for a cursory medical exam to make sure there were no obvious signs of sickness. The depot was set up and run along the lines of living on board ship. The aim being to prepare the emigrant for that experience. Rules, regulations, dormitories, mess seating and meal distribution were similar to ship living and even maritime terminology and language was used. Sleeping arrangements were very ship like. The large dormitories accommodated sixty to seventy families or 200 to 300 people.

Two rows of berths, two storeys high, ran the entire length of the room on both sides. The berths were no more than shelves less than two feet wide and six feet long divided by eighteen inch planks standing on edge. Jane and Richard having lived together with the seven children in what was really less than two proper rooms were not so much troubled by the tight sleeping arrangements as the actual number of bodies in one room. The atmosphere was close and oppressive and the night continually punctuated by snoring, loud breathing, crying babies, hollering, singing, swearing, praying and bad smells. When the 6 a.m. bell rang they were glad it was all over, although it was not a pretty sight to see more than 200 people all struggling out of their narrow berths at once. Mattress, blankets, bed spread and pillows had to be rolled, wrapped up shipshape and stowed.

All things considered the depot was remarkably well-run with order, discipline and accompanying civility prevailing for the most part. If anyone seriously misbehaved they could have their sea passage cancelled. Jane kept the children in hand by reminding them if this happened to them they might be left ashore while the rest of the family sailed away. Although particular attention was paid to cleanliness, fleas, lice and bed bugs were a recurring problem in an environment where so many people were coming and going.

After two nights in the depot they were advised that they would board ship that day and spend their first night in Plymouth harbour at anchor. The passengers for *Trafalgar* were mustered together and equipped with their essential kit for the voyage by the Depot Master. Everyone got two blankets, a bed spread, tin plates, drinking mug, cutlery and canvas bags to stuff in a month's change of clothes and linen which would be stowed beside the bunks. This was their carry-on luggage and the cost of these issued items was covered by their passage deposits. They would be allowed to retain them on arrival in the colony provided they had all behaved well on the voyage. Depot staff did a final check of all other luggage before it was delivered to seamen for transporting and stowing aboard ship. Jane had one last chance to grab from her boxes any essential items she might need on board, as once underway passengers could only access their luggage in the ship's holds once a month, and that was subject to good weather. After much waiting the *Trafalgar* passengers, loaded with all they could carry, were herded down to the docks. Jane welcomed the chance to escape the depot. She had never spent so much time with so many people in such a small space. No one wanted to spend another day there.

They recognised their personal provisions among a great pile of boxes sitting dockside waiting to be loaded. Teams of sailors were busily hoisting freight aboard small boats intended for various ships. Barrels, coils of rope, pigs in crates, boxes, sacks, rolls of canvas and a miscellany of other freight and provisions, even a cow were heaved on. Among the *Trafalgar* passengers there was a great deal of chat and a lot of nervous laughter. Ship's carpenters could be heard banging about, some sailors and dockworkers yelled and swore and others sang. Clergymen of various denominations appeared and offered prayers over the emigrants and granted them God's blessing as pigs "oinked" and grunted in the background. It was Sunday the 15th day of October 1848.

Before coming to Plymouth Jane and Richard had not ventured much further than their own parish boundary and had never seen a proper seagoing ship. They knew nothing about them and although there was no place in the eighty mile length of Cornwall where you could get more than twenty miles away from the coast, they knew little about the sea. Like everyone living in Cornwall they were frightened of its power. Cornwall had about 200 miles of rugged coast and along one small stretch of about forty miles, 131 vessels and a dozen fishing boats were lost between 1823 and 1846. Some 200 seamen and fishermen were drowned. They did know that the sea was a dangerous place to be, that they had never travelled over water on a ship before and that no one in the family could swim. But, they really had no idea what was in store for them.

Part Two

THE VOYAGE

1848–1849

Chapter 10

TRAFALGAR

Trafalgar stood with a number of other ships in the harbour. The emigrants were ferried out to her in sailing barges which operated on the Tamar River and around Plymouth Sound. They were cutter rigged with a well shaped hull and a fine run which presented them as attractive vessels when under sail. But they were industrial boats, completely open for the greater part of their length, used for hauling all sorts of cargo including coal, sand and gravel and not set up for passengers. After being loaded with general ship's provisions and passengers' personal luggage, the emigrants simply climbed in on top of everything else for the short trip to the ship. As they sailed out to her, *Trafalgar* waited with her sails furled at the yard arms, placidly it seemed, although perhaps a little sulkily. Once alongside, able-bodied persons boarded the ship up wooden steps slung between substantial rope cables hanging over the side. All the passengers managed this except one 70-year-old lady who was hoisted aboard with one of the ship's davits in a chair made from a barrel by the ship's carpenter.

On reaching the deck wide eyes and opened mouths expressed the family's awe at having entered a world totally alien to them. Necks craned as they gawked at the rigging and squinted at the confusing bits of ship's tackle and equipment. Like all square rigged tall ships she was a combination of thousands of parts designed, perfected and finetuned by individuals and committees over hundreds of years to epitomise function, power and grace under sail. To Jane she represented a dream of escape and adventure; a machine that would transport her family to a new and different earth through time and space.

Trafalgar had been built in a shipyard on the river Wear at Sunderland in 1845. Lloyds Register classified her as a ship of 739 tons of A1 character for hull and storage with an overall length of 129 feet and a beam of twenty-nine feet two inches. She had a square stern and three massive wooden masts – the main mast amidships, the mizzen mast at the stern and the foremast towards the bow. Each mast and the yards that crossed them to hold up the square rigged sails were supported by a very complex system of ropes (halyards, braces, stays, gantlines and others) which required constant attention and adjustment from highly skilled sailors to keep the ship safe and properly functional.

In the typical style of the time she was a dumpy looking vessel with a solidly built roundish, full hull that was flat underneath so that she could rest easy and stay upright on mud flats when the tide ran out of harbours. Her bows collected a lot of water in front of her instead of slicing through so she was not the fastest ship at sea. She did not sail very well close to the wind (with the wind coming towards her) and while she was a buoyant little ship, like all vessels of the time she leaked continuously and needed to be pumped out regularly by the sailors to keep her afloat. She would be a good little ship so long as she had a competent crew on board and did not meet extreme weather conditions. Lines of imitation gun ports were painted in black squares on the sides to create the impression, when seen from a distance, that she was heavily armed. In fact she only had a couple of small deck cannons. This standard decoration was a legacy of the Napoleonic wars and was applied almost without exception to all British merchant sailing ships in the 19th century.

On the main deck a slightly raised short section at the front housed the crew's quarters in a cramped little area called the forecastle (pronounced "fo'c'sle") where they had the crashing sea as their constant companion. Between the foremast and the mainmast, in the area known as "midships" there was a deckhouse that contained the ship's kitchen or galley with a large cast iron stove, set on a platform of stone slate slabs, with double ovens and not a lot of room for anything else except the cook, his assistant and a workbench. The area behind (abaft) the main mast to the mizzen mast at the rear was called the quarterdeck and beyond that to the stern another section, raised eight to nine foot higher than the main deck, was known as the poop deck which also formed the roof of the cabins underneath where the captain, his officers and full fare passengers were accommodated.

The best cabins had windows opening over the stern at the very back of the ship. The ship's wheel and binnacle housing the compass were mounted at the rear of the poop deck where the officer of the watch stood next to the helmsman on the wheel. Only officers, crew and full fare passengers were allowed on the poop deck or any elevated part of the quarterdeck. Steerage passengers were not permitted to use these areas unless invited to do so by the captain. The poop deck was the captain's favoured

A typically rigged ship of the time.

[*Illustrated London News*, 31st August 1850. Mary Evans Picture Library Ltd., London.]

position. From there he had the traditional military advantage of high ground and could see all around the ship.

Sailors were busily getting everything loaded, stowed and ship shape to sail. Using blocks and tackle at the end of davits they hauled and swung aboard bundles of sacks, boxes, barrels and crates to be stowed in the cargo hold. Two nanny goats were heaved aboard with the assistance of belly bands slipped beneath them and dropped into their stalls on the main deck. They would provide milk and, if needs be, meat for consumption. For the officers and cabin passengers, a dozen live chickens were lifted aboard in coops to be installed on the poop deck. Ten little pigs were delivered to a small sty constructed under a lifeboat in front of the main mast close to the galley, the refuse from which would fatten them during the voyage. In addition to the ship's provisions general cargo going into the hold included, among other things, boxes of sheet glass, barrels of sugar, rum, brandy, porter and tar, bars of iron, bundles of flat steel, several anvils, bags of cocoa, bales of paper and a case of castor oil.

Trafalgar had arrived in Plymouth the previous day after a nine day voyage from London with 193 passengers on board and had now shipped another 82 more at Plymouth, including 31 from Cornwall, making a total of 275. In addition she had a crew of 35 men and seven boys which totalled 317 individuals on board. With passengers milling around the main deck and scampering children running about among the ropes, ship's boats, hatchways and the deckhouse it was so crowded that the sailors found it difficult to do their work. Most of the children seemed entirely oblivious to the ordeal they were about to confront. Young Richard, Ben and Henry (12, 11, and 10 years of age respectively) were greatly excited by the adventure and had all sorts of fantasy expectations about the future. Wearn, Mary and Ann (8, 6 and 3 years) were much quieter and stayed close to their mother. Like most of the men Richard looked sombre and serious but resigned and determined. Jane gazed blankly out over the ship's side as she nursed little Lizzie and noticed for the first time that the banks of Plymouth Sound were extremely well fortified with cannons and looked very formidable from the ship. She had worked so hard to get on this ship but just now felt a little disconnected from the reality of it all.

The steerage accommodation where the emigrants would spend most of their time during the voyage was built on the floor constructed above the cargo hold and below the main deck. This area was petitioned fore and aft to create three separate steerage quarters. The fore area was set aside for single men and the rear area for single women. The largest area in the middle was for married couples and families.

The Chief Commissioner for Emigration Mr. Wood accompanied by the local government emigration agent Mr. Carew had boarded and inspected *Trafalgar* when she arrived in port the previous day. Mr. Carew, whose job it was to supervise the embarkation of the passengers, had drawn up a plan of the berths in steerage, properly numbered them and allocated them to individual passengers so that when they arrived on board they were directed to their own berths and there was no arguments or fighting over berth spaces.

In order to gain possession of deck space for working purposes the sailors had to send the emigrants below and Jane and the family found themselves being ushered through a hatchway down a steep set of steps. "Always go down the ship's ladders backwards," Jane was told by a grizzled old sailor with a white walled eye. She braced herself and descended carefully into the dim light of the steerage deck. It was a gloomy long cavernous area lined on each side with double-decker bunk berths built-in among the great beams, stays and bolts of the ship at right angles to the hull so that the only way into the berths was over the foot end. Running down the centre of the ship dividing the two rows of berths was a long wooden fixed trestle table that continued forever until it disappeared into the shadows at the other end. Seating was on wooden planks fixed along both sides. The only way in or out of this area where a total of 210 emigrants would spend the next three months was via two ceiling (called the deckhead) hatchways at the top of steep stairs each end. These hatchways, together with two small deckhead trapdoor ventilators in the middle of the dormitory (midships) provided the only ventilation and natural light. There were no portholes. Canvas wind sails fixed around the hatchways helped to push air below in good weather and reflect down a soft yellow light.

It was a completely weird environment to Jane and she found it difficult to see at first until her eyes became accustomed to the dullness. She recognised a strong smell of fresh straw coming from the newly stuffed mattresses that reminded her of the large barn that the family slept in on the wagon in Liskeard while travelling to Plymouth. Other smells were not so appealing. The place was already crowded with people talking at once and making new friendships. Emigrants' boxes and bundles of luggage were piled up at the end of berths. Children buzzed about among everything as they explored every nook and cranny. No less than seventy-five children aged ten years and younger would live in this area during the voyage. Of them, twenty-four were aged two years or less and most of these were still in nappies.

Richard was appalled at the idea of living in this confined space for the next three months. Not happy Jane, he thought, but did not articulate. The expression on his face gave him away prompting

Jane to berate him for being so miserable and to do something worthwhile by helping her organise the bunks. The children, meanwhile, disappeared into the bowels of steerage on their own expeditions of discovery, making new friends on the way.

Plymouth Harbour in the 1840s.

[National Maritime Museum, Greenwich, London. PU1124.]

Chapter 11

SHIP BOARD RULES

After having found their berths, dumped their carry-on luggage and introduced themselves to their neighbours it seemed no time before the Dunstans and all other emigrants were ordered to muster back on the main deck. They were called to order by the first mate standing next to the captain on the poop deck.

"Silence, all pay attention!" he yelled.

The captain, who had been the last person to board the ship having left the on board departure preparations to his first officer Mr. Blythe, then briefly introduced himself as George Richardson. He was a tall good-looking fair haired man with an authoritative stance and steel grey eyes, wearing his best uniform – mid-length bluecoat, large lapels and turned cuffs with brass buttons, a dark red waistcoat, a deep white shirt with lace at the throat and gold buttoned sleeves emerging from the coat. Breeches, stockings and buckled black shoes corroborated the impression that this was a man with knowledge and power. He welcomed all, hoped they would all have a safe and enjoyable journey to Australia and then introduced the Rev. T. C. Childs, minister of St. Mary's Devonport, to conduct a farewell religious service and said that he would have more to say soon afterwards.

The Rev. T. C. Childs was an indefatigable clergyman who took a lively and active interest in the spiritual and temporal welfare of all emigrants leaving the port of Plymouth and ministering to their comfort. He welcomed the emigrants, assured them they were in good hands with Captain George Richardson at the helm and then read from psalm 107:

"They that go down to the sea in ships,
that do business in great waters;
These see the works of the LORD,
and his wonders in the deep.
For he commandeth, and raiseth the stormy wind,
which lifteth up the waves thereof.
They mount up to heaven, they go down again to the depths:
their soul is melted because of trouble.
They reel to and fro, and stagger like a drunken man,
and are at their wits end.
Then they cry unto the LORD in their trouble,
and he bringeth them out of their distresses.
He maketh the storm a calm,
so that the waves thereof are still."

He then said to the keen listeners:

"Though you may be all sinners and unworthy and liable to perish may God go with you and grant you mercy should the need arise and may you all be truly assured of God's love, God's wisdom and God's power and God bless you all."

There followed the singing of hymns in mournful strains and then the Lord's Prayer all of which were a comfort to the passengers in general and Jane in particular.

Captain Richardson then addressed them. He said that while Her Royal Highness Queen Victoria represented the English nation, he the Captain, represented the Queen on board ship and also therefore England and as captain his word was law and behind his word lay the full authority of the English Parliament. Any order he gave to his crew or the passengers was an order with the full authority of England and her Royal Highness the Queen. He said that in his absence at any time from the deck the first mate Mr. Blythe, or his delegate, would be the senior officer and have control of the ship. He explained that as captain he had absolute power to punish anyone who disobeyed orders or directions including the power to withdraw rations or privileges, the power to place offenders in irons or the ship's brig and finally the power to order flogging.

He then introduced the ship's surgeon Dr. Tweedale and explained that he and the doctor had power to make absolutely any rules and regulations concerning the health, welfare, safety and moral conduct of the passengers and that all such rules and regulations must be obeyed. Further, that Dr. Tweedale himself had direct power to administer some punishment to offenders including withdrawal of rations and also the power to make submissions to the captain relating to the administration of more serious punishment such as placing offenders in irons.

Dr. Tweedale then spoke and said that he was also the direct agent of the Queen and the government on board ship and had all the powers of a duly appointed government medical officer of health on land, and a great deal more. He said he would not hesitate to recommend to the captain to administer corporal punishment to an offender if the need arose but hoped everyone would obey all the rules and regulations on board ship which were there to protect the health and safety of passengers and advance their general welfare. Those rules included matters relating to hygiene, cleanliness (including personal cleanliness), diet, ventilation and preservation of good order. He said that he believed dirt in all its forms and noxious smells encouraged bad health and that his motto was "A clean ship is a healthy ship." Regulations dealing with cleanliness, meals and bed times, prohibitions on gambling and drinking and general behaviour were posted up in steerage quarters for all to read who could.

Dr. Tweedale made it clear that he would apply the instructions of the Colonial Office to daily hygiene and public health routines with the utmost zeal. Emigrants must wash their clothes and themselves regularly, steerage quarters must be kept scrubbed clean, well ventilated when possible and fumigated when required. In general the highest standards of sanitation would be insisted upon at all time. Dr. Tweedale had a powerful, determined but charismatic persona that commanded respect from everyone and conveyed the impression that you should do as he said. He had been well-trained, and had an excellent knowledge of the techniques that would promote the health of all on board.

He then announced that after consultation with the captain it had been decided that emigrant Miss Caroline Bacon would be appointed the ship's matron. Her primary and most important role, explained Dr. Tweedale, was the protection, welfare and moral guidance of the single women on board. In that capacity, subject to the control and supervision of Dr. Tweedale, she had the full delegated authority from him to order, direct and carry out all the rules regulations and policies that come under his jurisdiction including the giving of practical and spiritual directions and seeing that the ladies were kept occupied. On arrival in Australia she would be paid a gratuity of three pounds for her services, provided they had been satisfactory during the course of the voyage.

Next, he said he had to appoint four constables from the married male passengers. They also would be paid gratuities. Three of them as ordinary constables would receive two pounds for supervising persons rostered for sweeping, deck scrubbing and cleaning, watch duties and fumigation. They would also organise and oversee the mess captains, making sure that each mess received its fair and proper allowance of rations. On a call for volunteers there were far more applicants than positions available. While the payment of the gratuity was a powerful incentive to get the job, it was also regarded as an honour to be appointed a constable.

The fourth position was that of special constable whose duty was to attend to the water closets and privies and keep them clean and in good order. The job also involved other "special disinfectant duties". Because the job was important, and involved dirty work, it would provide a gratuity of £4. This was nearly twenty-five percent of a year's income for many people in the poor parts of Cornwall and was a good stake to get started in the colony.

"It can be a dirty job at times," said Dr. Tweedale. "I want someone who is not afraid to deal with dirt."

This time there was a scarcity of applicants. The first voice to be heard was Richard Dunstan's.

"I'm used to workin' in dirt and I'm not a'feared of it! I'll be your man!"

It was clear to the doctor that Richard had the build and body muscle of a man who was used to hard physical work. That, together with his short physical stature made him a good choice for working in tight spaces and getting in and around the bunks, furniture, fittings, and water closets of steerage. He got the job but had no idea what it really involved. At least it would give him something to do and he would earn some money on the voyage. For the single women's quarters one of the more senior single ladies was appointed a special constable with duties similar to Richard. If necessity required she could call on him for his assistance which, of course would be supervised at all times by Matron Bacon. Dr. Tweedale also carefully selected and appointed Mr. Henry Congreave as his assistant and Mrs. Ann Pollard to act as his nurse in the management of the ship's hospital and patients generally.

These important ship keeping matters having been attended to, Captain Richardson thanked Dr. Tweedale and congratulated the constables and his assistants on their appointment. The ship would sail he said, weather permitting, early next morning. All passengers were dismissed and directed to see that their belongings were properly stowed, to organise their mess groups and appoint their mess captains. It was their job to collect the rations doled out by the ship's stewards who would only do so on production of a mess card detailing the names of each member of the mess. With their seven children the Dunstan's formed an acceptable number of nine for their mess.

After any necessary preparation of the food on the long trestle table in steerage the captains would then take the food back up the steep steps of the hatchway and along the deck to the galley where the cook was requested to deal with it according to the instructions delivered by the mess captain. When ready, the captain had to collect and carry it back down to steerage via the steep hatchway ladder, hopefully without spilling anything or being burned by hot liquids. It was then served up to the other mess members on the long trestle table and consumed. Being mess captain was an onerous responsibility and a thankless task usually done by men. Each male adult mess member was supposed to take their turn in the job, but Jane was adamant that she would do it herself for the duration of the voyage. There was no way she could trust Richard to take prepared dishes to the galley cook and accurately pass on her instructions. She would retain control of that and anyway Richard would have enough to do with his duties as a constable. Every mess had a slop pail to receive scraps and rubbish (at times even more unpleasant substances) which had to be emptied overboard at least daily and Richard and the boys could look after that.

They had a restless first night on board. Jane was frustrated because she had difficulty finding places to stow the family's carry-on luggage. Most of it was in bed with them. The business of organising themselves better in their berths occupied her mind. The children wouldn't stop talking and giggling. Richard tossed about and complained that there was not enough room. There was constant noise from families whispering about what might lay ahead. Every once in a while a baby cried. Eventually, the whispering died away to be replaced by snoring and other intermittent nocturnal noises. Just as they were almost asleep the stomp of sailors' feet on the deck above disturbed them. Eventually they dozed off.

As the sun rose over Plymouth harbour on Monday 16th of October 1848 the chant being sung by the sailors putting their backs into the capstan to weigh anchor woke the passengers on *Trafalgar*.

> *"We'll sing you a song of the fish of the sea*
> *Away down Rio*
> *We'll sing you a song of the fish of the sea*
> *For we're bound for the Rio Grande*
> *Then away lads away*
> *Away down Rio*

"Tugging Out".

[*Illustrated London News*, 13th April 1844. Mary Evans Picture Library Ltd., London.]

So fair thee well
My pretty young gal
For we're bound for the Rio Grande."

Weighing anchor was a long laborious process during which the shanty was endlessly repeated. More than an hour passed before finally the anchor was aboard and lashed down for the voyage. By then most of the passengers had dressed and gone up to the main deck where the sailors were busily making sure everything was tied down fast. The lashings on the spare yards and masts laid on the deck and the lines over the lifeboats on the galley roof were tightened and checked by able seamen under the supervision of the second mate. Anything at all that was movable was either stowed below or secured with rope ties.

Captain Richardson had decided to engage the services of one of the "newfangled steam tugs" to tow *Trafalgar* out of Plymouth Harbour. They had proven to be much quicker than the old arduous business of towing the ship by rowing boat and were safer for vessels always subject to wind and tide. The tow line in place, *Trafalgar* was soon underway with soot from the steam tug spattering the ship and everyone on deck where groups of passengers were warmly greeting and introducing themselves to others to engage in conversation about family, home and England. On shore a number of people had collected together to wave the ship off. The tug took *Trafalgar* out past the breakwater and lighthouse and with three long blasts on its steam whistle (the traditional seamen's goodbye) cast her adrift. It was like the severing of an umbilical cord.

Trafalgar collected a perfectly directed soft north easterly breeze in her topsails and edged away from Plymouth Sound to weather safely around Penlee Point into the English Channel.

The captain bawled: "All hands standby on deck – All ready for'ard."

"Ay ay sir," said Mr. Blythe the first mate.

"Then sail the ship Mr. Blythe – sail the ship!"

"Ay sir, sail her I will! – Sail her I will! Standby halyards," Blythe yelled. "Raise tacks and sheets."

As the first mate yelled each order it was repeated further along deck by the sailor or sailors whose responsibility it was to carry it out. Blocks and tackle squeaked as sailors heave hoed on the lines. Slowly great sheets of canvas flapped and rattled the rigging as they were unfurled by the men aloft on the yards. As the ship headed to wind more orders were issued.

"Standby braces – set mainsails."

"Ease away starboard braces – haul away port braces."

Sailors then worked furiously hauling and adjusting the braces and lines to trim the ship until all canvas was filled to the captain's satisfaction. With yards braced she stole forward and soon the ripple of water was heard under the stern. As she healed slightly to the gentle breeze she more than doubled her speed. In full sail, with a fair wind and in good trim, *Trafalgar* headed to Australia with some 14,000 miles ahead of her.

Captain Richardson yelled, "Steady your helm! – Keep her full!"

With Plymouth Harbour disappearing into the distance Jane was overcome with sadness. A tear trickled down her cheek as she nursed little Lizzie and looked back to England. Richard was silent with his arm around Jane. He held her tight. She turned to her husband and said, "Oh Richard what have we done?"

The week before *Trafalgar* left, the Irish nationalist and Member of Parliament, William Smith O'Brien, was tried before three judges on charges of high treason for his involvement in leading a fight against British forces in Tipperary, Ireland. When sentencing him the Lord Chief Justice donned his black cap and pronounced that he "be drawn on a hurdle to the place of execution, and then be hanged by the neck until you be dead, that afterwards your head shall be severed from your body, and your body be divided into four quarters to be disposed of as Her Majesty shall please."

You didn't have to look hard to find plenty of good reasons to leave England. There was all sorts of trouble in the kingdom and the free colony of South Australia offered a new start and new hope.

Chapter 12

BEYOND ENGLAND

The English Channel failed to live up to its usual reputation for uncomfortable seas. With a mild and kind breeze on her starboard quarter *Trafalgar* proceeded sedately at an agreeable pace of five to six knots without any significantly adverse effects on the passengers. Jane took the opportunity to organise the family sleeping berths. She was annoyed because, apart from some wooden pegs she had discovered on the uprights at the end of the berths, there seemed to be a total absence of any place to store things, and even in the berths themselves there was scant space for anything except bodies. She and Richard had only six by three feet for their combined bed space. For persons of small stature like Jane and Richard there was just enough headroom to sit up in the bunks. This space was reduced regularly by heavy wooden beams that crossed overhead adding to the claustrophobic effect. The children were in berths measuring six by two feet. But while

Steerage Quarters.

[*Illustrated London News*, 10th May 1851. Mary Evans Picture Library Ltd., London.]

Richard Junior age 12, Benjamin 11, and Henry 10, had their own berths, the four remaining children, Wearn 8, Mary 6, Ann 3, and baby Elizabeth slept two to a single berth in toe-to-toe fashion. In all, the family of nine had one double berth and five single berths separated in each case only by a single plank one-foot high.

The first thing that Jane did was tack up some thin calico sheets at each end of the Dunstan bed rows so that the family would have some privacy. Then using Richard's boot as a hammer, and the nails, hooks, screws and gimlet she brought with her, she added hanging points to the beams and upright stanchions around the bunks. On these and on the lines she would string between them she would hang clothes and calico bags with drawstring closures she had made to store things in – the most important one containing the cured flitch of ham from the cottage family pig.

An area of not much more than six inches was available under the bottom bunks to store things belonging to both the lower and upper berth occupants. The problem was that items placed there tended to work themselves up to the back of the six-foot space and prove devilishly hard to retrieve. They could also "travel" during the voyage due to the movement of the ship causing them to be mixed up with the goods of other passengers, resulting in arguments. And, things stored here could suffer water damage. Jane used it only as a place to put boots and shoes at night and to store soiled clothing until washing day.

On the second day, when the Dunstans went on deck after breakfast, they could still see in the distance the coast of Cornwall and Lizard Point. Light breeze had sent *Trafalgar* along gently at around five knots, but now she changed her course slightly to the south and pushed her bow into big Atlantic rollers coming into the entrance of the channel. With the first big roll, clattering, shrieks and laughter came from the steerage quarters. At the same time

"Goodbye England."

[*Illustrated London News*, 19th June 1852. Mary Evans Picture Library Ltd., London.]

a smart breeze appeared to take *Trafalgar* up to eight knots. The oncoming swells soon increased to a height of fifteen to twenty feet but they were well spaced and the wind was still mild allowing *Trafalgar* to rhythmically plough her way through as she rose and fell confidently like a cork. The sailors thought it quite pleasant and exhilarating to be on deck but those passengers still there all had sad and pale faces.

The ship was soon crossing the wide entrance to the Bay of Biscay off France, an area notorious for producing rough water and seasickness. Swells pushed by prevailing westerly winds that had travelled more than 1,000 miles across the thousand fathom depths of the Atlantic were pulled up abruptly as they hit the shallow continental shelf at the mouth of the bay, causing steep sided, breaking and confused seas particularly when, like at that very moment, they were met by oncoming winds. To the uninitiated seafarer the large swells experienced up to now were bad enough. Jane already felt unwell. She was not yet at the point of vomiting but felt hot and sweaty with a headache and queasiness. Now the pitch and toss and chop of the waves, the ploughing of the ship from stem to stern and its rolling first to port and then to starboard finished her off. The novelty of it all, which had first caused shrieks and laughter when they met big swells, was forgotten as silence now predominated, interspersed here and there with occasional cries from the children. As waves pounded the creaking ship, water washed in through the scuppers and swathed over the bulwarks causing the decks to be quickly vacated.

Down in steerage everyone began to feel more and more unwell. People took to their bunks or sat at the trestle table with their head in their hands. When little Ann Dunstan threw up on the floor this was the catalyst for another six or so children to quickly follow. Men groaned and women scurried about looking for mops and any kind of receptacle to catch the next lot of vomit. Courageous mothers of children who had spewed (by now a chain reaction had set up and nearly every one of the seventy-five children under ten years in steerage was going through the process) did their best to clean up their child's mess, but with the pitching and yawing of the ship much of it was trampled about by the 210 people in that section all of whom were unsteady on their feet. Stumbling was a certainty when a heaving ship was combined with seasickness. Conditions rapidly became revolting. In endeavouring to clean up their child's mess wretched mothers often found it impossible to cope with their face hovering in the semi darkness over a pile of vomit in the constantly moving ship with the result that they simply added to the pile. Other adults now started to lose their last meal.

Going on deck at that point was out of the question because waves were washing over the bulwarks and you would get wet if not washed overboard. The logistics in steerage were that there were simply not enough receptacles to go around for everyone to have their own vomit pot. When someone felt sick they would yell for the spew bucket and, if lucky, be handed the slop pail from their mess already containing several donations, before they heaved themselves. By this time the hatchway's leading to steerage that provided the main ventilation had been closed to keep out the sea. The twenty or more babies and toddlers were sick too or had tummy pains. Most of them grizzled, others cried, some screamed and many of them began to soil their nappies. The collective smell coming from all of the crammed in wretches and their retching was disgusting. Some women were violently sick and repeatedly retched and retched. A few men who had not yet been sick now joined in so that in the end there were only three or four women and a couple of men who abstained. Fights started when emigrants who had been lying in their bunks and could not reach a vomit pot in time leaned over and threw up on a neighbour or their bedding. Many vomited in their own bedding or on themselves. The mess, the stink, the heaving of the ship, the groaning and crying and wailing and whingeing and gut wrenching sickness made everyone wish they had not put a foot on *Trafalgar*. Some thought they were going to die. Others wished they were already dead.

The rough weather lasted almost three days and during that time most passengers clung to their berths and thought, to the amusement of sailors that they were going through a great storm when in fact it was not even close to one. During the first night Jane spent much of her time holding bowls for the children to be sick in and cleaning up vomit. She was thankful she had brought a good supply of bicarbonate of soda for upset stomachs. It proved a godsend, she thought. Many passengers brought none and suffered the worse for it. Women seemed to suffer from seasickness to a greater degree than men. After attending to the children's needs all Jane wanted was to lie in her bunk. Neither she nor the children could manage much at all to eat or drink. After almost three days in the bunks it was too much for Richard who asked each of his children and his wife if they intended to rise and shine again or whether they were going to sail to Australia between their blankets. He counselled them to lift their heads and put two feet over the end of their bunks and take in some fresh air on deck. Jane was still unsteady on her feet and some days away yet from getting her "sea legs" but at least the constant vomiting had stopped and, with the help of Richard, she managed to navigate up the steps from steerage to the main deck.

Once beyond the Bay of Biscay *Trafalgar* picked up a gentle trade wind and settled into a rhythm that the new seafarers found more comfortable. Within an hour of the weather having settled Dr. Tweedale appeared in steerage and began handing out orders to the constables and passengers to clean the place up. Mops, buckets and swabs were in great demand. Richard now found out what his job as sanitary constable really involved. Neither he nor Jane had seen a water closet (WC) before boarding *Trafalgar*. Due to the rough conditions they had not been cleaned for days and Richard now had the job.

The ship board toilets consisted of a basic wooden plank seat with a hole cut in the middle installed in what was in fact a closet or cupboard. Once you went in and sat down there was barely enough clearance at the end of your knees to close the door. Some people could only do so with their knees spreadeagled at 45°. Under the hole in the seat a lead lined chute found its way eventually out into the sea. A stiff leather flap fitted on the outlet of the chute between the sea and the sitter was intended to prevent water from the vessels wake back-firing the whole business back up the chute in rough weather. As an extra safety measure in really heavy seas a hinged hatch cover was bolted down over the hole. If deemed necessary the access door to the closet could also be barred and locked. In those circumstances the passengers had to revert to the original method with the mess slop pail of "in the bucket and chuck it". The only problem was that with it being too dangerous to go on deck during storms, and deck hatch covers being not only closed but sometimes locked, you couldn't "chuck it" and had to save it until the weather settled. That could take many days. At least, in good weather, the toilets in steerage could be flushed by tipping in a bucket of sea water filled from a tap leading from a tank on deck.

In steerage the WCs were intended primarily for the use of the female passengers and children. The men were allocated two on deck privies built in to little cupboards on each side of the deck in the bow near the forecastle. In stormy conditions they could not be used. It was physically impossible for the men to fight their way through waves sloshing over the front of the ship to reach them and even if they did make it to the seat it would be like riding a bucking bronco. In such conditions men used the WCs below in the family steerage deck if they were still operational and, if not, reverted to the slop pail.

Due to the punishing they had received during the three days of rough weather the steerage toilets were in a dreadful state. They had been subject to passenger inaccuracy due to the lurching ship and the recipient of slop pails containing vomit, food scraps, filthy rags and other revolting and unidentifiable substances most of which, but not all, had gone down the hole. With no ventilation they erupted with the smell from ammonia based stale urine, over spray from urgent diarrhoea bowel motions, spilt vomit and disgusting detritus on the floor.

With his handkerchief to his nose Dr. Tweedale carried out a toilet inspection with Richard and issued him with specific instructions. First the floors had to be swept. Second they had to be mopped all over with ordinary salt water. Then they must be scrubbed with a mixture of marine soap and salt water. Next they had to be disinfected all over with a solution of chloride of lime and vinegar and a squirt of creosote applied around the lead lined chute. This procedure, the good doctor explained, had to be carried out every day in future, and if required more than once a day. Finally, the doctor impressed upon Richard the necessity for him to thoroughly wash his hands and arms at the end of each day's duty and then to rinse them in a mild chloride of zinc based disinfectant solution or else he "might catch a sickness". For similar reasons he constantly instilled in all passengers the importance of washing hands after using the WC. There were times when Richard had to steel himself to roll up his sleeves to tackle the mess but the thought of the monetary reward at the end of the voyage and a sweet pipe of tobacco on deck at the end of the day's task to take the smell from his nostrils kept him going.

Chapter 13

DISEASE

After fourteen days sailing *Trafalgar* was approaching Madeira Island situated in the Atlantic more than 300 miles to the west of Casablanca on the African coast. With a mountain 6,000 feet high it could easily be seen from the considerable distance that the ship passed by. She was now well under the influence of the consistent and gentle winds of the northeast trades. A light, steady and trustworthy breeze on the port side quarter allowed the captain to hoist all the canvas she could carry. With her sails gleaming in the sunlight as she progressed over a sparkling blue Atlantic she presented as a stately and pretty picture if not the most beautiful moving man-made object in the world.

She developed a rhythmic sway under sail. The wind in her rigging made a continuous soft sound as though she was moaning with delight at the caress of the breeze. Dipping to the side off each swell, the gusts on her sails created a "wirrer, wirrer" sound that rose and fell with each dip. Down in steerage there were constant soft "tinkle", "ding", "tung", "dong" and rattling sounds from the emigrant's utensils and paraphernalia. The gentle "creak", "crack" of the ships timbers and rigging punctuated the lullaby of sounds. A hatch cover joined in occasionally with a squeak as it swung slightly on its hinges within the confines of its keeper. This was fair weather sailing where for the most part the running gear of the ship could be set and not require constant adjustment, which gave the sailors the opportunity to carry out necessary repair and maintenance work aloft and on deck while the passengers settled in to a ship board routine. But now they were heading into the mid-Atlantic, the world of the big sea with all its dangers and unknowns.

Lloyds Register of Shipping recorded in 1840 that ships were being lost at sea at the rate of one and a half vessels a day. In 1847 there were at least twenty-eight ships wrecked on the Australian run or operating in Australian waters with the loss of at least ninety-nine lives. In 1848 there were at least thirty of such wrecks with a loss of at least sixty lives. There were never enough lifeboats on board to cater for all persons and lifejackets were unheard of.

While shipwreck was to be feared so too was disease. Between 1848 and 1885, five percent of all ships that took the route from England to Port Adelaide buried sixteen or more emigrants at sea. In November 1838 the *Thomas Harrison* arrived in South Australia after a fifteen-week voyage from Plymouth and the deaths of thirty children at sea. Likewise, the *Moffat* arrived in December 1839 after thirty deaths on board during the voyage. Then in July 1840 the 570 ton barque *Fairlie* sailed into port Adelaide after having buried twenty-four emigrants at sea – mainly children. But *The Manlius* on its trip from Scotland to Port Phillip in 1842 far exceeded these figures with the death of forty-four persons on board averaging a new death in less than every three days for the entire 116-day voyage. While at anchor in quarantine in the bay a further seventeen died bringing the total deaths to sixty-one which was just short of twenty-five percent of all the passengers. Most of these deaths were caused by typhus, an acute infectious disease which in 1910 was found to be caused by the body louse. It was very common where people were crowded together in unsanitary conditions and did not have regular changes of clothes, often being named after its location as "gaol fever", "ship fever" or "camp fever". Victims developed a listless stupor with a dry and heavily coated tongue, suffered from severe headaches with painful joints and muscles and got covered with a bright red spotted rash. They were feverish, sometimes delirious and smelled very badly as their skin began to darken. Death eventually resulted from the accumulation of toxic substances in the blood – toxaemia.

Great dangers existed due to the difficulty of detecting early-stage infections of diseases such as typhus, whooping cough, scarlatina, measles or even influenzas before a ship sailed. Such diseases, and even all too common diarrhoea, had the potential to develop once a ship was underway into full on-board epidemics with the capacity to cause multiple deaths particularly in the case of children. The more of them on board, the greater was the risk of increased mortality. Larger families suffered more deaths and the risk increased with the number of children under the age of seven years. Richard and Jane had three: Mary 6, Ann 3 and Elizabeth 1. Coming from a relatively remote rural area in Cornwall the Dunstans did not have the same acquired immunity that emigrants from populated urban areas had. The risk of one or more of the family having come aboard with a serious illness contracted from others at the emigration depot was also substantial.

Despite the insistence of Dr. Tweedale on the washing of

hands after toilet use and the cleaning and disinfecting of the WCs diarrhoea was prevalent. Dirty nappies, changed infrequently then stowed for a period before being washed inadequately, increased the risk of spreading infection in the poorly ventilated close quarters of steerage. The bowel complaint could cause serious dehydration in children resulting in death.

In steerage there were always some young children with stomach pains and fevers who fretted, grizzled and cried to the discomfort if not misery of adults. Little Lizzie had been having that effect on Jane, who had been very worried about her for some time. In addition to diarrhoea she had inflamed gums, was feverish and sweaty and had no appetite. She was weak and listless and refused all offerings of food but was keen to drink a lot. Dr. Tweedale attended regularly and prescribed her an arrowroot mixture drink to take as thick as she could. She did not vomit but passed a green and bilious foul-smelling stool. Richard and Jane took it in turns to wipe her forehead with a cool wet rag and lie with her in the bunk, and she would give them her little hand to hold or sometimes lay it across their neck. For three days she was very ill and Jane thought she might be lost to her forever. On Dr. Tweedale's instructions the cook prepared a special thin broth which Jane managed to administer to her a teaspoonful at a time. This she seemed to enjoy and ever so gradually began to improve until at last she fully recovered. Jane said to Richard that she thought she would be committing her little darling body to the deep and would have done so had it not been for the divine intervention of God. Richard thought that Dr. Tweedale and the ship's cook had more to do with her recovery than the Almighty.

While diarrhoea was one problem, the on board ship's diet made sure that constipation was another. Dr. Tweedale readily and freely made available "opening medicine" to those who suffered in the form of castor oil – a pale yellow foul tasting substance made from castor beans with a strong laxative effect. Only the desperate came back for a second dose. Worms were another common bowel complaint in children and for this the doctor had an excellent medication which often resulted in specimens over twelve inches long being evacuated after treatment.

Because ships doctors were paid at the rate of ten shillings for each emigrant landed, including babies born on board, they had a vested interest in preventing deaths. Apart from diarrhoea and constipation the run of the mill patients suffered from coughs, colds, fevers, seasickness, stomach cramps and indigestion, infections of eye, ear, throat, nose and chest, boils, infected wounds, toothaches, lice, skin rashes, and of course pregnancy and childbirth. There was a range of on board medicines available to the doctor to dispense for diagnosed complaints. On special occasions a broken limb or amputation needed the surgeon's skills.

Cuts and abrasions had a tendency to turn septic fairly quickly at sea – particularly in the tropics. Sailors were constantly suffering small injuries which often became infected as a result of poor hygiene on their part and contact with sea water heavily laden with bacteria. Dr. Tweedale regarded all septic wounds as serious and before bandaging applied leeches from his medical kit to facilitate bleeding and clean the wound – a procedure used commonly by many doctors at the time to avoid the onset of gangrene and the consequent necessity of amputation. Apart from his well equipped medical kit Dr. Tweedale took on board with him an extensive library of books relating to medical matters and maritime health in general. While he was not over endowed with "bedside manners" he was professional, polite and civil to all regardless of their station. Jane was delighted with him and thought that he took a special interest in the family because of Richard's position as sanitary constable. The Dunstans had never been able to afford a doctor's consultation in the past and it was quite a luxury to them to have free access to the ship's surgeon about any of their complaints. Jane also thought he was good because he, like her, hated dirt. He had no knowledge of bacterial science or the germ theory of disease but knew from experience that whenever people lived closely together in filthy conditions sickness was sure to appear. He knew that cleanliness and good housekeeping went a long way towards disease prevention and made sure that these two things were applied to *Trafalgar*.

He gave instructions to the constables for the daily sweeping and scrubbing of the decks in steerage, the use of disinfectants and fumigation procedures and ordered special cleaning duties where circumstances required it. He checked on the operation of equipment such as wind sail ventilators to steerage, WCs, stoves and boilers, the proper cleaning and scouring of eating and cooking utensils and the cooking and distribution of rations. He conducted regular inspections of bedding, berths and bodies in steerage keeping his nose tuned at all times for suspicious odours. He often sniffed out smelly treasures that had been squirreled away such as dirty nappies, soiled underwear and used menstrual napkins which were then condemned to be thrown overboard or ordered to be washed straight away. He took a special interest in all the children on board and rounded them up for regular medical inspections by bribing them with a sweet at the conclusion of each consultation. He counselled all passengers to eat their meals on deck in the fresh air whenever possible and was completely opposed to anyone remaining below decks all day if the weather was good. Anyone caught in their berth in those circumstances, and not sick, was ordered up to do six laps of the main deck.

Those who failed to toe the line and follow exactly all the rules, regulations and orders of the doctor were summoned to attend a person to person conference with him in his surgery where they were admonished at length about the importance of cleanliness, orderliness and discipline on board ship and reminded about the punishments available to deal with disobedience.

Chapter 14

LIFE ON BOARD

Three days after passing Madeira *Trafalgar* sailed within sight of Palma Island, the most westerly of the Canary Islands, with its mountainous peak of 7,900 feet. The passengers had soon learned to hang onto any available part of the ship as it lurched constantly, even in good weather, from one side to the other. "One hand for the ship and one for yourself," was the rule advised by the sailors which occasionally a passenger would forget and find themselves pelted by the next lurch into some part of the ship. But mostly, after nearly three week's sailing, the passengers had found their sea legs.

After arising around 7 a.m. and attending to personal cleanliness, blankets and bolsters on beds were then folded and stowed. Following breakfast the emigrants had to remain on the upper deck (weather permitting) and while they cleaned the breakfast dishes the men rostered for the day swept out steerage and washed and scrubbed its deck, the table and the bottoms of any berths under the direction and supervision of the sanitary constables. Disinfectant comprising chloride of lime or zinc mixed with vinegar was then applied as directed. All passengers would then collect and take on deck their bedding to shake and air out by throwing it over the ships hatches, boats, rails or rigging – but not on the gunwale. Every second day, or more if necessary, the whole of steerage quarters would be fumigated in an attempt to sweeten up the stinking air, by men swinging a little iron stove fumigator containing burning charcoal, tar and a solution of vinegar and chloride of zinc as they walked through steerage. This produced a pungent vapour.

Other detailed rosters were devised for the men including galley assistants with the job of peeling potatoes or preparing other food under instructions, delivering of hot or cold water and anything else that needed regular attention. The full-time position of assistant to the cook, which came with a gratuity of £3, was given to emigrant Mr. Charles Winchester.

In many ways life on board was an imitation of life back home on land. Enterprising passengers tried to make the most of their time by endeavouring to earn an income. One man who set himself up on deck as an engraver would, for a few pennies, tap the initials of the owner on tin plates and mugs with a punch and hammer he had in his kit. Several people established themselves as barbers offering shaves and hair and beard trims for a very reasonable fee. There was a woman who told fortunes for a penny. Even Jane made a little money from selling small calico storage bags with drawstrings that she had sewn and she let it be known that she could do anything with a needle for an appropriate payment. Other women offered to sell crochet or embroidery that they had done. Literate emigrants performed penny readings from books for groups of non readers. One of the passengers publicised that he had skills as a cobbler and could sole and heel anyone's shoes for a very fair cost. Even the ship's carpenter found time to whittle up a number of wooden tops from rubbish wood he had to sell, he said, to keep the children amused. Some passengers had come fully prepared to set themselves up as specialist shopkeepers on board. One sold cottons, needles and threads, another laces and brass buttons, another looking glasses and small scissors, while someone else had a range of handkerchiefs for sale. A lady selling lollies and pickles cleared her stock in no time. Although most items were offered at a mark up of 75 to 100 percent the vendors were surrounded by keen shoppers, including sailors, as soon as they appeared on deck. Some emigrants were quite ingenious at making things for a profit. One was an expert at creating rings, jewellery and ornaments out of pennies and halfpennies which he then polished and recycled back into the economy at triple the original face value. Another wrote letters for those that could not and an old man sharpened knives from a whet stone he kept in his pocket.

Occasionally articles would be auctioned off – usually to pay for gambling debts. Although gambling was prohibited, card games were allowed if there was no betting, which was impossible to police. On fine days there was always a card game going in a corner of the ship that was not obvious. Most men did not play for money, but for tobacco and prized possessions such as pocketknives.

By far the most popular pastime was talking. After breakfast and any morning chores were attended to, the women would congregate in yarning groups on deck, all wearing white aprons and frilled caps tied under the chin. Some were keen smokers and enjoyed their "Blackjack" tobacco in large clay pipes with tin covers to shield out the wind. There was always a great deal of reminiscing about the life they had left behind in England and an equal amount of speculation about the life that they would live in Australia. Many passengers developed strong friendships that lasted long after the voyage had ended.

Men, too, had their discussion groups where they exchanged their favourite entertaining stories and outlined their plans and expectations for colonial life. They played draughts and chess and deck quoits and tried their hand at fishing if the conditions allowed. Some made good friends with the sailors who entertained them with amazing stories and taught them valuable new skills. Strong men often readily helped in the working of the ship which gave them a knowledge of matters nautical as well as something to do. The sailors were always glad of their help which was usually executed without adverse consequences except in the case of one emigrant who had two fingers amputated after they were crushed in a block while helping the crew with ropes. After being dosed with a glass of brandy he was held down while Dr. Tweedale did the job.

It was good that the British Colonial Emigration Department did not simply throw the emigrants on board and leave them to their own fate, as the demographic breakdown of persons on board included no less than ninety children aged fourteen and under. Recognising that young minds and bodies such as these needed to be educated and kept busy the government appointed official teachers on all emigrant ships. On *Trafalgar* the task was given to Mr. Robert McTaggart, a teacher by occupation, who was travelling to Adelaide with his wife and three children. His duties also extended to the conducting of Sunday church services, as well as a general pastoral care as the ship's chaplain. For the discharge of these responsibilities, which would be substantial,

Mr. McTaggart was granted a free passage for himself, and if his performance was satisfactory he would also receive a £4 gratuity on arrival.

All children between five and fourteen were supposed to attend formal classes on board ship unless excused by the surgeon or captain. On *Trafalgar* there were sixty-five in this group which meant classes of thirty or so each for boys and girls. Straight after breakfast each morning the children assembled on deck and were called to attention by Mr. McTaggart who conducted an inspection as to their cleanliness. Anyone who did not "pass muster" was told to report immediately to Dr. Tweedale. Non-attendances were noted in a book and reported to Dr. Tweedale and Captain Richardson weekly. The children were then culled into two classes, with Matron Caroline Bacon, whose duty it was to assist the teacher, leading the young ladies to the quarterdeck area and Mr. McTaggart ushering the boys up to the other end of the ship. Reading, writing and arithmetic were the main subjects taught with needlework every afternoon for girls and rope making, tying and splicing for boys. School was two hours in the morning after breakfast and two hours after the midday meal, each day including Saturday.

On Sunday morning there were two hours of religious instruction for the children after divine worship. Writing was taught using slates and copying with chalk in copperplate style maxims such as "a stitch in time saves nine", "waste not want not", "a fool and his money are soon parted", and others. The older experienced scholars were given the job as monitors to teach the younger children. Matron Bacon and Mr. McTaggart made sure there was plenty of respect shown by the students for their positions through the liberal application of the strap and the cane if there was any foolery or excessive talking. As an incentive to the students the most deserving child in each class would receive a prize of a book signed by Captain Richardson, Dr. Tweedale and Mr. McTaggart on arrival in Adelaide. By the end of the voyage there would be children who could read and write for the first time in their life and who, in a few months on board, had received more formal education than ever before. Included among them were Richard Dunstan aged 12, Ben Dunstan aged 11, Henry Dunstan aged 10, Wearn Dunstan aged 8 and Mary Dunstan aged 6.

The Government Emigration Agency also provisioned the ship with educational texts and supplies for the passengers use. There were books on arithmetic and spelling, instructions on how to teach, slates and chalk and paper, pens and ink. A quantity of literary books were also provided and a few passengers brought their own which were shared among friends after being read. Dickens was popular and there were several copies of *Sketches by Boz*, *The Pickwick Papers*, *Oliver Twist*, and *A Christmas Carol* going around. Copies of Jane Austen's *Pride and Prejudice*, Emily Bronte's disturbing tale *Wuthering Heights* and her sister Charlotte's book *Jane Eyre* were also on board. Mr. McTaggart established a library and appointed a person to be in charge.

A number of philanthropy and church groups, which took a great deal of interest in emigration at the time made available copies of the King James Bible, biblical tracts, institutional pamphlets and books together with sewing kits, materials and wool for the women, and ropes, leather and basic tool kits for the men. With these materials at their disposal Mr. McTaggart and Matron Walters organised educational classes with volunteer teachers for adults to attend if they wished. The captain gave permission for an adult literacy class to be set up in a quiet part of the poop deck to teach reading and writing. The religiously inclined could attend daily Bible groups to hear lessons, scripture readings, sermons and homilies from their fellow travellers and join with them in appropriate hymn singing. Craft groups provided instruction on fancy knitting, crochet, quilting and sewing skills where the women made maximum use of the free materials and wool that had been delivered to the ship. Lessons set up especially for men included the popular rope making and tying, mat and brush making, basic wood carving, and instructions on a variety of other skills that would prove useful in the colonial world such as straw plaiting, bag making and weaving, leather craft and shoe cobbling.

Both the captain and Dr. Tweedale made it clear to all emigrants that laying about doing nothing was not what they should be doing and that it was expected that all passengers would make the best use of their time on board to learn new skills through the educational facilities provided. The doctor was determined that with the assistance of Matron Bacon and Mr. McTaggart the passengers on board would not only be sanitary, healthy and sane, but that as many of those as possible who were barely literate at the beginning of the voyage would have a fair chance of basic literacy by its end.

Although Jane's two youngest children (Ann 3, and Elizabeth 1) and her regular on board domestic chores absorbed a fair part of her day she was still left with more time to herself than she ever remembered having before in her life. She resolved to make the most of opportunities given and with great enthusiasm enrolled for as many adult classes as she could manage. She would never have had the time to fit in proper lessons at Tolcarne even if they were available. On board ship she could go every day and for free. She decided that by the time they reached Adelaide she would learn as much as she could.

When not attending school classes the children amused themselves with a variety of games. Ball games were popular at first but sooner or later the ball went overboard never to be seen again. Marbles were out of the question on a hard deck that was never perfectly level. Hide and seek was popular, although there were many "no go zones". Competition races around the deck were promoted by Dr. Tweedale to encourage the children to exercise. The simple game of "tag" was popular. All it required was for one person to be the chaser and everyone else to be chased until someone was caught when he or she was then "it" and then had to become the chaser. "Blind man's bluff", a game in which a blindfolded player tries to catch others while being pushed about by them, was played. It was popular with the girls as was skipping rope and games such as leapfrog and hopscotch with grid chalk lines marked on the deck. Another game that the girls liked was accompanied by a song which everyone sang about "Oranges and lemons, the bells of St. Clements ..." – while a line of children ran under an archway created by two players holding their arms up. The song ended with the words "The last one through gets the chop, chop, chop!" – and on the last "chop" the arch fell trapping one of the runners who then replaced one of the archway players. It was young Mary Dunstan's favourite game.

The boys preferred a more aggressive game called "hoppo bumpo" where they held onto one foot and hopped aggressively into the melee towards a selected opponent with the aim of bumping him off balance so that he had to put both feet on the deck, in which event he was "out". The victor then moved on to the next opponent. The last one standing was the winner. It was not a very fair game as the little ones always got the worst of it, though at times the small and nimble footed, such as Henry and Wearne Dunstan, could out-wit larger opponents by ducking away from the charger and causing them to overbalance.

On days when the weather was too bad to play on deck some

games could still be played in steerage. A game called "cat's cradle" was played with a simple knotted length of string from which a web of patterns could be created with a few hand movements. Mothers could amuse young children for a few moments at least by playing "This little piggy went to market" with their toes or involving them in hand clapping games with lyrics such as "Pat a cake, pat a cake, bakers man, bake me a cake as fast as you can". Hide and seek could still be played and the ever popular game of "Simon Says" where one player called moves and the rest had to follow worked quite well in confined quarters. One game that Jane had made sure she had packed was "Jacks" which consisted simply of five or more knuckle bones from sheep legs. The game was played by holding the five Jacks in your hand, throwing them in the air and catching as many of them as possible on the back of your hand. Further degrees of difficulty included throwing a single Jack in the air and picking up from a table surface as many single Jacks as you could before catching the Jack in the air with the same hand without dropping any. The game helped to develop eye and hand coordination. Noughts and crosses and "hangman" were played on slates with chalk. A simple but popular game called "pinny ninny" was played with a pudding bowl placed upside down on the table. Each child would take turns to slide an ordinary dressmaker's sewing pin (of which there were always plenty available) down the side of the bowl so that it would land on the table surface. When a pin landed on one or more other pins then they would be confiscated by the player until whoever had the most pins when a count was taken was the winner. Whoever got the least was the "pinny ninny".

Chapter 15

THE DOLDRUMS

The Northeast Trades blew to near the equator and then *Trafalgar* entered the doldrums, an area of 200 to 300 miles notorious for its light and variable winds, complete calms, thunder storms and heavy rain. Overnight the ship ran out of wind and there was an unusual silence about next morning. Even the sailors were quiet – without their normal running and yelling. For a while there was still a slight swell in the sea but after three days of no wind even this abated. Now, as far as the eye could see lay a green, oily, unbroken surface with only the slightest of undulating ocean swells on which *Trafalgar* rolled very slowly from side to side for a while and then sat motionless with her sails hanging limp before again repeating this process.

Every part of the ship was scorched by the tropical sun. The deck, made as hot as a stovetop, caused the pitch and tar mixed with the oakum caulking used for waterproofing deck seams, to bubble up and melt through the deckhead into steerage below. Down there conditions were intolerably hot and stuffy so that nearly all emigrants were forced up on top where they spent most of their time under temporary canvas awnings erected by the sailors.

At night it was so hot and humid in steerage that everyone left it till the deadline of 10 o'clock before going to bed and then lay tossing about for hours with clothes dripping wet with perspiration unable to sleep. While Richard and the eldest boys eventually slept half naked on the top deck Jane and the other children sweated away in their steerage bunks fully clothed. Meanwhile, the ship developed its own dirty little ring of rubbish. Flotsam, from the vessel comprising, garbage from the galley and slop pails, soiled babies nappies and evacuations from the water closets encircled the ship's hull and did not move. Then, as if by magic, swarms of flies appeared – no doubt having picked up the smell of the ship from the mainland.

The tropical humidity caused a population explosion of ship board bugs which now literally came out of the woodwork in ever increasing numbers. The cockroach population in particular seemed to double overnight every night. Jane, who loathed all "crawlers", was disgusted by them. Just before tropical rain storms they would swarm in herds all over the ship and were their busiest after dark. They scurried through everything and ate everything. If they could not find food they would eat the paint and varnish off the ship's wood work or even the wood itself. They seemed to revel in haunting the precincts of the water closets and, to Jane's horror, had a penchant for crawling over her bottom when she sat on the hole. At night they gently nibbled at the ears and noses of sleeping passengers and happily crawled into any mouth left open in search of food morsels. Young Wearne loved to squash them because when he did they popped and stank. They became a staple diet of the ship board rats that in turn waxed fat and went forth and multiplied.

There was a ship's cat who was an indefatigable ratter when it suited him. He could sit for half a day or more on a rat run in the darkened hold waiting to ambush his selected victim. Unfortunately, he was spoiled by the seamen and passengers who gave him tid bits to eat so that his motivation for rat catching was diminished. He often scampered up the rigging after the men when they were ordered aloft but never to their full height. The sailors demonstrated he was a good swimmer when they tossed him overboard in the doldrums and he quickly clawed up a thick rope cable thrown to him and hauled himself back on board.

Bedbugs were also becoming a problem. They lived in seams between the wooden bed boards and came out at night to suck the blood of passengers. Their bites often caused allergic reactions with large wheals accompanied by itching and inflammation. The children in particular suffered from their depredations and Jane's three girls Mary, Ann and little Lizzie with their fair skins were tormented more than the boys in the family.

In an attempt to control the cockroaches, bedbugs and rats and at the same time "sweeten up" the place, Dr. Tweedale ordered everyone out of steerage so it could be given a heavy duty fumigation. On Dr. Tweedale's instructions Richard lit a slow burning fire of charcoal, birch bark, brimstone, tar and a few other extra secret ingredients added by the doctor, in a big iron pot set over ballast stones laid on the deck in steerage. All hatches and vents were then blocked, any open seams and cracks stopped up, and the fire left to "cook" for most of the day. When finally reopened and aired a few slow moving clearly stifled rats were found and finished off. The cockroaches, fleas and other bugs had mostly left the premises to take up temporary refuge elsewhere before returning at the first available opportunity.

As *Trafalgar* drifted in the doldrums the captain made sure the crew were kept occupied in attending to the ship's maintenance. Calm weather provided an ideal opportunity to scrub the barnacles and growth off the sides of the ship and several teams of sailors suspended in boatswains chairs hanging on ropes tied to the gunwales were given the job. This was also the time to completely change every sail on the ship. Like all working ships *Trafalgar* carried a full set of spare sails as well as a good store of extra canvas for patching repairs should it be needed. On leaving Plymouth she had masted her best, newest and strongest set to cope with northern latitude winds. These were now changed for an old, patched, fair weather set that were quite adequate to wave in the winds of the doldrums. The best set would now be stored below until they were critically needed for the roaring 40s westerlies in the Southern Ocean. While the wind was free, sails were expensive and had to be looked after. The changeover procedure took a full day and involved most of the crew. The largest sails weighed close to a ton and had to be manhandled in and out of the storage hold during the process. Each day drooping sails hardly moved except once in a while to give two or three sad flaps against the mast. *Trafalgar* sulked and lolled and rolled slowly and sullenly on the glassy sea that disappeared without horizon into the misty atmosphere.

To keep up the sailor's morale Captain Richardson gave permission for any seamen off duty to lower one of the ship's boats to go swimming if they wished, after having rowed a respectable distance from the ship – or if they desired, fishing. The privilege was not extended to passengers although they could, if they wished, fish from the ship.

Passengers, however, could take advantage of an on board sea water bath to cool off. Large half barrel wooden tubs were placed for the men in the forecastle area of the ship's bow as far away from the women's single quarters as possible and a temporary canvas screen erected for privacy. Women had a similar bath space prepared for them towards the stern of the ship on the quarterdeck. The area was virtually a small room made out of old sail canvas that included a tarpaulin roof so they could not be observed by sailors in the rigging. It was kept under constant supervision by Matron Bacon whenever women were engaged in bathing.

In the forecastle area the men had the use of a pump mounted on a pipe made out of a bored out elm tree trunk that went down below sea level. The ladies had the use of a portable wash deck pump that required four persons on the handles to pump it up and down. It made a clank, clank noise when operated and shifted a great amount of water in a short time. After some practice, the women emigrants soon learned how to use it. Through the use of these pumps, pails for pouring water and the large half tub barrels a very satisfactory bathing system was achieved.

Once a week, so long as the ship was not rolling so much as to make it impossible to stand on deck, Dr. Tweedale ordered the young boys to strip and jump into one of the large tubs where they would be doused with numerous buckets of cold salt water by a couple of laughing sailors. Young girls were a little more gently washed by their mothers under the supervision of the matron who also gave instructions to young mothers on correct washing procedures for babies. From time to time Dr. Tweedale would order a "general wash" for everyone on board with the aim of rounding up those who seemed to have a complete aversion to water as was the case with one young man in the single men's steerage quarters. Complaints were made about his dirtiness and lack of hygiene.

Dr. Tweedale ordered that he report to him and found that he was both lousy and filthy and clearly had never washed himself since coming aboard. He refused outright the doctor's orders to wash, so clandestine arrangements were made for him to be ambushed at an opportune moment by a posse of six fellow passengers, who stripped him, threw him in the tub and scrubbed him mercilessly until squeaky clean. Thereafter, whenever the doctor suggested that someone should have a bath they readily obliged.

Jane and the children were delighted with the ablution arrangements which they took advantage of every day in the tropics and had never before had so many baths. When it rained, as it frequently did in the doldrums, rainwater was caught in canvas collectors made from old sails and drained into barrels. When available a bucket of this was used to wash off the sticky finish that a salt water bath always left.

There was never enough fresh water for the washing of clothes or dishes, activities which were prohibited in steerage because of the importance of trying to preserve dryness between decks at all times. After the slop pail was emptied of its contents and cleaned it was used on deck with cold seawater and so called "marine soap" that refused to soap up properly, to wash anything that needed it. Washing clothes was only permitted twice-weekly on days designated as washing days which, subject to suitable weather, was on Tuesdays and Thursdays on *Trafalgar*. The task was impossible to perform in rough weather. In the meantime, babies, often suffering from diarrhoea, continued to soil their nappies which the mothers stowed under the bottom bunks until the next available wash day creating a stink in steerage that was chronic and increasing the risk of cross infection and re-infection.

Items really in need of a thorough clean, such as clothes from a sick person, filthy nappies or menstrual napkins were placed in a net bag at the end of a line or tied on the end of a rope and thrown overboard to be towed behind the ship for a pre-rinse treatment and then retrieved and washed. Washing was hung all over the ship on lines specially strung for the purpose or on convenient pieces of ship's gear. Clothes dried quickly with a stiff crusty salt residue that made them so uncomfortable and itchy to wear that rashes often resulted. The worst part was that the salt crystals left behind in the fabric attracted moisture from the damp sea air so that the article never felt really dry, soon went smelly again and was prone to rot.

Rot was a problem on board ship as some passengers found when they were given the opportunity at last to access their boxes from the hold when they were brought on deck. Some boxes seemed damp inside, others stunk with dirty damp clothes that had been jammed into them back at the emigration depot and were now spotted with black mould and in the process of decaying. Every once in a while there was a shriek or a groan or an "Oh no!" when a lid was opened. Leaking jars of jam, or bottles of oil or vinegar had spoiled new dresses and bonnets. Colonies of silverfish and cockroaches had taken up residence in some boxes while a few had been penetrated by rats seeking the articles of food squirreled away therein. Jane's boxes were fine of course. She, being the meticulous, totally in control person that she was had made sure that the lid closed tight on carefully packed contents with her own moth repelling sachets containing lavender, rosemary and cloves placed among the clothes to help keep pests at bay.

Chapter 16

CROSSING THE LINE

The calm periods were broken several times by rain squalls accompanied by thunder and lightning. After one such event, the first mate Mr. Blythe was peering through his telescope at faint flashes of lightning on the horizon in the southwest quarter from which a hint of a breeze was coming, when young Ben Dunstan beside him asked, "What can you see sir?"

"I can see young fellow the line that cuts the world in half called the equator."

"Can I see it too please sir? Can I please have a look?" Ben pleaded.

"Noo me lad, you could'na see if ye looked. Ya' have to be an experienced seaman to see those sort o' things."

At other times he had placed a thin piece of cotton on the end of his glass to trick the children, and even the emigrants themselves, into believing that they could actually see the equator, but right now he was trying to give the weather his full attention. While there was no wind to speak of the sky was covered with ominous looking black clouds and the atmosphere seemed electric. The lightning continued with its faint flashes on the horizon and then the ship was hit with noisy raindrops the size of pennies that splattered loudly on the deck. Within seconds thunder clapped and lightning darted in all directions over the ship. An ear splitting "crack a crack" noise came from above the main deck which lit up with an orange flash and *Trafalgar* trembled from fore to aft. Shrieks and screams followed by plaintive cries came from steerage and without further words the passengers were on deck in a minute.

The foremast had taken a lightning strike. It split the upper and lower top sails which were left blackened and smoking and ran down the mast and over the deck but appeared not to do any structural damage to the timbers. Attracted by the ship's anchor and cable it travelled through the hawsehole and burst into the crew's forecastle quarters with a red zap which was the last thing the men in there remembered. They and several sailors on deck were thrown into the air and dashed down again by the shock. No one was killed but several sailors and one passenger were rendered unconscious for a period. For a minute or two there was total dismay and confusion until Captain Richardson's voice took charge. Dr. Tweedale was quickly on deck to examine the affected, all of whom promptly recovered except for two men who were ordered below to the ship's hospital for further treatment. No one was more active during the aftermath of this event than Dr. Tweedale. He was everywhere.

In the meantime a group of emigrants with astonished expressions formed a prayer group on deck and began singing hymns. As they did so they were interrupted by another deafening thunder burst that clapped almost on their devoted heads. "Praise be to the Lord for the warning that sinners in the end must face their God!" someone yelled.

While the sailors didn't like big black clouds at any time, at midday they didn't like clouds of any sort as it was important to be able to see the sun at its zenith at noon to establish accurate local time with the use of a sextant. Captain Richardson would then give the order to his first officer Mr. Blythe to "Make it noon". He would in turn give the order for eight bells to be struck. Once this was done the captain would compare the time with Greenwich Mean Time set on his reliable ship's chronometer and calculate his longitude, as each hour of difference meant he was 15° away from the Greenwich meridian. By referring to tables, latitude could also be calculated from the same noonday sighting of the sun.

On cloudy days without sun the calculations could not be made. The ship then had to proceed by dead reckoning, or what the captain thought would be right allowing for the wind, waves, currents and estimated distance travelled. There was one day in the doldrums, after Captain Richardson checked his bearings at midday that the ship was found to be thirty miles closer to England than the day before due to the drift of the current and the prevailing swell.

Trafalgar was baffled in the doldrums for more than two weeks making no progress at all. With the oppressive tropical weather everyone soon became bored, frustrated and then depressed. Occasionally the monotony was broken by a school of flying fish flashing by as they were chased by a mob of bonito, or a great squadron of porpoises bent on some migratory route. At times they appeared in huge pods of 200 or more making a scene that thrilled everyone. Even the small things were noticed like the jelly fish, with conspicuous floats splashed in colour, that the sailors called "Portuguese men of war". Flocks of storm petrels which the crew called "Mother Carey's Chickens" and boatswain's swallows visited the ship.

On one oppressive quiet day when *Trafalgar* was dead in the water a cry was heard from the watch "Turtles off the starboard bow!" A collection of serpentine heads could be seen some 100 yards away intermittently popping up from the flat sea. Turtle meat was highly valued by all seasoned mariners most of whom had eaten it at some stage. They tasted like veal and turtles caught alive could be stowed in the ship's hull to live for months as a supply of fresh meat. Two large turtles were soon captured by sailors launched in small boats who, after quietly getting as near as possible to their quarry without disturbing them, simply hauled them aboard by a flipper. Next day there was turtle meat soup for all those willing to try it. Those that did enjoyed it greatly and praised highly the skills of the cook whose turtle soup recipe had been honed to perfection during years of practice at sea.

In the tropics the hot days and cold nights plus the constant varying wet and dry periods caused the ship's rigging to stretch and shrink alternatively so that the sailors had to make constant adjustments in order to properly tune its setup. When a faint breeze finally appeared the captain kept the men hauling the yards around constantly, night and day, chasing every tiny puff of air. As soon as the ship was braced up on a gentle tack the breeze would swap to another quarter so that the sails had to be set again. Then it would go dead calm with utterly no wind at all with the ship rolling about in the swells causing the sails to flap and bang against the rigging with the risk of fraying and tearing. To prevent such damage the captain would order the sails to be brailed up, gathered in and secured; and as soon as this was done another slight breeze would appear so that the men had to undo all the work just completed and reverse the procedure to again try and catch the latest faint puff of fickle wind. Tempers shortened under these conditions and the men were soon tired of the continuous hauling of braces and halyards. Eventually *Trafalgar* limped across the equatorial line and Captain Richardson gave the crew permission to conduct their crossing of the line initiation ceremony which would be an amusing diversion as well as a morale booster for all on board. Preparations for the performance of this pantomime had been going on for days.

The set for the theatre included a canvas tarpaulin erected at the bow end of the ship across the forecastle area behind which the sailors could dress and attend to their preparations in secret. The rest of the ship was the stage. On the quarterdeck a canvas pool made out of old sail was filled with water and a plank set across it for a seat. Captain Richardson, the ship's officers, Dr. Tweedale, Mr. McTaggart and Matron Bacon together with the cabin passengers, a Mr. and Mrs. S.G. Dorday and their five children, had box office seats of the proceedings from the poop deck while the remaining passengers from steerage stood around the circumference of the main deck.

At four bells (2 p.m.) the proceedings began with the performers parading forth from behind the canvas screen led by a Scotsman playing the bagpipes accompanied by a man on a squeezebox, a fiddler and a tin whistle player. Then followed King Neptune and his wife, selected from one of the ugliest crew members. They were made up for the occasion with long flowing hair and whiskers of rope yarn and oakum that looked a bit like seaweed. Neptune looked fearsome naked to the waist with face, arms and chest painted red to simulate the effect of the sun. He wore a crown made from old shells and bones and held a five pronged spear, normally used for spearing fish, as his trident. Mrs. Neptune wore a lady's bonnet and a huge old dress she had borrowed from one of the passengers and carried a bag in one hand and handkerchief in the other. Both appeared dripping with sea water that had previously been poured over them for effect. Then followed a "barber" carrying a huge "razor" over his shoulder, dressed in a white canvas coat that looked like it was spattered with blood, a "latherer" carrying stiff brushes and a pot of foul-smelling slush grease from the galley mixed with tar and oil and a "doctor" looking more like a funeral director dressed in black with a battered top hat, a tray of "medications" and a very red nose. Three "enforcers" armed with canvas waddies stuffed with old rags accompanied the entourage. After an elaborate parade around the deck the players finally stopped in front of the canvas pool on the quarterdeck where Neptune and his wife were seated on their "thrones".

Captain Richardson formally welcomed his Royal Highness and gave him permission to proceed with the conduct of his Royal Court but reminded him that his proceedings were to be confined to the crew and passengers who volunteered, like young Richard Junior, who foolishly offered himself as a participant.

King Neptune called for order and announced that the purpose of the proceedings was to initiate the new midship boys, or anyone else who had not crossed the line before. The initiates were "seized and arrested" by the enforcers, through the liberal application of their rag filled canvas waddies, stripped to the waist, blindfolded, handcuffed, marched around the deck and then, when their names were called, individually placed on the plank over the water filled canvas pool to face their "trial" before King Neptune. Using the stiff brushes which were dipped into the stinking slush lather pot the candidate was lathered all over, including his hair. During this process the barber questioned the sorry stooge who, whenever he opened his mouth received a gob full of lather. He was then "shaved" off by the barber using the giant rusty old iron shaver, and examined by the doctor who diagnosed the necessity of prescribing a little "opening medicine", whereupon he was given a dose of castor oil. Still blindfolded and handcuffed he was dumped into the pool of sea water where the enforcers, encouraged by the cheers and hoots of the passengers, gave him a thorough ducking and softening up with the canvas waddies. He was finally allowed to scramble out and given a stiff glass of grog to drink the health of King Neptune accompanied by more cheers from the passenger audience.

Several passengers allowed themselves to be initiated and at the conclusion of proceedings all participants were given a hearty three cheers. A collection was then taken up in favour of the performing sailors and the captain gave orders for them to be issued with extra rations of grog. The festivities then degenerated into a water throwing melee with buckets of it being thrown about. Matron Bacon copped it a couple of times but took it in her stride. It was not the first time she had been drenched. Once, when half way down the hatchway stairs leading to the single women's steerage quarters, she received an anonymous bucket of salt water from the upper deck. The girls were always playing tricks on her and one young woman who had been clearly insolent was ordered by Dr. Tweedale to remain below in steerage until she apologised.

Caroline Bacon's job of being the guardian of single women's morals and making sure that while at sea the virtue of thirty-eight females was preserved at all times was a demanding, thankless and unpopular task. She was well suited to the job and had a tongue like a lash that whipped out orders and admonitions from her mouth in a flash. Unfortunate miscreants who committed on board misdemeanours were verbally flogged until they cringed and begged for mercy. When in full flourish with a large red face, black bushy eyebrows and a chin like the stern of *Trafalgar,* she was the very model of intimidation. A perfect choice as Matron. Jane marvelled at the way she made Richard jump to attention and do her bidding with a single demand, when in similar circumstances Jane might have to ask him half a dozen times before he showed any sign of action.

Chapter 17

Night Time

The best thing about being in the doldrums was the nightly on deck festivities that took place during perfect tropical evenings on dead flat seas. Everyone had already discovered that heaving seas and lurching decks were no good for fiddle playing and dancing. But in calm equatorial waters under a tropical moon and millions of stars twinkling in an ink blue sky, dancing to the tunes of an on board band was a wonderful tonic that provided passengers with the best memories of the voyage. Dr. Tweedale encouraged such activities as a means for passengers to get valuable exercise. The action started before the last of the huge orange sun disappeared, leaving as it faded a transient river of sparkling gold flowing towards *Trafalgar*. Deck lanterns were then lit fore, aft and midships.

A simple tune from a penny tin whistle was all that was needed to get some passengers dancing. But there were on board a variety of instruments including several concertinas, six or more violins, two proper flutes, a tambourine and a couple of harmonicas as well as a number of tin whistles and one set of bagpipes. The musicians divided into groups and formed three different bands playing the style of music they enjoyed. One had a repertoire of rattling jigs, reels and hornpipes that they played at the forecastle end of the deck for the sailors who, by and large, moved with surprisingly precise and calculated courtesy towards each other during their dances. Up on the poop deck a band had been given special permission by the captain to play music for more formal dancing including waltzes, polkas and quadrilles, and here single men and women engaged in the most sober form of dance under the watchful eyes of Dr. Tweedale and Matron Bacon. Standing a few feet apart in rows opposite, the movement of feet was minimal while the dancers looked at each other with a smile. Down on the quarterdeck the loudest and largest bunch of musicians specialised in playing full-blooded English country dances such as *An Old Man's a Bed Full of Bones*, *Cuckolds All Awry* and *All In A Garden Green*. This area had the greatest flutter of skirts from the ladies and from the men actions that at times looked like a "war dance". Mary Dunstan joined in, improvising with other girls her age on the edge of the circle, but the Dunstan boys always linked up with a group of males that preferred to be spectators.

At the rear of the poop deck near the helm a small group of women who were not in favour of these activities gathered, with the captain's permission, to sing hymns and pray. Unlike them, Jane Dunstan did not prefer prayers and hymns to dancing opting instead to prance around the deck with Richard doing country dances in their own style. While all these activities were occurring on the main deck, down below in steerage a senior solo fiddler was going through his repertoire to entertain some of the more mature passengers.

Each night it was the practice to take around a hat for donations to the bands to keep them playing. A penny or two from some of those enjoying the music was more than enough to keep them happy and added up to a considerable sum by the end of the voyage. As the ship's rule was lights out by 10 p.m. all festivities on deck were brought to a halt an hour before to allow everyone to settle down and prepare for their bunks. As arranged by Mr. McTaggart the lament of a lone bagpiper droning from the poop deck was the nightly signal to terminate the proceedings. From that time until lights were out Matron Bacon and Dr. Tweedale kept a constant vigil to make sure that the young unmarried men and women kept a respectable distance from each other and made certain that they went to bed at the opposite ends of the ship.

While the onboard activities helped to keep the sanity of most people intact the oppressive tropical conditions seemed to have an adverse effect on some. With each week in the doldrums tempers were shortened and sharpened. A number of male emigrants who brought with them their tendencies towards domestic violence began to practice their proclivities. One man who bashed his wife, giving her a severe black eye and cut lip was, on the recommendation of Dr. Tweedale, followed by the orders of the captain, put in irons and chained to stanchions for two nights on a bread and water diet. At the end of it he was greatly remorseful and did not reoffend. Most women on board were even-tempered, polite and well mannered, but some who were loud-mouthed, crude and argumentative seemed to get worse with the tropical heat.

Another man became a major concern to the women and children. When he first came on board he was noticed only as a dirty slow witted fellow who kept to himself. But he had now developed the habit of creeping around the deck and jumping out at children from behind the ship's boats or galley yelling, "Whoo Whoo Whooo! If I don't get ya' then the devil will! Ha! Ha!" This frightened the children out of their wits and often left little girls crying. Mary and Ann Dunstan were terrified of him. At night in steerage he would wander around talking to himself and waking people up. He never showed any sign of violence but was caught twice taking ladies clothes off the washing lines and throwing them overboard. Dr. Tweedale found that a regular dose of laudanum, an opiate based medicine, kept him under control but as a backup measure had the sail maker stitch up a straight jacket which he could then prescribe in case there was a total loss of reason. With the continued oppressive heat and humidity the usual rule that females were not allowed on deck at night was relaxed allowing those women who wished to sleep topside, but the captain always placed a watch on each side of the deck to patrol for their safety.

Down below in steerage regular night guards were appointed on a roster basis from the married men to watch the hatchways and generally keep an eye on the sleepers as a means of curbing theft. Close quartered conditions made it easy to steal things and passengers worried constantly about the security of their few possessions. The night watch guards also made sure there was no pipe smoking or naked flames such as unprotected lit candles below. Smoking in steerage, or anywhere "between decks", was prohibited because of the danger of fire. Straw mattresses in wooden ships created a virtual "tinderbox". Anyone caught breaching this rule was liable to be confined in chains for a period of time on a bread and water diet. The lighting system in steerage at night was provided by brass gimbal-fixed oil safety lamps with the flame contained in glass lanterns that were locked and could only be lit or extinguished by the authorised person with a key. They were extinguished at 10 p.m., except for one at each hatchway which were kept on low leaving a faint yellow light at each end of steerage that disappeared altogether in the middle. Due to safety concerns in extremely rough weather all lights were put out for fear that the rocking of the ship might cause the oil to splash about and start a fire. In a wooden ship a fire was an extremely dangerous event. If it had to be totally dark then people simply proceeded around by touch and feel as best they could.

When it came to bedtime, changing clothes was a struggle because everyone dressed and undressed in full view of each other. Privacy was not available. Jane soon learned to change under the cover of a blanket draped around her neck while standing at the foot of her berth. Others fought clothes on and off while lying under a blanket in their bunks. Some didn't change clothes much at all. When it came to love making most married couples managed it quietly and furtively and if, like Jane and Richard, they had a top bunk then at least with a little more privacy than down below. Some passionately coupled anyway and didn't care.

With 210 people in the married quarters of steerage (including 101 children aged fourteen years and under of which seventy-five children were aged ten and under with twenty-four of them aged less than two and nine babies under one year) a good uninterrupted night's rest was not possible. At the start of the best nights when adequate ventilation was coming down the hatchways there was always a peculiar sickly, musty smell of unwashed bodies in old clothes mixed with the smell of straw mattresses that were beginning to develop mouldy bits, smelly blankets and smoking lamps. That was as good as it got. During the night a great number of the 210 human beings had to urinate. Some also had to defecate. Some made it to the WC in the dark. Most used the slop pail. Babies used their nappies. By early morning an overpowering smell of faeces, urine and ammonia mixed with flatulent emissions and bad breath permeated the deck. During the night a significant number of the 210 persons snored, some called out in their sleep, others coughed, babies cried. Sometimes someone would knock something over in the dark or put their foot in something nasty and curse loudly so that others were woken.

Rats were on the increase and squealed and scurried about, at times running over the emigrants in their bunks. One night when Jane had the bunk to herself because Richard was sleeping on deck, she woke around 5 a.m. all hot and perspiring to become conscious of a scratching noise near her feet. Raising her head she saw a monster rat nibbling the boards at the bottom of the berth. She froze as it turned its attention to her toes. She felt the tickling of its whiskers as it sniffed. She was terrified but did not move, fearing every moment that he would bite. Having decided that toes were not on his menu "rattus giganticus" then turned away and quietly walked up Jane's left side and over her pillow. In the process the nails on his paws got caught up in her hair, at which point she simply wanted to scream her head off. He soon freed himself, walked around the top of her head, down her right side and jumped off at the end of the bunk. Jane lay there in a lather of sweat and thanked God that she had the courage to not move. At night rats seeking food scraps crawled into the pockets of clothes that were hung up and defecated before they left. They ate holes in hankies and the bottom of pockets, climbed in and out of slop pails and walked all over the trestle table down the centre of steerage leaving their droppings and urinating as they went.

There was no stopping the cockroaches either. Several times at night Richard was woken by a tickling sensation at the end of his nose which he made a grab at, catching a number of them in the process.

Sailors were always a noisy lot. If there was any shift of wind, sails had to be trimmed. Orders would be yelled to "square the yards" or "ease away port" or "let go" or "clew up" or "haul away starboard" or any number of other things. There was always an appropriate "aye, aye sir" yelled just as loud in response. Whenever a halyard or brace line was hauled by a group of sailors together it was accompanied by a lot of bellowing at the least if not a sea shanty. Every order was followed by the stamping and tramping of sailor's feet on the deck as they ran to their posts to execute it. All these noises reverberated through the deckhead to the steerage passengers below several times every night as even in light conditions the yards might have to be trimmed to meet the wind shifts. In addition there were always the usual noises a sailing ship made as she progressed. In fair weather they were pleasant creaking and sloshing sounds, but strong winds created all sorts of whistles and whines in the rigging. Squalls boomed in the sails and hail stones could make a hell of a din on the deck. Waves made their own thundering sound and anything not tied down banged, clattered or rattled; and then the movement of the ship itself was of a whole separate dimension to deal with. Learning to live with and accept nights of disturbed sleep was an essential part of a long voyage on a sailing ship.

Chapter 18

SOUTHEAST TRADE WINDS

A pod of sperm whales, often seen in large groups in equatorial waters, was congregating 300 or 400 yards off the ship's bow. There were twenty or thirty in the group. Jane and Richard had never seen a living thing as big before. Huge blunt-headed animals glistening dark brown in the sunlight with bodies as long as ninety feet and flukes fifteen feet long, they appeared indeed as leviathans to those on board the 129-foot *Trafalgar*. These animals had the biggest brain of any living creature and lived for up to eighty years if they were not killed by whalers in the meantime. A curious member of the pod came so close to the ship that Jane thought she could have thrown a penny on its back. She and the children saw clearly its grapefruit size eye and huge mouth and were agog at the huge noisy waterspout that blew from its blowhole.

Everyone on board was sick of *Trafalgar's* wallowing on the long Atlantic swells. Breeze was entirely absent except for the odd puff here and there. First she would roll right over to port side until it was hard to remain standing on the steep sloping deck; then she would hold for a couple of disconcerting seconds before making a continuous, sickening slow roll back to a similar angle on the starboard side. Sailors and passengers alike slid into the bulwarks. Every time she turned to roll the other way blocks, tackle and gear creaked, rattled and banged.

There were two recognised ways of hustling up a wind in the doldrums. You could pray for it or you could whistle for it. The rule was that passengers, being landlubbers, were never allowed to whistle while on board. If they did it could bring bad luck. Sailors could whistle if they wanted to stir up a better breeze, but not if the wind was already blowing as it would cause a storm. You could also cause a storm by spitting into the wind. Prayers for a perfect breeze were offered each day at a short divine service held at 10:30 a.m. and again on Sundays at 10 a.m. when a full one-hour service took place. Eventually of course, they were answered and a gentle but consistent wind appeared from the northeast to sweep *Trafalgar* out of the tropics and on her way.

Religious services were conducted on deck, weather permitting, by Mr. McTaggart acting as ship's chaplain with the assistance of Dr. Tweedale and the support of Captain Richardson. The Sunday service was attended by many of the crew and nearly all passengers who always wore their best available clothes for the occasion. The service opened with everyone joining in the Lord's Prayer followed by a fatherly address by Captain Richardson in which he counselled all to have goodwill to each other and make the most of their time on board by being occupied in learning new skills.

He then dwelt upon the shortness of life and the need to be ready for its end at any time. Next, Mr. McTaggart read some selected passages of scripture after which several hymns were sung and a short sermon delivered. Dr. Tweedale then took the opportunity to preach his usual homily about cleanliness being next to godliness and the importance of harmony and peace on board. A period of silent prayer followed with the Lord's Prayer again to finish off. The service ended with the captain's thanks for their attendance and – "May God Bless You".

Jane enjoyed the service very much. She, like most passengers, received great consolation from religion and the pleasure of singing hymns which went with it. In bad weather when on deck services had to be cancelled, it was still sometimes possible to hold a short service down below in steerage.

Captain Richardson's sailing plan was to take the "Great Circle Route" which had only just begun to be used by sailing ships. This course took vessels close to the east coast of South America before heading southwest to catch the "roaring 40s", strong westerlies which had the potential to considerably shorten the voyage in time and miles. Earlier emigrant ships had followed the coast of Africa before heading due east after the Cape of Good Hope. From now until she got beyond the Cape of Good Hope into the 40° latitudes the predominant winds that *Trafalgar* had to deal with came from the south, mostly in the form of the southeast trade winds but sometimes winds from dead south or south, southwest. This meant that a fair amount of tacking would be required to deal with winds tending towards the ship resulting in a lot of work for the sailors and some discomfort for the passengers.

Jane and Richard had not long fallen asleep when they were woken up by a change in the attitude of the ship. *Trafalgar* had been sailing into the wind on a close hauled port tack and with her heeling over in that orientation they dozed comfortably with their heads higher than their feet. But now the ship had been put

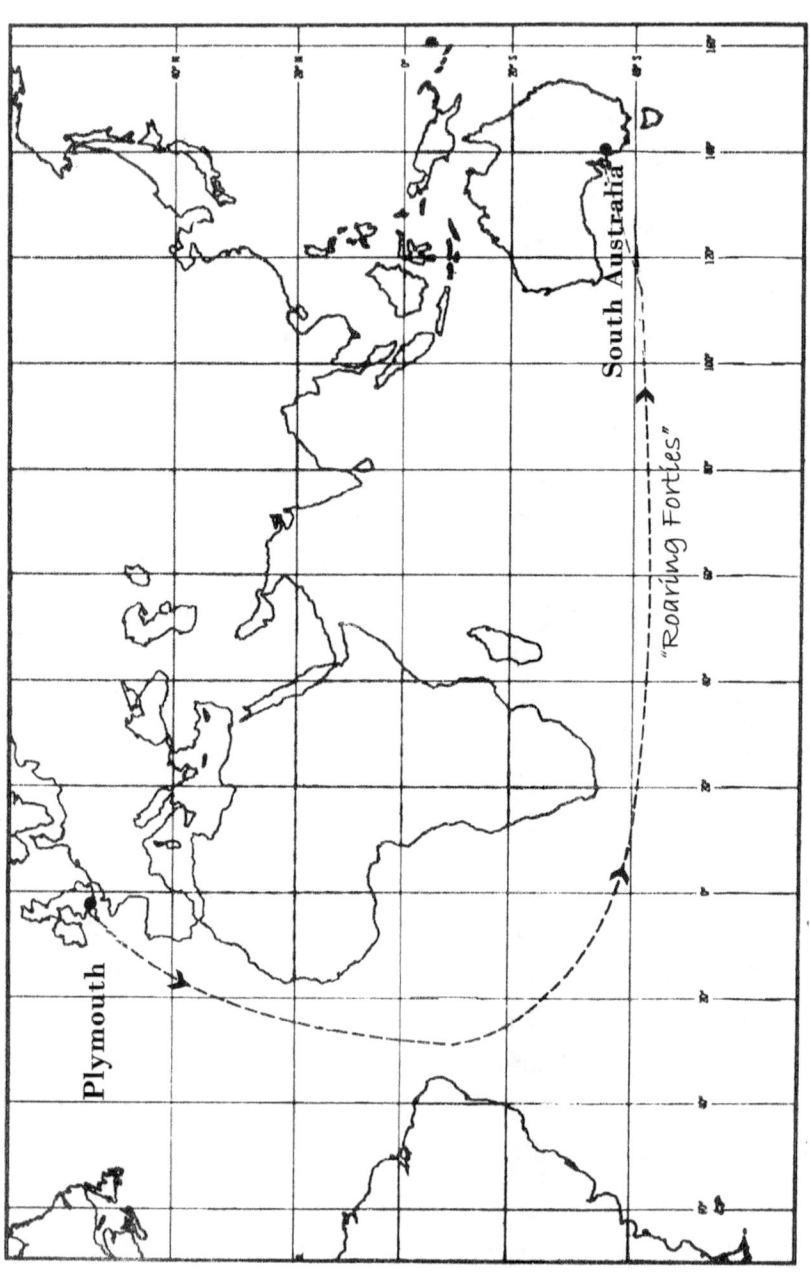

Great Circle Route – the approximate route of *Trafalgar*,
16th October 1848 to 17th January 1849.

about into a close hauled starboard tack that heeled her over in the opposite direction causing their feet to be higher than their heads so that they had to rotate 180° and change their pillows to what was previously the foot of the berth. After the passing of another couple of hours *Trafalgar* tacked again and they found that they were back to where they started and had to rotate once more. Each time this occurred there were collective groans and mutterings from all in the ship as ends were changed. Waking up with your head lower than your heels gazing at your feet in the air was an all too common circumstance.

When it came to tacking ship, every seaman had his station, knew his place and knew that he had to be there and be responsible for the ropes given to him when the order was made to put the ship about. When all hands were in position the commands came – "Raise tacks and sheets!", "main topsail haul", "ease away port", "let go and haul", "haul taut to windward", and others until eventually it was done and all trimmed with each man having neatly coiled up and tied away the last end of the rope line at his position.

The work of the sailors was never finished. Constant examination of the ship's rigging was required to detect any worn or unfit part of the running gear that needed replacement or overhauling. Numberless ropes and lines became worn or chafed and had to be bound, tarred or replaced. Ship's carpenters repaired broken spars and masts and were called upon generally to repair or make anything in wood. Torn sails needed repair or replacing. Rigging continually became slack or needed adjusting and had to be loosened off here or tightened up there. Then there was the continual knotting, splicing, washing, polishing, scraping, scrubbing, painting, varnishing, oiling, greasing and tarring required during the course of every voyage in addition to reefing, bracing, furling and making and setting sail and being ordered to climb over the ship in every direction and pull and haul to the point of exhaustion. After all that was done, there were always helm and watch duties to attend to.

Every day they climbed aloft 100 foot or more on the footropes and ratlines of the rigging, up masts and along yards to fight flapping canvas. They hauled heavy lines to a repertoire of sea shanties which had endless verses or often to a simple stretched out hauling singsong such as "Ee yah oh yah!" and "Ee ay ay yo ho!", emphasising the "yah!" and the "ho!" when they all pulled together. Often their rhyming chants ended with a chorus of "fal dal diddley di oh!", and they had their own slang which frequently included adding the letter "o" to words such as "beefo", "porko", "watero" and "mind your feeto".

They were a rugged, illiterate, superstitious bunch but none of them was short on courage or shirked hard work when it had to be done. Excessive expression of their masculinity was their main characteristic. They showed little sympathy for anyone who was injured in their work or sick at sea, were all thick-skinned and had to be to survive being the constant butt of jokes and ridicule from fellow sailors and the lashing tongues of ships officers. Except for common, tar marked, baggy canvas trousers they wore no uniform. Some had neckerchiefs. Some had their hair in pig tails. They wore a variety of hats and all carried knives on their belts.

The face of one of the older men was very deeply pockmarked and he had only one working, bloodshot eye that pierced through everyone like a ball of fire. His other eye was badly disfigured, white walled and useless. At first the children were frightened of him but he turned out to be a very friendly, caring and amusing storyteller making him so much in demand that in the end they followed him around like the pied piper. By and large, the sailors enjoyed having the emigrants on board as they generally provided much amusement and contributed to a friendly and more relaxed atmosphere.

To be an effective captain of an emigrant sailing ship required more than the ability to handle her well under sail, you also had to be master of endless but important details relating to ropes and rigging, pumps and passenger's trifles, their health and welfare, salt pork, vermin, dry rot, church services, burials at sea, and much more. Burials at sea were one of the least pleasant duties a captain had to perform especially, as was the case with the first death on this voyage, when the deceased was a young child. A dear little girl in a bunk not far from the Dunstans' berths had become critically ill. Emily Spriggs who was just one year old had been suffering from hydrocephalus, a condition in which fluid accumulates in the brain, typically in young children, enlarging the head and sometimes causing brain damage. She also had terrible diarrhoea for the duration of the voyage and was reduced to skin and bone due to severe dehydration. Her tongue, covered with white skin, seemed to rattle in her mouth and overnight she had strong convulsions. Her mother became very distressed and a group of people, including Jane who had helped nurse the child over the past few weeks, gathered around as it became apparent that she was clearly dying. Dr. Tweedale was in attendance but there was nothing he could do and on 9th of November she died. He gave the mother some laudanum to ease her distress and removed the body to his small hospital so it could be prepared. The sail maker was called to sew the corpse up neatly in a canvas shroud with stones at the feet from the ship's ballast to make it sink. Out of respect for the family of the deceased Dr. Tweedale ordered that all music and entertainment be cancelled for the rest of the day, that no unnecessary work should be done and all on board should keep as quiet as possible. The burial was scheduled for 4 p.m.

The idea of committing bodies to the deep sea distressed many bereaved who wished that they were on land to conduct a proper burial in a cemetery grave. Jane was not alone in thinking that without a traditional Christian burial in the earth the deceased's ghost might remain restless forever. If someone died on land you could follow the body to the grave and a stone would mark the spot. But if they died and were buried at sea you were left with nothing. There was nowhere you could go and leave flowers and stand and mourn. You knew where your loved ones were when safely laid to rest under six feet of earth, but when jettisoned feet first into the depths you had no idea what would become of them or what further terrible ordeals their body might be subject to. It was the stuff of nightmares. In any event, sea burials had to proceed as it was vital to the health of those remaining on board to dispose of corpses promptly.

The service took place in the presence of most of the passengers and a large complement of the ship's crew. The tolling of the ship's bell announced the start of proceedings. As the last toll died the emotive tones of "Amazing Grace" came from the lone bagpiper on the quarterdeck as the tiny body of little Emily, laid on a board and covered by the Union Jack, was carried by four family friends in a short procession from the forecastle area to midship where one end was laid on a barrel and the other on the gunwale. Although this took only moments it seemed an eternity to Jane and many of the onlookers. When the piper stopped, Captain Richardson came forward with prayer book in hand and stood at the head of the deceased as passengers and crew members gathered around. He began in a strong voice to read the beautiful burial at sea service according to the ritual laid down in the *Book of Common Prayer* but towards the end he choked and handed the prayer book to Mr. McTaggart to complete the service.

"The Lord gave and the Lord hath taken away; blessed be the name of the Lord. We therefore commit this body to the deep."

The two men who stood at the head of the board lifted it so that the tiny corpse of baby Emily in her heavily weighted shroud slid out from under the Union Jack to plunge with a soft splosh into the dark blue sea. It was followed all the way down by a heart rendering cry of continuous anguish from the child's mother. Except for her uncontrollable sobbing, all was quiet. Little Emily disappeared without trace. Jane had stiffened herself and silently sobbed as tears streamed down her cheeks, but in the end failed to contain her emotion as she gulped a full breath, howled out loud and wept into Richard's shoulder.

Dr. Tweedale ordered that all bedding and clothes connected with the child's last days be jettisoned as soon as possible overboard into the sea. As sanitary constable Richard was then directed to carry out a thorough disinfection procedure, using vinegar and chloride of zinc, on the berth and surrounds where she had died. All who had attended the deceased were counselled, yet again, by Dr. Tweedale on the importance of personal hygiene and the washing of hands.

It was getting cooler in the evenings. The southeast trade winds had increased and blew strongly on the port quarter. As she headed into heavy seas, with large waves making it difficult to walk on deck, *Trafalgar* was making eleven knots. There was great interest each day in the log line reading that was taken at noon. This was a light rope that when thrown overboard and allowed to run out recorded the ship's speed. It was divided at standard distances by knots and the faster the ship went the more knots would run out during a fixed interval measured by a sand timing glass. The number of knots run out during that time was the ship's speed.

Many birds now followed the ship. Boobies, petrels and cape pigeons (a bird about the size of an English pigeon with black and white wings) seemed to be able to soar about the ship tirelessly. Gulls screeched in *Trafalgar's* wake, hovering then swooping and diving at the wash, some landing on the ship's rails. They had learned already that ships were a convenient and reliable source of food scraps. The sight of so many birds was comforting to those who had never been away from land so long before. Land they thought, could not be that far away. *Trafalgar* had changed course and was now heading southeast some 400 miles off the Cape of Good Hope.

There was much excitement when a cry of "Sail ho!" came from the watch aloft. In a long voyage, meeting a homeward bound ship was a major event. If she was English and the weather fair, both ships could draw together to exchange news and mail. Ships heading to the port from which the other had departed could carry the good news that the latter had been "spoke" to and was proceeding well. *Trafalgar's* location would also be reported to Lloyds of London where anxious relatives could obtain details of its whereabouts. The other ship proved to be an English barque heading back from China and the East Indies with a cargo of tea and spices, but although they skilfully steered within twenty yards of each other they were unable to exchange mail as each was making a fair pace with the wind and neither captain was prepared to reduce sail. Using loud hailers they managed to exchange longitude, details of ports of departure and destination, length of journey to date and *Trafalgar's* request to report to Lloyds "All is well".

Jane watched the barque as it slowly disappeared from view over the horizon – first her hull, then her deck and slowly the masts with the top mast last to be seen. She thought that if the world was flat it would have gone away quickly over the edge and therefore it must be true that it was round. She half wished that she was on the barque heading back to Cornwall and thought she would never see a Cornish sky again. Down here even the stars were different. But someone had told her that the moon was the same. She realised that if it wasn't for her pushing the family would not be on *Trafalgar*. Richard would never have agreed to go without her insistence. She knew now that she hadn't thought through all the details before they left. She'd had no idea what a long sea journey was like or how disgusting the conditions in steerage would be at times. What if life in Australia turned out to be worse than life in Cornwall? What if they didn't survive the journey? So many "things" could go wrong. She was afraid that if their venture did not work out well it would be her fault. But she still had faith and found comfort in the belief that God would deliver them all to a better life. Whether better or not, it would be different she thought.

Chapter 19

SHIP'S FARE

Food was constantly discussed among steerage passengers. Most of them in recent years had not had enough. Printed copies of the official daily food allowance were displayed in prominent places throughout the steerage deck, and Jane made it her business to find out what the family's entitlements were so that she could make sure that the correct portions were doled out to her each morning by the food stewards when she joined the line with her mess ticket after they yelled "Yo mess! Yo mess!"

Good quality fresh potatoes were easy to keep, travelled well in the ship's hold and were a familiar staple to all those in steerage, but the stores of these had already run out several weeks ago. While there was no shortage of food it was uninteresting, unappetising, repetitive and boring. There was a good supply of staples such as ship's biscuits, salted beef and pork (known as "salt horse" or "salt junk" by the sailors), flour, barley, split peas, raisins, molasses, treacle, oatmeal, tea, coffee and sugar as well as sago and rice for the children. There was also plenty of highly salted ship's butter, stored and sealed from the air in small casks so that it would remain edible for two or three months, and plenty of a substance that was alleged to be mixed fruit jam. Steerage passengers never tasted any of the pigs and poultry housed on the main deck. They were for the officers and cabin passengers. Some milk from the goats was available to children who were sick and the cook was always willing to follow the instructions of mothers in the preparation of appropriate broths or mash for babies and toddlers. Some mothers simply chewed the salt pork, or whatever shipboard food was available, into a pap in their mouths and then pushed it into the mouths of their infants.

Every day Dr. Tweedale issued a dose of lime juice to the passengers, most of whom enjoyed it very much. By this time it was well accepted as a protection against scurvy; the British government having mandated its use to ships' crews in 1844. The emigrants had no access to alcohol on board as on government sponsored ships like *Trafalgar* it was prohibited under the *Passenger Act* of 1842 which had banned the on board sale of liquor to steerage passengers. Dr. Tweedale did have the power to prescribe a drink of brandy, wine or porter from the ship's stores under the provisions known as "medical comforts" but it was a power he seldom exercised. After more than a month Richard was really missing the regular pint of ale he used to buy at the Tolcarne pot shop, and resolved to himself that if he survived the *Trafalgar* experience the first thing he would do when he got to Adelaide would be to buy a couple of pints from his earnings as sanitary constable to wash the taste of the job out of his mouth.

The galley stove was a large rectangle cast-iron device with the fire box in the middle and a large oven on either side. Each morning it was lit around 6 a.m., stoked with coal and kept going until it was extinguished at night about 8 p.m. The top was surrounded by an iron rail to prevent pots from sliding off onto the floor in rough weather and other iron rails could be adjusted and fixed across the surface to help prevent the movement of cooking utensils. In very rough and wild weather, which might sometimes last for three days or more it was too dangerous to light the galley fire. In such conditions cooking pots could be flung off the edge of the stove regardless of the retaining rails to scald people and there was always a chance of fire escaping and burning the ship. During these times passengers were reduced to nibbling ship's biscuits. However, in normally solid rolling seas and swells, even in conditions where the sea came over the side, the galley continued to operate.

On one such day Jane delegated her mess captain's duties to young Richard by handing him her mess captain's ticket. Without a mess captain's ticket you were not allowed into the galley. His task was to collect a pot of barley broth soup for the family. Having done so he waited for what he thought was a "smooth spell" to navigate the deck back to steerage. He got as far as the end of the deckhouse when a huge sea broke over the bows to fill the main deck and sweep him off his legs. The soup went one way and he went the other finishing up aft in the starboard scuppers still holding onto the pot which now only contained sea water. Young Richard was more distressed at losing the family rations than getting a ducking as having lost the soup he could get no more from the galley.

Fortunately, as soon as the other passengers heard of the tragedy many readily came forward to donate a portion of their broth so in the end the Dunstans had some soup to go around. Jane managed to avoid any serious personal mishaps for herself.

Her worst experience occurred when going up the stairs of the hatchway with a pot of cold water and a quantity of dry oatmeal, the ship gave a lurch and she finished on the floor covered in both substances which upset her personal decorum, and disrupted her sense of control, but caused no lasting adverse effects.

The cook was in charge of the stove and controlled when and where the mess captains could place the pots for cooking. He was on duty from morning till night and had a thankless job cooking for all those people with limited ingredients and most times dishes that the mess captains, and not he, had prepared. He was commonly grumbled about and abused beyond earshot. But it paid to stay on the right side of him as he was a man of particular power who could quickly turn nasty if he heard his culinary ability being criticised. If you stayed in his good books he might let you dry your socks and mittens near the stove. While he answered to the name of "Cookie", he was happy to be addressed as "Captain Cook" so long as the real ship's captain was not around.

On a day-to-day basis he was probably as equally important to the passengers. He had a squarish face from which fleshy jowls drooped on each side, a large hook nose, dimpled chin, full lips and popped out bloodshot eyeballs. Receding grey hair tied back in a pony tail presented his profile like the figurehead of a ship stuck on the hull of his very large stomach. While he was ugly enough to frighten the ladies and little children he demanded civility and politeness from everyone and upon receipt of same returned it in spades. Because Jane joked with him, showered him with compliments about his cooking (mostly not justified) and offered him sympathy for the impossible task he had to perform they both got on famously. But any man who abused or upset him found himself the recipient of a storm of invective the like of which he had never experienced on land. He was proud of his ability to cope with the basic means available to him and kept himself and his galley clean, tidy and "shipshape" unlike most ship's cooks who were renowned for their slapdash approach, their untidiness, their rudeness and lack of attention to basic food hygiene.

Thick "stirabout" oatmeal porridge of one sort or another was the staple breakfast for the Dunstans, though with her smoked ham and preserved eggs, the latter of which would last until half way across the southern Indian Ocean, Jane was able to do up a frying pan of ham and eggs from time to time. For them this was really good living. To make a basic stew from the highly salted pork or beef, Jane would soak chopped up portions overnight in sea water which was then discarded. She would then add an onion from the few she still had left in her stash, some barley, split peas and flour dumplings. The few potatoes she had brought with her had, like the ship's potatoes, long since run out. With a splash of fresh water and heat applied in the galley the eventual result was a stew of sorts.

Jane also prepared, as best she could with what was available, her traditional meat or dessert boiled puddings. The bag of dried apples she brought with her proved invaluable for dessert dishes to which she also added some ship's raisins. She prepared and baked plain loaves and raisin loaves and made puddings from rice when it was issued, which she served up with butter and treacle. Ship's bread was also baked and distributed by the galley four times a week – weather permitting. It was a welcome alternative to the always available "ship's biscuit" infamous for its teeth breaking propensities. They were made from a basic dough mixture of flour, water and salt, measured one inch thick by four inches square and were baked two or three times until very hard, to assist their preservation. The sailors called them "hard tack" which was a term used to describe a broad headed nail but they were much valued as a staple on a long voyage. They ate best when broken up, which usually required a suitable implement such as a hammer, and then soaked for some time in a soup or light broth. Being prone to verminous infestations it was a good idea to give them a good bang on the table as a first precaution to rattle out any loose bugs or maggots. If this confirmed their presence then a follow-up re-bake in a moderate oven usually motivated any residual occupants to abandon biscuit. There was quite a list of different insect beasties that liked to inhabit them.

The water had started to taste and smell badly and Jane was glad that she had brought her raspberry vinegar with her to help mask the taste. Cold water was doled out to the mess captains every day and whenever the cook's assistant yelled out "hot water" down the hatchway the mess captains would pour out on deck with their tea and coffee pots to jostle for position at the door of the galley. Tea and coffee in the hot water tended to diminish its smell and it was better for the passengers having been boiled. Hot soup was also popular.

In rough weather the business of eating and drinking on a constantly moving platform was an acquired skill. It was often difficult to get a cup to your mouth and a sip could turn into a gulp or a bath of hot liquid if you were not on the ball. People frequently made a mess of themselves and others. Richard once received a dose of boiling liquid on his legs causing them both to be scalded and making him jump up and down yelling "Jesus holy Christ!" and "You bloody bastard, I'm burnt!" To try and prevent the movement of plates and utensils in steerage, the fixed trestle table was surrounded by a raised edge and had a vertical baffle board running down the centre to separate the dishes of port and starboard passengers. These measures helped but in rough weather you still had to hang onto your plate with one hand and

Emigrants at Dinner.

[*Illustrated London News*, 13th April 1844. Mary Evans Picture Library Ltd., London.]

eat with the other or your rations could be upended on the table or worse still land on the floor. Under the tables there were racks for plates and battens to hold small casks.

Both sailors and passengers took every opportunity to supplement their very basic and deficient diet from what they could catch and kill on the voyage. In addition to turtles in the tropics, flying fish, which at times went by in huge flocks, were caught when many of them landed on the deck and were pounced on. The Dunstan boys were adept at nailing them. They were one of the best pan fish around and were fine eating with a flavour similar to fresh sardines. At every opportunity Richard and his boys fished for sharks on hooks baited with old bits of salt meat, or barracuda on hooks trailing astern baited with a red rag.

Small sharks or "couta" baked whole in the cook's large oven were a delicious and welcome change to the usual salt meat meals. Any surplus fish caught, after bleeding and gutting, were salted and hung in the rigging to dry in the wind where they would keep for weeks and improve with age. Seabirds caught on baited hooks were skinned, gutted, salted and hung in the same manner. Albatross had a reputation for being palatable and was much relished by some sailors. They were easy to catch either on a baited line or sometimes by simply grabbing them when they landed on deck as they were not quick at taking off.

Preparation was a key part of the recipe. After gutting and skinning the bird was soaked in salt water overnight, par boiled, the water discarded, and the meat then chopped up and cooked in a traditional stew. Intrigued, Jane asked one of the sailors for a taste and thought it was like goose. Porpoises riding the ship's bow wave were targeted with harpoons and dragged on board by the men. They considered their flesh a great treat after being dealt with appropriately by the cook who was an expert in such matters. Richard accepted an offer of a cutlet from a sailor that he then shared with his boys. Jane and the girls refused it. The flesh was red like beef and most thought it was delicious although some found it disagreeable and complained it had a strong oily taste.

To Jane and Richard who were used to hardship and making do under trying and difficult conditions at Tolcarne, the food that they had on board was a great improvement on what they had been used to. By the end of the voyage all of the family, except little Lizzie who remained a constant concern to Jane, had put on weight.

Chapter 20

THE ROARING FORTIES

After tacking into alternate south easterlies and south westerlies for some days *Trafalgar* picked up a kind wind blowing steadily from her aft starboard quarter and rode a long soft swell that kept her lolling gently from side to side. She was interrupted only by a bit of a squall now and then and for the most part bowled along at seven to eight knots with much blue sky, a few fleecy clouds overhead and big splashes of bright warm sunshine every day. At night the southern sky twinkled with the brilliancy of its constellations. This was good sailing.

As they ran steadily south the evenings grew colder and Dr. Tweedale made arrangements with the captain for passengers' trunks to be brought on deck again so they could access warmer clothes. The garments they had worn in the tropics were not warm enough for southern latitudes. Every day the wind seemed to lose a little more of its soft caress and gain a slightly increased edge.

Captain Richardson now gave the order to replace all the lighter and older good weather sails on the yards with the ship's best quality heavy-duty storm canvas. Sailors were ordered to check all the rigging and repair or replace any frayed or worn lines. Spare masts, lifeboats and all other ship's paraphernalia on deck were checked again to make sure they were properly tied down and secured.

The usual on deck entertainment activities that were popular in the tropics began to peter out earlier each night with most passengers seeking the warmth below deck in steerage. After putting the children to bed Richard and Jane would make the most of the opportunity to use the comparatively quiet upper deck to have a few moments together, strolling under uncountable stars as they listened to the sounds of a fiddle coming from steerage or the notes of a tin whistle in the crew's quarters. Leaning over a rail amidships they watched the last of an enormous pale moon sink over the horizon to briefly leave a sliver of rippling silver flowing to the ship. Soon it was gone and they were left in the soft glow of the deck lanterns. Only then did they become aware that *Trafalgar* seemed to be floating on jewels. On each side of her bows there were billions of tiny twinkling white, green and blue phosphorescence sparkles which unwound down her hull leaving a trailing luminous milky way in her wake. While to Jane it was "just magic", it was due to living organisms ranging from bacteria to many species of plankton, including phytoplankton, especially dinoflagellates, that produced bioluminescence from a chemical reaction when disturbed by the ship's hull.

That night she and Richard felt especially close as they cuddled together to keep warm on deck. With the passage of time Richard's admiration for Jane had increased. He marvelled at her courage, her industry, her vision and the unselfishness of her love for him and the children. They clung tightly now, gazed in wonderment at the sea and had no thought for the future. He would have followed her anywhere in the world. Later, when he climbed up to the top bunk Jane was waiting for him. It had been ages since they had made love and she longed for his touch. They sank into each other's arms and loved passionately, intensely, quietly and inconspicuously. At that moment their peace and happiness was unencumbered and while *Trafalgar* sailed on, time stood still for the Dunstans. Although they did not know it, while one life had already expired on *Trafalgar*, a new one had begun that night.

Eventually the blue sky they had been enjoying disappeared and rain drenched the decks for the first time in weeks. As *Trafalgar* began to round the Cape of Good Hope the wind turned and began to blow and bluster from the west with the promise of more serious weather to come. Then, on Saturday 16th December, after sixty-two days at sea, there was another death. Benjamin Bailey, aged 23, suffered a stroke brought on by debilitating complications arising from a chronic bowel condition which culminated in an uncontrollable fever. He left a young wife, Sophia aged 21, with a baby under one year of age. After the burial at sea service a collection was taken up to assist her support and contributed to by almost everyone on board including a number of sailors. Several days later Benjamin's sea chest was brought up on deck and an auction of its contents conducted. Items sold included his pipe, trousers, jackets, shoes, a tin whistle, belts, shirts and hats, all of which brought far more money than they were worth due to the charitable bidders keen to help the family. Sophia and her child were supported by a number of good women, including Jane, who gathered around her for the rest of the voyage.

Every day it blew stronger and stronger and the swells rose higher and higher until, by the time they had finished rounding the Cape, they were breathtaking. They had now entered the Roaring Forties westerly wind system encircling the earth south of approximately 40° latitude where, due to the fact that there is no substantial landmass to interrupt their path, prevailing winds can produce exceptionally huge waves and severe storms. Trimmed of most of her sails *Trafalgar* still made around seven or eight knots from the wind caught on her rigging as she was followed constantly by a threatening sea building and rising high above the stern with every wave. The little ship seemed to recognise the danger and lifted over each mountain of water with measured determination. *Trafalgar* was sailing magnificently now and for several days logged nearly 200 nautical miles as her noon to noon day's run. But seasickness returned with the rough waters and Jane and most of the family soon lost their stomachs. Rain fell in torrents, the main deck was frequently awash with sea water and it was cold.

The Dunstans spent much of their time braced in their bunks as the ship pitched and lurched and felt to them it would roll over completely at any moment. At night time in particular she had a tendency to develop deep, long, hypnotic and heavy rolls in the big swells. One minute Jane's head would go bump against the ship's hull and the next her feet would be pushing against the footboard as she clung to Richard with all her might to prevent herself being shot out the end of the berth. At times it was better to get up and sit at the table rather than be bruised and battered in bed.

It was almost a week before the weather broke to allow *Trafalgar* to rise and fall with much better manners. The sky turned blue again and the wind fell to a gentle breeze enabling her to career along happily under full sail in the bright sun. After days of nothing but the putrid vapours of steerage it was a pleasure to be back on deck inhaling the pure sweet air of the Southern Ocean.

Under full sail.

[*Seascape* by H. B. J. Everett. National Maritime Museum, Greenwich, London. BHC2447.]

Richard sucked in luscious lungfulls of it before tackling the water closets. He noticed that he had lost his persistent cough and that the ingrained dirt from under his fingernails and skin had gone. He missed the smell of the earth he had lived and worked in but he had also grown to love the smell of the sea.

Just before Christmas and after sixty-nine days at sea a son was born to John and Amy Whittle on Saturday, 23rd December. Dr. Tweedale had comfortably accommodated her in the ship's small hospital the day before the birth and when it happened it proceeded quickly and without complication. The baby was the couple's third son and fifth child. John Whittle was a carpenter and no one was more pleased than he to have another son to join him in his dreams of carpentry enterprises in Adelaide. There was much rejoicing in steerage about the arrival of a Christmas child, and had there been any suitable liquid refreshment available there would have been a thoroughly sound wetting of the baby's head. In anticipation of the birth many women in steerage had been secretly knitting babies' boots, bonnets and clothes so that Amy was quite overcome when they all came forward and showered her with their efforts.

Everyone hoped that the good weather would last as it was planned to hold a grand concert on Christmas Day. The sailors fixed to the mast a bunch of holly that they had somehow managed to preserve thus far and children practised the singing of Christmas songs and carols. Jane's thoughts turned to Tolcarne as she pictured in her mind the traditional lighted candles burning in the windows of most cottages on Christmas Eve – placed there to guide all family members home safely for Christmas – and the sprigs of evergreen holly heavy in red berry and garlands of ivy hanging on cottage doors and windows. Jane never had enough money for a big family Christmas celebration but she always managed to buy some special sweets for the children. This Christmas would be no different. Prior to leaving Tolcarne she had purchased and secretly squirreled away the children's Christmas treats in her shipboard luggage. By Christmas Eve the weather had turned quite cold again and the wind had picked up causing it to be too uncomfortable for activities on the main deck. Down in steerage several groups of children moved along both sides of the trestle table singing Christmas songs and carols accompanied in each case by two or three adults playing tin whistles, squeezeboxes and fiddles.

Although it was cold with blustery conditions, next morning there was a beautiful clear and sunny sky so that the Christmas Day religious service proceeded on deck. Jane had managed to put together a Christmas pudding with a couple of eggs she still had left, flour, baking powder, dried apples and ship's jam, butter and raisins with a dollop of treacle. She mixed everything together thoroughly, making sure that every family member stirred the mix three times with their eyes shut and made a wish. She then took it to the cook in a pudding cloth to boil for a couple of hours. Although Christmas dinner was more of the same fare dished up regularly, the portions were larger and on the captain's orders several pails of so-called "Christmas punch" were ordered to be shared among the passengers. The on deck grand concert had to be cancelled because of the weather and instead everyone in steerage sang Christmas songs and danced to tunes beaten out on tin mugs and plates with the accompaniment of the collected tin whistle, fiddle, mouth organ and squeezebox players. The celebrations eventually broke up amidst cheers for Captain Richardson and Dr. Tweedale with the draining of mugs and voices bidding a Merry Christmas to all. There was indeed goodwill to all mankind on board *Trafalgar* that night, followed by peace on earth for most of them as they slumbered soundly through the night.

Chapter 21

Storm

With the cooler weather the cockroach population seemed to diminish somewhat. The same could not be said for the fleas and bedbugs that seemed to be in multiplication mode – or perhaps it was just that they more persistently sought the warmth of human bodies when the temperature was down. The blustery conditions of Christmas Day died away that night to leave *Trafalgar* almost becalmed the next day. As Captain Richardson and first mate Mr. Blythe stood together in relaxed conversation on the poop deck with quadrants and sextants in hand waiting for the arrival of noon to ascertain the ship's latitude, a smart westerly breeze appeared. The ship was soon trimmed to full sail and bowling along again at a respectable pace with her bow pointed east. Towards dusk a series of squalls added a cold bitterness and increased velocity to the wind. Steely-grey clouds rolled in and changed the colour of the sea from silver blue to greeny-grey and the wind suddenly shifted from west to southwest to bring with it a threatening aspect to the seas as well as a further drop in temperature. *Trafalgar* was now well past the 40th parallel of latitude and in the realm of giant legendary seas that circled the world without interruption.

Wave heights in the open ocean are caused by the strength of the wind and the distance over which it blows constantly at that strength. A wind blowing at sixty knots for twenty-four hours over a distance of 500 miles or more can create a wave fifty-five feet high. Stronger hurricane force winds of sixty-four knots or more blowing a greater distance and for a longer time can create wave crests up to eighty feet tall. Rogue wave monsters of more than 100 feet, bred by storms that have blown for days on end, have been recorded.

That night *Trafalgar* sailed into the teeth of a roaring gale. Captain Richardson had been expecting it and was prepared. Just an hour before dusk the wind suddenly started to howl and blow spray off the crests of the waves drenching the ship in horizontal swathes of water. A big wave boomed like thunder as it hit and rattled everything.

"Here it comes," yelled Captain Richardson. "Call all hands Blythe."

As a storm approached sails had to be furled along the yards to prevent the canvas being torn to shreds or putting too much pressure on the yards or masts causing them to break. To do this the sailors had to go aloft high in the rigging and gather up the loosened canvas by clawing at it with their hands and arms as they hung over the yard arms with their feet on a foot rope. Without a moment's hesitation Blythe yelled for all hands on deck and bellowed out the usual "braid up," "clew up" and "furl up" orders. As the men ascended like apes in the rigging the wind increased rapidly to sub gale force and laid an aching chill on their bodies through wet clothes. Waves started to look like hills rolling over a plain with deep hollows and breaking crests. Every sail and halyard and block and tackle and brace hummed and moaned in agony as they were overstretched by powerful south westerlies that bent masts under the strain and set sails as hard as iron.

When a sail was "let go" or loosened for furling a quarter of a ton of wet canvas shivered and shook the mast with frantic flapping and yards bent in the fury of the wind. Rigging vibrated and hummed a threatening tune as men inched out along the yards among loose canvas and lines flying about like a cat o'nine tails. One good flick could remove a lump of flesh or take out an eye. They fought and clawed with freezing hands at the stiff heavy wet canvas to furl it up and lash it down.

Daylight was starting to fade and the wind, whipped up to a frenzy, belted up a fog of sea water to reduce visibility further. The ship pitched and heaved as she hit each swell. Passengers in steerage thought that one minute she would stand on her tail and the next on her head. She gave shuddering jerks as she ploughed through waves. Roller after roller surged up, exploded on the bow and swamped the decks to the extent that the scuppers were barely able to cope.

The main deck was often covered with a foot of water. Sailors hauling lines on deck were hit with huge washes of water that knocked them off their feet and belted them into the scuppers like helpless children. The deck was frequently angled at 45 to 50° and although safety ropes were strung the full length of the ship it was almost impossible for the men to work their way along in the teeth of the storm unless they dragged themselves hand over hand on belaying pins and other pieces of rigging. In order to be heard above the noise of the wind and the sea you had to shout into someone's ear at the top of your voice.

By now the sun had gone down and darkness added a further degree of difficulty to all tasks. The men aloft hung on desperately to the yard arms as the ship bucked and pitched and the masts whipped from bow to stern and side to side. With the rolling of the ship in the swell the masts swung up to 45° off vertical causing men clinging to the yards high above the deck to get a sideways ride from port to starboard of fifty to seventy yards. Men trying to furl on the end of the highest yard arms got the wildest rides. There it was like being on a gigantic see-saw where for an instant you looked down on sailors on the other half of the yard arm, and the next you were looking at them way above you. When the ship did a really deep roll, the men at the very end of the yards could get a quick dip in the ocean.

A rolling ship in rough weather with a full complement of men aloft fighting the elements to furl sails was the perfect environment for accidents and injuries. Anticipating the certainty that his services would be called upon, Dr. Tweedale donned his sou'wester, sea boots and overcoat to stand ready. Up in the ship's top sails a line parted under the wind pressure and cut the torso of one of the men like a powerful lash. Dripping blood all the way he made it back to the deck and was ordered below into the warmth of Dr. Tweedale's surgery where he was stitched with surgical needle and thread and prescribed a measure of brandy. Then one of the ship's boys fell from a lower yard on the foremast having misjudged his footing in the wet and windy conditions. He survived with a dislocated shoulder, broken nose and a cut across the forehead which would leave him scarred for the rest of his life. He was a lucky boy as many sailors were killed in such falls.

The wind and swells were so strong that it took two helmsmen working together on the wheel to keep the ship straight. When there was only one man at the helm in a storm, it was possible, due to the power of the swells and wind exerting pressure on the rudder for him to be completely thrown over the wheel as it spun and he lost the battle to control the ship. To prevent being thrown overboard in the event of a huge wave coming over the stern, both men were tied to a safety line – known as being "lashed to the wheel". Increasing mountains of water did come to lift the stern and fling the little ship down the face of huge waves but although her rear was pitched high in the air only once did *Trafalgar* suffer a mild "pooping" that put out the compass binnacle lamp and washed the two helmsmen off their feet for a brief moment. *Trafalgar* rode like a duck. The task of the helmsmen was vital in extreme seas as it was critical to keep the ship on its correct orientation. If it slewed around sideways to the wind it ran the risk of being "broached" or overwhelmed by the huge swells side on. Many a ship founded in this manner.

With the wind threatening to blast them off the yards, the men aloft fought and battled to control flapping lines and heavy wet canvas which flew back over their heads before being caught by the wind and belted away again nearly dragging them off the footropes. Grim determination and blue and bloodied hands eventually won the fight so that after more than two hours of the toughest work the sails were furled – in a fashion. That they had been furled at all was a miracle. Captain Richardson would score the men ten out of ten for effort, but four off for neatness. When, in the dark, they eventually descended frozen and exhausted to the deck they could hardly speak. The captain gave the order to "Splice the mainbrace", which was sailors code for an issue of grog. Each man received several additional tots.

With everything now snug Captain Richardson was satisfied that for the moment he had *Trafalgar* under control with sails trimmed to the conditions. The wind soon increased to hurricane force so that the little ship often had her leeside rail in the water as she came up out of the troughs. At times the dead eye blocks eighteen inches above the gunwale went under. Captain Richardson ordered as many men as he could risk to go below and rest but still kept a substantial number at the ready on deck where they hung on for their lives with both hands. After remaining for more than thirty hours at his post next to the helmsmen on the poop, with meals being delivered to him there, the captain's beard was encrusted with salt crystals and his eyes black with fatigue. In the end sheer exhaustion drove him to his cabin.

Chapter 22

STEERAGE HELL

Jane had started to get used to the constant motion of the ship. She felt unwell but was not sick. She was frightened but also excited and felt a cautious kind of exhilaration derived from the ship's ploughing and plunging as it crashed through the waves. She knew God was on her side anyway but seemed to be discovering surprising things about herself, like the enjoyment she got from taking risks, and watching the strong, courageous and skilful sailors working aloft yelling and using coarse language that made her blush. She had certainly learned many new words on this voyage. But she respected the sailors in their work and felt sorry for the ordeals they had to endure, even though she thought some were a little short on brains and most a lot short on manners.

Down in steerage, in an endeavour to keep the sea out, the hatchways leading to the main deck were closed and bolted as was the doorway and lid on the WC. Due to the violent motion of the ship all oil lamps were extinguished because of the risk of fire, leaving passengers in total darkness. Water leaking into the passengers' quarters caused major discomfort. Scorching hot weather in the doldrums had caused the tar to melt in the deck caulking, allowing water to seep through the seams between the deck timbers whenever a wave swept over the ship. Down below, it dripped from the deck head and beams and trickled down upright stanchions onto passengers' berths and the whole of steerage. It also spurted in through the chinks and cracks around the hatchways. Passengers did what they could to combat the problem by collecting drips in containers, or covering berths with canvas if they had any, to direct water away. But containers soon got knocked over with the movement of the ship and in the persistently stormy and wet conditions all efforts eventually failed so that everyone was sleeping in damp beds. Once the straw in the mattresses got wet with sea water it soon compacted and began to rot and smell very badly. All over the floor and under the bunks an accumulation of water several inches deep began to slosh about, collecting everything with it. There was no heating and in the cold conditions everything that had not suffered a direct wetting was covered in condensation. Every item of clothing and all blankets felt damp.

The water that leaked into *Trafalgar* through the hull, or taken on board through the deck in a storm, eventually gravitated to the lowest part in the bilge along the keel. All sorts of soluble and waterborne detritus ended up there, fermenting away in a foul mixture and continually producing a dreadful stink that seeped up through the ship. When this emulsion was shaken and stirred, as it was with the present rough weather, the stench wafting up to steerage was gut wrenching and added to everyone's discomfort. Bilge water was pumped out regularly from a well constructed around the main mast extending through all decks. During the storm two pumps were manned continuously by shifts of four sailors at a time.

When the ship rolled or pitched everything movable moved. Bottles, cups, saucers, water jars, and tea and coffee pots left on the table together with cutlery and tin plates, cans of treacle, containers of sugar, butter and ship's jam, salt, pepper and sauces were all swept onto the floor. There the conglomeration sloshed about in the watery mess which included boots, dirty nappies, scraps of old food and slop pails rolling around after having lost their contents of, among other things, vomit, urine and faeces. Loose items stowed at the back of bunks such as bags of flour and people's clothes were flung out to join the soupy mire. Passengers could not leave their berths to try and retrieve things, even if they thought of it. Most were too sick and frightened to care and it was impossible to walk around in the dark with the lurching of the ship and the slippery mess on the floor. Even sitting was uncomfortable and required hanging on with both hands.

As the ship rolled from side to side the ever growing pool of water on the floor collected and clattered and banged the pots, tins and everything else adrift in it, first over to starboard and then a minute later back to port causing all the tumbling objects to repeat the din. As long as the storm lasted so did the noise. Through the howling and roaring of the wind and the crash of the sea, the rush and stomp of sailor's feet could be heard as they ran about frantically on deck and jumped down from the rigging. The captain's voice could be heard faintly above the storm, bawling out orders to his officers and they, in turn bawling them out to the men. Around 3 am it blew so hard that the upper top sail on the foremast tore off its spa and plunged to the deck with its tackle, knocking one of the ship's boats to the deck. The tumultuous commotion and subsequent pandemonium had everyone in steerage believing that their world was about to end.

The ship's rats were washed out of their usual hidey holes below the bottom berths and forced to seek higher ground. Every now and then they would squeak and dive in the dark over bodies in the berths after returning from splashing about in the muck on the floor where they had been quarrelling over food scraps. This caused frantic shrieks from the women and caustic curses from the men to be added to the noise mix.

For the most part everyone lay in their bunks and held on to the side boards in the dark to prevent being turned over into their neighbour's bed. Jane and Richard clung tightly to each other and were rolled around as one from side to side in their berth with every lurch of the ship. Jane couldn't stop thinking about Tolcarne and her little cottage with the dirt walls and the dirt floor. It was damp in the winter time but compared to this, with its big hearth log fire, it was as warm and as dry as toast. Her mind also turned to the wonderful times she had on board ship in the tropics. She had enjoyed so much her daily baths on deck and had never felt so clean as then. Now she felt filthy. Damp clothes stuck to her body. She had developed rashes in her armpits, under breasts and in the crotch. Her hair was matted and itchy. Her clothes stunk of vomit and God knows what else. The rest of the family were all the same – in fact everyone in steerage was just as bad. They were all revolting and the place was disgusting. She wished she had not brought the family to this and that they were all back in their little cottage that smelt of Cornish earth. She then remembered the winters that were not so warm because they could not afford to keep the fire going all the time and reminded herself that that was why they were now on board *Trafalgar*. If only she and the family could be clean and dry and warm and still, then everything would be all right. She would have settled for just being clean. She would, she resolved, be clean at the first available opportunity.

With the cavorting of the ship throwing you from side to side constantly it was almost impossible to sleep. If you did doze off it was only for a matter of minutes before the next thump or crash jolted you awake again. As they lay there in the dark one passenger started singing a hymn and others soon joined in. Many people prayed, including some that had not until that time thought a lot about God. Women passengers, exhausted by continuous seasickness lay in bed and groaned or screamed whenever the ship lurched violently or hit a big wave. Most of the seventy-five children aged ten and under grizzled and whined until, having reached the point of exhaustion, they fell into a fitful sleep. Some women and men cried and shook with fear. Others just cursed. In the dark they were sick, cold and wet, frightened by rats, bitten by bedbugs and fleas, had little to eat, were bruised and battered by the storm, had to suffer a terrible stench, and a conglomeration of frightening noises, and were terrified and thought they would die.

During the continuous blow which lasted nearly a week, New Year's Eve arrived and left unnoticed and uncelebrated. Dr. Tweedale, equipped in his wet weather gear, continued his rounds of the sick and instructed sailors on a regular basis to attend in steerage to help the emigrants. Some of the men wiped and cleaned up children of couples who were too sick to help themselves let alone others. Seamen did what they could to empty vomit pots and toilet pails and offered water and what little food was available – mainly in the form of ship's biscuits as the galley stove was closed down.

Chapter 23

DECONTAMINATION
AND DESPONDENCY

It was the quiet that Jane noticed most of all. For the first time in ages she had actually slept soundly for more than an hour. She was now awake and noticed sunlight sneaking through the cracks of one of the hatchways. Everything was still. No flapping of sails or sailors running around the deck. Even the ocean was still. No orders were being yelled out. No screams or crying came from between decks. There was little talking at all and, such as there was, was hushed in a whisper. The rest of the Dunstans were still sound asleep. Everything and everyone was spent. It was over.

The feet of sailors were soon heard on deck and then the creaking of salt encrusted hinges on hatchway doors as they were opened. The stench that accompanied the cloud of vapour rising out of steerage caused the men to step back. On the instructions

183

of Dr. Tweedale everyone was ordered topside for a muster. As emigrants emerged squinty eyed to gather on deck in the sunlight, a misty steam rose from their damp bodies. They looked poor sickly creatures and all stunk of stale perspiration, mildewed clothes, filthy blankets and much more.

The first task was to feed everyone as appetites were very quickly rediscovered. After the galley stove was fired up and hot porridge and tea delivered in the sunshine to all on deck, Dr. Tweedale ordered everyone below to bring back up all items of clothes and bedding, including mattresses. As soon as this was done the constables and other appointed cleaners were sent below to begin the task of cleaning. The whole of steerage including upper and lower bunks, trestle table and every part of the floor, especially under the bunks, was then swept. Dr. Tweedale insisted on removal of the boards on the bottom berths for full and proper access. There was found there a considerable quantity of revolting garbage that was uplifted and jettisoned over the side. The trestle table, berths and floor were then washed, scrubbed and disinfected after which the entire space was fumigated. Meanwhile Richard, with the assistance of a couple of helpers, made sure that the water closets were given the full treatment as per Dr. Tweedale's instructions.

On deck, the sun shone brightly and a gentle breeze wafted over the bluest sea. Dr. Tweedale had ordered the emigrant's boxes to be brought up from the hold to provide access to fresh clothing. On the rigging and every other available part of the ship, hung trousers, shirts, jackets, socks and all types of apparel including blankets and mattresses to dry in the sun. The doctor walked around inspecting everything and any item found to harbour lice or bedbugs or, in his opinion, to be too filthy to properly clean was immediately tossed overboard and then the owners identified and, if deemed necessary, "treated". Both the men's and women's on deck washing facilities were quickly set up and availed of by many passengers. Jane was one of the first into the tub although the water temperature was quite cold. Every available ship board pail was quickly cleaned and employed as a clothes washing bucket. Filthy mattresses were shot overboard and rotten straw emptied out of others, although the spare supply of fresh dry straw was insufficient to fully replenish them all.

The bright sun and light breeze were perfect for drying all *Trafalgar's* wet sails. In full canvas she progressed sedately through the bluest of water. Sailors were busily checking rigging and ropes, some of the latter of which were like ragged lint where they had been beaten by the wind. They were repaired or replaced where necessary and neatly coiled away. Other sailors scrubbed and swept the deck. It was a scene of ordered activity. By the end of the day *Trafalgar* was shipshape.

Twenty-four hours later the light breeze turned into a good strong wind from the southwest quarter that allowed *Trafalgar* to still keep most of her sails up as she gracefully dashed along, heeling over to the port side with her scuppers occasionally underwater. It was hard to believe that only a few days before, this proud little ship had been groaning and complaining in every timber as she battled the fury of the sea. On Thursday, 4th of January 1849 when the ship was some 300 nautical miles southwest of Cape Leeuwin, Western Australia, Ann Bee, the wife of John Bee farm labourer, gave birth on board to a little baby sister for her two sons aged one and three. There were no unusual difficulties or complications and Jane and other steerage ladies again came forward with gifts of booties, bonnets and clothes they had made for the baby. Unfortunately a gloom was cast over this happy event when only six days later, six-year-old Susan Julian died after eighty-one days at sea. Like Emily

Spriggs, she had been suffering from hydroencephalus, had also been unwell with diarrhoea before the storm hit, and developed a fever during the rough weather. Her inability to accept food or water lead to dehydration and death. She was one of five children in her family.

As the ship sailed further into southern waters, the air grew colder and more birds appeared to keep the ship company. Jane could not believe the wildlife at sea miles away from any land. She marvelled at the strikingly graceful albatrosses with their long narrow wings. They flew continuously up and down the waves and troughs of the sea without a wing beat and followed *Trafalgar*, gliding and wheeling effortlessly, scavenging every bit of galley refuse and floating waste that left the ship.

Powerful squalls which hit *Trafalgar* from time to time causing her to heel over considerably and sometimes carry away the top sails, kept the sailmakers busy replacing lost canvas and the sailors on their toes as they endured repetitive adjustments and changes to the rigging. Strong winds kept the ship running on her side in a constant tilt from the vertical which together with the rolling action made it extremely uncomfortable, if not dangerous, to be on deck. The weather now was predominantly cold, damp and grey. There were days on end when there was a mixture of mist and drizzling rain that Jane fairly and accurately described as "mizzle". At times a dense and impenetrable fog lay over the sea which could only just be seen as you looked over the gunwale while standing on deck. As it condensed in the rigging the mist turned into large drops and intermittently plip-plopped on the deck below. It condensed also on the beards and clothes of sailors and passengers giving them a "frosted" look. The fog made it impossible to take bearings at noon and dictated quiet as everyone on deck listened carefully. It was also depressing.

Emigrants on Deck.

[*Illustrated London News*, 20th January 1849. Mary Evans Picture Library Ltd., London.]

In an attempt to keep warm, passengers took to their beds fully clothed and topped up their blankets with anything available including coats, clothing and sacks. A problem began to reappear in the form of bedbugs, fleas and lice. Arguments broke out among the passengers about who was to blame for bringing them on board in the first place. Best attempts were made to deal with the problem, weather permitting, through scrubbing, disinfecting and fumigation. In the end everyone stayed lousy.

Many passengers stayed in their bunks all day and crawled out at meal times only if they thought they could face the food, which had now started to deteriorate. The ship's biscuits were mouldy, butter was rank, the water was foul and everyone was heartily sick of salt meat. Most passengers had run out of any little extras they had brought with them. All Jane had left was a little flour and some baking powder.

It was too cold for church services on deck. They had not seen any land for ages and had a profound feeling of isolation. Many had lost track of what day of the week it was. Boredom and misery set in. Rat numbers had multiplied during the voyage due to their propensity to breed and they were becoming more aggressive as the ship's provisions diminished and some of their food sources dried up. During daylight hours they would now run under the trestle table, and even along the top, as emigrants sat and ate their meals. A combination of sheer exhaustion and exasperation caused some passengers to become short tempered and rude which led to quarrelling and physical clashes. Others resorted to playing childish practical jokes for their amusement or became lethargic and ran out of conversation. Children got into fights over trivial matters. Everyone just wanted to get to Adelaide. Rumour had it that they might be there in less than two weeks, all things being well.

Running in these southern latitudes there was always a risk of meeting an iceberg. While such encounters were much rarer during the southern summer months they did occur, and at times ships' captains had reported seeing them only a few degrees south of the Cape of Good Hope. For every ton of ice floating above the surface there are eight to nine tons below and it is this hidden part that is the biggest danger to ships. While the side of an iceberg may appear to descend vertically into the sea there could actually be an ice shelf or spur hidden just a few feet under the surface extending a considerable distance. The visible part of such icebergs were sometimes noted to be two or three miles in circumference and several hundred feet in height with the top covered in snow. The main danger they presented was at night when, with an overcast sky, even the keenest lookout found it difficult to see a flat topped berg just a couple of yards above the water and who knows how many yards below.

On a moonlit night the seaman on watch on board *Trafalgar* yelled out "Sail Ho! – on the port bow!" Then, as the moon popped out further from a cloud bank he changed his cry to a scream of "Iceberg! Iceberg! – on the port!" Ahead, some 850 yards away, was a glistening mountain of ice. Captain Richardson, cool and calm, quietly gave the order "Hard down to starboard" to the helmsman as some nervous looking sailors stood by close to the lifeboats ready to rip off lashings and covers. There was another yell that the 'berg was closing fast on the ship and it did appear to be moving on *Trafalgar* although the opposite was true. Then, utter silence as no one moved or spoke. White faced men in oil skins and sou'westers strained their eyes to port and listened for the expected crunch and crack of *Trafalgar's* hull as she impacted on submarine ice. She bumped heavily into a ledge causing several hands to lose their footing and finish up against the scuppers, and then slid along an icy wall making a long drawn out scratching noise like fingernails on a blackboard. After several crunches and then a final bump she cleared and shot out into the open sea again.

Chapter 24

AUSTRALIA

Just as *Trafalgar* began to enter the waters south of the Great Australian Bight huge grey-black shapes broke the surface, blew noisily and disappeared. A juvenile humpback jumped clear of the water, turned and did a back-flip as it showed off its white underbelly. Others rolled and slapped their flukes while some tossed their tails in the air and flopped them down with a resounding whack. They seemed to Jane to be a happy exuberant lot enjoying their fun. With tails three times as wide as the height of a man, flukes fifteen feet long and weighing up to fifty tons, they were an impressive sight as they breached.

On the pleasant evening at the end of that day, the emigrants on deck had their attention drawn to the horizon in the distant east where the sky was darkest and noticed a speck of flame spiking and then fading before flickering again. In no time *Trafalgar* was abreast of a British whaler and they could see the flames licking from the try works on its deck heating huge iron pots filled with blubber. She was a dirty foul-smelling ship and, as she was passed by, steam from the cauldrons drifted a putrid stench over *Trafalgar's* deck causing the passengers to gag. There was good whaling to be had in Australian waters at the time. The Port of Hobart alone was the base for thirty-seven whaling ships and more than 1,000 men working in the industry. One ship's captain reported seeing 300 whales on a voyage from Sydney to Hobart.

After several days of good running *Trafalgar* had traversed most of the bight when her course was altered from due east to more northeast. Captain Richardson announced that it would only be a matter of days before they would be in Adelaide and arranged for passengers to get access to their luggage to obtain good clothes for the arrival. Jane had a fine time going through boxes, setting aside the good (not the best) clothes the family would wear ashore and reorganising and repackaging everything soundly. There were a quantity of clothes that she collected from every family member that were, even in her judgment, totally beyond redemption – worn out, stinky and good for nothing. These she threw overboard with delight and in her mind they seemed to take with them memories of the family's worst times on board ship.

The crew were ordered to make *Trafalgar* shipshape, spruced up and presentable for her arrival. She was cleaned, scrubbed and, where necessary, painted to give the best appearance. Patched working sails were taken down and only best canvas hoisted. Anything glass or brass was polished. The ship's bell and compass binnacle were transformed from the verdant green colour they had acquired during the voyage to sparkling brass. Rust was pounded off the anchor, chains, bolts, fastenings and all iron work which was then blackened with coal tar or treated with fish oil. Finally, the anchor was freed on the cat block in anticipation of its release. Everything useless was thrown overboard including empty tar barrels which the sailors, for a lark, tossed over at night after setting fire to them. They lit up the ocean for miles as they blazed astern.

As Adelaide got closer the ship bustled with the activity of both crew and passengers. Everyone was in high spirits and the weather – temperature and wind – were pleasant. A sense of excitement mixed with anxiety began to spread throughout the ship. Thoughts turned to the future and wondering what it would be. They smelled the land well before they saw it. A different smell, but sweet and full of flavour. "Kind of like a spicy hay stack with a hint of lavender and camphor," said Jane. It was fragrant and enchanting to people who had endured only the smell of the sea and the stink from the bowels of *Trafalgar* for three months.

Before land was sighted a fog came up thick and quick. The afternoon sun disappeared as it was engulfed in a watery mist. The ship was closing in on Kangaroo Island, just south of Adelaide, and the reduced visibility concerned Captain Richardson. Extra watches were kept on deck that night, listening and peering through the mist, and extra lights lit on deck. As sailing ships could not be quickly turned about or stopped smartly, the concern was that *Trafalgar* might, in the reduced visibility be driven into the lee shore of Kangaroo Island by the prevailing westerlies. Many a ship had been wrecked in such circumstances. There was no proper dawn next morning, just a white glow in the fog that announced night had finished. Captain Richardson was on deck early and joined the first mate Mr. Blythe near the helm. "Listen sir," he said. The captain heard the sound of the sea rippling under *Trafalgar's* stern, the splosh splash noise as her bows broke the waves and the usual shipboard creaks and clatters from the sails and her rigging. Then he heard the unmistakable sound of the sea breaking over rocks and cliffs on the starboard side. "Take her port side 25 degrees," the captain ordered and followed with, "Call all hands on deck to stand by." Moments later the warming sun lifted the mist sufficiently to reveal a brown smudge at a safe distance on the horizon which by midmorning became clearly visible as the south western end of Kangaroo Island. On deck there was an overwhelming sense of relief and excitement among passengers and crew as they watched with awe their destination coming into focus.

By the time *Trafalgar* rounded Cape Borda at the bottom of the island all mist had lifted. It turned into a perfect sunny sailing day with an accommodating southwesterly breeze coming over the port quarter. *Trafalgar* relaxed and with all sails pulling, slid along the surface of Investigator Straight at a steady clip on the way to Adelaide. Looking out from midship at the endless coast and up at the sheets of white canvas shaped perfectly above, Jane could not believe her good fortune and good fortune of the family. She was serene, almost ecstatic. Time seemed to have stopped.

Trafalgar sailed into the outer harbour anchorage area marked at the entrance to Port Adelaide by the stationary lightship *The Ville de Bordeaux*, a three masted wooden French vessel of 822 tons that had been confiscated by the South Australian government for alleged smuggling. Captain Richardson, judging carefully the strength of the following breeze and the space his ship would need to swing on her anchor, waited for the optimum moment and then gave the order to take in sail. As her forward momentum gradually diminished the captain signalled "Let go!" The anchor fell from the cathead and dragged out the cable through the hawsehole with a rattle and bang as it hit the water with a satisfied splash to announce *Trafalgar's* arrival. It was Wednesday, 17th January 1849.

Due to both good luck and good management *Trafalgar* made it to Adelaide with only three deaths on board. The week before she left Plymouth there had been thirty deaths in London from cholera. It had been lucky that none of the passengers that boarded in London brought cholera with them, and lucky that at the time the Dunstans and *Trafalgar* passed through Plymouth it was not prevalent there. It was an unpleasant disease with horrible symptoms including violent vomiting, uncontrollable watery diarrhoea and painful convulsions. Severe dehydration sets in, the lips and face turn a leaden blue-colour, shock follows and finally death in an atmosphere of sickening stench. There was no cure and the mortality rate was at least fifty percent. Some 50,000 people died from it in Britain between 1848 and 1850. In July 1849, after arriving from London, the barque *James T Foord* set sail from Plymouth to Port Phillip Australia and lost thirty-six lives on board during the voyage, mainly from cholera. During the following month of August when there was now an epidemic of cholera two vessels that sailed out of Plymouth for Australia suffered twenty-three and twenty-one deaths respectively on board, mostly from cholera.

Trafalgar's arrival in a superior state of cleanliness with healthy and grateful emigrants on board was due largely to the professionalism and good management of the ship's surgeon Dr. Tweedale and the industry, discipline and attention to detail he applied to his task. He administered the health and morale of the ship with a firm hand which had included, with the captain's consent, the placing of two rebellious men in irons.

In the year *Trafalgar* arrived, there were at least thirty-three ships wrecked on the Australian run or operating in Australian waters with a conservative estimate of at least 130 lives lost. Small wooden sailing ships like her could be easily demolished by devastating storms en route. In the same year *Mohammed Shah*, a three-masted barque of 615 tons with 246 emigrants on board was hit by a huge storm in the roaring forties south of the Indian Ocean causing twenty-five men who were aloft at the time taking in sail to be washed off the masts into the sea. Amazingly seventeen men were recovered but eight were lost. Eventually the ship made it to Australia. Captain Richardson's navigational skills, the ability of his crew and seaworthiness of the ship all contributed to *Trafalgar's* safe arrival. She had been a good little ship and continued to bring emigrants out to Australia until May 1860 when on a return trip to London from Australian ports she sprang a leak sailing the Atlantic and sank when the pumps failed to deal with the water. Only one life boat was picked up with a few survivors.

Part Three

South Australia
1849–1851

Chapter 25

DISEMBARKATION

South Australian law prohibited any ship from entering the port without a pilot from the eight-man pilot service based on *The Ville De Bordeaux* anchored permanently at the entrance. *Trafalgar's* anchor had been in the water only moments when a couple of whale boat-styled four-oared rowboats were alongside with smart looking gentlemen on board from the pilot service. Upon arrival on the quarterdeck they were besieged by the passengers and cross examined for information about the colony. Quickly exchanging the usual greetings and enquiries, Captain Richardson rescued them from the rabble and took them into his cabin to deal with formalities. He delivered his written report of the particulars of the voyage together with all letters, parcels of the post and newspapers under his conduct (for which he would receive a penny per item) and then handed control of the helm to the pilot.

Trafalgar now had to navigate the Port River to get to Port

Adelaide more than eight miles away from the lightship and there was no steam tug to assist. With a difficult wind, "tacking up the creek" was a tiresome process that could take all day even with the assistance of four oarsmen in a whale boat working as a tug. *Trafalgar's* luck held and with anchor aweigh and a fair and very slight breeze she proceeded gently towards the port under the pilot's guidance calling out to the helmsman "starboard a little" or "port" and pointing out the best line in the channel to avoid sand and mud bars. With yards squared she floated pleasantly up the muddy narrow creek lined with mangrove trees, tea trees and melaleucas. Pelicans and herons glided effortlessly up and down, cormorants nested in colonies and the occasional wild duck quacked past with a bunch of ducklings in tow.

As a vessel carrying cargo to discharge, *Trafalgar* was entitled to preference berthing at the port wharf pursuant to harbour regulations. Stowed beneath the steerage quarters in the ship's hull were a variety of goods including numerous boxed cases and packages of freight to order, assorted iron, thirty hogsheads of Taylor's Porter, 200 casks of Dunbar's Porter and Ale, 100 cases of Hunt and Pages port, thirty-nine hogsheads of rum, ten hogsheads of brandy, twenty barrels of tar, stationery, ink stands, school books, works of literature and of course the passengers' luggage. Captain Richardson soon discovered that preferential wharfage rights were not much use if there was a long queue of ships with prior rights in time in front of you. As *Trafalgar* reached the entrance to the north arm of the river he was astounded to see a veritable forest of ships' masts ahead of him in the little Port of Adelaide. There were twenty-four tall ships at anchor comprising thirteen barques, five brigs, four schooners and two ships. Open whale boats, barges and lighters were also tied up plus the cutter *Petrel & Midge* and the packet *Jane & Emma* that serviced local waters including Port Lincoln. There was great excitement among everyone on board. This was civilisation like they had not seen for ages. Neither would they see much of it now. The logjam of ships meant they would have to anchor in the north arm. There was no room at the wharf.

Jane noticed during the slow traverse up the river that the absence of ocean breeze in the confines of the mangroves seemed to concentrate the heat and thought that it was as hot as she had experienced in the doldrums. The sun at last was losing its sting as it headed towards the horizon. *Trafalgar* settled down for the night with a clutch of other tall ships in the north arm and the smell of 316 unwashed bodies on board acted like a magnet to draw squadrons of mosquitoes from the mangroves. For the first time in months the ship was motionless all night as she sat in still waters, but with the constant buzz and bite of the mosquitoes, the heat and stuffiness below deck plus the excitement and anticipation of tomorrow, sleep did not come easily for those on board.

Next morning the ship was boarded by South Australian Immigration Agent Charles Brewer. After checking the surgeon's and captain's reports of the voyage he mustered all the immigrants on deck and asked them if they had any complaints about food, treatment, the surgeon or crew. There were none except from the two men who the captain had put in irons and which Mr. Brewer dismissed as frivolous. After examining the condition of the passengers he signed a letter to the Colonial Secretary certifying that all the assisted immigrants were satisfied with their diet and treatment during the voyage. He then outlined the type of employment opportunities that were available in the colony, gave general advice about the kind of wages and conditions they could expect and finally gave some details as to the actual places

[S.T. Gill, Australia, 1818–1880. *Port Adelaide looking across Gawler Reach*, 1848, Adelaide. Watercolour on paper, 28.2 × 46.1 cm. Gift of the South Australian Company 1890, Art Gallery of South Australia, Adelaide.]

they might go to enquire about work. He advised that he had been requested by Mr. Henry Ayres, the secretary of the South Australian Mining Association, to inform all immigrants that there was work in the mines at Burra if they proceeded there.

The Dunstans were lucky to arrive at a time when the colony was short of manpower. Only a week before a strike of miners at Burra that had continued in one form or another for nearly four months ended. The miners lost when management ruthlessly dismissed 400 of them and ordered them out of their dwellings on mining land. Except for a group of hard-core ringleaders many of the men were re-employed but during the period of the strike quite a number decided to leave the mine permanently so that when the strike ended only around 300 men were left available for re-employment, leaving a 100 or so vacancies. Burra was 100 miles north into the dry interior. Proceeding there was going to be no walk in the park. The Dunstans were told that they could travel there for a reasonable cost by bullock dray which could take a week.

It was decided to unload *Trafalgar's* immigrants from the North Arm with the assistance of several four-oared rowing boats and their boatmen. Seamen hauled and heaved blocks and tackle to extract boxes and baggage from the hull and heap them on deck where confused passengers tried to locate and sort their possessions. Other sailors lowered nets full of items, whether sorted or not, into the boats below provoking more confusion and resentment among the immigrants when they were told they could sort their luggage when it and they reached the wharf. The deck was full of steerage passengers with their belongings and children who rushed to and from the bulwarks shouting, jostling and pointing with excitement. Passengers talked vociferously and waited patiently in their family and friendship groups for their chance to be rowed ashore. It took many trips and several hours before they were all there. As each boatload left good luck messages were exchanged with friends and shouts of "good-bye" yelled. On the wharf, flustered immigrants rifled through the piles of bags and boxes from the ship's hold until they had found and secured their property in their own individual piles. Most of them never looked back at *Trafalgar*.

The ninety-four days that the passengers had lived together on the ship had welded them into a community that would now be fractured as most people went separate ways. While some would be glad to see the backs of others as they left the ship hoping they would never see them again, many had formed bonds they would remember for life. Adults and children felt a sense of loss as the realisation came that they would soon be separated from ship board friends. Among the women there were some wet eyes and even real tears as they left the ship. Matron Bacon's eyes welled up when she was presented with some needlework and crocheted articles by some of the single girls endorsed with the embroidery "To Matron Bacon, – ship *Trafalgar*."

The Dunstans were different people to those who had left Tolcarne. Jane had reinvented herself on the voyage out. She had learnt a lot about people and herself and how to read a little and how to play a squeezebox accordion. The five eldest of her seven children had learnt how to read and write. The experiences they all had of close quartered living during the storms and equatorial doldrums would never be forgotten. Jane, who always hated dirt could now distinguish between the "clean dirt" she had back at the Tolcarne cottage and the filth she had endured on board *Trafalgar*. Nothing would ever be the same again. They had all arrived safely and, except for young baby Elizabeth who remained a sickly child, they were in robust health. Jane thanked God for the deliverance. Richard thanked Christ that they had made it!

Chapter 26

PORT ADELAIDE

The port reminded Jane of home. It had many of the characteristics of a Cornish seaside village. There were some obvious differences like the bullock wagons on the wharves, the different sorts of trees, the funny straw hats that many of the men wore, the heat, the flies and even the seagulls sounded different although they looked similar. The sights, scents and sounds of tall ships, sailors and the sea were the same as in England – the cluster of ships' masts, the smell of tar and rattle of chains and rowlocks mixed with gravelly male voices. The wind was hot and dry but had a certain fragrance about it. Jane liked and felt welcomed by all of it.

It was a functional little town with two good wharfs, several warehouses of large capacity, a Customs House, a resident magistrate, businesses such as blacksmiths, wheelwrights, ship-wrights, ship chandlers and sail makers – even block and mast makers for ships. Also numerous stores including butchers, bakers, grocers, tailors, shoe makers, a chemist and a number of eating houses plus of course residential dwellings and no less than five hotels.

On the wharf Jane gathered her family about her, conducted a quick head count to make sure she still had seven children and one husband and gave them all a stiff lecture about staying close together and guarding their belongings. It felt strange standing on a stable platform after three months of ship board motion and the planks of the wharf seemed to rise up to meet them with every step. It made Jane feel a little sick.

Richard took note of huge piles of canvas bags stamped with the letters SAMA stacked up outside the warehouse of the South Australian Mining Association at McLaren Wharf and confirmed through enquiry that they were bags of ore awaiting shipment to Swansea in Wales for smelting into copper. He estimated the pile to be thousands of tons and felt excited at the prospect of starting work in the so-called "Monster Mine" at Burra. The ore had been carted to the port by some 800 bullock teams comprising 6,000 to 7,000 working bullocks trudging from the Burra mine over 100 miles of unmade road using drays carrying two to three tons hauled by teams of six bullocks.

The luck of the Dunstans seemed to be lasting as there were presently many drays standing empty and ready for hire to Burra with young and old teamsters spruiking out competing fares for freight and passengers. Before heading north teamsters called at the wharf with the hope of getting a back load to Burra. On return trips they often carried supplies of timber, ore bags, tools, nails, implements, candles, bricks, charcoal, rope, slate, shingles, hay for working horses, blasting powder and an array of food items and domestic requirements. If general freight was not available passengers and their luggage were better than going back empty.

Richard faced up to a feral looking teamster with long reddish hair poking out from under a wide cabbage tree hat. Months of dust were impregnated in his woolly beard that probably would have looked reddish also if it had been washed. He smiled with the remains of a much depreciated set of green teeth and spoke through very bad breath with an Irish accent. He said his name was Ned but they called him Red and he would take the family to Burra for £4.00. Richard bargained him down to £3.05.00 and they shook hands.

There were, however, two conditions, said Red. First, if he happened to pick up freight on his way through Adelaide they would have to ride with it or on it. Second, if the road was rough and the pulling tough they would all have to get out of the dray and walk and if needs be, help by pushing. He had a flannel shirt that was the colour of dust and wore heavy boots with green hide laces and moleskin trousers held up with a substantial leather belt on which hung several pouches carrying knives, matches, pipe and tobacco. His trouser legs were tied below the knees with green hide straps called "bowyangs" to prevent the upward movement of dust and any insect or animal nasties and the cuffs were frayed and covered in dirt. A large kerchief tied around his neck looked as though it might have once been coloured something.

Red confirmed that the journey to Burra via Adelaide might take a week and that apart from some inns on the way there were few opportunities to shop. They would stop at Adelaide where they could get provisions to sustain them on the track. At Red's invitation the family loaded their luggage onto the dray as he stood back and ordered the mean looking dog he had chained to the axle to "stay!" He told them he was a working dog and warned them not to try and pat him unless they wanted to lose some fingers. He was a mongrel breed with a fair bit of bull terrier in him, had a

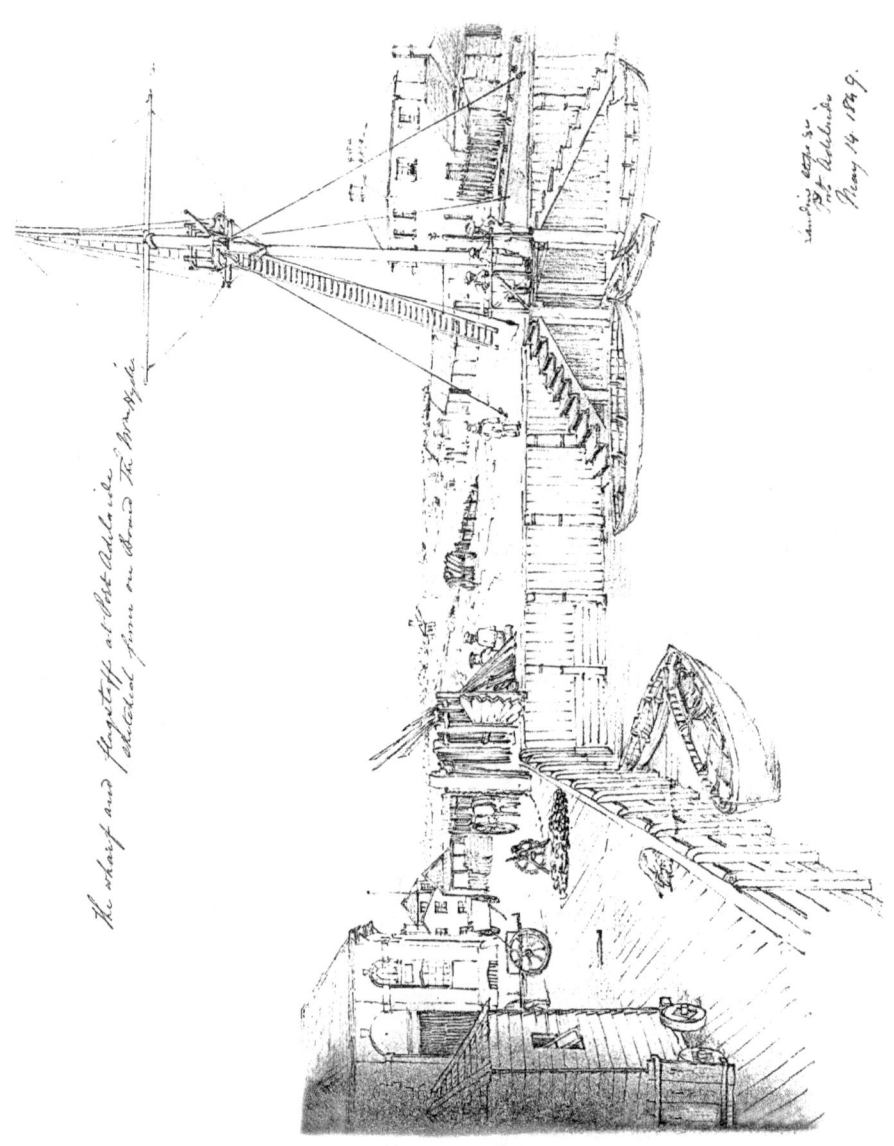

Wharf at Port Adelaide, 1849.

[Drawing made from the deck of the *William Hyde* moored in Gawler Reach on 14th May 1849. Ink on paper by Walter Light. Christine Courtney Collection]

permanently disgruntled disposition and was missing his left ear. His name was Scrapper.

Jane was a little nervous at the new experience of being hauled by bullocks but thought that after *Trafalgar* she could deal with anything. The six big chestnut bullocks with staring eyeballs and slobbering mouths looked quiet enough as they sat on their haunches on the side of the dirt track chewing their cud. With everyone on board Red walked alongside of the team trailing in the dust his long whip. Made of twelve feet of plaited green hide leather bound to an eight-foot long tapered handle it was his most important tool as a bullocky. He yelled to the lead bullocks "Hey Nelson! Hey Blucher!" And as they rose, the other beasts followed with a rattle of chains.

The dray was a crudely built, huge, unwieldy, unsprung mass of wood and iron. It was about five-feet wide and eight-feet long with a solid wooden floor and sides that had extra "hungry boards" added on so you could fit more in. It had a single, centre hauling pole at the front and ran on two four-foot diameter twelve-spoked wheels with three-inch iron tyres. It was built for endurance and not speed or comfort. Teamsters preferred two-wheeled drays to four-wheeled wagons as they could be turned more readily and were easier to get out of bogs. Conditions on board were fairly cramped by the time the family of nine climbed in on top of their luggage.

First stop was the Port Boiling Down Establishment where whole sheep carcasses were being made into tallow to export for use in candle and soap making. Jane could smell the place long before they got close and it turned her stomach. Red explained that it was the cheapest place in South Australia to buy meat. Fresh leg joints of mutton weighing eight to ten pounds were only sixpence each. When they arrived there were a number of other newly arrived immigrants with their bullock drivers making purchases. After eating three months of basic ship's fare Jane seized upon the opportunity of feeding the entire family for sixpence on fresh mutton. This was the first time in her life that she could afford to buy a whole leg.

The road to Adelaide was the settlement's busiest. Each working day it was trampled by a mixture of more than 200 head of horses and bullocks pulling a diverse collection of gigs, spring carts, drays and wagons hauling all sorts of freight and more than 300 people. Although most of the road was level and firm over the eight or so miles to Adelaide it was potholed in places, had some very deep ruts and was subject to clouds of dust. It was a bone jarring ride in the dray and Jane thought the road was quite unsafe. Fortunately, she was unaware that this was a "silk road" compared to some she would soon traverse.

Jane now realised she had another problem. She was six weeks pregnant. The symptoms were well familiar to her. Feeling sick in the mornings was just one of them. She was not pleased with her condition. Already she had seven children with four of them under the age of 10. The thought of eight children with no certainty as to what the future held filled her with great anxiety. An attack of the miseries overcame her, she felt sad, depressed and dispirited. Their situation, she thought, was wretched and all she seemed to do year after year was rear babies in an endless slog as though she was on a treadmill with never enough sleep or rest. She felt like screaming but prayed instead, dealt with life one day at a time, counted her blessings and thanked God for them.

After travelling only a short distance Red announced that he was stopping at "The Old Halfway House" on the road to water his bullocks from a trough outside the inn. Up until now Jane had managed to keep Richard moving past all the inns but ever since leaving the ship he had been thinking of a big glass of colonial ale and when Red went into the inn's tap room there was nothing Jane could do to stop Richard following. He emerged soon after wiping his mouth with the back of his hand as he spat on the ground declaring that "Cornish ale was better". Red agreed and described the ale as "bloody damnable" which in deference to Jane, who was within earshot, was the most polite derogatory phrase he could recall from his extensive vocabulary of that genre.

Chapter 27

ADELAIDE

It was late in the afternoon when they reached the outskirts of the Adelaide settlement situated on a slightly elevated fertile and lightly timbered landscape beside the River Torrens and several other creeks with the Mount Lofty Ranges in the background. The Dunstans were surprised at the size of Port Adelaide, the open expanses along the road and now the vista of Adelaide before them. It greatly exceeded their expectations influenced by a lifetime of living in small Cornish hamlets like Tolcarne. While still a work in progress Adelaide was clearly past the stage of being just a colonial village and starting to develop its own character.

There were public offices including a Treasury building, Government House, court house, police station, post office, a gaol, a hospital and lunatic asylum, also several theatres, three banks, building societies, a stock exchange, Chamber of Commerce, Mechanics Institute, libraries, two fire engines and even a botanic garden. The population of about 10,000 was serviced by twenty-eight registered and qualified medical practitioners and twenty-two solicitors with practising certificates. No less than six regular weekly newspapers were published. Well-planned streets were laid out in a grid pattern with three wide thoroughfares running from north to south and from east to west with open "squares" at their points of intersection.

In the colony there were more than twenty breweries, about 200 licensed inns and around 100 churches of all denominations plus a number of schools. There were also about a dozen steam flour mills as well as others of water and wind power, various foundries, tanneries, a woollen mill, a distillery and quarries. In the entire colony there resided more than 56,000 white inhabitants. All this was some achievement for a place that had started in the bush from nothing thirteen years before.

The dray lumbered down Hindley Street and joined in with others going slow motion in both directions. Teamsters shouted encouragement between whip cracks but nothing made the beasts move any quicker. It was just too hot, too dusty and too busy. Each side of the red dirt road there were stores, warehouses and dwellings varying from large stone establishments to small timber shops and with vacant lots scattered between them. As they got closer to the intersection of King William Street the buildings grouped closer together and there were less vacant lots.

Houses built of stone looked as though they would last forever; other rough built wooden ones were already falling down. Fruit trees and vegetables grew on some vacant lots, children played beside goats and cows tethered on others. People bustled from one side of the street to the other dodging piles of dung, riders on horseback, all sorts of beastly drawn vehicles, dogs and the occasional half-naked black men armed with spears and waddy.

Jane had noticed that there were not many women in the street and that while she saw a couple of top hats it seemed that straw hats were the local preference for the heat. Many of them sat on the heads of rough, fully bearded, ugly and very dirty characters with short clay pipes jammed between their teeth standing outside hotels. Richard didn't notice the men but did think about the possibility of quaffing a deliciously cellar cool beverage of local ale from any of the many inns he saw. On the other side of the commercial centre of town Red pulled up the team next to a tiny roadside vegetable stall.

"Right," he said. "Tonight there'd be boiled mutton, potatoes and cabbage!"

Mouths watered at the prospect of fresh food. Jane bought some onions as well and only a mile or two further on Red drove his team off the road to a clump of big eucalypts where several other teamsters had already lit their campfires and settled for the night. Jane had packed one big iron pot onto *Trafalgar*. Quickly retrieved, a fire lit, some water from Red's water barrel, a dash of salt and a big family stew of chopped mutton, potatoes and onions was underway with cabbage on the side.

That night they slept rough but well. They had been allowed to take their bedding with them when disembarking and took blankets and bolsters but left behind smelly mattresses. Jane, Mary, Ann, Elizabeth and young Wearn all slept on the top of the dray while Richard and the three eldest boys slept underneath. Red made a simple tent by slinging a tarpaulin over the dray's centre hauling pole after he had secured it to a forked stake driven into the ground. The mid January night in Adelaide was not cold so they had a comfortable sleep except for a few persistent mosquitoes.

Red was up before the sun, had the fire going and, using a flour and water mix with some of his own "extra ingredients",

[S.T. Gill, Australia, 1818–1880. *Rundle Street, Adelaide*, 1845, Adelaide.
Watercolour on paper, 27.3 × 40.5 cm. Gift of the South Australian Company 1890,
Art Gallery of South Australia, Adelaide.]

had begun the makings of a big breakfast damper before anyone else had moved. He said he had business to attend to in Adelaide, that they would have the morning to shop for provisions while he headed off with the team, and that he would meet them back at the camp around noon. He recommended that they buy a large tarpaulin to throw over the dray at night in the unlikely event that it might rain or get cold. Apart from that the main thing they needed to buy was food to last them all for up to a week. Anything else they might want was a matter for them, although an axe might be handy if they hadn't already packed one from Cornwall.

The family were on the streets before most shops had opened. There was some activity at the horse bazaar, coach stables, auction rooms, a few offices and even public houses. Jane thought there was far too many of the latter. She was impressed by the number and variety of businesses and the quality of goods on sale, and was fascinated by the display of ladies' worked muslin robes at Messrs Miller & Lucking, their corded petticoats, lace falls and veils, shawls and velvet cravats. It was all beyond her means except for a large fancy summer bonnet which she deemed a necessary purchase for dealing with the hot climate.

Meanwhile, Richard and the boys had wandered into an ironmonger's store full of every type of article that could possibly be made of iron or tin and assorted tools and hardware all of which, he thought, was absolutely essential for colonial life. He settled for the tarpaulin that Red told him to buy and a knife in a sheath he could wear on his belt – everyone else seemed to have one.

Jane conducted a quick inspection of three grocers' shops in Hindley Street to find that she could buy potatoes for a penny a pound, onions at threepence a pound and cabbages for one shilling and sixpence. Stocked up with these basic items she then bought tea, salt, sugar, flour, barley, raisins, salt meat and bicarbonate of

Hindley Street, Adelaide West End, 1849.

[J.B. Austin. Courtesy of the State Library of South Australia. B2268.]

soda. From a butcher shop close by she bought more fresh mutton which this time cost threepence a pound and from a bakery a little further down the street a couple of two-pound loaves of bread for threepence each. Richard bought tobacco and a box of the new Lucifer matches which, to his delight, readily produced a flame when struck against a hard surface. A proper camp oven from an ironmonger's shop was Jane's last purchase.

It was now late in the morning, the sun was getting high, it was hot and the smell of animal dung and urine in the streets was pungent if not nauseous as the family trudged back to the campsite pursued by a cloud of little black flies. Red was true to his word and arrived at almost precisely high noon, albeit with half a load of general freight that had been tossed in on top of the Dunstans' luggage. After a little sorting and repacking the party were soon on the road again.

Although impressed by Adelaide Jane did not like the smell of the place, the dung and urine in the streets, rough looking characters outside the inns and the flies. The infant city had problems with its sanitation. Commenting on its condition in the *South Australian Register* newspaper on 10th February 1849 Adelaide doctors variously described it as "filthy in the extreme … we are literally living in a dunghill of thirteen years standing. The … filth of the city is in such a deplorable condition as would be dangerous." The problem was caused by "necessaries" (toilets) all over the town from three to five feet deep – most of them overflowing and pigsties, tanneries, slaughter yards and rubbish heaps.

Jane was glad to be moving on. After the sweet smell of the sea, Adelaide stunk. The bad sanitary conditions contributed to the high rate of infant mortality in Adelaide that year – 316 children under the age of two years (two percent of the entire population) died.

Chapter 28

THE ROAD TO BURRA

All dray men named their carts and referred to them as "she". Burned roughly into the wood with a hot iron on the back of Red's dray was the name *Constance* and she was not the only vehicle leaving the wide, unpaved, dirty streets of Adelaide. The road was busy with bullock teams like theirs heading north, but there were a few teams coming south and some horse drawn carriages as well as horseback riders moving in both directions.

They were soon on what was called "The Great North Road" although it was neither great nor a single road. It had begun as a series of rough bush tracks that meandered in a generally northern direction through the natural environment and became a "road" mostly through constant usage and very little man-made construction. When it became too difficult because of deep wheel ruts, huge boggy sections, fallen trees or anything else, the teamsters made a new and better track through adjacent country.

There was, however, no difficulty in determining the main route as the trail of empty liquor bottles glinting in the sun on the track formed sparkling dots between the inns on the way. They had travelled past two inns in the first 6 miles and then at Dry Creek there were another two. Red stopped at "The Bird in Hand" to water the bullocks from the abundant supply provided and while leaving them in the care of Jane and the children he and Richard slipped into the tap room for a quick tankard of ale.

The distance to the Burra mine from Adelaide was about ninety miles and a good three days' ride on horseback. A bullock wagon with a load of ore travelling south to the port might take ten or eleven days depending on the weather and state of the road. Lumbering back to Burra with an empty dray or light load could be done in eight or nine days in good conditions. Bullocks travelled at a speed of around one and a half to two miles per hour – equivalent to a man's walking pace. Depending on the track ten to fifteen miles was considered a good day's travel. The aim was to reach water and if possible good feed by mid-afternoon and then camp for the night. Distances had to be adjusted accordingly and some days a team had to be pushed further than was desirable. A string of watering places a day's journey apart became the camping grounds for bullock drivers and their teams and often the site of a solitary inn.

The day had turned into a scorcher. In the great gums that grew along the creek the road followed, cicadas started up their tree-top din. They could be heard but not seen and were a mystery to Jane and most other new immigrants, some thought it was the gum trees that gave out the loud buzzing sound. The country was stranger than she had imagined. In the distance hills rolled out covered by a sky that had a blue vastness without end. It was just a great expanse of new world. England could fit comfortably into the State of South Australia more than six times.

As they travelled over the predominantly flat open country between Dry Creek and the Little Para River known as the Salisbury Plains they came upon an area the teamsters called "The Glue Pot" because in winter it was one gigantic muddy bog. It was surrounded and criss-crossed by countless circuitous tracks and now, at the end of a dry summer, had been pulverised by the traffic into a huge bowl of fine talcum-like dust. Dry bog holes almost knee deep in dust could be quite dangerous to bullocks and drays that might stumble into them. Red used a stick, which he stored on the side of the dray, to check their depth. Even on good parts of the track the twenty-four hooves of the six bullocks in the team constantly stirred up dust that coated everything and everyone in a fine light powder, choked throats, blocked nostrils, smarted eyes, penetrated clothes and infiltrated the food supplies.

When there was no breeze it hung like a low mist along the full length of the track and was impossible to escape. At times it was so thick that when Red was working at the front of the team with the leaders he could not see the dray when he looked back. Red's dog, Scrapper, tethered by chain to the dray axle, copped the worst of it. It was all right with a cross wind or tail wind but a headwind or no wind forced passengers to vacate the dray and walk ahead near the leading bullocks to avoid nearly suffocating. As a result, by the time they got to Burra, the Dunstans found they had walked for more than half the distance they had paid for as passengers and after a lack of proper exercise during the three months on board *Trafalgar* they discovered walking was very difficult. Blisters were a problem. Jane had to carry baby Elizabeth and even though she didn't weigh much found the task particularly hard. Richard helped – but only some of the time. Little Ann, aged 3, could not walk any long distances and resorted to hiding under the tarpaulin in the dray to try and avoid the dust. Mary, aged 6, joined her most of the time and the two of them cooked in their refuge as the sun beat down. All of the children had begun to ask of their parents, "Are we there yet? How much further is it?" Although Red sometimes tied a bandanna over his mouth to try and keep out the fine powdery dust from his throat, years of swallowing the stuff on the trail combined with sucking on a pipe filled with cheap colonial tobacco had given him a constant rattling cough which he relieved by clearing his throat and spitting every two or three hundred yards or so.

It was getting late in the afternoon when they reached the Little Para River and Harvey's Inn, described by one traveller as a place "susceptible of much improvement". The area around the inn and along the banks of the river was one of the regular camping places where horse-drawn vehicles and bullock drays stopped for the night. Like all inns on the Burra Road, Harvey's supplied watering facilities for the bullocks as well as liquid refreshments for the drivers. There were already some fifteen to twenty drays pulled up in the vicinity of the inn with cattle unyoked grazing about in hobbles. Some teamsters had started campfires and tossed kangaroo skin swags under their dray in readiness for their eventual retirement when they staggered back from the inn. Others had slung hammocks under their dray or made a rough tarpaulin tent.

Within moments of arriving there was a clunk-clash sound as Red tossed a bag of bullock bells from the dray. The noise signalled to the bullocks they were finished for the day and they tossed their heads around in excited anticipation of their moment of freedom making it difficult for Red to de-yoke and bell them.

"Whoa Nelson you bastard!" he yelled. "Whoa whoa whoa! Whoa Sampson. Whoa ho wo Curly," and so on until the last of them wandered off in hobbles creating sonorous clonkety clonk clonks and donkety donk donks – a bit like a bullfrog band in full swing.

On going to bed that night they all emptied cups full of sand from their boots. Jane kept Richard on a "short tether" and refused to allow him to go anywhere near the campfire festivities of the other teamsters. After something to eat Red wandered off "to wash the dust from my throat" he said. As the night waxed on so too did their drinking, volume of talking, singing and swearing until eventually it went quiet and the last dray man rolled into bed.

Next morning Red's dog Scrapper really proved his worth. While each of the bullocks had distinctive sounding bells around their necks with different tones so they could be found and rounded up, with so many bullocks wandering about the camping area it was hard for Red to ascertain exactly where his beasts were. No problem for Scrapper. He knew his bullocks and when sent off by Red to round them up had them back at the dray in no time. Scrapper's job was also to hold the bullocks steady while they were being yoked.

Each bullock had his own special place in the team. The leaders, Nelson and Blucher, were the most valued and highly trained pair, selected by Red for their intelligence and ability to readily and willingly respond to orders. Behind them were the plodders, Curly and Arthur, known as "body bullocks" – not the smartest in the line. Nearest the dray were the "polers", Sampson and Big Bob, whose job was to support the weight of the dray's pole and help pull it around when turns were made. They also acted as brakes to control the forward momentum of the load when going downhill. They were the biggest and most powerful beasts in the team. Although weighing up to a ton each, they were all for the most part as gentle as lambs and enjoyed being patted by the children who soon learned their names. Blucher was the only one that could be strong willed and cantankerous at times. Like Scrapper he was nervous and apprehensive when approached by strangers. Red reckoned he was too smart for his own good. They were trained to be always hitched on the same side of the team with the same pulling partner. By working together they soon formed a bond and became "mates". When unyoked they often stayed close as they grazed, and when Scrapper rounded them up each morning they usually lined up in front of the dray in their correct pairs and correct places. Red attributed this to Scrapper's ability and said that dogs were like people. There were good ones and bad ones. Scrapper was a good dog at some things. He could handle bullocks, but was not much good with people.

Chapter 29

BULLOCKS AND BULLOCKIES

Another long day's trudge would take them to Gawler some twenty-six miles north of Adelaide. Once underway, the creaking wagon, crunching wheels, clanking chains and clomp of bullocks' hooves interspersed with their occasional lowing provided a soporific kind of orchestral rhythm to their slow and steady progress. Red was the conductor of this performance which he punctuated where he deemed appropriate with cracks from his whip or a burst of obscenities designed to motivate any wayward bullock. Walking on the near side (left) with the whip over his shoulder and the long lash dragging in the dust behind him he applied the butt end of the handle from time to time to prod any slackers. He used only a few simple orders to control them. If he was up front and said "Come here" they would follow him. To stop he would say "Whoa" and if he ordered "Whoa back" they would step backwards. Veer left was "Come over" and go right "Gee off". Orders to individual beasts were given such as "Wake-up Curly! Move on Blucher" or "Come over Nelson". When going around a turn, the inside bullocks were called by name to slow down and their outside mates called to speed up. If needs be, a light touch of the leather or a whip crack in the air reinforced orders. Seldom was any order given without an accompanying profanity. As he spoke to them and gave orders Red constantly walked up and down alongside the team. In the end he walked much further than they did.

A succession of stony ridges crossing the track over the Gawler plains jolted the dray and rattled its occupants as they continued on. About half way to Gawler at Smith's Creek they passed Smith's Hotel and then some two and a half miles south of Gawler they came upon the Harp Inn situated on eighty acres of land and with the best stockyard on the Burra Road. Jane was relieved when Red drove his bullocks on past both inns. Time was running short and Red had other plans at Gawler.

The township was an important stop on the route. Settled in 1839, it sat near the foot of the Barossa Mountains on the junction of two small rivers, the North and South Para, after they emerged from the hills and joined into a wider more open area that provided fording possibilities. Approaching the town they passed a native camp along the river. Although they had seen quite a number of black people around Adelaide there had been few along the road. Both men and women were almost naked. Jane could not stop staring at them and thought that they did not look well with their thin legs and bloated stomachs.

Gawler was a thriving place with a number of houses, a steam flour mill, several shops, a large store, a butcher, a baker, a brewer, a tinsmith, blacksmiths and three good inns of which The Old Spot owned by Henry Calton and reported as being "a good Old Spot" was supposed to be the best.

Down along the river there were already groups of bullock drivers clustered together around smoking campfires that had not yet flamed into life. Red parked *Constance* at the end of the furthest group where the grass feed was good for his team. It was a noisy place with the thwack of axes and crack of sticks connected with making fires, rattles and thumps to do with unpacking, the banging of stakes into the ground, the clonk of bells hooked up to bullocks, the chatter of travellers relieved at having stopped for the day and the laughter of children who had found new energy to run about and play. After unyoking the team and seeing to the welfare of Scrapper, Red politely excused himself advising that they would have a little time in the morning to shop for provisions before continuing on. He headed off to the Old Bushman Inn for a night with his bullocky mates.

Next morning as they drove out of town towards Burra, a mealy mouthed Red, even more sullen than his usual self, fired oaths with increasing rapidity at his bovine charges. His swearing always increased as his degree of satisfaction with the world declined. Nearly everything a bullocky said was prefixed by the word "bloody". He was always "bloody wrong" or "bloody right" and never just whatever he was and if he got stirred up was capable of swearing not only several times in one sentence but even in the middle of a word. Such profound profanity sounded out aloud was not just ridiculous but "ri-bloody-diculous". Jane tried to count how many times a day Red swore but gave up after she got to more than 200 and then delivered an icy rebuke to the teamster.

All he said was, "Mrs. you have to swear at them to make 'em go. No one ever drove 'em politely."

It was accepted as an eternal truth that bullocks could not be motivated to move unless you swore at them and bellowed their individual names between curses.

The Old Spot Inn, Gawler Town.

[Sketch by Samuel Galvert. Courtesy of the State Library of South Australia. B9483/8.]

"Garn ya mongrel bastard Curly – git up!" yelled Red and "Yah Big Bob – move your bloody arse," or "Damn you Nelson – dig your bloody hooves in", and much better, or worse, depending on your point of view. Jane put her hands over her ears as he bawled "Come on you buggering useless slack bastards, put your bloody shoulders into it!"

From Gawler to Burra there was a choice of three alternative main routes. Red took the eastern road because it had the most secure watering places during a hot summer. That night they camped at the She Oak Log, a tiny settlement comprising an inn of that name, a blacksmith shop and cottage. Although only some eight miles north of Gawler it worked out a satisfactory days run as they had been late decamping that morning due to the combined effect of Red's hangover and the need to purchase some provisions. "The Log" was popular among teamsters as a place where they could get bullocks' hooves shod while they partook of refreshments in the tap room. It required special blacksmithing skills to shoe a bullock, each cloven hoof requiring two shoes – needing eight for a full set.

Red pulled *Constance* up to a group of four other drays that had begun to form a circle around a substantial fire in the middle. Smaller individual fires were soon lit for cooking but later that night the teamsters sat in a group around a big log crackling away on the central blaze, spinning yarns and telling jokes. It was a tough life with long hours for bullockies and this was their happiest time. Someone always produced a concertina, fiddle or tin whistle to provide the impetus for a sing along, but talking "bullocky" was their main entertainment. Apart from yelling at his bullocks Red never said much during the day. After a few grogs around the campfire at night he would talk about bullocks flat out for a week if you let him, articulating on the merits of

229

different drays and wagons and their construction, and then on the different personalities and pulling propensities of each of his individual bullocks, and then on the design of yokes and chains, and then on the respective merits of wood used in yokes and whip handles and on the amazing things he could do with a whip. The teamsters formed a close fraternity and there was a great deal of good humour and good feeling that prevailed among them.

Constance made an early start next morning and headed off through gentle undulating country with several flat plains. They had a long day ahead of them if they were to reach the River Light and township of Kapunda more than fourteen miles away. It had been settled in 1842 and copper mining began there in 1844. It had only one inn called The Miners Arms.

After spending their fifth night camping on the banks of the River Light at Kapunda the party left the river's course and travelled north over the Waterloo Plains some ten miles to where they again met the river and followed it north. There were another two inns in this area, The Light Arms on the Burra Road and the Royal Oak on the River Light. The river contained several large and deep waterholes which were an important source of water to the dray men and their bullocks as they headed north.

For five days now the temperature had been over 100°F and Jane wondered if it would ever be cool again. It was so hot she thought the steel in the yoke bows and harness chains would singe the hair on the bullocks. She had discovered that English clothes were not really suitable for these conditions and why big cabbage tree hats were so popular among the men. She noticed that the teamsters wore a piece of old flannel shirt, or any available material, hanging down the back of their necks and the spine to lessen the heat of the sun and quickly fashioned copies of the device for the protection of all family members. It was not just the constant heat.

Every day, dust caked around their eyes and mouths and blocked their nostrils. Hot winds made eyes dry, red and sore. Persistently annoying little black flies were a constant aggravation. There was usually little talk. It was better to shut your mouth to keep out the dust and flies.

As the morning advanced so did the heat and the wind picked up. It was now a driving stinging thing that carried not just dust but substantial dirt dislodged by the bullocks' hooves. Jane tried to protect the girls and herself in the dray using the tarpaulin as a wrap. This was a meagre, wretched, scrubby countryside she thought. A dry and parched place that would never show the verdant green of Cornwall. All it had was grass that was yellow and brown forever. It was, thought Jane, a completely different earth – a place that God had forgot. Charles Darwin, who had visited Australia in the 1830s, thought that if God had been involved at all then it must have been a different God to the English one.

Jane was worried about little Lizzie who continued to be frail, and was frightened of what may lie ahead for the family. She had thought that once they were off the ship everything would be all right. But it wasn't. She was full of trepidation and doubt and wished she had not brought the family to all of this. She wondered, if they ever got to Burra, where they would live with seven children – and there was another one coming in about seven months. She prayed that God would look after them and believed he would. Richard and the boys plodded on stoically next to Red at the front of the team. There was something in them that enjoyed the great adventure. They were off to seek their fortune and this track could turn out to be the yellow brick road that would lead them to it.

Chapter 30

A BURRA HOME

After another night's camp on the River Light, the next four days journey took them to Tothills Creek in surrounding undulating, lightly grassed and timbered country and then north to Apoinga where Messrs Penny and Owen had set up a copper smelting works that had fired up for the first time eleven days before the arrival of *Trafalgar*. Red was happy to park *Constance* in the vicinity of the Apoinga Inn. It had been a couple of days since he had seen one. They were now seventy-eight miles north of Adelaide and he was pleased with their progress and thought he would have a little drink on the strength of it. On this occasion Richard joined him in the tap room. Under these conditions every man had to wash the dirt from his throat now and then.

An early start next morning took them to the Black Springs that provided a supply of clean fresh water channelled into a large wooden trough for animals with a separately quarantined supply available to those humans who did not wish to imbibe at the local inn called The Emu. On each side of the hard sandstone range at the springs the country was flat but the road from here went through country that undulated over the Sod Hut Range through an opening known as the Stony Gap and then to Burra. Jane alternated between riding on the dray and walking as she found the bumping and jolting arduous after a while and had to get down and walk.

As they crawled into the precincts of the Sod Hut Inn only eight miles and one day's bullock tramp out from Burra, Jane stared with wide eyes at the violet hills in the evening light. When the sun went down the colours changed so that the hills were washed with cobalt blue and deep purple framed in the softest of pink skies. But she could not see a blade of green grass or green anything anywhere. Even the normally green leaves on the few gum trees had changed their hue to a greyish colour in the light and everywhere the sun bleached grass had turned to the palest straw colour. Unlike Cornwall, yet truly, bizarrely, uncommonly, beautiful Jane thought.

The "Hut" was run by Irishman Daniel O'Leary in an original sod hut once occupied by a shepherd. Although a sorry, shabby place with a scant and muddy water supply, it was, nonetheless, a popular stamping ground for Burra's bullockies. They travelled about a mile past the inn until they found several bullock drays and horse vehicles drawn up around their campfires and joined them for the night.

Next morning it was still dark when everyone began to pack up and decamp with a deal more enthusiasm than usual as they looked forward to their last day of travelling and arriving at Burra. The well beaten road wound through hilly terrain with remarkably barren ridges and their rocky outcroppings running north and south. Approaching Burra they could see towards the north a series of bald rounded hills. Stumps scattered through the landscape were all that remained of trees that had been cut down within several miles of the town. They had been harvested for shoring timber and fuel for boilers. This was mining country, thought Richard.

The site of a thick stream of white smoke and then its chimney caught their attention. Burra at last! The dray soon rolled into Burra's main road of Commercial Street, stopping in Market Square where there was a collection of other drays with bullocks yoked to them lying down. When Red threw his whip on the ground the team knew it was the signal that they too could lie down in the dirt, rest and chew their cuds. The first business that Jane had noticed as they entered the town was a hotel on the right. Since leaving Adelaide they had passed no less than sixteen inns although some of them were little more than wayside shanties. She thought there were far too many of them in this country.

While it had been less than four years since the first charge of gunpowder had been fired at the mine in September 1845 the town looked as though it had already decided to be more than a frontier settlement. There were several good shops and general stores, a baker, three dairies, a couple of butchers and a chemist shop run by Mr. Tom Powell that also operated as a post office. Several blacksmiths and a tinsmith practised their skills. The main street was lined with a number of substantially built stone houses and commercial premises. After seeing so many hotels at the port, in Adelaide itself and along the road to Burra, Jane was relieved to find that there were only two in Burra, the Miners Arms and Burra Burra Hotel. Many more would soon be built.

In the town there was a police station complete with lock-up and stables manned by four constables. They enforced the law as interpreted by resident Magistrate and Coroner, William Lang, who conducted his court in a rented mining cottage until a proper courtroom was built. A Wesleyan Chapel and schoolhouse already existed while a similar Anglican establishment was in the course of construction and there was also a small private school. The community included people with a range of other skills including charcoal burners, sawyers, smelters, carpenters and joiners, stonemasons, wheelwrights, shoe makers, saddlers and harness makers, clerks, brick makers and layers, tailors, domestic servants, tanners, shepherds and a "cabinetmaker and undertaker". There were also two doctors, appointed by the mine, whose salaries were paid by a weekly deduction of sixpence from the wages of each miner which entitled them to free medical treatment if they were sick or injured. The doctors could supplement their income through private practice such as services rendered to the miners' families for which they would be charged a fee.

There was plenty of activity in the square with bullock drays and horse drawn vehicles coming and going and people bustling about but Jane thought the place looked drab and cheerless surrounded by bare hills with sunburnt grass and stone buildings sprinkled with Burra dust the colour of the ground. She noted, however, that in Adelaide and Burra there was a great deal that had a clearly recognisable British flavour.

The family's first priority was accommodation. The rapid development of the new mining settlement had led to a desperate shortage of housing for ordinary mine workers. The mine management had built some miners' cottages and were currently building others from stone, roofed with wooden shingles and flagged with local slate. These were all allocated to a long list of waiting miners. From the very early days of the mines' development the lack of housing had forced miners to rely on their own resources to put a roof over their families' heads. They resorted to excavating cave-like dwellings in the steep banks of the Burra Creek using their mining skills to create underground dugout homes. By the time the Dunstans arrived the dugout huts extended for some three miles on both sides of the bank and housed a population of around 750 people. Lack of title deeds for these dwellings did not prevent their occupiers selling their "possessory rights" to the premises. Because a number of mining families had decided to leave Burra permanently during the miners' strike that ended a week before the arrival of *Trafalgar* and a small group of strike ringleaders had been banished from the town by the mine management, vacated dugouts had become available for very little money.

Richard secured a small two-roomed dwelling for a consideration of £1.10 shillings. One room with a fireplace and chimney that lead to the top of the bank Jane could use as a kitchen and they would all sleep in the other until, as time went on, they could excavate extra rooms. The dugout was constructed by cutting into the bank until a perpendicular of almost ten foot was obtained, a doorway was then cut out and the interior excavated. Supporting walls about three-foot thick were left to hold the place up and windows cut through to give some ventilation to each room. Shelves were made on each side of the fireplace by cutting storage cavities into the dirt walls. It was whitewashed inside but the stained and scored walls needed another coat. The premises came complete with several hordes of fleas left embedded in the earth courtesy of the previous owners. There was no glass in the windows and the "door" was just an opening. But whatever it was it was better than the steerage of *Trafalgar* or the back of a bullock dray. It was home, and there was no rent to pay.

Red delivered them to the bank of the creek on top of their

house and their goods and chattels were unloaded. Along both sides of the bank smoke was seen wafting out of hundreds of stubby ground level chimneys made from old barrels or mud bricks. Walking along the footpath that wended its way between the chimneys they could see in use the fireplaces, tea kettles and frying pans below and savour the cooking smells rising up. As they carried their meagre possessions down rough hewn steps to their hut, neighbours from both sides came to welcome them and offer help with fresh water, wood for the fire and pannikins of tea. They received a barrage of questions about Cornwall and England and were delighted with the warm and friendly reception from Cornish families living in the creek.

It took several days to set up house. Along one wall in the second room a sleeping shelf or chamber had been dug out of the earth to provide an elevated area above the floor of sufficient size to use as a bunk. Richard and the boys constructed other beds by driving four forked sticks into the dirt floor and slinging horizontal sapling poles between them which had been threaded through hessian chaff bags to provide a base for a mattress made out of more old hessian bags sewn together by Jane and stuffed with dried native grass. She made pillows from smaller old flour bags using the same stuffing and sewn together at the ends. Furniture was made from all sorts of old wooden boxes used for packing a variety of freight shipped to Australia and then Burra in bullock drays. When finished with by storekeepers, they were sold cheaply to become tables, seats and storage systems in miners' huts. They made ideal bedside tables or clothes stores and, stacked on top of one another, became cupboards. Richard dismantled several broken ones and used the timber to build a rustic kitchen table with local saplings as legs and made bench seats to run along each side. The previous owners had left a blackened chain hanging down the chimney which, with the aid of a wire hook fashioned by Richard, Jane could use to hang her iron cooking pots from.

Boxes and blocks of wood cut from logs and placed on each side of the fireplace served as seats, and sapling pegs driven into the wall were good for hanging things on. Several of them were used to support a packing case plank that made an ideal shelf for plates and Jane's small collection of tins containing important ingredients. A couple of slush oil lamps were made by hanging a wick over the edge of a cut down tin filled with mutton fat from the frying pan. The small yellow flame created black smoke and a sickly burnt fat smell but enough light to subdue total darkness. The fire provided most of their light. There were no kerosene lamps as that fuel was not yet available, and candles were costly. By the time Richard hammered together a front door out of rough packing case timber, Jane scattered a few leftover old chaff bags around the dirt floor for mats, made some hessian curtains for the windows and placed a bunch of flowering gum tree sprigs in an old pannikin on the kitchen table, the Dunstans had turned a hole into a home.

But a journalist reporting on the conditions in the creek in the *South Australian* newspaper on 2nd February 1849 sounded a warning – "The medical men here will have a rich harvest this summer in consequence of the stagnant water settled in the creek surrounded also by homes dug out in the ground without the least ventilation. For humanity's sake they ought to be all rooted out. Fever of a malignant nature is already very prevalent."

Chapter 31

BURRA

The Burra mine was a two-mile walk that took about ten minutes from the creek dugouts through the village. The surface workings were in an area of little more than six acres which contained huge piles of earth spoil intersected with heaps of green, blue and red coloured ores. Next to the shafts were a series of extensive sheds in which men and boys banged away with flat headed hammers breaking and dressing ore while others stood knee deep in water washing it by jerking jigging machine handles connected to big sieves up and down. Stacks of canvas bags full of pulverised and washed mineral were lined up waiting for removal by bullock drays that rattled their chains and crunched their steel wheels as they moved in slow motion around the site. The mine's blacksmith shop contained a special shoeing shed and several forges where smiths created hammer-on-anvil clangs that seldom stopped for more than a few minutes during the day. In addition to shoeing they sharpened miners' picks and drills. There was a general store that stocked all articles miners required, extensive stables for horses, and office buildings for the mine management. Next to a pile of logs being unloaded from a bullock dray a team of carpenters sawed and hammered away as a new mine shed was erected. A pall of dust hung over the lot.

The mine had at least thirty vertical shafts to a depth of mostly around 180 feet where they stopped because of the water level. It was a wet mine with streams of water in some places one inch thick pouring out of the subterranean walls to flood the drives and shafts. When a steam pumping engine was later installed greater depths were reached. From the sides of the shafts tunnels ran in all directions at different levels to the lodes of copper.

Working conditions at the Burra mine proved to be much better than in Cornwall. At worst, depths were no greater than 200 feet whereas in Cornwall they went to 1,000 or 2,000 feet. The miners were not faced with a strenuous and dangerous climb out of the earth on rickety ladders that might take more than an hour as in Cornwall. The shallower workings at Burra also made for easier and better underground ventilation. It was not as hot as a Cornish mine. Underground at Burra felt cool in summer, was a good place to escape the scorching summer heat on the surface and in winter it was a haven from icy winter winds above. Good quality ore was much easier to win at Burra where much of it was deposited in surrounding spoil consisting of relatively soft clays, shales, limestone and sandstone which was easily worked with a pick and shovel and quite different to Cornish hard rock mining.

The downside to these conditions was that a lot of timber shoring was required which resulted in the demise of nearly every large tree around Burra for a radius of about twenty miles. Gunpowder was not used as often as in Cornwall and when it was safety fuses were employed. Miners considered it a "safe" mine. The average of one death due to accident per year was much fewer than recorded fatalities in many European mines. In Cornwall, Richard and the boys had to walk for nearly half an hour to get to work, while in Burra it only took a few minutes.

The high-grade copper ores that the miners kept discovering resulted in a financial bonanza for the mine owners and good income returns to the miners. Some of the richest ore bodies were discovered while the Dunstans were mining there. Under the tribute system that Richard Senior and Richard Junior worked together as partners, miners could earn an average around £2 per week each or £100 per annum which was a great improvement on the average rural worker's wage in England at the time of £25. per annum. Some miners at Burra could earn a lot more than £2 a week if they happened to be on a good patch of dirt or "pitch." From time to time there were reports of men earning £5 or even £10 per week.

Based on the experience he had in Cornwall with his father underground, young Ben, who would be twelve in May, got a job as a "ton" or piece worker picking out copper ore for which he was paid at the rate of 18 shillings per ton. While a grown man could pick out two tons a week young Ben was doing well if he managed a ton. The two youngest boys, Henry aged 10 and Wearn, aged 8, also got jobs. Henry sorted ore as a "picky boy" at long tables in the ore shed where he set aside the clearly good ore for bagging and threw the poorer pieces on to the sieve bases of jigging machines to be washed. For this he earned around fifteen shillings a week. Wearn, aged 8, was employed as a whim boy driver which entailed walking in circles all day around a 36-foot diameter path behind two horses that rotated a capstan winding a rope of more than four inches in diameter to raise and lower big slightly egg-shaped iron buckets called "kibbles" in the mine shaft. They transported men and equipment up and down and were then the chief means of extracting ore and water. The whims operated around the clock to keep water at a manageable level with a change every eight hours of horses and boys who were paid around nine shillings for working a six-day week.

At the time there was no law that required parents to send their children to school and Richard and Jane, both being illiterate, did not see the need to provide a formal education for the children.

With five breadwinners in the family earning much more than they could in Cornwall and no rent to pay, the Dunstans had never had it so good. The family lived comfortably and managed to save a tidy sum from their income. As in Cornwall the procedure on payday was for Richard and the boys to hand all their earnings over to Jane and she would then dole out their respective allowances. The difficulty was that the mining company never paid wages in cash but always in the form of promissory notes. Jane had no faith in these "paper flimsies" as she called them and made sure they were converted to the silver coins circulating in the town as soon as possible. There were times it was not possible due to a shortage of coin and then shopkeepers issued their own promissory notes as change. The hotels usually had plenty of cash but Jane could never feel confident about sending Richard there with a pocket full of money orders.

The family savings were deposited in a cavity excavated in the wall of the dugout which was then mud bricked up and white washed over so that it could not be identified. There was no bank in Burra until 1859.

After working all day in the mine Richard would return home late in the afternoon to again go underground at home. Outside propped up on a sapling tripod was a tin dish Jane had filled with

Burra Mine.

[S.T. Gill, c1850. Courtesy of the State Library of South Australia.]

water so Richard and the boys could wash the worst of the days working dirt from their faces and hands. Richard did not like the idea of living in a dugout. He thought he spent enough time underground during the day without going there again for the night and that so long as he had breath in his body it was better to reside above ground. In the end he would be underground long enough. The creek was full of Cornish miners who had worked all their lives in dirt, lived in dirt houses made of cob and now having come to the new world with their skills had gone back to working in dirt and living in the earth.

Jane worried that, like all miners, Richard would be diminished and then destroyed by his occupation before his time. Born and bred a miner, his whole life had been spent digging for copper and tin. When she thought about it tears came to her eyes. She was three months pregnant and starting to show and Richard, now aware that he was to be a father again, despaired at the thought of having his family of ten living in two small rooms underground.

With the assistance of his four boys he began to excavate another room for the family. After digging in the earth all day underground and returning home to eat his main meal of the day with the family, he and the boys, would again resume digging the earth underground at home for several hours into the night. During the day Jane and Mary, aged 6, did what they could to continue the work and even young Ann, aged 3, threw her weight into the project with a handful of dirt every now and then. Eventually it was done. Mindful of her forthcoming confinement Jane was anxious to have everything in the dugout as best she could manage before then and so decided to whitewash the walls of the entire premises. The wash was made from a mixture of common salt, lime and water with the addition of a little sour milk to "give it a bit more stick". Best results were obtained if it was applied thinly with a brush. Jane used an old rag and with practice got good results.

During the day Jane had the opportunity to escape the dugout to breathe and enjoy the open air. Richard envied people who could do that. The clean, sweet ocean air he breathed on the deck of *Trafalgar* was the best he had in his life. The air at work and at home underground had no life in it and as each day went by he seemed to need more of it. Strangely, the one place that he felt he could breathe freely was in the smoke-filled bar of the Miners Arms hotel in Market Square. While church on Sundays was Jane's salvation, after a six-day working week, the Miners Arms on Saturday nights was Richard's. There he felt released from the clutches of mother earth and free to relax and enjoy the humour and camaraderie of his fellow miners. Customers of many nationalities gathered in groups on the sawdust strewn floor of the bar speaking their language as they imbibed their pitchers of beer. The hubbub was remarkable with inputs of dialogue from Welsh, German, English, Scottish, Irish and Cornish miners and occasional choruses of song from particular ethnic clusters. At times a tin whistler piped up or a fiddler played a jig. There were drinkers in every state of trim – argumentative, intoxicated, sober, elated, depressed, happy, and pugnacious but above all talkative. Richard could lose all his cares there. Official closing time of 11 p.m. often extended beyond midnight.

Depending on how he pulled up next day Richard might return for another round of "fresh air" on Sunday when the trading hours were from 1 p.m. to 3 p.m. and 8 p.m. to 10 p.m. and he could watch the bare fist boxing or "prize fight" matches that were run from time to time on "convincing grounds" at the back of hotels. Hundreds of miners watched gruelling matches being slugged out to the end in which sums from £1 to £5 were bet. A wide range of fighting techniques including holds and throws were allowed by the rules. If a man was downed by a punch or a throw he was given thirty seconds to rest and another eight seconds to come back to the centre of the ring and square off with his adversary, failing which he would lose the fight. There were no limits to the number of rounds with some marathon battles lasting several hours and for more than ninety rounds. In practice, rounds could be quite short when fighters took advantage of minor blows to go down for a thirty second rest. Although these bloody-bare knuckle fights were illegal police took no action against them.

Cornish wrestling matches were also popular and were often held at the back of the Miners Arms in a sawdust ring where contestants wore strong canvas wrestling jackets and pitted the strength and dexterity of their legs and feet against one another to score a back fall. Unlike bare-knuckle boxing these contests were legal and although betting was not it still took place "on the quiet". In his younger days in Cornwall Richard had often earned himself a little extra drinking money by winning a few bouts of wrestling but there was no chance of that now. If there were no boxing or wrestling contests then there was always a cockfight or dogfight on somewhere. The venue could often be located by watching for men sneaking into a secluded spot in the backyard of an inn with a rooster smuggled under their shirt or following someone leading a mongrel dog with ears and tail cut off to minimise places their opponents could latch on to.

Chapter 32

The Creek Hamlet

The women left in the creek after their husbands went to work in the mine were a sisterhood with a commonwealth of interests, fears and desires. They needed each other for moral support, to help with sick children, for babysitting, to assist as midwives, for a shoulder to cry on when the need arose, and even to help lay out the dead. They bartered and shared goods and recipes with each other, taught each other skills and assisted one another when big tasks arose such as whitewashing dugout walls. Above all, they talked and talked, laughed together and discovered the importance of having friends you could rely on. They had their own little community in a kind of separate de facto hamlet away from the rest of Burra society.

Each day local bakers, butchers and grocers would do the rounds of the dugouts by travelling along the bank tops and yelling down the chimneys to announce their presence. Jane would then ascend the rough steps in the bank to do business with the callers. A woman put up a sign outside her dugout advertising that she would write letters for anyone for a small fee. Shoes left at another dugout could be repaired in a day or two for little money and there were several barber shops. Tailoring services were available at several places including Jane's, who also made for sale, aprons and potholders from old tightly woven jute bags. She continued to regard her sewing basket and its contents of pins, needles, threads thimbles and scissors as though they were treasured jewels. They were part of her capital and really mattered.

Outside many dugouts was a small pen made from saplings containing a pig whose job was to get fat consuming the family garbage. Nearby against the bank of the creek a lean-to pit "necessary" (toilet) contributed to the stench from the pigs and the unhygienic conditions. Some people tethered cows or built chicken coops among the chimney pots on the roof of their dugouts so that vital space in front of the dwelling was not used. Others ran a few ducks or geese in the creek or tethered a goat or even a horse in the vicinity. Dogs barked about on the loose and added their defecations to the area. Most of the dugouts had miners' shirts and children's clothes fluttering from a clothesline hung from saplings driven into the bank and a wood heap near the front door.

Wood was carted in by bullock dray from the Murray Mallee twelve miles east as there was none left to cut or collect around the mine. Jane had to purchase it from a licensed timber merchant at five shillings a ton. This was a substantial expense for the family. When the wood was delivered to the bank on top of the dugout, Jane and the children carried it down to be stacked close to the doorway to discourage theft. Some dugouts had rustic shingle verandas over the frontage which provided shade in summer and kept the doorway dry in winter. Richard scrounged some flat local stone to pave the entrance to their place and Jane started a little herb garden along the front with a mint plant given to her by a neighbour.

Women were busy boiling clothes in tin tubs set over outdoor fires filling the creek valley with smoke, or hanging clothes out, scouring pots, collecting water from the brown trickle that ran down the centre, collecting eggs from their chicken coops, tossing leftovers to their pigs or just gossiping in groups. Swarms of children bustled along the banks, some playing in water and mud, some in groups of two or three creating fantasies in the dirt with sticks and stones, some little ones hanging on to their mother's skirt while she was trying to do the washing, others squealing and running about in the dappled shade of the few remaining gum trees and she oaks. All had smudgy faces and bare feet, wore scanty patched clothing and had skin browned by the sun and dirt. To keep the younger children within the bounds and close precincts of the dugout at night Jane instilled in them all a fear of darkness through telling stories about a hairy bush bogeyman, giant eels in the creek and blackfellow ghosts that came out after sunset. The ghosts were the biggest worry because, being black, you could not see them in the dark. The stories had the desired effect.

A favourite trick of boys not old enough to be employed but savvy enough to create mischief was to throw a bag over the chimney of a dugout to smoke out the occupants. By the time the angry resident reached the top of the bank there was no sight of the offenders. Children acting in pairs played tricks on their mothers when an above ground villain lowered a line with a hook attached down the chimney to his subterranean accomplice who attached it to a kettle or even a whole joint of meat which then disappeared vertically. The trick had the potential to drive overwrought mothers hysterical.

The dwellers of the creek had destroyed its beauty. It was mainly humanity, rubbish, mud and a cradle for filth. Its waters, that had run swift and clear before copper was found, were sluggish and a repository for waste water from the mine, seepage from "necessaries" and pigsties, wash water, the contents of the family bucket filled during the night and rubbish. Animals wandering and defecating in the precincts of the creek added to the problem as did men who urinated outside the dugout in the middle of the night with little concern about where or on what.

As the water in the creek was subject to all kinds of polluting influences, Jane procured hers mostly from the nearest public well and carried it in buckets hung from a yoke over her shoulders back to the creek and down the bank to her dugout. It was back breaking work and harder than in Cornwall where barrels around the cottage collected plenty of water from the thatch and the creek close by had cleaner water than Burra. She could have had a quantity of water delivered for sixpence by one of Burra's water carriers who used large barrels on drays as water carts, but was unable to justify such expense in her mind.

The washing up, family laundry and personal ablutions were all done in the same dented tin tub that sat on the sapling tripod in front of the dugout. Jane worked there barefooted on the sloppy banks for hours scouring, rubbing and rinsing the laundry for her family of nine. Handkerchiefs, made from old rags hemmed up by Jane, and any other seriously soiled items were boiled up in the tub on an outdoor fire after first undergoing a thorough soaking. Hand wringing of water from wet clothes over many years had given Jane powerful wrists. If ironing had to be done she would do it on the kitchen table after first heating a flat iron on a stone at the side of the dugout fire

It was impossible for Jane in the environment of Creek Street to have a proper bath. The best she could do was to sponge herself down from a tub of water as she did in Cornwall. She wished she could have a hot bath like the one she had experienced at the emigrant depot in Plymouth and replayed in her mind many times the fun she had bathing in big barrels of sea water on board *Trafalgar* in the tropics.

She sprinkled old soapy washing water, half a handful a time, over the floor of the dugout to help keep the dust down. Before doing this chaff bag mats were removed to be beaten outside. This caused the fleas that resided underneath to turn their gyrations into a rampage and Jane to pound them with her heels without any marked effect. Once, in desperation, she poured boiling water over a mob of them which served to reduce their numbers slightly but mainly turned the dirt floor into mud.

There was plenty of company in the dugout: swarms of sticky black flies, lines of crawling ants that bit and got into every morsel of food not quarantined from them, local cockroaches, mosquitoes that stung through clothes, bedbugs and lice that had migrated with them and various other unidentified flying critters that gained entry on hot evenings through the open door and windows. At night moths flew into the flame of the slush lamps adding the smell of their burning bodies to the air before they fell into the fat. If Jane failed to cover the lamp next day it was not unusual for the mix of solidified fat and insects to become a repository for maggots left by visiting blowflies. The smorgasbord of insects acted like magnets to attract large huntsman spiders, which everyone called "Tarantulas", seeking to dine out. Jane hated them and kept a long length of she oak branch made flat at one end as her favourite spider execution device. Large centipedes escaped from logs placed ready near the fire and took up residence in the cracks and crannies of the walls and roof. At night they would perambulate around on their numerous legs making strange scratching sounds. Jane soon learned from the neighbours to set the legs of their makeshift table in dishes of water, to which a teaspoonful of castor oil was added, in order to discourage the ants and she made little crochet doilies with beaded edges to cover milk and cream jugs to keep out flies.

In the creek environment bowel complaints were common with diarrhoea and its dehydrating effects an ever present cause of infant illness and mortality. As winter months approached the cold and damp of the dugouts promoted colds, sniffles and sore throats. Children and toddlers had constant yellow drizzles coming from their noses. More serious infections resulted in congestion of the lungs and sometimes pneumonia and death. Measles, mumps, tonsillitis and whooping cough made their visits. The latter was a common cause of death in children under one year old. A further aggravation to the unhealthy environment was the offensive state of slaughterhouses behind local butcher shops where complete bullock's heads, sheep's heads and offal of various sorts were dumped in the open. These nauseous heaps, together with pigsties, animal dung, rubbish piles and "necessaries" full to the brim became breeding grounds for millions of flies that spread their germs along the creek and over the whole of Burra. Before the year was finished, typhoid fever appeared in the creek. Outbreaks of typhus were also common. Children, in particular, living in the creek suffered from poor health due to the unsanitary conditions. Still, living in the creek was better than in Mevagissey in Cornwall where in a population of 1,800 cholera killed 111 in mid-1849.

Little Lizzie was now nearly two years old. She was an affectionate little girl and readily responded with a hug and a smile when she was picked up by Jane or Richard. She had a pretty face with long eyelashes, fine eyebrows and big pastel grey eyes that

Dugouts at the Burra Creek.

[W.A. Cawthorne, c.1850. Courtesy of the State Library of South Australia. The only known sketch of the dugouts – original in the Mitchell Library, Sydney, New South Wales.]

never seemed to sparkle. For her age she was smaller than normal, had a sickly complexion, did not attempt much communication and had a poor appetite.

Towards the end of March 1849, a cold wind blew in from the south confirming that winter was not far away. It had been more than two months since the family arrived in Port Adelaide and in that time Elizabeth's health had declined. A chronic cough prevented her from getting a good night's sleep so that Jane had to often hold her in her arms and rock her back and forth for hours to get her to doze off. One night when Richard and the boys came home from the mine they found young Lizzie lying listlessly in her cot. She looked pale and drawn and her lips had a faint tinge of blueness. She was hot to touch, had perspiration under the eyes, her breathing was short and every now and then she gave a faint plaintive cry. Jane did her best to get her to sip a mixture of water, sugar, milk and arrowroot but whatever she swallowed she vomited back up. All night Jane sat with her, put water on her lips, a damp cloth on her forehead, addressed the toilet needs of her constant diarrhoea and spoke loving motherly words. In the morning when Lizzie stopped her little cries her sister Mary went and gathered a small posy of flowers to place in her dead sister's hand.

Jane had known in her heart for some time that her little girl was not going to live for long. She had been born at the height of the "Hungry Forties" potato famine and Jane's malnutrition then meant she was unable to provide sufficient breast milk or milk of the right strength to give Elizabeth proper nourishment. Poverty had contributed to her death; that and the strain of the long journey out, and also living in the dirt in Burra. She had survived for only two months and two weeks in Australia. Perhaps if they had stayed in Cornwall she would have lived. Or was it the will of God anyway? In any event Jane had too many responsibilities remaining to her surviving family to mourn or dwell too long over her loss. In the 1840s in South Australia fifty percent of all deaths were those of infants. The mortality of children was a fact of life. Jane had been lucky that she had only lost one child out of her seven.

Jane knew her duty. She washed the child, brushed her hair and dressed her in her best dress. She then with the help of her neighbour from next door sewed up little Lizzie's unbleached fine calico shroud stitch by stitch, top sewing and hemming, until it was finally done. They carried and laid her in a crude box coffin made hastily by Richard from planks and scraps of timber given by the creek dwelling community. Women came forward with sprigs of lavender and rosemary to place in the coffin. A small handbell was rung on the march to the cemetery, and, as was the custom in such cases, the mourners all wore something white. The bottom of the grave was lined with native grass to make a softness to lay down an innocent child who had died too soon.

Chapter 33

LIFE IN THE CREEK

When the fire in the dugout's fireplace was ablaze, the white washed walls were brilliantly lit. In winter they acted as a heat bank and kept the dwelling cosy at all times. In summer, when the fire was still necessary for cooking, it could turn the home into a hot box. On hot summer nights with eight people sleeping in the dugout the atmosphere was very close with the only ventilation, not including the chimney, being two small window holes and the doorway. On extremely hot days, though, it was always cooler inside than outside. It was the hot, dry and dusty north wind days with temperatures 100 to 110°F in the shade that Jane dreaded. The heat cooked the garbage piles and cesspools near the pigsties and made them stink. In front of the dugout the ground, covered in fine clay dust after months without rain, was swept up in a blistering wind already full of grit and grass seeds collected from Burra's treeless landscape, and blown into every nook and cranny of the dwelling to cover bedding, furniture and food with a coat of fine sand. On the worst days, when the dust browned out the sun to reduce visibility, Jane and the girls would retreat inside the dugout with the door closed and hessian curtains drawn to sit it out beside a slush lamp. Arriving home from the mine Richard and the boys would have red eyes, ears and nostrils caked in dust and muddy streaks of perspiration on their faces. Sometimes Richard's beard was so impregnated with dust, sweat and dirt that it was more like a solid mass than hair. Jane always had a tub of water waiting for them which she had laboriously filled by carting buckets from the well in the afternoon heat. In Cornwall the earth was covered in green grass and the mine dirt readily washed off. In Burra it was not easy being clean.

After heavy winter rains the space between the bank and the creek became a churned up mass of sloppy and slippery mud that stuck to boots and was tramped through the dugout. Creek Street became Clod Street. Jane ruled that all boots had to be left outside. She tried bare feet but found that unless she washed them every time before entering she carried almost as much mud inside. Burra streets were churned up into such a mass of mud that they became nearly impassable to pedestrians and difficult to navigate in horse drawn vehicles. Storekeeper Mr. Coates took matters into his own hands and constructed at his own expense a length of footpath leading from each side of his store with the result that his patronage increased substantially. The road from Adelaide was also churned up, with the mud slowing bullock wagons so much that they took up to three times as long to get to Burra with supplies, resulting in higher freight costs and increased price of goods.

Meat was cheap and Jane was amazed that it seemed everyone in Australia could afford to eat it three times a day if they wanted.

Due to the proliferation of sheep, joints of mutton were common. Several butchers in Burra did their own slaughtering each day and sold fresh meat. The price of beef and mutton averaged two and a half pence a pound. This was a vast improvement on the famine conditions they had left behind in Cornwall. Jane also bought, at incredibly cheap prices from the butcher, bones and pig's trotters for making soup, lamb's tongues and tripe and tins of dripping for fuelling slush lamps and for cooking. Mutton fat dripping spread over hot toast and sprinkled with a little salt was a popular breakfast dish and a welcome change from the barley porridge in Cornwall or the "burgoo" porridge on board *Trafalgar*. Potatoes, onions and tripe were always a favourite and cheap family dish. Salted and cured beef or lamb, available from the butcher was common in the warmer weather because it did not deteriorate as quickly as fresh meat.

It was important to cook and eat meat without too much delay or it would "go off". Flies were the problem. On the worst days small ones would almost blacken the surface of the kitchen table and cover every inch of any bag containing meat. Big blowies seemed to love the comparative coolness of the dugout. Jane did her best to keep them out by hanging more hessian over the windows and cracks in the door but it made no difference as they simply zoomed down the chimney to torment her with their constant drone. The flies could blow almost anything if it suited them including clothes and bedding if they contained wool which was one of their attractions. Jane complained constantly about them. She thought they must be the work of the devil and prayed that God would strike all the evil little wretches dead. If they weren't laying maggots in the meat they were buzzing her ears all day long and smothering every square inch of her body. They made talking hazardous and hardly a day went by when she did not swallow one or two. She wished the devil would fetch them all back to hell from where they obviously came. One day when the dugout became so full of flies that the place hummed like a beehive she lit a fumigation fire in the camp oven on the floor in an endeavour to drive them out but succeeded only in evicting them temporarily and making the whole place smell smoky. In the end she had to acknowledge that it was a waste of time killing them for they came in their millions.

Fresh meat could be flyblown in hours if not looked after. Kept away from flies and treated with care it might last in the relative coolness of the dugout up to three days in summer, while in the cool of winter it might still be consumed with safety after a week or more. It was possible to dry and smoke meat in the chimney but it had to be lean, boneless and cut into small strips. If Jane didn't cook the meat the day she bought it she would rub it well with coarse salt and hang it in a closely woven jute bag tied tightly at the top. A dish underneath caught any liquid drips from the bag and when they stopped the meat was transferred to a "meat safe" made from an open weave chaff bag that had a piece of deal board placed on the bottom to create a shelf. This was tied off and suspended from the top. While the open weave of the chaff bag allowed ventilation, if the meat touched the sides flies could lay their maggots through the weave. To prevent this Jane put the meat in a calico bag before placing it on the board. Sometimes, despite all her precautions the meat had begun to deteriorate before it was cooked, or worse, had become flyblown. If that happened she calmly cut or scraped off the flyblown or decayed parts, dressed the meat with vinegar and proceeded to cook it in the normal way. This was accepted practice at the time.

While the family had plenty to eat, their diet was basic. There was very little in the way of fruit and vegetables grown in the area.

Those that were on sale in Burra were hauled from long distances by bullock wagon and were therefore expensive. Jane found that potatoes at one and a half pence a pound and pumpkins (when she could get them) kept well if she stored them in the dark on a shelf layered with dried native grass. Onions were fine, simply hung in bunches on the wall. In addition to meat, these three vegetables formed the main part of their diet together with bread, treacle, tea, sugar, salt and butter. Heavily salted to preserve it, butter was still turned into a pool of yellow rancid grease in the heat of summer which also soured milk and dried up and shrank loaves of bread. Jane regularly made her own butter from cream she had allowed to sit for a day or two to mature. This allowed it to "ripen", have a better taste and made it easier to churn. Milk was readily available in Burra from either one of the several dairies in town or from family cows the miners were allowed to graze on the mining company's land.

Goats were more popular with the Cornish community. Nearly every family along the creek, including the Dunstans, kept a nanny goat to provide a ready supply of fresh milk. The animals were easy to handle and Mary, aged 6, worked as a goatherd for a few days and a few pennies each week. Goats were also cheap to feed but their habit of stripping herbage and shrubs to the roots contributed to the bare hills of Burra where a number of them soon went feral and formed their own herds.

One of Jane's greatest pleasures was to sit down and have a cup of tea. It had been too expensive to buy in Cornwall because of their low income and government import duty nearly doubling its price. Tea was cheaper to buy in Australia and the family had much more money. It improved the taste of local water and Jane drank cup after cup. A pound of tea still cost two shillings and at that price Jane made sure it lasted as long as possible by not emptying the tea leaves from her quart teapot. When the water got low she simply added more and put it back near the fire to stew so that the last hint of flavour was extracted from the leaves. Old tea leaves were left in the pot at the end of the day and next morning, after more water was added the pot was boiled up again. Only then, if it was still too weak, would she add a quantity of new leaves. The brew acquired a peculiar harsh flavour.

While the boast of the Burra business houses was that you could buy everything from a pin to an anchor in the town was not completely true, most things were available in the shops. The main thing missing was fresh fruit and vegetables, but they had been missing for years from the lives of the great majority of the residents anyway. After they had discharged their loads of ore at the port the constant stream of bullock drays returning to Burra arrived with almost everything anyone needed including smoked codfish and salmon, dried apples and apricots, English jams, bottled gooseberries, salad oil, pickles, ginger, rice, coffee, tea, currants, raisins, mustard, sago, chocolate, cheese, prunes, tobacco and American clocks. Jane enjoyed the occasional visits of "Cheap Johns", a new class of dapper salesman, who brought their wares to town to auction, such as "The Professor" who conducted his auction on the last Saturday in July standing on a tub in Market Square. His entertaining, jesting repartee was of more value than his cheap goods and reminded her of the spruiking vendors at the Cambourne market.

"This 'ere tweed coat – observe the weave and cut – this 'ere tweed coat was made for Prince Albert after a pattern drawed by the Queen Victoria 'erself!" announced the Professor.

Every item presented had a pedigree story which the "Professor of Puffing" pushed beyond credibility so that, while no one believed it, all were entertained and put in a good humour. Jane was tempted by the shawls alleged to be from England, Scotland and France and the "De Laine Dresses" but, having due regard to her present circumstances and thinking ahead, purchased material to make a dozen diapers and some cheap mattress ticking instead. In a little more than five weeks she would be a mother again. This was, she thought, likely to be her last visit to the town shops for some time as the social mores of the day deemed it not polite for patently pregnant women to walk the streets or socialise.

Chapter 34

A BIRTH AND CHRISTMAS

As the end of her pregnancy approached Jane found it more and more difficult to carry out domestic chores requiring substantial physical effort such as carting buckets of water, lifting and emptying the washtub and chopping wood. The women in the creek were generous with their support in helping her with these duties and her shopping requirements and never walked past Jane's place without calling in to ask if they could do anything to help. Often they came with hot bread, cakes, chicken broth, eggs and even joints of cooked mutton in hand for the family. Young Mary, aged 6, surprised Jane with her capability and was a great help.

As her time drew near Jane did all she could to put her house in order and keep the place scrupulously clean and sweet just in case there were any complications with delivery that might incapacitate her for any longer than absolutely necessary – or worse, that she did not survive the labour. For the entire nine months of her pregnancy she had received no medical attention and would not receive any at the birth. There was no functioning hospital in Burra in 1849 and travelling to Adelaide to attend hospital was untenable. It was not a reasonable proposition to put a nine months pregnant woman on a bullock dray and jostle her up and down over a dreadful track for a whole week. Coach travel was an alternative but too expensive and that, together with the cost and difficulty of organising accommodation in Adelaide, made it out of the question.

Jane had only midwives attend her during the births of her seven children and fortunately there were a couple of women residing in the dugouts at the creek who would assist her. While it was certain that they had no medical training and had no conception of surgical cleanliness at least they had practical experience gained through being present at numerous births through the years and through having babies themselves. In the event of serious difficulties there were two doctors at the mine who could be called upon for assistance. When it came to giving birth Cornish mothers preferred to be attended by women and in their own home even if it was underground in an unhygienic, less than germfree environment with little privacy. Since the establishment of the creek community there had been plenty of babies born in the dugouts and some carried out in coffins not long after. Women too had died including some in middle years after giving birth many times before. Still, it was probably a better place to be than Redruth in Cornwall where cholera killed twenty-eight people in this same month.

For some reason many babies like to enter the world in the early hours of the morning and so it was with this one on 3rd September 1849. The midwives had been in attendance for several hours when they gave clear instructions to Richard and the boys to stay well away until they were sent for. Calling on help from God, all her prior experience and with the care and encouragement of the two midwives, Jane gave birth without complications. In the candlelight of the dugout one of the women held up a tiny crinkled thing with a pinkish red, screwed up face, eyes puffed up and closed, thick black hair, arms and legs thrashing about and making a loud "erk errk acck acck!" noise. He was well and truly alive.

It was the practice to keep mothers in bed for a good several days after the birth. Jane seemed to enjoy this as it was the longest period of rest she'd had for a long time. Again, the creek women were lavish in their support, providing help with chores as well as hot bread, cakes and other food. For a while there was an almost constant stream of visitors wanting to see the new baby.

Richard was delighted to have a son but always felt awkward and not in control at these times. He busied himself by making a cradle out of an old packing case, making sure that the wood was soft and had no splinters. Jane made a cover for it out of some gauze to keep the flies off and therein the tiny baby, now called William, began to thrive. Within months it was clear that he was not going to be a small child like Elizabeth was. He was a solid little chap with strong features and anything but delicate. Jane thought it was a mystery that he thrived so well considering the peculiar circumstances in which he had been conceived and born. She wondered if it was the Burra climate that made all the difference.

Richard tried his best at nursing William but was not good at it. After a few minutes William would start to squeal and Richard would have to hand him over to Jane where, after a moment's cuddle and rock in her arms, he would be silent and then giggling when Jane blew raspberries on his forehead. Perplexed, Richard resigned himself to the fact that women were better with babies than men.

While the dugout in the bank of the Burra Creek may not have been the best environment for a toddler to take his first steps, Jane knew, peering down at her sleeping baby, that she was very happy with her little Australian. Apart from Elizabeth, she and the family had survived many trials, a few hazards and numerous tribulations. The future was, of course, uncertain and no doubt would have its dangers, but for the time being Jane was content in the Burra Creek.

At the end of 1849 a census taken by the South Australian Mining Association found Burra's population totalled 3,708 persons including 1,142 children (almost a third) aged fifteen years and under. To all of them, albeit in different ways, Christmas would be important. When it should have been cold the hot weather came. It was heat like they had never known at this time of the year. At the end of a hot night, shortly after dawn several large flocks of galahs flew south east towards the River Murray, and then the heat began in earnest and blistered until dusk. The contrast with a Cornish Christmas was stark. While in Cornwall Christmas was a time for evergreen holly and ivy decorations, the residents of Creek Street decorated the front of their dugouts with green eucalyptus branches sold to them at a few pennies a bunch by bullockies returning from the Mallee scrub in carts heaped high with foliage.

In Cornwall Christmas was always a time for visiting friends and relatives and for general conviviality and so it was in Creek Street with the ladies engaging in lots of visiting, drinking tea, eating cakes and reminiscing about the home country and how different it was there at this time of the year. Each seemed to have their own special cake that they wanted everyone to taste a small piece of, claiming that the more you tasted different cakes and puddings, the greater your happiness would be in the year ahead.

On Christmas Eve there was little enthusiasm for work at the mine and the shift finished early. By mid-afternoon the mine was deserted except for a few men who stayed to make sure that the newly installed steam driven beam engine kept on with its relentless "kerplonk – kerplonk". As soon as the sun was gone small groups of children holding miners' "fatjacks" or tallow candles in their hands, or set in an old treacle tin with holes punched in, started to wend their way along the dugouts on both sides of the creek bank to stop at each doorway and sing Christmas carols hoping to be remunerated with a few pennies or sweets.

Once dark, the long line of dugouts in the creek with orange light from their fireplaces flickering out the windows and doors, and the array of candles and lanterns in groups or moving slowly along the creek bed making fluttering yellow dots provided an imposing sight. Although it was a humble circumstance there would be many children who would fondly remember Christmas in the Burra Creek where on that night there was much tenderness and laughter amid the dirt and squalor.

For those men like Richard who fancied it, Christmas was traditionally a time of drinking, celebrating and letting off steam. The hotels competed for their custom with various amusements and competitions including climbing greasy poles, wrestling bouts, dipping for apples, Aunt Sally's and jingling matches where blindfolded players in a large ring tried to catch an unmasked "jingler" who rang bells in each hand and then ducked out of the way. Outside the hotels and in the Market Square small groups of musicians set up their tin whistle, concertina and fiddle ensembles to play their particular brand of Christmas music in the hope that some pennies would fall into their upturned hats on the ground.

In competition, a group of young ladies collected together on a street corner to sing in harmony their hymns and carols in celebration of Christmas while older women gathered in their churches and chapels to sing praises to the Lord. Jane was one of them.

As always Christmas had its detriments as well as its benefits. The legal drinking age was twelve years and by that age many boys, like Richard Junior and Ben, were mine workers and so quickly adopted men's habits which included drinking. Beer was only a couple of pence a pot and after having imbibed a few ales young drinkers got up to all sorts of mischief such as the popular practice of dropping unwelcome articles down the chimneys of dugouts or covering them with a sack to smoke out the occupants. Other young men pushed unhitched carts or wagons several blocks away from where they were parked, threw stones on roofs, tied up door handles on houses and "necessaries" or simply got into a fight or made rude remarks to passing young ladies.

The two-day race meeting held at Christmas was Burra's largest annual event. On race day the shops closed at 10 am after which a procession of drays, carts, gigs, horses and people headed out to the course on the flats about a mile and a half out of town. There were races to suit the capabilities of all riders from a mile run for novices to the Burra Plate of two miles, the Hotel Keepers Stakes, a race for hacks, a Lady's Purse and a race for the losers. A "Hurdle Race for All Denominations" held on Boxing Day over a distance of one and a half miles in which there were only three starters was described by a correspondent in the *South Australian Register* newspaper:

"The Maid and The Bride with much labour were got over the first two hurdles but refused any further leaps, not liking the uncouth appearance of

*the barriers. As to Thunderbolt he stood stock still and ... returned to the
starting post, when it was decided to give it up, the stakes to be put in the
next flat race."*

The numerous publicans' booths at the track decorated with flags
were well patronised by Richard and his mining mates. A band
played in the grandstand and the local constabulary ensured that
the large crowd was well-behaved. Except for the dust, the weather
was fine. Jane and other church going ladies like her did not go to
the track as attendance was discouraged by the Minister of their
church. Richard and his eldest boy had no such inhibitions.

The boys of Burra conducted their own race meeting on
holidays. Young Ben, Henry and Wearne Dunstan all took part.
Harnessing their billy goats to the shafts of primitive box carts
they drove them flat out around a suitably laid out track with as
many as 10 or 12 competitors in each race. The winner received
a prize of lollies or marbles. It was a fun day with carts colliding
and tipping over, goats charging and head-butting anything they
took annoyance with including people, other goats and carts.
Some goats "jibbed" and refused to move while others bolted and
refused to stop after passing the finish line.

Christmas Day for the Dunstan family was one of celebration.
Jane made ginger beer and several types of biscuits and cakes
including Christmas cake as well as Christmas pudding and
sacrificed chickens (specially fattened for the purpose) from the
pens on the roof of the dugout to roast together with potatoes,
pumpkin and onions. She purchased sweets from the shops
as gifts for the children and all in it was the best Christmas the
Dunstans had celebrated for years.

Chapter 35

FLOOD AND DEATH

In 1850 the population of Burra exceeded 4,000 people and it was then the largest inland town in Australia. Bullock carts were hauling 45,000 tons of ore a year along the dirt track between Burra and Port Adelaide.

A pound of oatmeal cost six pence, beef and mutton were only two pence a pound or for the same price you could buy two pounds of potatoes. Sugar was just three pence a pound and flour one and a quarter pence per pound. You could buy a bonnet for four shillings and six pence and a handkerchief for eight pence. Straw hats cost two shillings and six pence or you could get a shirt for the same price. If you needed trousers, moleskins cost ten shillings while cheap canvas ones were only five shillings. At these prices the Dunstans, with five breadwinners in the family and no rent to pay, were doing fine.

The year started phenomenally hot and dry. Strong winds

blowing from the northern deserts for days on end turned Burra into a dust bowl. One afternoon in February, the sky suddenly darkened with clouds of copper coloured dust in which leaves and twigs from trees whirled about in wild confusion. Lightning flashed and crackled out of the soupy sky followed instantly by rolling thunder. For a few moments the wind stopped and there was a frightening stillness. Then it began. Hail came first, whipping up more clouds of dust as it pelted the earth, followed by muddy rain with big water drops impregnated with dust. Soon it settled into drenching sheets of water that fell almost vertically.

The Burra Creek, sourced from ranges to the north, flowed south collecting hundreds of little water courses on the way before funnelling between red clay banks in the Burra township. With a heavy downpour the catchment quickly gathered large volumes of water. The rain was welcome at first but then it continued in torrents for the rest of the day and late into the night. By early next morning the creek was full. Some months earlier the copper smelting company had built an earthen embankment across the creek to create a causeway for drays delivering ore from the mine leaving only a small tunnel for the water to flow through at the bottom. This became blocked causing the water to back up on the high side and flood the dugouts. On the 6th of February *The South Australian Register* newspaper reported:

"The water soon rose above the roofs of many of the huts, the inmates being glad to escape with their lives. Upwards of 80 huts were utterly destroyed, the furniture floating about in all directions … It was a sad sight to see the women and children midst the heavy rain endeavouring to save their furniture from the flood which had destroyed their dwellings, and having no place to go to for shelter. Many found shelter in the stables belonging to the Smelters Home public house, and in Messrs Thompson and Keckwick's

stores. *The officers of the South Australian Mining Association rendered assistance to the unfortunate sufferers by sending the carts belonging to the mine to assist in conveying such furniture as could be saved from the flood to a place of shelter, and as many families were admitted into the storehouses now erected as could find room."*

Another thirty families were temporarily housed in a large building known as "Robbins Stables" while others found refuge in churches and in cottages whose occupants had extended their hospitality.

As the Dunstans' dugout was further up the creek at a higher elevation they escaped most of the inundation with water coming in and flooding only the first room of their dwelling for a few inches depth. Jane had the sense to grab the family's stash of promissory notes and cash before vacating hurriedly with five-month-old William in her arms and Ann and Mary in tow. Richard and his four boys formed a chain to pass the family's possessions up the bank to place on the roof of the dugout where Jane and the girls stood guard over them. All this took place in the mud and the rain and the dark with treacle tin candle lanterns the only light source. Luckily, it was summer time and not a cold winter night. When daylight came small groups of drenched women, some frightened, some weeping, some holding their pregnant bellies, could be seen still standing guard with their children next to their pile of wet belongings on the creek bank. When the water subsided many miners found that their huts had "caved in" and all they could do was start excavating a new dugout further up the creek as alternative accommodation was expensive and in short supply. As soon as they could get access the Dunstans lit a big fire in their place and kept it going for days to dry the house out. In the meantime they managed with temporary accommodation.

As usual Jane sought solace in her religion. The creek community was largely made up of Cornish people with regular church going habits that followed one of the three Methodist branches of Wesleyans, Primitive Methodists or Bible Christians. Each with their own petty differences, these groups flourished in Burra, but in times of need like the present the members of their congregations gave to each other vital support and encouragement of both a practical and spiritual kind. Every Sunday morning Jane and the children joined the great assemblage of well-dressed persons coming from the creek and wending their way to different houses of worship. Jane made sure that on Sunday the family was well turned out in their best clothes. Rising early she heated flat irons in the fire, then cleaned their bases on a damp hessian pad so that they would leave no mark on the clothes before ironing them on the family table.

Any spare time she could find was devoted to duties at the Wesleyan Chapel which in addition to regular church sessions included tea meetings, choir practice, temperance meetings and special occasions such as annual picnics and Easter celebrations when on Easter Monday the church members marched with flags and banners flying to Market Square where they formed a circle and sung some hymns before marching back for their tea.

While Jane escaped from constantly living in dirt to the pristine sanctity of the church, Richard's consolation was the frivolity and fellowship of the tap room. Although by 1850 there were four hotels in Burra, he and his fellow Cornishman always drank at the Miners Arms in Market Square and certainly not at the Burra Hotel frequented by mine management and business professionals. After six days working and sleeping underground Richard felt he would go insane if he did not get away from Creek Street for awhile. His persistent cough had returned and he found that after a few drinks the relaxing effects of alcohol seemed to give him relief. At least he felt better, and who could blame a man for washing mining dust from his clogged throat with a drink or two, or three, now and then. Richard had always been a moderate and responsible drinker but since arriving at Burra he was drinking more. He blamed his thirst on the hot weather but his poor health, responsibilities for a wife and seven children, their present living conditions and no immediate prospect of improving their circumstances caused him to have bouts of depression so that he needed more often to have what he called a "serious drink". Most hotels remained open "on the sly" past the official closing times. Although being "found drunk on the Sabbath" was a serious offence enforced by the local constabulary it failed to prevent some miners over indulging to such an extent that they were unable to work the next day known as "Maze Monday".

The terrain of the Burra Creek made it difficult for miners to find their correct dugout when returning in the dark at night from the Burra pubs. There was no street lighting in Creek Street and men walked into and tripped over the chimneys on top of the bank or used the sides of them as urinals, often with little accuracy. At times they blundered into poultry pens or pigsties, tumbled down the embankment, tripped over log pews, wandered into the creek or entered the wrong dugout. After Richard made such a grand homecoming one Sunday night and then vomited in the bed he discovered next morning that one of the world's greatest misfortunes was to be on the receiving end of a tongue lashing from Jane.

While his head was still aching and swirling with guilt she bundled him off to one of the regular Monday morning Wesleyan Temperance Meetings where he was harangued by the incumbent Reverend William Lowe and several reformed drunkards on the evils of drink. The first man, Adam, he was told, was a teetotaller. Among the evils incurred by drunkenness there were no fewer than forty-two diseases of the body. Teetotalism had proved the best news in the world next to the Gospel. Drunkenness was the worst kind of slavery. Poor drunkards trying total abstinence would soon find the benefit of it. At the end of the meeting Richard and a number of his sorry mates signed the pledge book to abstain in future. He was a model of sobriety for two weeks and then again reverted to the numbing effects of alcohol. He was labelled a "backslider" and thereafter Jane had to march him to Temperance Meetings about once a month to re-sign the book. He always had plenty of mates to accompany him. At one meeting twenty-nine names were added to the pledge book but despite such mass signings the demon drink continued to prevail.

Very few miners had unaffected lungs by the time they reached forty. Richard was now thirty-eight but looked older and was showing the symptoms of serious silicosis damage or "miner's complaint" as a result of inhaling dust particulate all his life. His cough had now become persistent, his cheeks were hollow and he always looked weary and half asleep. He had lost weight over the past year and was starting to look gaunt. Only a few weeks after the family moved back into the dugout he caught a nasty cold. If Jane had been in Cornwall she would have ground up the roots of some stinging nettles in a mortar and pestle and then squeezed the pulp in some muslin to extract the juice. This she would have mixed with honey and dosed Richard with several teaspoonfuls each day in a glass of warm water. But stinging nettles did not yet grow in Burra, so instead of their juice she substituted a little vinegar. His cough developed into chronic bronchitis and the medicine didn't stop it. He had to stop work.

Soon he was coughing all day and night with only a few

minutes between episodes. His chest crackled and he spat a coloured sputum regularly into a tin he kept near the bed. Now he had pneumonia. He lost all appetite and as each day went by got thinner and weaker until his eyes seemed to recede into his head and he became increasingly confused. One day his jaw dropped, the coughing stopped, his breathing slowed and every now and then it stopped. But he was not yet dead and he lingered in this state for days when every now and then he would suck into his rattling chest a few more rapid breaths as though he was trying to make up for the ones he missed. From time to time he opened his closed eyelids but his gaze was empty. So that he was never left alone family members, including young Ann, rostered turns to stay by his bed to share his suffering and torment. The gaps between the heavy sucking breath increased but always began again with a horrid snorkelling sound. From the appearance of his waxen face he might as well have been dead but his body refused to recognise the fact and kept up with its useless, agonising, intermittent, noisy inhalations until at last there was a complete and silent stillness in the room so that Richard could rest in peace. Jane had known for weeks that he was dying but when he did she could not contain the deepest soulful cry rushing from the very essence of her being. He died underground where he had spent much of his life. It was the 7th May 1850.

Chapter 36

FIRES AND DEATH

The mining community was familiar with death and Richard's had been expected. Two of Jane's neighbours who were women of some maturity and experience came forward at once to console and assist her with the laying out. With a heavy silence they slowly and deliberately cleaned his body with warm water, soap and a wash cloth, clipped his nails, trimmed and combed his hair and gave him his last shave. Leaky orifices were plugged before he was dressed in his best and placed with his clay pipes and some tobacco in a rudimentary coffin which the boys had purchased from a local furniture maker and carried back to the dugout. Jane did the final arranging of his limbs and secured his mouth shut with a band of cloth around his head. The rustic front door that had marked the threshold between Richard's place and the rest of the world was removed and each end placed on two large boxes in the front sleeping room to provide a platform upon which his coffin could rest with his feet pointing to the exit. He had died on a weekday and as the non-working day of Sunday was the most common day for working class funerals it would be several days before the body would leave the dugout. For Jane and the rest of the family this was an awful time of disorientation and shock. There was a fear associated with going to sleep in the same house as a dead body so it was the practice to have someone sit up all night with the corpse. Because it was important for the boys to get their sleep so they could carry on working at the mine this task was undertaken by Jane, on a roster basis, with the ladies who assisted in the laying out. Candles and slush lamps kept burning all night provided a subdued yellow light for the person on corpse watch. To help "keep the body sweet" a large dish of salt was placed on Richard's chest to absorb odours and sprigs of lavender bush and some fresh eucalyptus leaves placed in the coffin which was kept open but covered constantly with muslin to keep out the flies.

As was the custom, people from the community called in during the day to pay their respects. Every visitor brought something – sprigs of lavender for the coffin, candles to keep the light going, cakes, scones and hot bread, pots of broth and even legs of roast mutton. When someone died the first thing friends and neighbours did was to cook some scones or pasties or make some soup. Jane kept the kettle on the fire and made lots of tea for the callers. By the end of each day she was exhausted but glad to have been kept occupied. On Saturday evening, about an hour before sunset, a small group of ladies gathered at the front of the dugout and sang all the hymns they knew and then repeated their favourites.

It was a blessing that Richard had died towards the end of autumn when the weather was cool, for by the time Sunday arrived there was a distinct stench of death in the dugout. His skin had yellowed and the lines of fatigue and pain that had become his permanent features of late had left his now expressionless face. He looked really dead. The lid of his coffin was fixed by Richard Junior and his brother Ben just before it left the dugout.

As chief mourner, Jane prepared for the day by making a dress and blouse out of a piece of black serge. A neighbour on one side lent her black stockings and a friend further up the creek provided a black hat and veil. If the funeral had taken place in Cornwall, Richard would have been buried in the neighbourhood church graveyard but here, in the colonies, dead bodies were banished beyond the realm of the living to a cemetery outside the limits of the township. After a service at the Wesleyan Chapel the Reverend William Lowe led the coffin carried in relay by two teams of six miners with Jane and the children next, followed by the church choir singers and then a long line of mourners, comprising nearly every resident of Creek Street, walking in pairs. The choir and mourners sung hymns all the way to the cemetery led by the Minister who recited one verse at a time before it was sung, which was the usual Sunday church method used to accommodate the many who could not read. To hear the rich natural voices of Cornish singers echoing down the valley of the Burra Creek and fading as the long line of mourners in black marched slowly into the distance towards the cemetery was a moving experience.

After the burial service was over and nearly everyone had gone, Jane, heavy with grief, sank to her knees on the grave's edge and began a discourse with Richard. It was her fault, she said, that she had taken him away from his beloved Cornwall and the house he had built above ground out of cob. She knew he would not have come out here but for her insistence. She was so sorry and would miss him so much, loved him even more and sobbed that she didn't know what to do. She wished she could turn back time and if only she had not been so stubborn and stupid and selfish. And, but for the children, she would gladly join him in the grave. For him, she would try, try to make a better life for the children and upon his grave that was her promise and her solemn oath. She continued in this manner going over the same recriminations and promises again and again for some twenty minutes until eventually her eldest son, Richard, now male head of the household, took her by the arm and led her back to their dugout.

For the next twelve months, custom required Jane to wear full mourning dress and a widow's cap of the deepest black when she left the house. Moreover, it was considered disrespectful for a widow to leave the house at all for the first few weeks after her husband's death or in the next twelve months to accept formal invitations or be seen in a place of public entertainment. After twelve months the dress code could be relaxed to "half mourning" which would allow the colours of grey or lavender to be worn. Ladies' dress shops in Adelaide devoted entire departments to "Mourning Bazaars" where all sorts of paraphernalia signifying grief could be bought including mourning brooches, hats, rings, parasols, dresses and veils.

In all of Victorian England marriages never lasted more than fourteen years on average before the death of a partner. Richard and Jane's marriage had lasted fourteen years and eleven months.

Jane's new black dress and chilling grief seemed to go well with the shades of grey that settled over the creek valley and blotted out the sun as mid winter approached. Back in Cornwall at the zenith of the summer solstice the evenings were magical when the sun at its furthest point north seemed to stop for long moments on the horizon before setting. At Midsummer celebrations in June each year, in accordance with a very ancient custom, the Cornish held bonfire nights to celebrate the grandeur of high summer, with the sun at its full strength and glory in the sky promising ripeness to the growing fruits and grain. Although it was midwinter in Burra the Cornish community still insisted on celebrating Midsummer Day, on the 24th June and calling it by that name. At the start of the half day holiday granted to miners it was customary to fire salutes from a line up of hollow logs charged like cannons, but only with gunpowder, and fired at a safe distance with fuses. Some blew up, some misfired and those that did go off were more impressive for the smoke they created than the noise they made. Children began building bonfires as an essential part of the activities several months before the event. Any available timber, shrubbery and burnable rubbish including old rags, tar barrels and animal bones were heaped up. The cleanup of rubbish was of great benefit to the community.

When lit, the fires flared quickly and soon after, thinking that they might miss out on a better show, boys would be running from fire to fire with fire sticks, waving them around, and yelling "Hip Hip hooray, Midsummer Day is passing away". Eventually the bonfires collapsed sending a shower of sparks up in the evening air and later, when they were reduced further, potatoes were produced for roasting in the embers. Some people practised leaping through low flames in the belief that it ensured good luck and protected the performer from bad influences. Daredevil children did it just for fun. Home-made fireworks added colour to the scene. One recipe required a mixture of sulphur, chlorate of potash, lamp black and nitrate of strontia to be lit in a tin dish for the production of a devilishly looking red flame and smoke. Cornish children were also enthusiastic lighters of rockets and crackers. A favourite trick was to blacken their hands with soot, sneak up behind someone sitting in front of and dreamily watching the fire, then rub black all over their face before bolting into the darkness. Naughty boy laughter would then be heard from numerous untraceable directions.

Bonfires were lit in Market Square. Trestle tables were set up piled with pasties, cakes, buns and biscuits for sale and a pile of potatoes to roast when the fire died down. Publicans set up liquor booths, several bands of musicians plied their particular trade, young girls in their best smocks joined in dancing, and singing, wrestling and hurling continued until dawn.

Jane's recent widow status kept her quarantined from these festivities so she remained in the dugout with 10-month-old William and allowed young Ann, aged 5, and Mary, nearly 8, to accompany the four boys Richard, Ben, Henry and Wearne while attending the bonfires on the creek bank, after first extracting undertakings from them all that they would be very careful, look after each other and remain together. She had confidence in the boys who were now the only breadwinners in the family and felt that they needed what relief they could get from their constant drudgery at the mine. Without their father's income there was less money to support the family but fortunately the mine management had declared Richard Junior, now in his fifteenth year, "capable of doing a day's work" which allowed him, as a fully qualified miner, to operate his own pitch under the tribute system like his father had done so that money was not the problem it might have been.

When the fires had gone down on bonfire night young Ann had watched with envy the children having fun leaping through low flames on the edge of the fire and wanted to try it herself but was restrained by her older siblings. Some three months later a small group of children decided that they would have their own mini bonfire among the chimneys on top of the creek bank. They all had great fun jumping through the flames until Ann stumbled and fell head long into the embers. She rolled out of the fire with her hair and dress alight and ran screaming in pain along the bank. The faster she ran the more the flames burnt and the more agonising were her screams. By the time she collapsed at the front door of her dugout the flames had gone out but most of her dress and nearly all her hair were burnt away. Her screaming had stopped. She just shivered and moaned and could not speak as she lay hunched up in the dirt with smoke wafting from her little body.

She had suffered major burn injuries with shock from heat and pain, respiratory distress and fluid loss arising from increased permeability of blood vessels in the burn areas. Jane was distraught but there was little she or anyone else could do. The correct treatment of burn injuries was not understood and there was then no oxygen or intravenous fluid resuscitation available. Ann died about four hours after the accident on Saturday, 19th October 1850.

An inquest into her death convened by Magistrate and Coroner William Lang was held at the Miners Arms hotel on Monday 21st October 1850. It was the normal practice to swear in a jury of twelve men to decide the facts of the case but on this occasion the Coroner swore in a jury of twenty-four men to preside at the hearing which was an indication that the community regarded this death as a particularly important matter to adjudicate on. One witness testified that he had seen Ann running along crying with her clothes on fire. Dr. George Bull gave evidence that her injuries were so severe that recovery was hopeless and stated that on the previous day he had seen Ann and some other children making a fire and jumping over it and that he had cautioned them of the danger. The jury returned a verdict of "accidental death". Curiosity, trying to imitate what the children had seen others do on bonfire night and a lack of understanding of the dangers of playing with fire had resulted in tragedy.

A surprising number of mourners turned up to Ann's funeral. Though only five years old, she had touched the hearts of many along the Burra Creek with her always cheerful and polite personality. Her coffin was carried from the creek to the church and then, after the service, to the cemetery by six young girls dressed in white. As it passed along the streets people who had stood in silence fell in behind the small but growing crowd of mourners. Many had been genuinely moved and disturbed by her tragic death. When the coffin bearers stopped for a rest they all spontaneously sung a popular psalm.

Jane felt numb with the loss of a third member of her family in little more than nineteen months. When the hot November northerly winds started to blow she found it difficult to breath. She was sick of the dust, flies and mosquitoes and hated living in the dirt of the Burra Creek. She was always amazed when thunderstorms blew in with no warning. Some of her friends and neighbours had also died from undiagnosed fevers. But she still had her eldest daughter Mary, four working sons and baby William to live for and, to her, Australia, although a harsh and different earth, remained a land of abundance and freedom compared to Cornwall. She couldn't afford the luxury of extravagant grief. There were too many things to do and too many blessings to count.

The upside of living in a dugout was that at least there was little furniture to polish and she was delighted when a pair of swallows took up residence. They flew in and out of the fixed open window as they pleased and constructed a marvellous little bottle shaped nest out of mud pellets on the dugout roof. It was only a few weeks after it was finished that she heard the "peep peep" of baby chicks. She told the children that swallows brought good luck and while they could watch them they could never disturb them or their luck would fly away.

Although for much of the time Richard and Jane had not needed to talk to each other she missed being able to do that more than anything. She often found herself thinking that she would discuss "this or that" with him when he got home – then realising he would not come.

Chapter 37

MORE TROUBLE

The burgeoning population of the Burra Creek was becoming a fertile breeding ground for all sorts of quarrels, disturbances, public nuisance and even crimes. A government census taken in January 1851 found that 1,800 people now resided in the creek dugouts comprising 340 families with 653 children under fourteen years. The close quartered environment of creek side living caused stresses resulting in neighbour falling out with neighbour and sometimes civil or police court cases. Heavy drinking among the miners led to spousal arguments with wife beating an all too common consequence. Stray goats ate washing and fights between children generated arguments between their parents.

Resident Magistrate William Lange was kept busy in his tiny court room with cases from the creek and the rest of Burra. Drunkenness, disorderly behaviour and petty theft of clothing from lines or small items left outside dwellings were the most common offences. Minor assaults, such as stone throwing and hair pulling by the women in the creek and indecent language charges were also regular cases, as were assault charges between drunken men. One creek dweller claimed that his next-door neighbour had stolen eggs from under his fowls and went next door and kicked up a row. After receiving a lecture from his Worship and apologising to the court he was discharged. Cases alleging that the keeping of pigs in the creek was creating a danger to health or an intolerable nuisance were common with the defendants usually being released on their undertaking to pay court costs and remove the pigs. Every once in a while someone was charged with "furious riding" down the main street and fined £2 or fourteen days' gaol.

Larrikinism was sometimes a problem on Saturday nights when drunken youths hanging around the town square in the dark offended passing young ladies with bad language or obscene songs. Nearly every week the court dealt with cases of forgery involving promissory notes or money orders circulating as local currency, where crude alterations of the words and figures of monetary amounts were made. More serious crimes of burglary and robbery and even one case of murder also came before the court.

Before the year had finished Burra would boast nine hotels which was one for less than every 500 people including women and children. Jane was not impressed – to her Burra was a sinful place. At the other extreme there were ten separate religious congregations, many in open opposition to the hotels and all competing among themselves for souls to save. Along High Street and around Market Square shops and businesses were flourishing. There were four or five hairdressers, three chemists, and a public doctor – even a practising solicitor. Stores and shops included milliners, tailors, cobblers, a watchmaker, eating houses, drapers, ironmongers, general stores, blacksmiths, and there was a subscription library open to all members of the public.

The year 1851 was not a good year for Burra. A continuing drought had depleted pasturage available for bullocks causing the carting of wood from the Murray Scrub for the copper smelting works to almost cease. Of twenty-one furnaces only five were burning by April. Hay carted from Adelaide now cost £10 per ton compared to the usual £3 per ton. Wood was so scarce and expensive in Burra that it resulted in families conducting clandestine night-time raids on mining company trees and wood stockpiles.

Everything about the weather changed when on Monday, 12th May 1851, around 5 p.m. storm clouds over the Burra Hills turned a solid black. After a few stabs of forked lightning two thunderstorms described as "waterspouts" burst over the township. Within half an hour a wall of water was rushing down the creek again at a record height pushing everything before it including horses, a heavy dray, fences, planks and posts, thirty or forty pigs, empty casks, huge logs of wood, fowls and ducks. Men carried away little pigs, women, and children in all directions, and women waded up to their knees in water calling out for their children.

The water again banked up on the causeway bridge to the smelter and again many dugouts were flooded and destroyed but again there were no fatalities. Jane's dwelling received a more serious flooding this time with the water level reaching higher than before but there was still no structural damage done as her dugout was built higher than most. It was the mud and the mess and the stink of rubbish left by the flood that upset her more than anything. A child's rag doll caught in a branch, a drowned pig, dead chickens and broken furniture – all a frightening reminder of what might have been the worst for the family. She missed Richard.

Once again the community came to the help of the homeless. The Reverend James Pollitt of the Anglican Church opened the church schoolroom to receive them. The Postmaster, Mr. Powell and his wife provided assistance and Captain Henry Roach from the mine provided sheds for shelter and horses and carts to transport belongings. This flood washed out over the cemetery, which was then situated on the lower western side of the Burra Creek, and swept away many of the modest wooden crosses and mounds of dirt marking the graves, including Richard's, Elizabeth's and Ann's, to the great distress of Jane. Now she was uncertain as to precisely where their bodies lay. There was no exact spot where she and the children could stand and place a small bunch of flowers and remember. The cemetery trustees said they would try and re-mark the graves but they never did, and instead moved the burial ground to a slightly higher elevation on the eastern side of the creek where all future internments would take place. The earth that he had exploited all his life had now truly swallowed up every trace of Richard Dunstan.

The second flood of the year arrived four weeks later on the 8th June. A dreadful storm of hail rain and thunder hit the township around six o'clock and after dark the creek rose considerably higher than the last flood. By about seven o'clock all the houses situated on low ground in the township were a foot deep in water; and there was great concern that lives would be lost in the creek. The *Adelaide Observer* newspaper reported on the 14th June that the causeway again caused problems when it collapsed around 11 p.m. with the result that:

"the immense mass of water which was dammed by the obstruction of the bridge suddenly rushed down the Creek at a fearful rate, carrying away everything in its course. Immediately on observing the bridge give way, some men who stood by run (sic) along the banks of the Creek, crying out in the greatest alarm – "The bridge is gone; turnout, turnout." – The signal of danger thus given passed down the creek with the rapidity of electricity, and in an instant all was bustle and confusion. The distressing cries of women and children were heard a long-distance. Some of the families were in bed at the time, and so rapid and fearful was the rush of water that they were compelled for the safety of their lives to turn out in their nightclothes and make the best of their way in many places through three and four feet of water to gain the tops of the banks."

Men, women and children on the far side bank were left stranded, huddled in their nightclothes to suffer the piercing cold and pitiless rain which continued through the night. One man, a widower, who left three surviving and now orphaned small children died when his dugout roof fell in on him while he was trying to remove his furniture. Entire sections of bank were washed away leaving huge holes where there had been homes. The Dunstans' dugout suffered more damage this time and would require a good deal of shoring up as well as drying out before it could be re-occupied. This was the third time in 16 months the family had been flooded and Jane had endured enough of them. Again, public houses, churches, chapels, stables and all manner of sheds were utilised as temporary shelter.

Motivated by the occurrence of the first 1851 flood on 12th May, and at this stage unaware of the second flood on 8th June, the secretary of the mine in Adelaide Henry Ayres wrote on 9th June to the accountant at Burra to post a notice on the door of the blacksmith shop at the mine reading:

"NOTICE TO PERSONS LIVING IN THE BANKS OF THE
BURRA CREEK.
Notice is hereby given that from and after the first day of December next
no person residing in the caverns of the Burra Creek will be employed by the
South Australian Mining Association and all parties continuing to reside
therein after the above date, will be regarded as Trespassers and treated as
such.
This Notice will be peremptorily enforced.
By Order of the Board of Directors. (Signed) Henry Ayres. Secretary."

The day after Ayers sent his notice, and before it had a chance to be posted in Burra, the creek dwellers were hit with yet another flood two days after the last and the third within four weeks. The weather had been fine without any material fall of rain in the vicinity during the last night and day, when people cleaning up in the creek heard a strange rumbling sound coming from upstream. It was water tumbling and roaring along the bed of the creek. There were no fatalities but again the level rose rapidly tore down all obstacles in its path and washed them away in the muddy torrent including thirteen bullock drays belonging to the smelting works, their wheels going round like paddles of a steamer.

Again the creek dwellers shovelled and mopped, washed and cleaned, dried out and recovered and rebuilt what they could. Creek Street was a scene of dreadful devastation. When floodwaters finally receded they left behind decomposed vegetable matter, pools of mud, destroyed and silted up dugouts, dead animals and wretched and impoverished people in a deplorable condition dependent for shelter on the kindness of their more fortunate friends. Complete strangers took in refugees from the flood. The Cornish had a motto of "One and All" derived from an old fellowship song and at times like these they stuck together and helped each other to persevere even when all rational hopes of success had disappeared.

Dismally depressed by the course of natural events the Dunstans and other families of the creek were now confronted with the ultimatum in the notice from Henry Ayres, Mine Secretary, that if they remained living in their dugouts after the 1st December they would be dismissed from employment with the mine and be regarded as trespassers.

On the 10th July democracy of sorts came to South Australia when its first election for the State Legislative Council since the foundation of the colony in 1836 was conducted. But as voting rights were given only to adult males who owned property worth £100 or rented a residence for at least £10 per annum, the creek dwellers living rent-free in dugouts valued at much less than £100 clearly didn't qualify. As a woman Jane was excluded on grounds of gender as well as property. Election day was a non event in Creek Street with work as usual.

Chapter 38

GOLD!

Three days after the last flood, news reached Burra on 13th June that gold had been discovered at Bathurst in New South Wales. By now many of the Creek Street dwellers had had enough of the creek and their fill of Burra. Miners looking for a new start began to talk about going to the goldfields. Burra did not have a local newspaper and the populace relied on news in the Adelaide papers which arrived by coach two or three days after being published. The New South Wales diggings were reported on 1st July as "large" with about 2,000 diggers and one nugget found that weighed forty-six and a half ounces. There was "ample room and gold for thousands" a report claimed. The news was enough for a few experienced Burra miners to proceed post-haste to the Bathurst goldfields but the cautious majority, including Jane and her family, stayed put.

On 1st July 1851 the Port Phillip District officially became the Colony of Victoria and by the end of the following week the Victorian press was reporting gold discoveries. By 15th August Adelaide papers stated that the discoveries had "become tangible with 100 men at work", and five days later (quoting Melbourne newspapers) that "wealth of unlimited extent abounds". One party was said to have obtained a quarter of a pound of gold in three days and another report claimed that gold had been discovered in the heart of Melbourne by two children playing in the dirt.

Kenneth Campbell in Melbourne wrote to his brother in Adelaide "that upwards of 1,000 people had left for the diggings ... There is nothing but gold. All business is at a standstill ... in point of fact they are all gold mad. There are several parties making £100 per day. This you may rely on as a fact". His letter was published in the Adelaide press on 20th October.

By this stage the glowing reports from Victoria were too much for many mining families to resist. Although the pursuit of gold was the catalyst that sent them on their way to Victoria their real motivation was the attainment of better lives for themselves and their families, to live in better homes and communities, and to achieve good health and happiness. To find gold was the best chance they had of bettering themselves, of gaining financial independence to provide for old age and sickness and to give a better education to the next generation. By mid October more than 2,000 South Australians began tramping overland to the goldfields.

Reports soon started to come in from the newly discovered Mount Alexander diggings indicating that they were going to be richer than anything yet seen. Over a period of four weeks in November-December 1851 the weekly gold escort from Mount Alexander brought down to Melbourne 6,486 ounces in the first week, 10,428 ounces in the second week, 13,783 ounces in the third week, and 23,750 ounces in the fourth week. These fabulous amounts reported in the Adelaide press removed any doubts in the minds of those still at Burra as to whether they should join the gold rush. Miners who continued to live in the creek dugouts after 1st December were facing dismissal under the terms of notice given by Henry Ayres anyway. By now most of them had developed plans to decamp to the goldfields after that date.

It didn't take Jane long to make the decision to leave. Burra had not been good to her family. She'd had enough of it. It was the possibility that things might change for the better that brought them to Australia in the first place. The decision now to go to the goldfields was based on the same, albeit perhaps remote, chance that this time they might remake their lives for the better. It was a risk, but with that went a feeling of elevated spirit, ambition and independence as well as adventure.

A sea journey from Adelaide to Melbourne for Jane and her six children was out of the question because of the cost. The cheapest means of transport was by bullock dray and her thoughts immediately turned to Red. He had brought the family to Burra safely and by the end of the journey Jane began to admire his skill and ability as a teamster. She already knew about his faults but figured it was better to deal with the devil she knew than any unknown quantity. Bullock drivers were now deserting Burra on a daily basis to head East with passengers and freight and enquiries soon located Red who had been thinking himself about going to the diggings. A bargain between them was soon struck, but he insisted on two special conditions. First, that young Richard would agree to work as his "offsider" in driving the bullock team and second, that Jane would do all the cooking. Before the end of November there were many empty dugouts in the creek that owners had simply walked away from. It was difficult to sell a proper above ground cottage in Burra and impossible to sell a dugout. What had started as a trickle of miners and others decamping for the goldfields was turning into a flood.

With their meagre possessions loaded aboard Red's dray *Constance* the Dunstan family joined a line up of conveyances early one mid December morning in Market Square. At the head of the line were several well horsed wagons and carts which were then followed by more numerous bullock drays yoked to teams of either four, six, or eight bullocks. Red and the other dray men, impatient to start, chewed their pipe stems and lent on their whip handles as the women and children climbed aboard. Jane climbed up with Mary, now aged 9, and little William, 2 years and 3 months. Richard Junior, Benjamin, Henry and Wearn elected to walk. Family cows and goats were tied with leaders to the back of drays and some had dogs tethered to the axle underneath. Chickens, contained in coops made from small saplings, and wooden water barrels were lashed to the sides.

The words "Gee up" directed to the horses at the front started a chain reaction that was soon taken up by the teamsters with appropriate hollers of encouragement and cracks of their whips down the line. Bullocks dug in their hooves to take the strain of the weighted drays, harnesses and yokes creaked, chains clanked, iron tyred wheels turned and they were away. Townsfolk remaining clapped and cheered hurrahs and shouted goodbyes, some of them promising they would see their friends later at the diggings when they followed on. As the convoy headed down the road towards Adelaide Jane took one last look in the direction of the cemetery where Richard, Elizabeth and Ann were buried.

It comforted Jane that she was travelling with Cornish friends and people she knew from the creek in their little convoy of five bullock drays. She was pleased also that Red still had the same bullocks in his team. Looked after, they were capable of a hard working life of ten or twelve years or more. Their familiar faces and names added to the family's sense of well-being, with an added sense of security provided by Scrapper although he was now missing a few canine teeth and showing more grey hair around his jowls. As the ponderous teams ambled past dwellings along Commercial Street in the direction of Adelaide residents waved and wished them luck. After passing the Burra Hotel it was a clear run to the Sod Hut Inn eight miles out. It was now a substantial building made from brick and stone and no longer built with sod. Bearded men in cabbage tree hats, moleskins and flannel shirts clustered under the veranda drinking beer and sucking on their clay pipes. The publican's business was booming with the passing trade. The problem was, it was passing one way and most of it would not return. The convoy joined a dozen or so other drays and carts stopped for the night with camps already set up and fires crackling.

The road between Burra and Adelaide had not improved since the Dunstans last travelled on it and, if anything, had got worse due to the constant use over the years by ore-carrying bullock drays and all manner of other vehicles and animals. They travelled south much the same way they had come north via Apoinga, along the River Light, then to Kapunda, She Oak Log Inn, Gawler, Harvey's Inn at the Little Para River and on through Dry Creek to Adelaide arriving there in little more than seven days.

In Adelaide they pulled onto a vacant acre of land between King William and Waymouth Streets near the post office where there were already several other drays of overlanders camped for the night. By agreement with Red it was decided to stay there for two nights to give everyone a chance to buy provisions for the trip and the goldfields.

Jane's first priority was to go to the office of the South Australian Mining Association at Waterhouse's building in Rundle Street where she could convert her stash of Burra promissory notes issued by the mine in payment of the boys' wages into cash. She then returned to the dray and secreted the sovereigns obtained in a little chamois leather belt she made and sewed into her corset's stay bodice which she would wear until she reached the goldfields.

Adelaide shopfronts quickly developed new displays to make the most of marketing essential requisites to the future diggers. Goods and chattels suitable for normal trade were relegated to the back of stores while wares and articles suitable for overlanders and gold mining were put on show. Walkways outside shops were stacked with goods to attract attention. There were shovels, picks, coils of rope, washing cradles, axes, hatchets, whips and wedges, camp ovens, cattle bells, hand saws, all manner of tin ware from quart pots to teapots, plates, pannikins, coffee pots, stacks of washing tubs and nests of buckets. If you wanted to really add to the load you could pick up a couple of crowbars and stone hammers.

As professional miners the Dunstan boys already owned the basic tools required but they did buy some gold prospecting pans with rims and handles. To them digging was not a problem. They had done nothing but dig in the dirt all their lives. They also bought half a dozen each of new hemp and hessian bags, some manila cordage, extra tarpaulins, a pair of good boots each, and two guns. A gun of some sort was an essential piece of equipment for an overlander. Self defence had to be considered where the correct presumption was that every man on the track would be armed with a weapon of some kind. Moreover, a good shot had plenty of chances to put meat on the table in Australia and the opportunity to hunt any native game without being charged with poaching was too good to miss. Back in Cornwall it was still a crime. The boys had to pay more money than the two old double barrelled muzzle loading shotguns were worth due to the demand from overlander's pushing up the price. More than just a few shots had gone down their barrels which were a little thinner now than when new and the chequering on the handgrips of the wooden stocks had worn smooth, but they would do.

The Adelaide newspapers were full of advertisements designed to attract the custom of overlanders. Mr. Philip Lee's Clothing Establishment in Hindley Street announced that he could supply every article for the bush and gold regions "at prices that cannot fail to astonish", claiming that "outfits you'll get very cheap at P Lee's if you take a peep". Others advertised gold washing sieves, washing dishes, comfortable tents cradles for gold marquees and tarpaulins. A plethora of advertisements proclaimed the beneficial effects of patent pills and remedies that every overlander should take with them. One advertisement claimed that "Doctor Graham's Antibilious and Digestive pills (were) the only medicine in the colony which can be taken with perfect safety to travellers". Another said that Holloway's Pills would cure asthma and fever "at the point of death" as well as "venereal affections," and piles. Jane purchased a bottle of Kearsley's Original Widow Welsh's Female Pills which were, among other things, "eminently useful in windy disorders", and Red bought some Parrs Life Pills which were said to "revive animal spirits and import a lasting strength to the body". Food advertised as suitable for travelling included dried fish, salted herrings, hams, bacon, cheese and ship's biscuits with one advertisement declaring "Don't go without biscuits".

Rundle Street, Adelaide, looking east.

[S.T. Gill, on stone, c1851. Courtesy of the State Library of South Australia. B2430.]

While Jane refused to entertain the idea of stocking up on the dreaded ship's biscuits it was no small matter to get together food provisions sufficient to sustain two adults and six children for the estimated six weeks it would take to get to the goldfields. She settled on buying basic supplies of flour, barley, oats, salted meat, flitches of bacon, potatoes, onions, salt, tea, sugar, treacle, raisins and dried apples which she calculated they would survive on. She was nonetheless hopeful that to a certain extent additional provisions could be got on the way. With the purchase of some soap, reels of cotton, Lucifer matches, vinegar, bicarbonate of soda and castor oil she thought her shopping was done until her "helpers" Mary and little William put in a requisition for a quantity of boiled sweets to sustain them on the track.

Staggering back to the dray with arms so full of supplies she could not see her feet Jane rolled her ankle in a pothole and the parcels went in all directions as she pitched face forward towards the ground. Moments before impact a strong arm hooked under her waist and saved her from what was going to be a nasty fall but did not prevent her and the owner of the arm both rolling around in a dusty embrace on the ground.

"I beg your pardon Mrs.," he said as he helped her up.

"Oh my stars! No, thank you for saving me. I was headed for a complete cropper only for you."

Her ankle was hurting and she found herself leaning into him as he supported her around the waist. He seemed a bit younger than her, taller than her, strong and lean of body. Judging by his clean-shaven face, short hair and smell of cologne he had not long been out of the barber's chair, she thought.

"My name is Thomas Rodda, and by the looks of you and your lot Mrs. you seem to be loading up for the goldfields. I happen to be going that way myself so maybe I'll see you on the track."

By now Jane was blushing. She thanked him profusely for his gallantry as he lifted his hat and, having satisfied himself that Jane was all right, begged to leave. She thought him a very fine fellow. He didn't have to try and save her and in doing so had incurred considerable inconvenience to himself and his clothing. Later, when the pain had left her ankle, she recalled the spark she had felt as he held her around the waist and looked with concern into her eyes. She admitted, to her shock, that she fancied him. It had been nearly nineteen months since Richard died and she had not thought about any other man until now.

When Red finally returned to the dray after doing the rounds of a number of Adelaide inns it was apparent that firstly he was in a very talkative mood and secondly that all he had bought (apart from ale) was a hessian bag full of fishing gear comprising lines, hooks, lead weights and a net, plus a screw bottle jack capable of lifting three tons – "In case of trouble," he said.

PART FOUR

OVERLAND
1851–1852

Chapter 39

TO THE DIGGINGS

Adelaide was in turmoil due to the rush for gold. In 1851, 15,000 to 20,000 people left the state for the goldfields travelling overland or by sea. At times a dozen or more ships lined up at the port advertised in the Adelaide press for passengers to take to the diggings. Shut up shops and businesses displayed signs in their windows "Gone to the Diggings" and departing diggers drained the banks and business community of so much coinage that shopkeepers remaining had to issue promissory notes for change in sums as low as sixpence and two pence.

The ability of the government to govern was diminished through the resignations of public servants afflicted with gold fever. On one day the *South Australian Register* newspaper listed seventeen who handed in their notice including the house surgeon and a wardsman at the hospital, two clerks of court, the engineer of the steam dredge and a lighthouse keeper at the port, four court bailiffs, the head turnkey and his assistant at the gaol plus two guards and three mail guards. Large numbers of police officers walked off their jobs leaving many small settlements with reduced or no police protection. As government reserves fell more public servants were retrenched or given leave of absence without pay. The economy almost came to a standstill and by 1852 there was so little money in the Treasury that civil servants remaining at work were not paid for three months.

To Jane the bush between Adelaide and Mount Alexander seemed like an ocean. It was strange and wild and suspected of being full of dangers. Depending on where you started and which way you went, the route to the diggings could be anywhere between 400 to 600 or more miles. The distance "as the crow flies" was only about 360 miles. The longest way was to follow the Murray River upstream until the Loddon River was found and then follow it up to the diggings. At least there was plenty of water along the way. The shortest route, directly east, which took travellers through a large tract of desert and dry country was fraught with difficulties especially during the long hot summer. The Adelaide press reported at the end of December that in the desert to the east of the Murray many bullocks travelling in overlanders teams had perished due to the lack of water. The most popular route, after crossing the Murray, was a southerly trek along the Coorong coastline to about the 37th parallel of latitude and from there over a choice of several routes in a generally easterly direction to the goldfields. The estimated distance was around 460 miles. Red decided to follow this trail. Apart from finding the route itself his main concern was obtaining good water and feed on the track for his bullocks.

It took a degree of skill to pack the dray properly. Heavy gear such as tools and sacks of flour needed to be placed at the bottom to keep the centre of gravity as low as possible with the weight spread and balanced each side of the axle so that the pole for the bullocks would neither weigh down on them nor tend to lift them up. Lighter bits and pieces such as small furniture items, clothes, food and gear for camping including bedding, tarpaulins or tents were then placed on top. A shovel and an axe were kept handy in the corner of the dray together with firearms in canvas wraps including Red's own shotgun.

Constance was a noisy contraption as she trundled along. Tin plates, pannikins, camp ovens and pans jangled and clanked together with every bump in the road. The timbers of the dray creaked, bullocks' chains clinked and the steel tyres crunched every stone they met. And then there was Red's voice which seldom stopped for any length of time. If he was not abusing his beasts he would talk to them gently, sometimes softly delivering a one-on-one monologue to an individual bullock lasting five minutes or more.

As the dray proceeded down King William Street in the early dawn light to Glen Osmond Road a variety of vehicles laden to the hilt with digger paraphernalia began to join the Dunstans from side streets. All were accompanied by three or more men on foot with looks of resignation on their faces. Some seemed enthusiastic, others thoughtful. It was an odd sight with a strange jumble of equipment and vehicles. There were carts that were quite new with harness fresh from the saddlers strapped to good sturdy horses while some dilapidated old drays and wagons were hauled by worn out old bullocks that looked as though they would not see the distance. A few rigs were covered by white duck canvas over steel hoops in the American wagon style but most were open. Teams of two, four, six or eight beasts did the pulling.

With new alluvial gold finds the first to the field usually

pegged out the best spots. Those who were the last to arrive often found little or nothing. Once the decision was made to go it was important not to delay. Everyone seemed to be moving as fast as they could towards gold – even if it was at bullock wagon pace. It was a case of "Eastward Ho the Wagons and Drays!"

They headed straight for the only crossing place over the Murray River at Wellington, sixty-five miles from Adelaide where a government punt operated. The well defined road headed south-east four miles to Glen Osmond, a mining and agricultural district that serviced Adelaide with its gardeners, vignerons and small farmers. Travelling through hilly country with fine fertile valleys and slopes to begin their climb around Mount Osmond, the party passed by the Vine Inn, the Miners Arms and the Mountain Hut licensed establishments. They then faced a range of hills clothed to the summit with a thick and almost impenetrable mass of trees and began an extremely steep, long, slow pull along a winding track towards Mount Lofty.

The team needed encouragement to make the ascent and it was now that young Richard's job as an "offsider" became crucial. Red, as the teamster, always walked on the nearside (left) beside the team and when the going got really tough he would have his hands full working the bullocks on that side. In such circumstances it was helpful to have an offsider on the offside (right side) to assist in motivating the beasts there. Red armed Richard with one of his old whips but instructed him only to wave it about and not lay it on the bullocks. His only other instructions were to "talk to them like me" and if they really needed goading to poke them in the ribs with the handle of the whip.

As the team led off, Red walked up and down both sides explaining quietly to the bullocks that they had serious work to do for a while and that he would not tolerate any slackers. Then, taking up position on the nearside next to the dray, he grabbed his whip with the seven-foot handle and ten-foot lash in both hands and, drawing himself up to full height, swung it around his head to crack it literally through the sound barrier like a rifle shot. If there was any doubt that this was important business it was altogether removed when Scrapper was released from the chain on the back axle so he could nip and goad any reluctant beasts into action.

It took more than two hours to get to the top of the range during which the bullocks were given several spells. Red had the ability to think like them and he knew when they were tired or hungry. During the ascent Jane and Mary were ordered down from the dray to walk but Red allowed little William, to stay on board. Teams of bullocks on the track scrambling for traction to haul their heavily laden wagons over the range left a lingering cloud of dust in their wake that hung like mist through the trees. The cracks and pops of whips wielded by bullockies echoed intermittently up and down the valley to punctuate the constant shouts from their gravelly voices. They trekked past Crafers Inn in the forest near Mount Lofty and camped for the night a short distance down the road. *Constance* had only managed a little more than 10 miles for the first day but it had been difficult country.

The downhill run over the other side of the range had its own challenges. Drays were difficult to brake or slow. If some method was not used to retard the heavily laden vehicle it would run down on the team with disastrous results. Red had to "sprog" the wheels by shoving a sapling between the spokes so that it jammed against the dray's floor to stop their rotation. If the descent was really steep he hooked up a heavy log with a chain on the back to act as an additional drag and as a last resort he could always take two bullocks around and tie them behind where he would encourage them to lift up their heads and dig in their hooves to hold back the dray. For safety reasons Red ordered everyone out of the dray during steep descents.

They continued on through hilly forested country over a road made rough due to all the exposed tree roots on the track to the Onkaparinga River where they crossed over a well constructed bridge and on the other side went past the Wheatsheaf Inn. Another four miles south east brought them to the little village of Echunga established in 1849 where there was a creek with good water, St. Mary's Church of England, a general store, post office and the Hagen Arms Inn. They had travelled more than twelve miles since their last camp and Red called it a day. He found an ideal camping spot with good grass close to the creek and not far from the inn.

Next day they headed for Macclesfield only six miles southeast of Echunga. Being an ideal half days run they stopped there for lunch. It was important to rest the bullocks each day around midday for a couple of hours to allow them to chew their cud made up of partly digested food returned from the first of their two stomachs to their mouths for further mastication. This took time and they didn't do it while moving. The rest period each day gave Jane sufficient time to light a fire, make tea and cook up a light meal with damper.

The lunchtime break was cut short by Red as he planned to get to Strathalbyn before the sun set and still had another eight miles to travel southeast. It was a pastoral and agricultural settlement and an important stopping place for overlanders where they could buy sundry provisions including flour from the mill run by William Colman who advertised in the Adelaide press that he had always on hand a supply of flour for drays passing to the diggings. As his was the last mill on the road Jane took the opportunity to stock up. The village with two churches and the Strathalbyn Inn was situated on the River Angus where the party camped for the night at a water hole.

Just nine miles from Strathalbyn they reached the little village of Langhorne Creek surrounded by flat country with light sandy soil. Travellers passing through the area could buy wheat at eleven shillings a bushel and some other supplies from property owner Frank Potts who decided to stay on the land and make money from the passing trade rather than be tempted by the goldfields, and refreshments were available at the Langhorne Inn. Red pressed on some four miles past the inn and camped at a water hole under some substantial eucalypt trees where there was good feed for his team. There were a dozen or so drays and carts already stopped there for the night and another six more pulled up after *Constance*.

It took them more than a day to travel the remaining sixteen miles to Wellington. It was heavy work driving the bullocks through the Murray scrub along a soft sandy road in the heat of summer. As the only place to run a punt or ferry across the Murray River, Wellington was an important settlement. Tucked below undulating sandhills sprinkled with she oaks and situate along a bank of large reed flats and swamps it had a post office, a small police station manned by three policemen, and two hotels, the Wellington Inn on the west side of the river and the Bushman's Camp on the east side. Near the crossing place there was a shed and a large bell that could be struck to summon the ferry if it was parked on the other side of the river some 800 feet away.

To the great benefit of the innkeepers, the gold rush had hugely increased traffic passing through the crossing. It was estimated by the Central Road Board that during the last few months of 1851 the punt carried 3,688 passengers and 738 vehicles. In February 1852 the *South Australian Register* newspaper reported that "upwards of 100 drays" were encamped waiting for their turn to be ferried across. In that month it was calculated that 1,234 people, 1,266 horses and bullocks, and 164 carriages of all description were floated across. The ferryman complained that he was exposed to great inconvenience in being compelled to work the ferry at all hours at the caprice of travellers and that traffic had increased so much since the discovery of gold that he was afraid his assistant would leave him unless his salary was increased. He estimated that 300 men from Burra alone would cross on the ferry in a week.

The bottleneck at Wellington crossing caused what was probably the first traffic jam in the history of South Australia. The Dunstans and Red had no choice but to join the queue and wait their turn. When it came, the Dunstan boys readily accepted an invitation by the ferryman to assist hauling the vessel across by heaving on a strong rope cable running over rollers on the sides of the punt and anchored on each bank. The stronger they pulled the faster the punt went. The tolls were threepence for each person and each bullock plus one shilling for the dray.

Chapter 40

THE COORONG

To reach the east side of the Murray River from Adelaide the Dunstans had travelled through six established settlements and passed at least 11 inns. Now they had to deal with a track much less travelled but it was at least a track and they were not faced with having to blaze a trail through the bush. The way along the Coorong and the location of the turnoff to the overland route to Port Phillip had been detailed in a map drawn by Thomas Burr, Deputy Surveyor General, who had accompanied Governor Grey on an expedition to the area in 1844. In his accompanying report Burr detailed eight freshwater locations (mostly wells) between Wellington and the turnoff. In 1846 an overland mail service from Wellington along the Coorong to Mount Gambier had been established. It was run by armed police troopers on horseback because the area the journey traversed was still relatively unexplored and sparsely settled where tracks were few and there were no roads. By the time the gold rush started, some four years later, the route along the Coorong had been pulverised and hammered by bullock wagons, drays, horses carts and gigs into a recognisable, established track.

After crossing the Murray the road headed in a southerly direction with the shores of Lake Victoria (later called Lake Alexandrina) on the right. 1851 had been a very wet year with floods reported in the Murray River system in the lead up to Christmas with the result that a large "fresh" had flushed into the lake to provide good water for the overlanders. They camped on its shores a little more than twelve miles from Wellington at a spot where Red found good feed for his bullocks. He always tried to have them pulled up and unyoked an hour or two before sunset as it was important to allow them sufficient time to water and graze before dark. The first thing they did was to sit down and chew their cud. They would then graze for a while, sleep from about midnight until four in the morning and feed up again until yoking time. To give them plenty of time to do so, a good teamster like Red would not muster his team until it least an hour after dawn.

Next day's journey took them through scrubby country with some difficult sandy patches to the shores of Lake Albert where they found the water salty and so continued on another six to seven miles where they camped with a number of other drays near a water hole. From here there was a choice of several tracks through the western edge of the Tatiara Desert where, according to rumour, many drays had been abandoned to McGraths Flat. All routes had their own difficulties with either a succession of steep sandhills with plenty of limestone rocks on the way or extended plains of soft sand covered with low brushwood and prickly heath. There was no water and the days were scorching hot.

They decided to avoid the steep sandhills and took the route through sandy plains to discover that the wheels of the dray often sank up to the axle. There followed much cursing by Red, repeated cracking of his long whip and calling out with derogatory adjectives the names of every bullock in the team before the wheels slowly rolled along with the added assistance of everyone's shoulder to the back of the dray. Along the track they came across bits of broken carts and drays including shattered wheels, broken axles and shafts plus items jettisoned from vehicles in a desperate attempt to lighten the load. They passed several dead horses and bullocks, cooking in the sun, blanketed with flies and giving off a dreadful stink.

Emerging exhausted from the desert, they sighted the Coorong Lagoon. Red decided to call it a day as his team needed a rest, Jane was requesting a halt to the proceedings and it was Christmas Eve. They pulled into McGraths Flat where there were four wells and set up camp under a clump of she oaks with a group of other overlanders. As soon as *Constance* stopped, everyone went to work. Young Richard helped Red to unyoke, bell and hobble the bullocks and make safe and secure the parked dray. To stop it from rolling or tipping over the wheels had to be chocked and the pole propped and tied. Ben assisted Jane in unloading tucker and other boxes, pots, pans, pannikins, buckets and tin dishes. Henry and Wearn were in charge of gathering wood and lighting the fire. Mary had to release the goat from the back of the dray, tether it near good feed and try to milk it, feed and water the chickens in the coops on the side of the dray and take charge of baby William while Jane started cooking preparations for eight hungry people.

The first thing to do was boil a big pot of water for tea making. It was amazing how thirsty everyone was by the end of the day and how much tea they drank. Red and Richard then set up the tarpaulins for the night – one on the ground under the dray for the boys to sleep on (which was big enough to double up and sleep between if it was cold), one over the dray for Jane, Mary and young William to sleep under and one slung over the dray pole supported by a forked sapling to form a makeshift tent for Red. Henry, Wearn and Mary were then designated cook's helpers and general camp rouseabouts while Richard and Ben went shooting in the hope of bagging a duck or a bronze winged pigeon for the pot. Red stoked up his clay pipe and joined a group of other teamsters to discuss the track and talk about bullocks.

The overlanders tended to form into large camping groups at night drawn together by the attraction of a good camping spot near water and the thought of there being safety in numbers. Clustered side-by-side they looked like a prosperous little settlement with the glow from their fires silhouetting figures on the edge of their camps at night. A solid log or two around their fires made good seats where many happy hours were spent reminiscing and yarning. They never bothered with lamps or candles – large fires giving them all the light they needed.

Richard and Ben shot half a dozen wood ducks and a couple of teal along the edge of the Coorong. Mary plucked and gutted them and Jane wrapped them individually with a strip of bacon and baked them in the camp oven with onions, potatoes and barley for Christmas dinner. For dessert she made a bush damper with currants and dried apple mixed through which she served hot with treacle drizzled over. Red declared it was a capital feast. Jane could not help reminding herself again that it was much better than many meals that the family had shared in Cornwall and wished that Richard was still alive to enjoy it with them.

It wasn't long before the usual nocturnal bush sounds at McGraths Flat were overlaid with those from the ubiquitous tin whistle, soon joined by a fiddle and a squeezebox. As it was

A bullock dray in the style of *Constance*.

[Photograph courtesy of the Naracoorte Branch of the National Trust of South Australia.]

Christmas, a full range of carols were sung followed by some renditions from the Wesleyan Methodist hymn book. Eventually the party livened up with jigs and hornpipes accompanied by several merry men using the bottom of a tin dish as a drum.

Jane and the children were content with their Christmas and grateful to be camped in the Australian bush among friends many of whom were from Cornwall. They were pleased to be back on their yellow brick road to possible good fortune and went to bed happy. As was the usual practice, they did so in "full marching order" so that next morning, after a yawn and scratch they could be straight into their boots and ready for the day.

The Coorong was a lagoon running parallel with the coast for about twenty-five miles with a maximum width around two miles. It contained brackish water influenced by the sea, the River Murray and several creeks and was protected from the ocean on the southern side by a narrow sandy ridge. It was a source of prolific food for abundant birdlife including large flocks of several species of ducks and black swans as well as geese, water hens, coots, cormorants, pelicans, sandpipers, terns, herons, ibis and several types of gulls. The waters were rich in mulloway, mullet, bream and other fish varieties as well as molluscs. These abundant food sources supported several Aboriginal tribal groups of the Ngarrindjeri people who made bark and reed canoes and were accomplished fishermen who used sophisticated fish traps and traded their produce with other tribes. When white people came through their land they traded fish, cockles, mussels and "crawfish" with them in exchange for flour, sugar, tobacco or goods like pannikins and sometimes even for money. This was a fortuitous arrangement for overlanders who benefited greatly through the supply of fresh fish. Red did the bargaining with them as Jane felt quite intimidated by their naked black bodies and strange dialogue. A couple of pannikins of flour and some sugar were soon exchanged for several large mulloway and a bucket of cockles from which Jane made a shell fish chowder soup which went down extremely well with a freshly cooked hot damper. They all slept restlessly during their nights camped along the Coorong due to the noise of the surf from the Southern Ocean thumping down on the beach over the sand hills on the far side of the lagoon. It had been nearly three years since Jane had heard the sea. Its sound and the smell of salt in the air caused memories of *Trafalgar* to come flooding back.

The route along the Coorong depended on the prevailing seasonal weather. The past wet year with big flows down the Murray resulted in a full Coorong which forced the bullocks on to higher sandy, or sometimes stony, ground where the going was rougher and slower. Jane thought the place was beautiful. The waters of the Coorong, always covered with prolific birdlife, were bordered on the ocean side by sand hills rising precipitately in some places and gently in others, interspersed with little glens and undulating plains covered with luxuriant patches of peculiar shrubs with fine green foliage; contrasted every now and then with bare white sand patches. As they followed the bank, the edge of the desert on the high side was covered thickly by she oak trees in some places and coastal scrub in others. Sometimes they crossed a short grassy flat running inland and little islands appeared at intervals in the lagoon as they passed by. It was so unlike Cornwall.

Chapter 41

TILLEY'S SWAMP

Travelling on past Wood's Well and Policeman's Well they reached
Salt Creek where Jane was amazed and Red delighted to discover
an inn called The Travellers Rest built mainly of timber slabs with
a shingle roof. The inn sold tobacco at sixpence a stick, flour and
beef at four pence a pound and a whole sheep weighing above fifty
pounds for only eight shillings. Jane stocked up on flour and Red
bought tobacco which he later reviled as equal to bullock dung,
but he still smoked it. The inn also served as a post office. With
good rains the Salt Creek flowed fresh water while in the dry
times the supply turned brackish which, although it might still be
suitable for bullocks, made a very bad cup of tea. The stream was
shallow and easily forded.

After Salt Creek the road continued over a succession of
stiff sandhills and black flats from a quarter of a mile to a mile in
length. Fine dust and sand from the pulverised track was picked

up and sprinkled by the wheels over the contents of the dray and anyone within 10 feet behind. For the most part thick coastal bush on the high inland side formed an impenetrable barrier and at times when it became just as thick on the coastal side the winding narrow track caused both wheels of the dray, as it moved along, to gouge into the scrub. When the wheels hit stumps and roots concealed under layers of dust and sand it jarred and rattled the contents of the entire vehicle and anyone on it, particularly little William who was regularly bounced up and down on top of the load. Jane and the boys dragging their feet with fatigue as they walked beside the dray often tripped and stumbled.

Ten miles south of Salt Creek the track divided with one route heading inland to Tilley's homestead situated on the north eastern tip of a large swamp where William Tilley had taken up land in 1847. This was the usual route of the overlanders with the swamp fed by creeks providing excellent freshwater and an abundance of birdlife for the camp oven. At the road junction someone had put up a fingerboard directing the way to the diggings. Tilley's station was regarded as a landmark and mileage point for travellers, but to get to it the extensive swamp, covered thick with rushes and bogs, had to be crossed. There was a choice of numerous different trails formed by intrepid overlanders deciding that their particular way was the best to navigate through the mixed stretches of water, slushy track and serious bogs.

Red had been pleased with their progress until suddenly, when they were traversing a pool about a foot deep, the wheels of the dray sunk up to the axles and everything jolted to a stop. He immediately ordered Jane, Mary and baby William out of the dray and then slowly waded around the team speaking softly and gently to each individual bullock, waving his unravelled whip under their noses as he went. Returning back to his command position on the near side, his tone and delivery changed as he issued military like orders to each of them by name and, with both arms, wielded his huge whip with great skill and considerable art to crack, pop and bang it within inches of their hides. His volume then increased as he opened right out with amazing words and phrases that only someone who had made a lifetime study and practice of swearing could produce.

As Jane's face turned pink she thought that the extreme intensity of such language might be capable of moving any object whether animate or not. All the time while Red roared, his whip continued to pop and bang away. Jane and the younger boys did what they could to assist by putting their shoulders into the back of the dray and Richard worked the bullocks on the offside by prodding his whip into their rumps and doing his best to emulate Red's hollering without using his more colourful adjectives.

Young Mary stayed out of the way and looked after baby William. Red's dog Scrapper was entirely useless as he didn't fancy water or mud. Red roared "Giddap Nelson and Blucher you pair of useless bastards!" to the lead bullocks and they moved their heads from side to side to put more weight into their yokes. When the other bullocks followed, the team had a combined pulling power of several tons. The chains tightened to near breaking point and the timbers of the dray strained and complained, then it suddenly lurched forward with a drawn out sucking sound and broke free of the bog. The loud cheer that followed from everyone was supported by more than a bellow or two from the bullocks.

Red kept the team moving until good ground was reached and then stopped them for a rest. They camped as soon as they came to the edge of the swamp at a spot within the site of the white house that was Tilley's sheep station. The bullocks needed a proper break, the dray was covered in mud and needed a cleanup as did everyone and they had just had enough for the day. As the heat went out of the sun, mosquitoes in their millions came out of the swamp to irritate, torment and create their mountainous stings on everyone. Returning from the edge of the swamp with a bucket of water Red declared, "There is a black cloud of them bitey bastards down there six feet thick!"

He tried greasing himself with mutton fat but with no effect and then resorted to lighting fires of dry bullock dung all around the camp to keep them away. He had heard from some of his bullocky mates that this was an effective mosquito repellent especially if green eucalyptus leaves were added to the fire. Jane and the children found that for best results they had to sit in the smoke which then permeated their clothes and hair so that after several weeks of such treatment with no change of clothes or bath the ability to repel almost anything was greatly increased. Thereafter dried out bullock dung found on the track was collected as a valuable item as the dray travelled along. Jane's other method of repelling both flies and mosquitoes was to rub the surface of the skin with a freshly cut onion which at the end of the day could then still be tossed into the camp oven. Rubbing an onion on areas already bitten also relieved the sting. For the youngest children Jane mixed castor oil with a little vinegar to act as a mild insect repellent and help protect the skin from the drying effects of the sun. For serious bites and stings she applied a paste of bicarbonate of soda mixed with water which was immediately soothing.

As the light disappeared curlews began to wail mournfully and the surface of the swamp rippled with legions of frogs, tadpoles and insects. To keep the mosquitoes at bay they wrapped the tarpaulins around themselves as best they could, although it was a warm night, and tried to keep the dung fires burning. Noise from frogs made it hard to go to sleep. The calls from different species fascinated Jane. There were "reek, reek, reek reeks", "crick, cricks", "chirps", "gbonks" and "pomp pomps". When their racket eventually died down the shrill song of little black crickets filled the night and then a willie wagtail began his chorus of "sweet pretty little creature" which he kept up until dawn to the irritation of everyone. Jane did have a soft spot for the little bird as on one occasion it had warned her of the presence of a snake in the bush, when she was heading off to attend her toiletries, with its different call of "chatter, chatter, chatter!" repeated. Where there were swamps and frogs there were snakes. They were definitely the evil enemy and if one was sighted it was a point of honour to make sure it was dispatched and did not escape.

Red had endless snake yarns. Stories about snakes under pillows, snakes in bed, snakes in bullock wagons, snakes up trees and snakes in the toilet hole. He always counselled Jane and the children to make sure they had a good look around before doing a toilet squat in the bush. Jane believed that even though a snake was killed it did not really die until after sundown. She thought that the proof of this was the fact that she had seen a snake with its head cut off thrown on an ant hill where she had watched it writhe in apparent living pain as it was attacked by thousands of ants and not until the sun went down was it still.

The laugh of a kookaburra, a bird that had a reputation for catching and eating snakes, woke them. Red called them "laughing jackasses". After decamping they stopped at Tilley's station where they bought half a sheep for five shillings and ten pence and then proceeded along level ground on the side of the swamp which was covered in trees following the track that was used by the police troopers carrying mail between Mount Gambier and Wellington. That night they had a good camp with few mosquitoes, good feed for the bullocks, plenty of water, wood at hand and roast mutton with potatoes and onions in the camp oven. At many camping or lunchtime stops along the way they found lots of inscriptions on trees left by others as a record of their transit. They served as messages to following friends, to record the safe progress of the scribes and marked the trail for others.

The trek next day took them past Baker's station situated on a sixty-two square mile pastoral lease with the homestead built on the north side of Reedy Creek. They then passed through flat and dry country leading up to the station house of James Brown on a lease of sixty-nine square miles of land where whole sheep were for sale at ten shillings each. There was scarce feed to be found for the bullocks in the area so they travelled on to better feed and a well some two miles further where they stopped and set up camp. Although not late in the afternoon, there were already several drays clustered around the well setting up comfortable camps for the next day – Sunday when all trekking stopped on the day of rest. The bullocks needed a break as much as anyone else.

Selecting a good camp site was important. It should never be near a dead tree or against a log or stump that may be a haunt for snakes. Ants, too, had to be considered. There were always numerous armies of them; some large, others small but most with a nasty sting and all with a penchant to quickly find anything edible. They wasted no time in exploring swags, boots, clothing and tucker boxes. The Dunstans soon learned to give everything a good shake before they packed and decamped and took extra care to make sure that a selected camp site was not on an ant nest. Quite early in the trip young Richard had put on a gymnastic performance when, in the failing light as the sun set, he had carelessly sat on a bull ant nest causing him to yell, kick and dance about as he ripped off his pants. He was painfully bitten with stings reaching to his personal parts.

On Sunday morning a short devotional service was held and attended by all from the gathered drays and wagons. Hymns were sung from the Wesleyan hymn book to the accompaniment of music from the fiddle and concertina. They prayed and thanked God for their safe journey to date and prayed again that they would safely arrive at their destination. After that there was time for Jane to do a little washing and mending of clothes. Red checked *Constance*, carried out any necessary repairs and regreased her axles from a can of smelly old tallow grease hanging off the back of the dray. He then inspected each bullock individually, paying particular attention to their cloven hooves. Having satisfied himself that all was well, he picked up his fowling piece and wandered off to see if he could shoot something for the pot.

The day of rest was an opportunity to sort out and re-pack the dray, to do some writing (if you knew how), to have a shave and even a bit of a proper wash if there was enough suitable water about. Jane put young Henry and Wearn to work re-stuffing hessian pillows with fresh soft native grasses and instructed Richard and Ben to give their guns a good clean and oil before they went shooting. Mary checked and fed the chickens, re-tethered and milked the goat, kept her eye on young William and helped Jane around the campfire with cooking preparations.

After lunch Jane tied a rope around William's waist and fastened the other end to the wheel of the dray, to curb his enthusiasm to explore the world at large, while she lay on the grass closed her eyes and again and again breathed deeply the aromatic scent of the gum trees. She loved their tangy smell and how they were so different from the trees back in Cornwall. She was at ease in this environment. Her Cornish background served her well for the task of overlanding. She knew what it was to survive on the minimum and had the skills to improvise and make do with whatever she had. She thought it strange that although she missed Cornwall it was often the contrasts in Australia that she liked most.

The shooters were successful and that night they had the best Sunday dinner of roast bronze winged pigeon, roast cockatoo, roast spur winged plover and roast potatoes all cooked together in the camp oven with onions and rice. As it was Sunday Jane had plenty of time for cooking and made a batch of raisin damper scones which she served hot with lashings of treacle. When it came to cooking a big dinner over an open fire she was a master chef. While waiting for the camp oven to produce its familiar hiss and sizzle to indicate the contents were cooking nicely Jane watched the sun go down and listened to the groaning of the gums as they rubbed together in the breeze. She was happy and so glad to be out of the dugout and out of Burra.

Another five miles down the track next day and they passed the station homestead of Isaiah Cole situated on a pastoral lease of thirty-six square miles occupied since the 1840s.

Chapter 42

VICTORIA

On the track, hardly a day passed without some sort of crisis or incident. The terrain of much of the land they now travelled through was made up of either difficult sandhills or swampy marshes covered with reeds and rushes that from a distance looked like solid grasslands covering hundreds of acres. There were days when *Constance* got bogged repeatedly which sometimes necessitated the temporary removal of much of the load by hand to firm ground to make it easier for the bullocks to drag out the dray. If the bullocks sank to their bellies and lost their footing they had to be unyoked, manhandled out, the dray completely unloaded, and hauled by the bullocks straining at the end of a long rope from harder ground. If the team got hopelessly stuck, but still had a good footing, the next driver coming along would stop, unhitch his team and hook on in front of the bogged team. This tactic, combined with a double dose of whip cracking and hollering by the teamsters, usually worked so long as something like a yoke or link didn't give way and break. When the men and boys were engaged in such serious dray extraction activities Jane with Mary and young William would walk ahead and select a stopping spot to light a big fire so that the workers could dry their clothes, boots and socks when the job was done and replenish themselves with lots of hot tea.

A few miles south of the 37° parallel of latitude the overland track turned east and the travellers came upon the tiny settlement of Reedy Creek where there was a basic inn and a rough eating house. Built of slab timber and stone with a thatched roof, it comprised two bedrooms, a kitchen, parlour, and a tap room which was simply an open space containing rustic trestle tables and bench seats where customers were served room temperature beer ladled out of an open barrel into tin or pewter mugs. It was typical of the bush inns that were built at remote but strategic places along the busiest bullock tracks leading to the stations of early squatters. Some were not much more than basic bark huts that sold nobblers of gin and brandy to all comers. They usually had at least a couple of small windows with no glass and wooden shutters that were closed only on very cold days and a large fireplace that radiated prodigious heat in the winter. Floors were mostly dirt, spittoons were rarely supplied and the men simply slagged their spit from pipes and tobacco chewing into the fire or the nearest corner. "Necessaries" and latrines were of the crudest kind and built a long distance away out back. Basic meals were sometimes available from a big iron pot into which all available ingredients were tossed and boiled together over the open fire.

Late into the night the tap room would be turned into a cheap sleeping dormitory. Rough as they were, it was always a welcome relief to come across an inn on the track which meant not only the possibility of light refreshments and a cooked meal, but also a chance to stock up on provisions, experience different human companionship and seek information on the road ahead. They were important watering holes for man and beast alike and dots on the map that linked together the main bush tracks which, for the most part, followed the shortest distance between watering places a day's journey along the trail where teamsters regularly camped.

The next inn was a bit more than three days away. They continued over the Reedy Creek range, which was simply a group of low hills running parallel to the coast, on through sandy country with several salt lagoons and then crossed twelve miles of flat swampy country known as the Mosquito Plains. Arriving mid-afternoon at the Merino Inn near the Naracoorte Creek, Red wasted no time in de-yoking and hobbling the bullocks and went straight to the tap room for the tankard (or two) of ale he had been thinking about during the scorching hot weather of the last few days.

Built and run by William McIntosh, a squatter in the area since 1845, the inn was part of a village he was trying to establish which at this stage included a store and a gunsmith and tinsmith business. With a detachment of South Australia police established there since 1849 and installed in a police station built to accommodate them, the village had made a good start by the time Jane and her family arrived. She was delighted to find the store where she bought some expensive cheese, and for that matter a police station, in "the middle of nowhere". But Red was not impressed by the inn's draught porter on sale which he described as "equal to horse piss".

Just eight miles along the track from the Merino Inn they travelled through the Hynam Station run situated on more than sixty square miles taken up in 1847. The bullocks were now doing

Victoria

it easy as they loped along in their slow rhythmic pace through flat well-timbered country. The day was seriously hot and above the tall gums the air did not move. Except for the cicadas with their harsh, piercing and monotonous notes, much of the bush was silent. Birds sought shady roosts to sit it out, brown snakes curled up in the shadows of grass tussocks and stump tailed lizards and death adders hid in the cool among leaf litter under trees. Above the track two wedge tailed eagles circled like fly specks as they rose in the hot air currents coming off the scorched land.

Everyone was drenched in sweat. It was actually cooler to walk beside the dray than ride on top as Mary had to in order to watch over her toddler brother William who was far too young to walk long distances. Flies were a constant nuisance. Clouds of little black ones swarmed over every piece of exposed, sweaty skin, attacked their eyes and clung to their backs as if they were stuck with glue to form dense black patches more than a foot square. The best defence was to carry a small branch that could be waved around to swat a few and keep others at bay.

Talking had to be done through a mouth half closed and with a hand in constant motion in front of your face to prevent gagging but if you had to draw a deep breath they were often swallowed. March flies had a ravenous predilection for blood and after inserting sharp pointed stings sticking out of their mouths into any exposed part of human or animal flesh sucked out the red juice like little vampires. Their piercing pricks caused animals to shy and buck and people to hop and curse. In some patches of bush their attacks were unrelenting.

A team of bullocks pulling a loaded dray needed water every ten or twelve miles on a fair day and sooner if it was very hot. They had completed seven miles and in this heat had gone long enough without a good drink. Bullocks could smell water ahead from a

331

long distance and when their steady sullen attitude became noisy and restless, Red understood they were telling him that water was close.

After camping beside a large swamp for the night they made an early start next morning, soon crossed the border into Victoria and some six or seven miles further on came across the Border Inn erected on Newland's station at the junction of several important tracks running northsouth and eastwest. The proprietor, Samuel Baird, also operated a general store and post office for mail conveyed on horseback between there and Hamilton. His business prospered from the passing trade of the many overlanders during the gold rush. While Red and the boys set up camp around the back of the inn on the bank of a swamp Jane and young Mary visited the store and bought a forequarter of lamb. Some years later a town was surveyed around the inn and given the name Apsley.

A twelve mile trundle the next day brought them to an overnight stop at Lake Wallace with a stretch of water full of gum trees about half a mile long and a quarter of a mile wide. As soon as a faint flush of pink appeared on the horizon next morning Jane was up first to stoke the fire for breakfast. Dew deposited overnight on the tarpaulins and dray glistened as the sun rose over the trees and shrubs on the east side of the lake colouring a light mist on the surface golden. In the stillness kangaroos came down to drink and reed warblers began their babble. Magpies carolled softly in adjacent gum trees and hundreds of waterfowl including swans, magpie geese, ducks, divers, coots, water hens and their young paddled and sat and honked and quacked about their business on the placid lake. As the sun rose the mist began to lift and the laughter of several kookaburras burst across the lake to signal the start of the ornithological racket that followed. Crows cawed, cockatoos screamed, lorikeets screeched and plovers ack-

acked about as huge flocks of corellas and galahs exploded from their roosts in the dead trees on the edge of the lake and took off with their noisy screeching to a given destination known only to them. Before doing so they flew around and around the lake making as much din as possible. Jane watched them with delight as they flew low over the water and then barrelled up into the air in all directions with the sun's rays highlighting their pinks, whites and greys as they twisted about.

Now everyone was awake. Jane thought that most people had never seen and heard such things and how lucky she was. It was an experience she would never forget and it made a deep impression on her. She thought it was all so beautiful and that no matter what happened she would never want to leave this for Cornwall again. For the first time since Richard's death she felt a renewal within her. She loved this country, knew it would be good for her family, and kept thinking about that man Tom Rodda.

After Lake Wallace a good track meandered in a north easterly direction past the station homesteads of the Hope Brothers, the Cook Brothers and then on to Mount Arapiles and George Urquhart's station at its base. They were now on the edge of the Wimmera plains and this was good grazing country with some very large flocks of sheep. By the middle 1840s at least 282 sheep stations had been established on the great plains of western Victoria which were more closely settled than any other rural area. Many station owners were happy to sell a sheep to passing travellers for their sustenance. By the time the overland rush to the goldfields took place the fairly light timbered and flat plains of the west were already crisscrossed with numerous tracks cut by the large steel rimmed wheels of drays and wagons servicing sheep stations and while they were mostly easy to follow they could be bewildering to newcomers.

Due to the detrimental effects that the spread of white settlement had on the Aboriginal population, scarcely any resistance was met by overlanders from Aborigines. Still, people travelling through the bush always considered them to be a hidden threat even though their numbers were greatly reduced.

Chapter 43

THE WIMMERA

The last year had been a good one for rain. Shallow depressions collected huge sheets of water that attracted all types of waterfowl and as the Dunstans headed east from Mount Arapiles they travelled passed several swamps that provided good freshwater camping spots and the chance of shooting game for the camp oven. Some waterholes were covered with so many ducks that when they flew up they nearly blackened the sky. After crossing the Natimuk Creek they reached the banks of the Wimmera River near Major William Firebrace's station named Vectis where they made camp under a cluster of sighing she oak trees. While in the winter the river flowed strongly, at this time of the year it settled into a series of large waterholes which were 30 yards wide and 200 to 300 yards long, with the occasional reed-filled billabong on the banks providing sanctuary to many species of birds.

It was never a silent night in the bush. Koalas made strange guttural noises. Possums snarled at one another, sometimes urinated from the trees on the tents and drays, and sneaked around campsites until one of the dogs spotted them at which time canine hell broke loose as every dog strained on the chain tied to their dray and went barking mad. When they finally settled and became quiet the howl of a distant dingo might set them off again. When camped near water, which was always the aim, there were noisy frogs and on the darkest and comparatively quieter nights the mopoke owl could still be heard punctuating the night air with his distinctive mournful cry.

Natural bush sounds were always overlaid by the sound of bells on bullocks necks. The teamsters preferred the big "bullfrog" bells that created a low-frequency deep toned resonant sound that travelled a long way. With five or six teams all unyoked and belled in the same place there would be more than forty "dongs and klonks" banging on into the night air as the bullocks grazed. They drove Jane mad and kept her and the children awake. Nothing seemed to disturb Red who snored away in his pile of rags oblivious to everything.

They moved along the south bank of the Wimmera and continued on a rough track following the circuitous winding of the stream until eventually they reached Horsham located on its banks where there was a convenient fording place. The settlement was already a village with twelve or fourteen houses, a headquarters for the district police, comprising a watch house, court house and accommodation for the chief constable and three policeman, a blacksmith shop, a post office, a store and a public house called The Four Posts Inn which, to Red's utter disappointment only had brandy for sale. Red was no brandy drinker and he was not happy. He discovered from intelligence gleaned from other teamsters he spoke to in Horsham that there was another inn not too far down the track and wasted no time in heading off in that direction. He was told that after fording the river they should travel upstream on the northern bank to its source near Mount Cole in the southern Pyrenees Ranges. This well-established squatters' track had been clearly detailed on a map compiled and published by Thomas Ham in 1847.

Constance rolled on through waving kangaroo grass bleached pale yellow by the summer heat and as high as the dray wheels. Quail sprung from the verge every four or five yards and zoomed up the track to disappear in the distance. The road kept as close as possible to the riverbank and ready access to water in the event of a breakdown. In the river bends and on the billabongs black cormorants sat vertically in clutches on dead tree branches while spoonbills and herons tiptoed through the reeds on the edges and little invisible finches chipped and tweeted through the rushes. Black swans with heads under water and bottoms up grazed on aquatic plants while magpie geese waddled around the muddy bank and squadrons of ducks paddled and paraded about according to their regimental species. Blue wrens flicked tenuously like butterflies in and out of their protected scrub habitats, noisy miners fought in the tree canopy, crimson rosellas and topknot pigeons flew down to the water's edge to drink and swallows were on the incessant wing chasing flying insects.

When the track veered away from the river towards the open grass plains they were often covered with flocks of grass parrots and parakeets. Bustards in large flocks from 10 to 30 or 40 standing more than three feet high in their brown and white plumage minced about or adopted a frozen stance as the dray went by. Brolgas, or native companions, a beautiful crane that stood up to four and a half feet with long legs and lavender grey plumage, performed in groups of twenty or more their routines like stately ball room dancers in triple time. When *Constance* rattled back towards the river a group of black wallabies might burst out from the edge of the billabong and disappear into the trees. Flowering gums, heavy with nectar, dripped in rainbow and musk lorikeets as grey galahs flew around them flashing their pink breasts in the sunlight veering every which way with their antics. As *Constance* again followed the track away from the river bronze-winged pigeons shot out of the scrub and flew ahead and a pair of emus with their chicks raced across in front.

When they camped they saw weird animals such as platypus, echidnas, goannas, barred bandicoots, marsupial quolls, feather tailed gliders, the ubiquitous native water rat, a variety of other native rats and mice and tiny hopping marsupials. At night miniature bats emerged and squeaked about chasing mosquitoes. There was life everywhere. In the western part of Victoria through which the overlanders travelled there were eventually recorded no less than 275 separate species of birds. The whole of it amazed and enthralled Jane and the children. She wondered what Tom Rodda might have thought.

All of the prime land on the banks of the river had already been taken up by squatters and along the way they passed through several sheep stations. They had been trekking for three days since Horsham and according to Red's information the next public house was not far away. Jane wanted to stop for the night as it was getting late in the day but Red, knowing he was within "coo-ee distance" of the next inn, resolved to press on in the fading light so they could camp near the licensed premises. He knew there would be no difficulty in finding it as in Victoria the publican was required by law to maintain a light outside his inn between sunset and sunrise to make it easier for weary travellers to locate the premises after dark.

The Four Posts Inn at Glenorchy was located where four posts on the Wimmera River (two on each side) marked the ford and at the intersection of well used tracks servicing surrounding sheep stations. It was near a swamp and waterhole on the river where bullock drivers regularly camped. Glenorchy was a hamlet with several houses, a store, blacksmith and post office. The inn had clearly been designed and built by the publican. It was an irregular shape and the bark roof that bowed inwards had little chance of removing water in the event of rain. Slab walls were reinforced with log props and decorated with dried possum skins, hoop iron and other unidentifiable paraphernalia. A couple of hessian draped squares served as windows. Lean-to additions had been stuck on here and there as the circumstances required and several rough outbuildings circled half around it in the mid-distance. A pile of bones and rotten sheepskins thrown behind one of them was being picked over by half a dozen motley looking chickens.

As you stepped through the threshold of the doorway of the inn you descended into a hole worn into the earth floor by countless feet. The smell of stale grog which permeated the place seem to act as a magnet to bush flies on hot days that hummed in little black clouds inside the tap room. It was the sound of male voices coming from the premises that acted like a magnet to draw Red inside as soon as the bullocks were hobbled and the camp established. Assisted by several pannikins of warm sediment-laden beer that still seemed to be brewing he settled in to the serious business of discussing the track with fellow teamsters. The inn had the reputation for being a notorious rendezvous for the worst characters. Alexander Tolmer, Commissioner of Police for South Australia, who stayed there in February 1852 on his way to the goldfields wrote "I did not at first like the appearance of either the building or the inmates, and in truth was not deceived;

the accommodation was bad, beds filthy, full of bugs, charges exorbitant and extremely uncivil withal". When returning to South Australia escorting a cargo of gold he stopped outside the inn and noted "immediately there came out half a dozen of the most cutthroat looking scoundrels I ever be held".

The land close to Glenorchy, and much of it adjacent to the river track, had been cleared of good feed for bullocks and horses by the large number of them that had passed through on their way to the goldfields. The terrain was flat, a relief to travel on after so many hundreds of miles of dreadful track, and heavily wooded on the riverside providing good camping spots and fuel for their fires.

As the team pulled *Constance* through the trees towards a big waterhole on the river, Red was assessing its suitability as a fishing spot. The sun setting through woolly storm clouds created pink and orange rays and then the ambience changed as sheet lightning began to flash in the distance. There was no rain to follow and very little wind – just a humid electric atmosphere full of heavy eucalyptus bush smells, millions of insects and myriads of bird calls that perforated the twilight with almost more sounds than Jane could agreeably cope with.

The warm evening with the air full of insects suited Red. An accomplished bushman, he knew how to find scrub worms and bardie grubs and to catch shrimps and yabbies for fishing bait. In no time he and the boys had half a dozen baited lines in the water. The river was fringed with reeds and rushes that formed a beautiful edging to the dark still pools abundant with fish and overhung by the water-loving gum trees. Red's favourite was the river blackfish which could grow to more than ten pounds and was a superb eating fish with soft white flesh. With two or three big ones landed there was more than enough food for everyone. Eel-tailed catfish which could grow to more than fourteen pounds were considered by some as the finest freshwater fish of all to eat, with white flesh and an excellent delicate flavour. Cod and golden perch could also be caught with some giants of either species occasionally exceeding forty pounds. If the fish weren't biting it was nearly always a certainty that in a net baited with any old piece of meat you could get a feed of crayfish or yabbies. The Dunstan boys became experts in catching them. After ten minutes boiled in water with a dash of vinegar and salt, they were delicious.

Continuing along the river track they saw numerous elevated and heavily timbered blue peaks of the Pyrenees Ranges to the south east which gave rise to a number of creeks and rivers including the Wimmera. They had been on the trail nearly five weeks. Everyone was sick of the daily ordeal of trudging and equipment as well as personnel were showing the effects of wear and tear. *Constance* had developed twice as many creaks and squeaks since they left Adelaide. The wood in her wheels seemed to have shrunk with the heat and her iron tyres were so loose that Red had to twitch wire around them and the wheel rims to keep them on. The dray pole had developed cracks and would have failed altogether if Red had not strapped it also with his wire binding.

The daily complaint of everyone was sore feet. Boots had been stitched and patched and leather inner soles inserted to cover worn holes but they were now nearly beyond repair. Red's dog Scrapper became lame through picking up prickles and thorns on the track and would have been left behind altogether if Jane had not fashioned a tailor-made set of lace up boots for him from scraps of chamois leather she had in her kit. At first he chewed at them and pranced around like a newborn foal but soon got the idea and now would not leave Jane's side.

More than anything, Jane felt filthy. She longed to have a proper bath and fantasised daily about the hot baths she had at the emigration depot in Plymouth and the fun she had on board *Trafalgar* fully immersed in big barrels of sea water. All of that seemed so far in the past and so far away. Everyone, even the bullocks, were suffering from general disgruntlement, had lost weight and sometimes showed disagreeable dispositions.

Near the junction of the Wimmera River with Mount Cole Creek they came upon the settlement of Crowlands where there was a police station, a few houses, a store and a public house run by an unwashed and smelly licensee with matted hair and beard, dirty ragged clothes and bloodshot eyes whose specialty was the sale of miscellaneous fire waters that he passed off as spirits. Jane thought that she had never saw in her life such a dirty place. Scattered around the premises were rings of broken bottles heaped up under several clumps of trees and mangy looking long horned goats tethered under others. Horse stables at the back consisted of a few lean-to slabs thrown together with a bark roof, an old gin case as a manger and floor strewn with a build up of dung. Three or four drayman sat on a plank seat under the front verandah drinking pannikins of warm cloudy beer and sucking on their clay pipes. A short distance away under another tree several Aboriginal men, suffering from the adverse effects of alcohol, appeared to be arguing. A heavy fog of dust that hung in the still air of the hot late afternoon enveloped the entire precinct. Even Red was unimpressed. The Four Posts Inn at Glenorchy was bad enough but this place looked worse. He hadn't felt too well the next day after the Four Posts and blamed that establishment as the cause of the all too frequent toilet stops he had to make on the track afterwards. Uncharacteristically, he gave the inn at Crowlands a miss. He knew, however, that they were now only about 60 miles from the diggings "as the crow flies" and there was at least one more good public house on the way.

Chapter 44

FOREST CREEK

They continued to follow the upper reaches of the Wimmera River towards Mount Cole until the peak of Ben Nevis stood full in their face. Following the track on the north side of the Mount they forded the meandering and diminishing stream twice until they eventually lost it altogether. They had enjoyed the benefit of its continuous water frontage and prolific supply of fish and game since well before Horsham and now would have to do without. At times the river and swamps had been covered with so many water fowl that when young Richard fired at a duck perched on a log preening itself within easy pot shot range, the echo of the gunshot was drowned out by the sound of birds taking to the air and the calls they made as they swirled and rose and fell in waves. They found the various species of duck all delicious in the camp oven except the musk duck which was a real stinker with a pungent odour that made it inedible. If more ducks were shot than could be eaten that day they were cleaned, salted, stuffed with dry grass and hung overnight in a hessian bag under a cool tree. Next day, if they travelled in a shady spot on the dray, they might still be candidates for the camp oven at the night stop. Black swans also went into the pot but were regarded as a less desirable food source unless a young cygnet was shot. Magpie geese, seen at times in flocks of up to 1,000 birds, were slow on the wing, low flying and very easily ambushed. Although their flesh was coarse with an indifferent flavour and texture their easy shooting caused many to end up in the camp oven.

Even when away from the rivers, lakes and swamps there was plenty of meat in the bush and it could all be got without fear of being prosecuted for poaching under game laws as in Cornwall. Back home Richard and Ben would have been gaoled by now, if not transported, for their shooting efforts. When it came to scavenging food from the bush the Dunstans had no reluctance. Tough times during the winters of the potato famines in Cornwall had caused them to scrounge what they could find to eat and memories of pies made with birds caught in the hedgerows were still clear in their minds.

Not all overlanders were like them. Apart from the occasional sheep purchased from stations on the way, some completed the entire journey living on salt meat, ship's biscuits and damper and had little idea how to get bush tucker. Cornish miners would basically eat anything and if it flew and could be shot it was destined for Jane's camp oven which cooked all sorts of native birds night after night, including parrots of all description and wattle birds which Red said tasted sweet because of their diet of nectar. Galahs were a favourite and formed the basis of many a good camp oven stew. They were delicious so long as you did not get one that was too old. They lived for many years and if you had an old one in the pot it was said you should cook it with a stone and when the stone was soft the galah was ready to eat! Then there were top knot pigeons, bronze winged pigeons, spur winged plovers, snipe and several species of quail all of which cooked up a treat. Cockatoos, both white and black, also went into the pot but were not as edible as galahs and it was important to get a young one.

Bustards or bush turkeys that stood up to three feet tall and weighed seventeen pounds or more were a greatly prized food source and easy to shoot. Anything that came within the sights of a muzzle loading shotgun was fair game even the noble native companion or brolga which one hunter complained "requires the greatest circumspection in the sportsman to get a shot at it". Emus were shot, particularly their chicks if they were about. Their flesh was said to be coarse and taste like beef. Even magpies, kookaburras, crows and jays or white winged choughs (also called "lousy jacks" because they were always covered in lice) went into the pot if necessity demanded.

Kangaroos were shot and eaten at every opportunity but Jane thought wallaby was much nicer as it was not as rich or "gamey" and more tender. The kangaroo tail soup she made was described by Red "as good as the best oxtail to be got in Ireland". He told the boys not to shoot koalas because they were tough and not worth eating. While eaten regularly by Aborigines, white people did so only when desperate. On a fine moonlit night possums were easy to shoot but sometimes had a peculiar eucalyptus taste, and were regarded, at best, a third rate meat. Still, a roasted leg of possum was better than nothing. Equipped with a gun and the desire to eat most overlanders had little difficulty in obtaining food for the camp oven. They shot their way from one end of the Wimmera to the other.

The track to Mount Alexander from Mount Cole was blazed

in 1836 by explorer Major Thomas Mitchell. On 23rd September that year he climbed the lofty granite range which he thought "resembled very much some hills of the lower Pyrenees in Spain" and named it Mount Cole. With his pocket sextant he took a bearing on what would later be called Mount Alexander and used it as a guide when he travelled in almost a straight line to it from Mount Cole. His expedition party of twenty-five comprised six bullock drivers and their teams as well as horses pulling carts and men on horseback. The steel wheels of the vehicles and the hoof marks of the animals cut deep into the soft ground as they proceeded leaving a trail which became known as "The Major's Line" that squatters and settlers subsequently followed and made into a permanent track.

After leaving the river, the route from Crowlands, around the northern base of Mount Cole and then east, led to the village of Burnbank situated on a fine creek at the junction of the squatters' western and northern tracks with the Major's Line. Mitchell described the area as "a valley of the finest description". Due to its strategic position on the lifeline to the Avoca River stations it had developed into an important centre prior to the gold rush. The Burnbank Inn was run by widow Janet Anderson and an official post office was established there in 1848. The village also had a store, a blacksmith and wheelwright shop to service the needs of teamsters and travellers, a tailor and a public pound, an Anglican church and Minister, a teacher, carpenters, sawyers and splitters and five carriers which reflected its importance as a depot town for a large district. It became a major supply base and stopover for those travelling to and from the goldfields.

One day out of Burnbank they were heavily rained upon. This was the first serious rain they had experienced during the trip and Red simply refused to travel. Apart from the mud and slippery conditions he was concerned that the bullocks were prone to rub the skin and hair off their necks with the yokes and bows in the wet. This could lead to sores and infection rendering the beasts useless as draught animals. After parking *Constance* under a big tree they slung the tarpaulins all over her and everyone huddled underneath to wait out the wet. Late in the afternoon the rain stopped, giving Jane just enough time to establish a good hot fire to cook the best meal of the day. As dark fell the crack of the lash could be heard in the distance and some thirty minutes later another dray arrived to join their camp.

The country now had changed again. The grass was different, large gum and stringy bark trees grew straighter and silver wattles and blackwoods were thick in the gullies that resounded with the screech of cockatoos. They travelled through hilly, forested terrain and then on grassy plains. There was abundant water and drays and wagons were often held up at the fording places of numerous creeks that crossed the track. Mishaps occurred with items falling off drays, wheels getting stuck or stock becoming disoriented and tangled up in harness. Men waiting in the queue would then proceed up to the ford and lend a hand. It was customary to do this as one day you may need help yourself. It also speeded things up.

After fording the Deep (Tullaroop) Creek they crossed a plain of kangaroo grass with its brown seeds waving like a wheat crop in the breeze. Pressing on, they splashed through Middle Creek to continue following the Major's Line which formed the southern boundary of Plaistow Station for six miles. The property was ideally situated on open native grassland and well watered by another creek named after station owner Alfred Joyce who boasted in his letter dated 26th March 1852 that the diggings "have been no loss to us at Plaistow but rather a source of profit. The main road from Adelaide passing by our head station has caused a great demand for stores and meat from the continued stream of persons coming overland".

For another five miles or thereabouts beyond Plaistow, they continued over a flat well grassed country and reached the River Loddon. Being at the end of summer it was now reduced to a chain of beautiful large waterholes deep and clear to the bottom. As they crossed the ford a short distance below the junction of Jim Crow Creek one of the wheels of the dray slipped off a rock on the downstream side into a hole which caused the load to tilt severely and submerge part of the dray. The lead bullocks that had reached the bank managed to haul *Constance* clear but everything, including some chickens still in the coops strapped to the side, were pretty much drenched which required the vehicle to be entirely unloaded when they camped for the night.

To the annoyance of everyone it was the tea and sugar that suffered most. They all wished the trip was over. *Constance* stopped for the last night before the diggings only a short walking distance from where Major Mitchell's men had set up their tents on their trek to Mount Alexander. In the vicinity there were twenty or more drays parked that tomorrow would all be pointed in the one direction to complete the remaining one days run to the diggings.

During a relaxing after-dinner walk among the camp sites Jane recognised and spoke to a number of old friends and acquaintances from Burra but caught her breath when she met face-to-face with Tom Rodda. The picture of his clean shaven profile had been kept in her mind and at first she did not recognise him behind his full beard. All doubt was removed when he spoke.

"Nice to see you have made it Mrs. – er Mam!"

"Well! Tom Rodda as I live and breathe! If you had not saved me, I may not have."

"I am sorry Mrs, I don't recall discovering your name at our last encounter."

"It's Jane – Jane Dunstan. I do hope you have good luck on the goldfields Mr. Rodda."

"Likewise, Mrs. Dunstan and if I may say so, happiness to you and your family as well."

He doffed his hat. She thanked him, and they bid each other good night. But he had made a mental note of the sparkle in her eyes and the curve of her strong feminine mouth.

Nobody slept well that night. There was just too much anticipation in the camp and next morning they were all up before the sun. There was a scurry of activity among the camps to compete for the position of first dray on the track. If not a race it was certainly a rush. The drays continued virtually in a straight line along the Major's track passing through undulating country where in the distance the thickly timbered mass of Mount Alexander could easily be seen from the top of the rises. They soon picked up Campbell's Creek and then followed the track along its course leading to the Forest Creek goldfield.

They could hear it miles before they could see it. At first there was a faint discordant racket punctuated with clinks, clunks, thumps, bangs, rattles, tings and dings. It was estimated that by the end of February 1852 there were between 25,000 to 30,000 people employed on the diggings in the vicinity of Mount Alexander and what they heard was the combined sound of several battalions of men rattling wash dirt, gravel and stones in thousands of cradles and picking, shovelling, barring and breaking dirt in pursuit of gold. As they got closer the noise welled up into a constant, resonant cacophony that sounded like a river rushing down rapids.

It was like no other scene that Jane had ever witnessed.

Thousands upon thousands of rough tents extended haphazardly through the gullies for about 10 miles in every direction. A huge cloud of dust covered a dreamlike vision of a multitude of men attacking the earth along the Forest Creek valley. They were either digging it, carrying it or washing it. They carried it in wheelbarrows and hand barrows made from two saplings poked through a sack. They carried it on bark sledges dragged along the ground and in bags slung over their backs and in tin dishes balanced on their heads. They washed it in the same tin dishes, in half barrels and in rough built sluice boxes and cradles rocked from side to side. They even washed it on the end of their shovels. Some found gold after the dirt was washed away.

The hills on each side of the creek were covered with yellow clay heaps and the ground honeycombed with square holes. One observer described the scene as "what one might suppose the earth would appear after the day of judgement had emptied all the graves". His thoughts were echoed by a correspondent to the *Adelaide Observer* newspaper who reported "My first emotions were those of indescribable sadness. I could not divest myself of the idea that I was standing in the midst of an immense graveyard. The grim appearance of the diggers; the anxiety depicted in every face; the horrid stench exhaled from the slaughter yards by a burning summer's sun, excited feelings which to be understood must first be realised".

As *Constance* wended her way along the track through the tents Jane thought that the diggers either looked wretched and forlorn or vile looking customers who were plainly headed for gaol. All were bearded, dirty and wore clothing the colour of clay. As the dray passed by, men stopped work, lent on their shovels and gazed at the newcomers. They were now a daily constant stream and everyone on the field wondered how many more people would come. Male arrivals outnumbered females by a ratio of about four to one. One of the diggers pointed at Jane sitting on top of the dray with young William and yelled to his mates "Look it's a woman!" The word travelled up the creek much faster than *Constance* progressed as men shouted out the news so that, by the time the dray trundled by, groups of men stood at their holes to gawk at Jane.

After more than six weeks travel over some 550 miles from Burra they had arrived with their boots split on the uppers and holed in the soles but they were all individually healthy and Jane still had the gold sovereigns in the leather chamois belt secured onto her corset's stay bodice. Their bodies stunk and their clothes were impregnated with dirt and all Jane wanted was to have a good bath and be clean again. All she could see everywhere was mining dirt like in Cornwall – only a different earth. She shook her head in despair and the words she spoke to Richard as they sailed away from Plymouth harbour resounded in her head as she said out loud "Oh Richard what have we done?"

EPILOGUE

Jane was 37 years old when she arrived at the Forest Creek diggings. Multiple childbirths, hard work and a basic diet had not enhanced her appearance over the years. But she had a lovely face with happy wrinkle lines in all the right places and still retained a good figure. Although a few grey strands now appeared in her hair it was still mostly so black that in a flickering lamp light it sometimes had a bluish sheen. She brushed it in a nightly ritual with a slow, soft rhythm and went into an almost trance-like state as she did so. At such contemplative times she often felt acutely the absence of a husband to share the responsibility of family. She had always been good at making decisions and Richard had agreed with nearly all of them. He was always a good backstop for her and she missed his support. She missed also his touch in those rare times when she found herself alone.

To most widows the desirable goal for the future was to find another husband. Economic necessity, emotional needs and the desire for a stable social status were compelling motivators to look for another partner. While Jane was always too busy with the day to day chores of looking after her family to have much spare time to think about herself, feel lonely and dwell on her widowhood, she did feel uncomfortable being dependent on her children for support.

The boys, being good Cornish miners, soon found gold and combining that with the gold sovereigns Jane had stashed in her corsets the family were quickly and comfortably set up in their own tent on the goldfields. Jane then began to learn that she still had the power to please men with her looks. She moved easily and enthusiastically, had a pleasant voice and smiled often. She could be personally gracious and was easy to get along with most of the time. She kept a good house and on a daily basis was just heaps of common sense and good company. She gave the correct impression that she was an unusual mix of strength, warmth and loveliness. She had also arrived on the goldfields when women were in demand. Men looking for wives found they were in short supply.

Thomas Rodda soon located her and looked no further. A little more than two years and six months after arriving at Forest Creek the pair married at the Wesleyan Church on the 1st October 1854. Thomas, a miner from Penzance Cornwall, was two years younger than her and had spent four years in South Australia before overlanding to the gold fields to continue his occupation in the Forest Creek area where he and Jane first resided. When a "rush" started at nearby Vaughan on the Loddon River the family moved there and Thomas decided to follow his father's occupation by setting up a butcher shop. He retained his interest in mining and later held a mining lease and registered a claim in the name of "Duke of Cornwall" which was eventually developed into a substantial, but largely unsuccessful, mining company.

Thomas fathered three children with Jane bringing her total issue to eleven babies. The first child was a daughter born 6th August 1855 at Forest Creek and named Ann after Jane's little girl Ann who died tragically at the age of six in the fire at Burra. Then a son named Thomas followed on 1st March 1857 at Vaughan. Sadly, a third child, Charles, born at Vaughan in March 1860 died three months later from pneumonia.

At age 23, Richard was the first of the Dunstan children to marry. His wife, Margaret, aged 19, from Lezerra, Wendron in Cornwall also had the surname Dunstan. They were married in the Church of England at Castlemaine on 3rd February 1859 and subsequently had eleven children, three of whom died in infancy. The family moved to Daylesford in Victoria in about 1873.

Jane's daughter Mary was the next one to pursue matrimonial bliss. At the tender age of 17 she married John Hicks, aged 24, a miner from Redruth in Cornwall. The wedding was held at Jane's house in Vaughan on the 25th of June 1860 according to the rites of the Wesleyan Church. As Mary was a minor Jane's consent to the union was required. The couple settled at Chiltern, Victoria near Indigo and had fourteen children. Mary had plenty of practice developing mothering skills when, as a child of seven years, she had tended to and carried her younger siblings Ann, Elizabeth and later William on her hip to keep them out of the mud at the Burra Creek. She had felt the loss of Elizabeth and Ann on their deaths and gave special care and attention to young William that established a bond between them lasting for life.

The marriage of Henry Dunstan, aged 24, to Jane Tregonning, aged 23, was the third in the family. Jane was born in Cornwall the daughter of a miner and the marriage took place on Boxing Day

26th December 1861 at the Bible Christian Chapel, Pennyweight, Strathlodden near Vaughan where they lived and had eight children.

Richard and Jane's son Benjamin was the next one to marry. At the age of 25 he married Hannah Phillips, aged 18, a lovely colonial girl born in Melbourne. Their wedding took place at the office of the Registrar of Marriages at Castlemaine on 16th of May 1862 with the consent of Hannah's mother as her daughter was a minor. The union produced twelve children.

Next to sign a marriage contract was Wearn Dunstan, aged 23, who by now had become a qualified blacksmith. On the 28th of December 1864 he married Annie Fogarty, aged 22, born in Dublin, Ireland, at St. Mary's Roman Catholic Church Castlemaine. The couple lived at Guildford where Wearn later became the licensee of The Family Hotel. He was reputed to have been a fine musician and also an artist. He and Annie had no children of their own but did foster two girls.

The last of the Dunstan children to marry was colonial lad William who had been born in the dugout in Burra. On the 18th April 1870 he married 18-year-old Elizabeth Speedie from Newburgh Scotland in the newly built Wesleyan church at Vaughan. William gave his age as 21 although he had nearly another six months to go. He and Elizabeth subsequently had 10 children. Following the occupation of his stepfather, he first became a butcher and later wrote a book on the trade of butchering. At one stage the family lived at Kyneton, Victoria, where William owned a string of racehorses. By 1892 the family had moved to Melbourne and resided at Collingwood where William established a business demolishing buildings. When he got the job to demolish the first bank to be built on the corner of Elizabeth and Collins Street he ordered the men to bag the topsoil and send it to his home where he and a John F. Joyner together washed about 100 bags of it to recover gold dust spilt from parcels brought into the bank by miners and finding its way through the floorboards. The returns were greater than the profit made from demolishing the building.

The marriage of Jane's first child with Thomas Rodda, Ann, then aged 18, with William Carlisle who was aged 23, took place at the Wesleyan Parsonage Castlemaine on the 6th December 1873. William Carlisle was a mining legal manager and the union produced four girls, Elizabeth, Tillie, Nettie and Ivy.

Jane's son Thomas Rodda became a schoolmaster and at the age of 22 married Frances Fare, aged 20, the daughter of a Geelong solicitor on the 29th September 1879 at the Rodda residence in Vaughan according to the rites of the Wesleyan Church. There are no known children of the marriage.

Jane had a total of fifty-nine grandchildren most of whom were a great joy to her while living the remainder of her life at Vaughan where she at last had a proper house. After her experience residing in a cob dwelling in Cornwall and in the dirt underground at Burra she swept, scrubbed and polished daily her new little home so that it was the cleanest in the village. She remained happily married to Thomas Rodda for more than thirty-one years until her death on the 12th March 1886. Thomas had come home at 3 p.m. on that day to find that she was lying in bed complaining of suffering great pain. She died about 5:30 p.m. An autopsy revealed "a large quantity of blood on the base of the brain", which according to the pathologist Dr. G.M. Reid caused death by "sanguineous apoplexy" (cerebral haemorrhage or stroke). Jane was aged 71 years. A eulogy on her death in a publication of the Castlemaine Local Preachers Association read:

"On the day that she died she did what she never was known to do before – made a house to house visit in the township. In one home she appeared to be particularly in bidding each of the children goodbye and on leaving sang to them 'We shall meet to part no more.' Her sudden seizure of illness produced great pain, and soon she was unconscious to all around her. For 53 years she had been a quiet and consistent member of the Wesleyan Church showing piety at home."

The Castlemaine newspaper reported:

"– a most estimate lady, and an old resident of Vaughan, Mrs. T Rodda, expired last evening at about five o'clock." and *"was a woman beloved by all who knew her, … No event has occurred in our community for a long time that has excited so profound a sorrow among all classes as the demise of this talented and goodhearted woman. The esteemed lady had a large family …".*

Relatives, friends and other respectful mourners filled the Wesleyan Church at Vaughan for a memorial service and then Jane was buried at the Vaughan cemetery in the same grave as her infant son Charles. Her grave is at the front of the cemetery just inside the gate on the left. The graveyard is a beautiful and peaceful place tucked into the side of a hill in the Loddon Valley among native box forests that harbour an orchestra of local bird sounds at dawn and dusk each day. A fine place for Jane to be, in an earth that she had grown to love. Her husband Thomas died some nine years later on 31st July 1895 and was interred in the same grave.

In 1974 it was calculated that Richard and Jane Dunstan had more than 1,045 descendants. Today there are many thousands. Some have obtained university degrees in engineering, science, medicine, dentistry, economics, commerce, education, arts, jurisprudence and law. Their diverse occupational skills have included blacksmith, carpenter, coach builder, bank manager, mine manager, journalist, hotel licensee, fighter pilot, newspaper proprietor, teacher, photographer, author, medical practitioner, lawyer, airline captain, book publisher, schoolmaster, radio announcer, theatrical agent, patent attorney and racing car driver. One became a customs and excise officer, another a Magistrate and Coroner, another an Air Vice Marshall in the Australian Air Force and one was appointed the City Engineer for the City of Melbourne. One became the District Commissioner of the Sepik District in Papua New Guinea where he served for eight years and was awarded the Most Excellent Order of the British Empire (OBE).

If Jane was alive today she might say, "Oh Richard look what we have done!"

Jane's legacy is the DNA she gave to her children, grandchildren, great grandchildren and so on. The only reason they existed at all in their particular composition was because Jane was one of their ancestors. We are all the sum of the people who have come before us. Our ancestors are important because at this moment of our life we are in part what we are because of them just as our children are what they are because of us.

Grave of Jane and Thomas Rodda and their son Charles,
Vaughan Springs Cemetry, Victoria.

Dunstan Family Tree

Jane Dunstan, 1815–1886
+ Richard Dunstan, 1812–1850 (m 1835)

— Richard, 1836–1899
  + Margaret Dunstan (m 1859)

  — Elizabeth, 1860–1926
    + George Green

  — Richard (Rev.), 1862–1917

  — Margaret Ann, 1864–1940
    + Richard Reynolds (m 1892)

  — Bennett, 1866–1887

  — Dorothy Mary, 1868–1944
    + Edmund Trembath (m 1889)

  — Ada Annie, 1870–1943
    + George Henry Barkla (m 1893)

  — Alfred James, 1872–1872

  — Ellen, 1873–1875

  — Amy Maud, 1877–1953
    + Frank Lade (m 1940)

  — Evelyn Mildred, 1880–1953
    + Walter Roberts (m 1909)

— **Benjamin,** 1836–1889
  + Hannah Phillips (m 1862)
    — Sarah Ann, 1863–1869
    — Benjamin, 1864–1933
    — Mary Jane, 1866–1940
      + Claus H. M. Gronn (m 1888)
    — Wearne, 1868–
    — Sarah Ann, 1870–
      + Charles Whitehouse (m 1890)
    — Sophia, 1873–1875
    — Thomas Phillips, 1875–1943
    — Frances, 1877–1901
      + Lorenz Victor Gronn (m 1897)
    — Richard 1880–1880
    — Amy Louisa 1881–
    — William Henry 1884–
    — Richard Alfred 1886–1886

— **Henry,** 1838–1906
  + Jane Tregonning (m 1861)
    — Henry, 1862–1914
    — Richard, 1863–1928
    — Thomas Tregonning, 1865–1946
    — Elizabeth Jane, 1867–1957
      + Peter Smith Kerr (m 1892)
      + Isaac Richard Watson (m 1898)
    — Ann, 1869–
      + William Tho. Williams (m 1890)
      + Higgins
    — Edmund, 1871–1942
    — Polly Doble, 1873–1939
      + Graham
    — Rose, 1875–1958
      + William Bransgrove (m 1898)

— **Wearne,** 1838–1893
  + Annie Fogerty (m 1864)
    (no children)

— **Mary Jane,** 1842–1917
+ John Hicks (m 1860)

  — Martha, 1861–1930
   + Richard Trevillian (m 1882)

  — William John, 1862–1863

  — William John, 1863–1939

  — Mary Jane, 1864–1944
   + William Eddy (m 1886)

  — Richard Dunstan, 1866–1915

  — Benjamin, 1868–1947

  — Wearne, 1870–1945

  — Thomas Henry, 1873–1951

  — Annie, 1875–1880

  — Walter, 1877–1945

  — Charles, 1879–1907

  — Sarah Annie, 1881–1951
   + James Milthorpe (m 1905)

  — Edwin James, 1884–1948

  — Emma, 1886–1965
   + Edward Skinner (m 1916)

— **Anne,** 1845–1850

— **Elizabeth,** 1847–1849

— **William,** 1849–1912
+ Elizabeth Speedie (m 1870)

  — Mary Emma, 1871–1940
   + Charles A. Horton (m 1893)

  — William Speedie, 1874–1958
   + Alice Miniken (m 1908)

  — Mabel Elizabeth, 1877–1947
   + Alexander (Alec) Beck (m1901)

  — Matthew Silvester, 1879–1949

  — Amy Hotham, 1882–
   + Charles Wm. Godding (m 1903)

  — Artemus Bede, 1884–188?

  — Alice Brighty, 1886–1961
   + Thomas D. Arnott (m 1906)

— Artemus Benjamin 1889–

— Victoria Myrtle 1892–1970
  + David C. Brister (m 1919)

— Millicent, 1894–1902

Jane Dunstan, 1815–1886
+ **Thomas Rodda,** 1817–1895 (m 1854)

— **Ann,** 1855–1916
  + William Carlisle (m 1873)

  — (Jane) Elizabeth, 1875–
    + Samuel J. Patterson (m 1897)

  — Anne Maud Matilda Rodda 1877– (known as Tillie)

  — Nellie Brighton, 1879–

  — Ivy, 1887–

— **Thomas,** 1857–
  + Frances Fare (m 1879)
    (no children)

— **Charles,** 1860–1860

BIBLIOGRAPHY

PRIMARY SOURCES

Brett R L Ed., *Barclay Fox's Journal 1832–1854*, Bell & Hyman1979, Cornwall Editions Ltd., 2008.

Census of England and Wales, Cornwall, 1841, Archive CD Books, 2003.

Charlwood Edward, *The 1863 Shipboard Diary of Edward Charlwood*, Burgewood Books, 2003.

Dana Richard Henry, *Two Years before the Mast 1840*, Heron Books London, 1968.

Drake P T, *Wendron Baptisms 1813–1837*, self pub. CD-ROM, 2001.

Duruz Rosamund, *The Long Voyage* – Robert McKean's diary of his voyage to Australia 1868, PAP Book Company Pty Ltd., 1979.

Greenhill Basil and Giffard Ann, *Women Under Sail* – Letters and journals concerning eight women travelling or working in sailing vessels between 1829 and 1949, David & Charles Publishers Ltd., no date.

Griffiths Tom and Platt Alan Eds., *The Life and Adventures of Edward Snell* – *The Illustrated Diary of an Artist Engineer and Adventurer in the Australian Colonies 1849 to 1859*, Angus & Robertson Publishers, 1988.

Grove James M, *The Echunga Diaries 1862*, Preston Lake Consulting, Ontario, 2003.

Haydon G H, *Five Years Experience in Australia Felix*, Hamilton Adams and Co., London, 1846.

Inquest Depositions concerning the death of Jane Rodda at Vaughan 13th of March 1886, (No. 311 of 1886), Public Records Office Victoria.

James G F Ed., *A Homestead History – The Reminisces and Letters of Alfred Joyce of Plaistow and Norwood. Port Phillip 1843–1864*, Melbourne University Press, 1949.

Letters from Victorian Pioneers, Archive CD Books Australia Pty Ltd., 2007.

Luke Tom and Libby, *From Burra to Bendigo 1852*, self pub. CD-ROM, 2006, detailing the diary of overlander Thomas Ninnes.

McNeill Carrol Ed., *Round the World Flying* – Journal of a Scottish emigrant's voyage from London to Melbourne in 1869, Fife Publicity, 2008.

Mills John, *Adventures of an Immigrant in Van Dieman's Land* (1840s), Rigby Publishers, Adelaide, 1973.

Mitchell T L (Major Sir), *Three Expeditions Into the Interior of Eastern Australia: With Descriptions of the Recently Explored Region of Australia Felix etc.*, 2 Vols. 2nd edition, T and W Boone, London, 1839.

Murray Andrew, *South Australian Almanac and Directory for 1851*, Archive CD Books, Australia Pty. Ltd., 2007.

Ragless Margaret E Ed., *Olivers Diary*, Investigator Press, 1986.

Randell Mark and Phillips Alan Eds., *Journal of Voyage to South Australia in 1837* by William Beavers Randell, Gould Books, 1985.

Registrar of Births and Deaths and Marriages Adelaide (www.sa.gov.au/ birth deaths and marriages).

Royal Geographical Society (London) *Journal*, Vol. 15, 1845, Deputy Surveyor General Thomas Burr's account of Gov. George Grey's expedition along the South Eastern seaboard of South Australia, pp 160-184.

Rule Charles S, *Logbook 1852*, State Library of South Australia, ref. D7486 (L).

State Records Office South Australia.

Stephens John, *South Australian Almanac and Directory for 1848*, Archive CD Books Australia Pty Ltd, 2008.

The Emigrants Friend or Authentic Guide to South Australia, J Allen, Warwick Lane, Paternoster Row; D Francis, Mile End Road, 1848.

Victorian Registry of Births Deaths and Marriages, Department of Justice Victoria, Australia (www.online.justice.vic.gov.au). (www.vic.gov.au.bdm)

Walsh Richard Ed., *A Voyage to Australia, 1838–1839*, James Bell, Allen & Unwin, 2011.

Wendron Parish Register, County Record Office Cornwall.

Were Jonathan Binns CMG, *A Voyage from Plymouth to Melbourne in 1839 – shipboard diary*, J B Were & Son, 1964.

Wise Edward Esq. Barrister at Law, *The Law Relating to Riots and Unlawful Assemblies*, Middle Temple London, April 1848.

SECONDARY SOURCES

Annear Robyn, *Nothing But Gold*, Text Publishing Melbourne, 1999.

Arden George, *A Sketch of Port Phillip – Being a Review of the Map of Australia Felix Compiled, Engraved and Published by Thomas Ham of Melbourne 1847*, Garravembi Press, 1991.

Ashenburg Katherine, *Clean – An Unsanitized History of Washing*, Profile Books Ltd., 2008.

Auhl Ian, Ed., *Burra Burra – Reminisces of the Burra Mine and Its Townships*, Investigator Press Pty. Ltd., 1983.

Auhl Ian, *Glimpses of the Past*, Investigated Press Pty. Ltd., 1979.

Auhl Ian, *The Monster Mine – The Burra Burra Mine and its Townships 1845–1877*, District Council of Burra Burra, Investigator Press Pty. Ltd., 1986.

Bach John, *A Maritime History of Australia*, Thomas Nelson (Australia) Ltd., 1976.

Barton D B, *Essays in Cornish Mining History, Volume 1*, D Bradford Barton Ltd., 1968.

Bateson Charles, *Australian Shipwrecks, Volume 1, 1622–1850*, A H & A W Reed Pty. Ltd., 1972.

Bennett Gwen, *Watering Holes of the West*, self pub., 1996.

Bentley Michael, *Politics Without Democracy 1815–1914*, Fontana Paperbacks, 1984.

Berry Claude *Cornwall*, Robert Hale Ltd., London, 1949.

Blainey Geoffrey, *A History of Victoria*, Cambridge University Press, 2006.

Blainey Geoffrey, *A Land Half Won*, The Macmillan Company of Australia Pty. Ltd., 1980.

Blainey Geoffrey, *Black Kettle and a Full Moon – Daily Life in Vanished Australia*, Penguin Books, 2003.

Blainey Geoffrey, *The Tyranny of Distance*, Sun Books Melbourne, 1966.

Blake Les Ed., *A Gold Diggers Diary*, Neptune Press Pty. Ltd., 1981.

Braden L, *Bullockies*, Rigby Ltd., 1968.

Bradfield Raymond A, *Serving A Sea Girt Land*, booklet, Castlemaine Press Publications, no date.

Brooke Brian and Finch Alan, *A Story of Horsham – A Municipal Century*, City of Horsham, 1982.

Broome Richard, *The Victorians – Arriving*, Fairfax Syme & Weldon Associates, 1984.

Brown Jonathan, *The English Market Town*, The Crowood Press Ltd., 1991.

Brown Stephen R, *Scurvy*, Penguin Books Australia Ltd., 2003.

Bryant Arthur, *The Search for Justice Vol. 3*, William Collins Sons and Co. Ltd., 1990.

Buckley J A, *The Cornish Mining Industry – A Brief History*, Tor Mark Press, 2002.

Cannon Michael, *The Roaring Days*, Today's Australia Publishing Company, 1998.

Cannon Michael, *Perilous Voyages to the New Land*, Today's Australia Publishing Company, 1997.

Carter Jennifer, *Burra 1845-1851, A Directory of Early Folk*, Shalimar Press, 1996.

Cawthorne Nigel, *The Amorous Antics of Old England*, Piatkus Books Ltd., 2006.

Cawthorne Nigel, *The Curious Cures of Old England*, Portrait – Piatkus Books Ltd., 2005.

Charlwood Don, *Settlers under Sail*, Victoria Press, 1978, 1981, 1991.

Charlwood Don, *The Long Farewell*, Penguin Books Ltd., Australia 1983 and Burgewood Books, 1998.

Chuk Florence, *The Somerset Years*, Pennard Hill Publishers, Ballarat, 1987.

Cole G D H and Postgate R, *The Common People*, Methuen & Co. Ltd., 1971.

Cooney Donald, *Bells of the Australian Bush*, self pub., 2005.

Couper-Smart John, *Port Adelaide – Tales from a Commodious Harbour*, Friends of the South Australian Maritime Museum Inc., 2003.

Crawford Dorothy H, *Deadly Companions – How Microbes Shaped Our History*, Oxford University Press, 2009.

Cummings Dianne, *South Australian Gold Seekers in Victoria 1851–1853*, self pub. C D Rom, 2007.

Daunton-Fear Richard and Vigar Penelope, *Australian Colonial Cookery*, Rigby Ltd., 1977.

Dean Tony and Shaw Tony, *A Cornish Christmas*, The History Press Ltd., 2008.

Deans Peter, *Seafaring Lore and Legend*, McGraw-Hill, 2004.

Dear I C B and Kemp Peter Eds., *Oxford Companion to Ships and the Sea*, Oxford University Press, 2006.

Denholm David, *The Colonial Australian*, Penguin Books, 1979.

Dingle Tony, *The Victorians – Settling*, Fairfax, Syme & Weldon Associates, 1984.

Dobson, Mary, *Disease*, Quercus Books, UK, 2007.

Domville-Fife Charles W Ed, *Square Rigger Days – Autobiographies of Sail*, (1938) University of N.S.W. Press Ltd and Seaforth Publishing, UK, 2007.

Douglas M H and O'Brien L Eds., *The Natural History of Western Victoria*, Australian Institute of Agricultural Science Horsham, 1971.

Dunmore John, *Mrs. Cook's Book of Recipes for Mariners in Distant Seas*, Australian National Maritime Museum and Exisle Publishing Ltd., 2009.

Dunstan Roy A and Finch Betty, *Spreading Branches – A Record of the Descendants of Richard Dunstan*, self pub., 1970.

Dunstan William, *The Butcher's Guide and Farmers Companion*, George Robertson & Company, 1898.

Evans Brenda, *Granny's Natural Remedies – Traditional Cures for Everyday Ailments*, Sphere Great Britain, 2010.

Faull Jim, *The Cornish in Australia*, A E Press, Melbourne, 1983.

Fletcher R A, *In the Days of the Tall Ships*, Brentano's Ltd., London, 1928.

Flett James, *Old Pubs, Inns, Taverns and Grog Houses in the Victorian Diggings*, The Poppet Head Press, Melbourne, 1979, 1981.

Fraser Rod, *The Champion of the Seas*, Pilgrim Printing Services Pty. Ltd., 2003.

Frith H J, *Waterfowl in Australia*, Angus and Robertson, 1967.

Goodfellow Caroline, *How We Played – Games from Childhood Past*, The History Press Ltd., 2008.

Goodman Jordan, *The Rattlesnake – A Voyage of Discovery to the Coral Sea*, Faber and Faber Ltd., 2005.

Green Percy J, *I Am Evergreen*, self pub., 1967.

Greenhill Basil and Giffard Ann, *The Merchant Sailing Ship*, David & Charles (Publishers) Ltd., 1970.

Greenhill Basil and Giffard Ann, *Travelling by Sea in the 19th Century – Interior Design in Victorian Passenger Ships*, A & C Black Ltd., London, 1972.

Haines Robin and Jeffrey Judith, *Bound for South Australia – Births and Deaths on Government Assisted Emigrant Ships 1848 to 1885*, CD-ROM, Gould Genealogy, Adelaide, 2004.

Haines Robin, *Doctors at Sea*, Palgrave McMillan, 2005.

Haines Robin, *Emigration and the Labouring Poor – Australian Recruitment in Britain and Ireland 1831–1860*, MacMillan Press Ltd., 1997, St Martin's Press, New York, 1997.

Haines Robin, *Flinders Occasional Papers in Economic History No. 3*, Flinders University of South Australia, 1996.

Haines Robin, *Life and Death in the Age of Sail*, University of New South Wales Press Ltd., 2006.

Halliday F E, *A History of Cornwall*, Gerald Duckworth & Co Ltd., 1959.

Hamilton J C, *Pioneering Days in Western Victoria*, Exchange Press, 1914.

Hamilton Jenkin A K, *Cornish Miner*, Westcountry Books (1927), 2004.

Hamilton Jenkin A K, *The Story of Cornwall*, Thomas Nelson & Sons Ltd, 1948.

Harrison Fraser, *The Dark Angel – Aspects of Victorian Sexuality*, Universe Books, New York, 1978.

Hattendorf John B Ed, *The Oxford Encyclopaedia of Maritime History – 4 volumes*, Oxford University Press, 2007.

Hill David, *The Gold Rush*, Random House Australia Pty Ltd, 2011.

Historical Souvenir, *Centenary of Clunes 1839–1939*, Clunes Museum Reprint, 1999.

Hitchins Fortescue and Drew Samuel, *The History of Cornwall Vol. 1*, W Penaluna Helston Pub., 1824.

Hoare Philip, *Leviathan or The Whale*, Fourth Estate – Harper Collins, 2008.

Hodder Edwin, *The History of South Australia*, 2 vols, Sampson Low, Marston, London, 1893.

Hull Rita, *Alexander McCallum and the Dunach Forest Run*, self pub., 1989.

Hull Rita, *Dunach in the Shadow of the Mount*, self pub., 1988.

Isaacs Jennifer, *Pioneer Women of the Bush and Outback*, Lansdowne Publishing Pty. Ltd., 1990.

Jones Alan & Cameron Karen, *Her Majesty's South-Eastern Mails*, self pub., 1999.

Joseph Peter, *Mining Accidents In the St Just District 1831 to 1914*, The Trevithick Society, St George Printing Works Ltd., Redruth, 1999.

Judd Dennis, *The Victorian Empire*, Praeger Publishers Inc., New York, 1970.

Keble Chatterton E, *Sailing Ships – The Story of their Development From The Earliest Times to the Present Day*, Sidgwick and Jackson Ltd., London, 1909, Kessinger Publishing – Rare Reprints, 1914.

Keneally Tom, *The Commonwealth of Thieves*, Random House Australia Pty. Ltd., 2005.

Kennedy Malcolm J, *Hauling The Loads – A History of Australia's Working Horses and Bullocks*, Central Queensland University Press, 2005.

Kiddle Margaret, *Men of Yesterday*, Melbourne University Press, 1961.

Lind Lew, *Fair Winds to Australia – 200 Years of Sail on the Australian Station*, Reed Books Pty. Ltd., 1988.

Linn Rob, *A Land Abounding*, Alexandrina Council, 2001.

Loney Jack and Stone Peter, *The Australian Run*, Marine History Publications, 2000.

Luke Tom & Libby, *Burra to Bendigo 1852*, self pub. CD Rom, 2006.

Lundy Derek, *The Way of a Ship – A Square Rigger Voyage in the Last Days of Sail*, Jonathan Cape, London, 2002.

Manning Geoffrey H, *Hope Farm Chronicle: Pioneering Tales of South Australia, 1836–1870*, self pub., 1984.

May Trevor, *The Victorian Undertaker*, Shire Publications Ltd., UK, 2008.

May Trevor, *The Victorian Workhouse*, Shire Publications Ltd., no date.

Mayers Lynne, *A Dangerous Place to Work*, Blaize Bailey Books, 2008.

Mayers Lynne, *Balmaidens*, The Hypatia Trust, 2004.

McHugh Evan, *Shipwrecks*, Penguin Books, 2003.

Morton Lesley J, *The Duke of Cornwall Mine*, self pub., 1992.

Naracoorte Jubilee 1850–2000, *Souvenir Programme*, Naracoorte Lucindale Council, 2000.

National Parks and Wildlife Division, Department of Conservation and Environment, *The Majors Trail*, 1990.

Newstead and District Historical Society, *Early Days of Newstead – Extracts from "The Echo" newspaper*, no date.

Noall Cyril, *The Cornish Midsummer Eve Bonfire Celebrations*, The Federation of Old Cornwall Societies, 2003.

Oulton Margaret, *A Valley of the Finest Description – A History of the Shire of Lexton*, Shire of Lexton & *The Pakenham Gazette*, 1985.

Parsons Ronald, *Migrant Ships for South Australia 1836–1866*, Gould Books, 1999.

Parsons Ronald, *Steam Tugs in South Australia*, self pub., 1972, 1979, 1983.

Payton Philip, *Cornwall – A History*, Cornwall Editions Ltd., 2004.

Payton Philip, Ed., *Cornish Studies Four*, "Cornish Health and Healthcare", Rod Sheaff, p131, and "*Reforming 30s and Hungry 40s – The Genesis of Cornwall's Emigration Trade*", Philip Payton, p107, University of Exeter Press, 1996.

Payton Philip, *The Cornish Overseas*, Cornwall Editions Ltd., 2005.

Perkin Joan, *Victorian Women*, John Murray Publishers Ltd., 1993.

Pescod Keith, *Good Food Bright Fires and Civility – British Emigration Depots of the 19th Century*, Australian Scholarly Publishing, Melbourne, 2001.

Pescott N, *Australia Early Settlers Household Lore*, The Sovereign Hill Museums Association, Ballarat, 2007.

Poole Daniel, *What Jane Austen Ate and Charles Dickens Knew,* Touchstone, 1994.

Priestley Susan, *The Victorians – Making Their Mark,* Fairfax, Syme & Weldon Associates, 1984.

Rapport Mike, *1848 Year of Revolutions,* Little Brown Publishing, Great Britain, 2008.

Reader's Digest, *Extraordinary Uses for Ordinary Things,* Reader's Digest, no date.

Resident A, *Glimpses of Life in Victoria,* Melbourne University Press, 1996.

Roud Steve, *The Penguin Guide to the Superstitions of Britain and Ireland,* Penguin Books, 2006.

Serle Geoffrey, *The Golden Age,* Melbourne University Press, 1963.

Sexton R T, *Shipping Arrivals and Departures – South Australia 1627–1850,* Gould Books, 1990.

Seymour John, *Forgotten Household Crafts,* Dorling Kindersley Ltd., 2007.

Sherer John, *The Gold Finder Australia,* Clarke Beaton & Co., London, 1853, Penguin Books Ltd., 1973.

Simpson K and N Day, *Field Guide to the Birds of Australia,* Penguin Books Australia Ltd., 1999.

Smith J W and Holden T S, *Where Ships Are Born. Sunderland 1346–1946,* Thomas Reed and Co. Ltd., Sunderland, 1947.

Smith Russell, *1850 a Very Good Year in the Colony of South Australia – Selected Items of Historical Interest,* Shakespeare Head Press, Sydney, 1973.

Talbot Cross Mary, *The Foundling,* Shalimar Press, 1998.

Tangye Michael, *Redruth and Its People,* self pub., Earles Press, Redruth, 1998.

Tangye Michael, *Victorian Redruth,* self pub., Redbourne Printers, Redruth, 2001.

The Burra History Group, *Burra's Monster Mine,* The Burra History Group, 2009.

Thomson F M L, *The Rise of Respectable Society* – A Social History of Victorian Britain 1830 to 1900, Fontana Press, 1988.

Tolmer Alexander, *Reminisces of an Adventurous and Chequered Career At Home and at the Antipodes,* 2 vols., Sampson Low, Marston, Searle & Rivington, London, 1882.

Villiers Alan, *By Way of Cape Horn*, Ibex for Heritage Book Group, 1952, 1996.

Villiers Alan, *Of Ships and Men*, George Newnes Ltd., London, 1962, 1965.

Villiers Alan, *The Set of the Sails – The Story of a Cape Horn Seaman*, Ibex for Heritage Book Group, 1949, 1997.

Villiers Alan, *The Way of the Ship – The Story of the Square Rigged Cape Horner*, Hodder and Stoughton Ltd., London, 1954.

Villiers Alan, *Vanished Fleets – Sea Stories from Old Van Dieman's Land*, Cat and Fiddle Press Hobart, 1931, 1974.

Viner David, *Wagons and Carts*, Shire Publications Ltd., UK., 2008.

Warsnop Thomas, *Warsnop's History of Adelaide*, J Williams, Adelaide, 1878.

Whickham Dorothy, *Women of the Diggings – Ballarat 1854*, B H S Publishing Ballarat, 2009.

Whidden John D, *Ocean Life in the Old Sailing Ship Days – From Forecastle to Quarterdeck*, Little Brown and Co., Boston, 1908, Kessinger Publishing, Rare Reprints, no date.

Whimpress Jack, *Echunga 1839–1939*, Lutheran Publishing House, 1975.

Whitelock Derek, *From Colony to Jubilee Adelaide – A Sense of Difference*, Savvas Publishing, 1985.

Wilson A N, *The Victorians*, Arrow Books, 2003.

NEWSPAPERS and GAZETTES

Adelaide Observer

Burra Record, South Australia

Geelong Advertiser, Victoria

Government Gazettes, South Australia, 1849, 1850, 1851, 1852

Illustrated London News

South Australian

South Australian Gazette and Colonial Register

South Australian Register, Adelaide, South Australia

The Advertiser, Adelaide

The Law Times, London

The Times, London

ELECTRONIC SITES

www.animalcontrol.com.au
   Animal Control Technologies (Australia) Pty. Ltd., Somerton, Victoria
www.southaustralianhist.com.au
   Flinders Ranges Research – South Australian history research
www.sa.gov.au/births/deaths/marriages
   South Australian Government – Births, Deaths and Marriages Registry,
   Adelaide
www.smh.com.au/news/Strathalbyn
   Sydney Morning Herald, Strathalbyn, 8th February 2004
www.theshipslist.com.au
   The Ships List – ships, passenger list and information
www.gale.cengage.co.uk/time
   The Times Digital Archive, UK
www.trove.nla.gov.au
   Trove Digitised Newspapers, National Library of Australia, Canberra
www.bdm.vic.gov.au
   Victorian Department of Justice – Births, Deaths and Marriages
   Registry, Victoria
www.wikipedia.org/Glenorchy and www.wikipedia.org/Macclesfield
   Wikipedia, the free encyclopaedia

Metric Conversion Table

Imperial measurements, as used during the period described in these pages, have been expressed throughout. The following table provides the metric equivalents,

Linear
    1 inch = 25.4 millimetres
    1 foot = 30.5 millimetres
    1 yard = 0.914 metres
    1 mile = 1609.34 metres

Liquids
    1 pint = 568 millilitres
    1 quart =1.136 litres
    1 gallon = 4.55 litres

Weights
    1 ounce = 28.3 grams
    1 pound = 454 grams

1 stone = 6.35 kilograms

1 ton = 1.02 tonnes

Monetary

1 penny (1d) = 0.83 cents

1 shilling (1s) = 10 cents (Australian)

1 pound (£) = 2 dollars (Australian)

Temperature

100°F = 37.7°C

32°F = 0°C

Nautical

1 knot (6,076 ft.) = 1.85 kilometres per hour (kph)

8 knots = 14.81 kph

10 knots = 18.5 kph

1 fathom = 1.8 metres (6 feet)

Land Measure

1 acre = 0.404 hectares

640 acres = 1 square mile = 259 hectares